STONE'S THROW

Thriller Publishing Group, Inc.

A "clever and engrossing mystery tale involving gorgeous women, lustful men and scintillating suspense."

"Part of what makes this thriller thrilling is that you sense there to be connections among all the various subplots; the anticipation of their coming together keeps the pages turning."

"This is one of the best thrillers I've read yet."

"A superb thriller and an exceptional read."

"Verdict: This fast-paced book offers fans of commercial thrillers a twisty, action-packed thrill ride."

"Another masterpiece of action and suspense."

"Fast paced and well plotted . . . While comparisons will be made with Turow, Grisham and Connelly, Jagger is a new voice on the legal/thriller scene. I recommend you check out this debut book, but be warned . . . you are not going to be able to put it down."

"A chilling story well told. The pace never slows in this noir thriller, taking readers on a stark trail of fear."

STONE'S THROW

R.J. JAGGER
JIM MICHAEL HANSEN

Thriller Publishing Group, Inc.

For Eileen

ACKNOWLEDGMENTS

Special appreciation goes out to Carmen Harris, South Africa, for devoting her massive editorial skills to the betterment of this title. Thanks, Camen! You totally rock!

Many thanks also go out to Roger Rittner for illuminating a variety of errors.

DAY
ONE

September 15
Monday

1

After dark Monday night, a mean thunderstorm pounded Miami with heavy demonic fists. It was absolutely perfect. The man punched through it down MacArthur Parkway with the wipers on full speed and heavy metal spitting out of the radio, eventually turning left into Hibiscus Island, which was an enclave of multi-million dollar waterway mansions not far from downtown Miami and South Beach.

A smile came to his face.

It was game time, baby.

The moment was finally here.

Winding into the neighborhood, he slipped on the latex gloves and the ski-mask.

They felt good, like old friends.

A hundred heartbeats later, driving down the street to the target mansion, he saw that all the lights were out and, as was his practice now, pulled directly into the driveway without making a pass by. There he immediately killed the engine. He waited for a few seconds to see if any lights turned on inside the house. When none did, he pulled the hoodie up over his head, grabbed the pouch, got out of the vehicle and walked briskly to the far side of the structure where he busted the laundry room window with his elbow.

In the wrath of the storm, the shattering of the glass hardly resonated. It was a minor thing at best; there one split of a second, and then just as quickly, gone; no doubt some trick of the storm. He reached through the opening, unlatched the window lock and climbed inside. Then he flicked on a small penlight, barely strong enough to make out his immediate surroundings, almost invisible if someone outside happened to drive past and throw an unintended glance this way.

No sounds came from inside the structure.

No lights turned on.

Oh, yeah.

From the laundry room he quickly made his way to the kitchen. There he pulled the jar out of the pouch and set it on the ritzy countertop. Inside that jar was the head of a rattlesnake that he'd cut off earlier today. He'd modified the lid of the jar to look something like a compass. The circular part of the top was divided into six pizza-like slices, labeled 2, 4, 6, 2, 4, 6. An arrow spinner had also been added.

He flicked the spinner and smiled when he saw where it landed.

Okay, good.

Now it was time for the fun part.

He pulled the syringe out of the pouch, made his way to the winding staircase and started up one silent step after another. Outside, a flash of lightning ripped across the sky and briefly lit the world, showing that the rear of the property opened to the waterway. The back yard had a pool, a large deck and a boat dock. A sleek powerboat was in a lift, resting cleanly out of the water.

He continued up, controlling his breathing and not making even a whisper of a sound.

At the master bedroom, he came to the most beautiful thing ever. The woman was alone, sound asleep on top of the covers, breathing deeply and rhythmically. She was face down on her stomach with her head buried in the pillow and covered under her long blond hair. She was completely and totally naked, with all her sensuous little curves on full display. He'd never seen anything so utterly perfect in his entire life. He stared at her, transfixed, knowing he should get on with the job but never wanting this moment to end.

Then he exhaled, took a final look at the woman and crept closer.

Then, just like that, wham!

He was on top of her and everything was in sudden violent motion. He shoved the needle into her ass and pushed the back of her head down as she struggled, keeping her locked in that position for a full five minutes while the drugs took effect, all the while being carful to make sure her mouth wasn't being pressed into the pillow.

The last thing he wanted was for her to suffocate.

When the drugs finally took full effect, he flung the woman's unconscious body over his shoulder, carried her downstairs and retrieved the pouch from the kitchen counter. Then he carried her out the front door, kicking it closed behind him, and headed into the storm. At the vehicle, he threw woman in the back tailgate area as if she was a sack of potatoes.

At that moment a flash of lighting lit the world.

To his disbelief, there was a jogger out in the storm, a female, running down the street at that exact wrong second, not more than fifty feet away.

She looked directly at him.

He didn't care.

He still had the ski-mask on, plus even that was buried under the darkness of the hoodie.

She couldn't ID him, not in a million years. That was his thought as he jumped into the car and got the hell out of there.

It was all good.

2

Monday night after dark, Nicole Stone jolted awake to find she'd drifted off in front of the TV. The phone was ringing. An empty bottle of wine lay dead on the floor; and outside, a wicked thunderstorm was busy punishing the windows and the roof and the walls. She didn't like it. Every time she'd almost died it had always been on a night like this.

The caller, from dispatch, wasted no time.

"We might have a situation. We got a report from a woman who was out jogging and thinks she saw a man coming out of a house with a naked woman slung over his shoulder."

Outside, lightning ripped the night.

Thunder rolled across the sky with a violent force.

Nicole muscled her 28-year-old body up into a sitting position.

"Yeah, I'm here. Go on."

"The woman's body was limp, like it was unconscious or dead. The guy threw her in the back of an SUV like she was so much trash and took off. A black-and-white swung by and checked it out. When they got there, the house was dark and locked and no one answered when they knocked."

"Did they go in?"

"No. They weren't sure they had authority. They said to let someone else screw it up."

Nicole weighed it.

She couldn't help thinking that if this was a medical emergency and the guy was taking the woman to the hospital, he would have been carrying her in his arms and not slinging her over his shoulders like a sack of potatoes. Even more likely, he simply would have called 911. The more she thought about it, the more it felt like someone stealing away with a body.

She exhaled and said, "Give me the address. I'll swing by."

She stood up with a swirly head and added, "Do you have the name and number of that witness?"

"Yes."

"Good . . . give me that, too, please and thank you."

The downpour outside was potentially crazy enough to break through the bank of old factory windows that filled the south wall, so out of an abundance of caution she dragged her mattress twenty steps across the worn, decades-old hardwood floor to where the glass wouldn't stab her in the face later if it decided to shatter and succumb to gravity.

Her movement was wobbly.

The wine still charged her veins. She shouldn't have indulged, not tonight, on account of being the detective on duty until morning. As the newbie of the department, this was only her fourth rotation of being on call.

During the first three shifts, the phone hadn't rung.

Now it had.

Your first case—

Don't screw it up.

Two minutes later she was dressed in jeans and a tee and bounding down the fire escape. The storm tore into her with a violence and had her soaked to the core by the time she got to the ground and into the protective confines of Penny Lane, a faded red Porsche 911 with 205,000 miles on the clock and more than four decades of dings, bruises and abuse.

Her long black hair was matted solid to her head.

She didn't care.

Start, she warned the vehicle, and meant it.

Then she turned the key.

The engine sputtered and chocked as if being dragged from the gates of hell. Then it reluctantly sprang to life. She gunned it twice, shifted into first and punched it.

The addresses in question turned out to be a waterfront mansion on Hibiscus Island where the rich and powerful and relevant laid their heads at night and muttered their oh-so-important offerings during the day. The structure in question was a two-story contemporary with a gated front yard and a large fountain in the center of a circular cobblestone driveway. Nicole came to a stop in front of the residence and killed the engine. She guessed the place was worth between five and ten million, but it could have been more.

The storm battered down, swinging the streetlights, flooding the windshield and ricocheting off Penny Lane's roof with a heavy, almost banshee scream.

Then, suddenly, the power grid defaulted and every light in the area went out.

Nicole pulled a flashlight out of the glove box, made sure it worked, and stepped out into the storm.

The rain was warm but felt more like nails than water.

One step at a time, she picked her way towards the dark, looming structure.

3

It didn't take Nicole long to find that one of the first-floor windows had been shattered. She climbed in, shouted her presence, loud, so as to get above the noise of the storm, and got no answer in return. As far as she could tell, she was alone in the house.

Over the next fifteen minutes she found strange, strange offerings; a syringe on the carpet by the edge of the bed, blood splatterings on the bed sheets, and, weirdest of all, a bottle on the kitchen counter with a rattlesnake's head inside and a spinner type thing on top.

She flicked it and got a two, then flicked it again and got a six. It was then that a noise suddenly came from behind her. Before she could turn, something smacked into the side of her head with the force of a tire iron. The flashlight dropped out of her hand and shattered. She wobbled for a few heartbeats and then fell forward in the dark. She tried to block the fall with her arms but they didn't respond quickly enough.

She hit the floor face first.

Pain came.

Everything turned thin and unfocused.

A frantic woman was waving a gun and a flashlight in her face, shouting, "Stay down! I'll shoot! I swear!"

She winced and put a hand to the side of her head and pressed in to get a feel for the damage. Pain shot back but it was the kind that would heal.

"I'm a homicide detective," she said.

"What are you doing here?"

Nicole put up a hand as a plea to not shoot, then strugged to her feet and said, "What's your name?"

"Fallon Bow."

"You live here, I'm assuming."

"Yes. What the fuck's going on?"

Nicole explained.

Fallon Bow had an air about her, one that Nicole, for whatever reason, gyrated to immediately. After calming down, the woman turned into a fountain of information, in a full-on effort to help in any way she could.

The missing woman, it turned out, was Danica Rose. She and Fallon had grown up together back in L.A. and had been lifelong friends ever since. She was out here in Miami visiting Fallon for a week or so while Fallon's husband, Conway, was doing a job in Tokyo.

"Do you have a picture of her?"

The woman did; it showed the two of them, Danica and Fallon, on a sunny California beach, smiling and carefree. Both of them were blond. Both of them were in good shape. Both of them were about the same age.

"You two can almost be twins."

"Yeah."

"Have you two been sleeping in the same bed by any chance?"

"Yes."

She almost asked the next obvious question, namely whether they were lovers, but decided to hold off, at least for now. Instead, she asked Fallon to call Danica. The connection rang to a phone in a purse sitting on the floor at the end of the couch.

It sounded like a death bell.

That's all Nicole needed.

She said, "With your permission, I'd like to get a crime unit down here."

Fallon didn't hesitate.

"Yes, yes, absolutely."

"I want to get a lab report on that syringe. We'll find out what was in it. I don't think it was a poison; otherwise the guy would have just left the body here. I'm hoping that we're going to find that it was just some kind of knockout drug; an opiate or something." She paused and added, "With any luck, there should be some blood residue on the syringe as well. We'll see if there's a DNA match to Danica to be sure it was her who got injected. We'll match the blood on the sheets too, just to be sure. There's a chance it could belong to the guy who took her but I'm not holding my breath. I'm almost positive it's Danica's, but we'll check just to nail it down one way or the other. We're going to leave the house now. It's a crime scene and the last thing we want to do is contaminate it any more than we already have. Stay right behind me and don't touch anything."

The woman didn't follow.

She just stood there.

After three steps, Nicole turned and said, "Is something wrong?"

The woman's lips trembled and the fear behind her eyes was palpable. Then, almost as if reading Nicole's mind, she said, "He came for me, didn't he? He got Danica by mistake—"

* * *

Fallon Bow, quite understandably, didn't want to be alone for the rest of the night, even at one of the big hotels downtown where she'd be safe, so Nicole brought her home to the loft, which was unquestionably against a hundred different department policies but right now at this hour of the night she didn't exactly give a flying fuck. The woman let her eyes take in the sight of the space as they stepped inside, seeing a large uninterrupted expanse, the entire fourth floor of the building in fact, with walls stretching long on each side and a ceiling that went up fifteen feet.

"I've been in countries that are smaller," she said.

Nicole set her gun on the kitchen counter.

Then she poured two glasses of wine, handed one to Fallon as she took a long swallow, and said, "This building was a boot factory back in the day. It sat empty for over thirty years. A couple of years ago Jay-J Juicy bought it. You ever heard of him?"

"Can't say as I have."

"He's a former basketball player who reinvented himself as a hip-hop producer. Anyway, he built a state-of-the-art music studio down on the first floor called Bizy Bizy Lo Records, paved the parking lot, got new heating and plumbing and electrical, and stuff like that. A lot of the music you hear on the radio is produced right here on the ground floor of this building, assuming you listen to rap."

"I don't."

"Basically I don't either, except for Jay-J's stuff. I get the top floor for free in exchange for keeping an eye on the place. You can't tell it now because of the weather, but we're right next to the Hialeah switchyard. In the light of day, this whole area is a pretty raggedy part of the universe."

"Sounds like a good deal for you."

"It is, so long as there isn't a fire."

"What's that supposed to mean?"

"It means that technically this isn't a legal occupancy because the interior stairwell's been welded shut to keep the studio secure. The second and third floors are empty and locked. The only way in and out of this floor is by the outside fire escape." She smiled and added, "So don't self-ignite or anything like that."

"Hasn't happened yet."

Five minutes later they were down for the night, sharing the mattress on the floor since that's all there was. The melody of the storm pulled Fallon into a deep sleep almost immediately. Nicole, however, wasn't so lucky. The blow to the side of her head was now a throbbing mess that wouldn't let her close her eyes. More than that, though, the events of the evening were demons in her brain.

Who was the target, Danica or Fallon?

And why?

According to Fallon, Danica was a close friend of hers since junior high school, back in the hills of L.A. where the two of them lived next to each other. Danica had always been insanely popular. She was one of those women that other women wanted to be seen with and men wanted to own. After graduation from high school, she got a bachelor's degree in marine biology from UCLA. All the while, at night and on the weekends, she sang in a band called Rude, which sort of had a grunge-type bent to it. They hadn't broken out nationally yet but locally in southern California they were pretty big, with live gigs on the strip four or five nights a week. A lot of the songs they played were actually written by Danica.

Here's the weird thing, though.

Last year, Danica got spotted bodysurfing at Muscle Beach by a guy named Adam Montrachet. It turns out that Montrachet was a director for Paradyme Pictures, which was gearing to up to make an action thriller called The Shoals. It was going to have a lot of exotic underwater swimming scenes and Montrachet was immediately interested in Danica. She had the chops to do the part, looked good in a bikini and indicated she would go topless, if the part called for it. He got an audition for her; she'd been swimming since she was three and could hold her breath for more than two minutes. She got the part, of course. At first she was just slated as an extra, for a non-speaking part. The more they got to know her, though, the more they liked the sparkle in her eyes and her slightly-crooked smile and the way she tossed her hair. They let her audition for a small speaking part. She blew them away. Then they let her audition for a bigger role, and a bigger one, and an even bigger one. By the time casting was finalized and they were ready to film, she had one of the leading female parts—the role of Jackie Jacks, who was the girlfriend of the man who was heading up a dangerous hunt for a sunken treasure.

As of now, the film had been shot and they were in the editing phase. The first trailers would land with full force next month. The movie was slated for a worldwide release at some point after that.

Until a few hours ago, Danica Rose was on her way to becoming the next big thing.

Now she was gone.

So what happened?

Did she rub someone the wrong way?

Did someone know about her upcoming fame and always wanted to own a silver screen actress all for himself?

Was someone trying to sabotage the film?

Was someone from Rude upset that she'd moved on?

Did she have a boyfriend that she'd outgrown, or would eventually leave behind if not yet, because of the impending stardom?

Did she witness something she shouldn't have?

Was someone going to hold her for ransom?

Nicole slipped out of bed without waking Fallon, then tiptoed her way over to the kitchen table where she fired up the iPad and did a Google search for The Shoals. A lot of information came up, including cast members, producers and directors, release dates, budgets, and the like. Sure enough, like Fallon said, Danica Rose was starring in her film debut as the sultry Jackie Jacks. The teaser photos of Danica from the shoot showed a young woman with a face and body custom built to light up the screen.

Nicole crawled back under the covers next to Fallon and pictured herself as a sexy actress on a beach with the big-screen cameras focused on her every move.

They made her feel important.

They made her feel wanted.

They made her feel like someone actually saw her.

Suddenly a shadow moved across the inside of the loft, compliments of headlights from outside. That was weird. No one ever came around this part of the universe in the middle of the night.

She made her way to the windows.

A hundred yards away, two menacing headlights were stopped in the weather, pointed eerily at the building. The rain was so insanely intense that nothing of the vehicle showed, not the shape, not the windshield, not anything except the lights, which stayed as still as death for two minutes and then slowly crept off and disappeared into the night.

Nicole's chest pounded.

Is that you?

Did you take the wrong person?

Did you really want Fallon?

Well, you can't have her, at least not tonight.

DAY TWO

September 16
Tuesday

4

Nicole got pulled out of a deep, deep sleep by hands forcefully shaking her body. "Nicole! Wake up! You're having a nightmare!" The voice belonged to Fallon Bow. "You're screaming, wake up! It's okay, everything's okay, it's just a dream. You're just dreaming! Everything's okay, wake up!"

Nicole bolted upright.

Her body was covered in sweat.

Her lungs fought for air.

Get it down!

Get it down!

Get it down now before it's gone!

She grabbed a 3 x 5 index card from the nightstand, ran to the kitchen table, turned on a table lamp and wrote what she could remember of the dream, before it disappeared forever:

I'm a kid—7 or 8, maybe. I'm on the floor playing a board game with a girl about my age. Suddenly two men appear from out of nowhere. They have rifles. They have mean, hateful faces. They stink like they haven't washed in a week. I can smell them. They smell like sweat and whiskey and smoke. One of them points at me and screams, That's her!

Suddenly, the other man grabs me tight and lifts me off the ground. My feet kick and my arms punch but they do no good. He carries me across the room and is almost out the door when a loud explosion of gunfire erupts and his face splatters into a bloody mess, spraying all over me. He continues to hold me for a second and then drops me to the floor. Before I can move, he falls on top of me.

She pushed the card away and put the pen down. From the bed, Fallon was watching her, knowing to not interrupt. It was four in the morning. Nicole turned the light out and got back in bed. She tried not to cry but knew it was futile. Tears came, hard and forceful, like a demon breaking out from under her face.

Fallon put her arms around her and held her tight.

Nicole let herself fall asleep in the woman's comfort.

She awoke shortly after dawn to the smell of coffee and eggs, compliments of Fallon, who said, "I remembered something. My neighbor next door has some security cameras. Maybe they picked up something from last night. I don't know if he records things or not but it's worth checking out."

Nicole headed for the bathroom, which had no walls, like all the rest of the space, but did have a curtain, which she pulled closed for privacy.

Two minutes later she was revived, with brushed teeth and a water-splashed face. She poured a cup of coffee, tapped her cup against Fallon's and said, "Sorry about all the drama last night."

"No worries."

"Do you want to hear something stupid?"

Fallon shrugged.

"Sure."

"I was fourteen, hitchhiking east across Florida on the I-10 on a rainy night," she said. "I got picked up by a couple. They weren't the normal type to pick up hitchhikers but I was a stray cat out in a stray night. They had a really nice car, something expensive. I sat in the back on a leather seat. They asked me questions but I didn't talk to them much. I didn't even tell them my name when they asked. I just said it didn't matter. They wanted to know why I was out there in the middle of nowhere all by myself. I told them I was heading to New York. That's about all I told them. I wasn't very much into talking."

Fallon took a sip of coffee.

"Okay."

"Anyway, an 18-wheeler merged onto the interstate with no taillights working. We didn't end up seeing it until the last second on account of the storm and didn't have time to swerve around. We crashed into the back end of it really hard and ended up rolling over a bunch of times."

"Were you okay?"

Nicole shook her head.

"Not exactly," she said. "I got busted up pretty bad. I ended up in a coma for over two months."

"Wow. I can't even imagine—"

"When I came to, I didn't remember anything at all," Nicole said. "I didn't remember who I was or where I came from or where I was going or anything. Everything I told you right now about me hitchhiking through Florida on the way to New York, I didn't even remember that. The only reason I know about it is because the couple that picked me up told me about it after I came out of the coma. I still have no personal recollection of anything in my life that happened before I woke up from the coma."

Fallon pictured it.

"Wow."

"Anyway, the couple that picked me up turned out to be a

Miami lawyer named Logan Stone, and his wife, Naya Stone. They felt responsible for what happened, even though they weren't, and came to visit me in the hospital every day. They said they talked to me a lot and read me stories but I'll be honest, I never heard any of it. When I broke out of the coma, I had nowhere to go so they let me stay with them rather than have me dumped into social services or whatever. They gave me everything a kid could ask for; food, a bed, shelter, safety and even love. They tried to help me find out who I was and where I came from. They hired a string of private investigators and threw a ton of money at it. They got nowhere. Neither did the police. Whoever I was, no one could figure it out. They hired psychologists and even tried hypnosis but that didn't work either. I continued to stay with them and they put me in school and just continued on with me as if I was their own daughter."

"And you still don't remember anything?"

Nicole shook her head.

"No," she said. "I have dreams. They say that some of those dreams may come from memories. So, what I try to do is write down every dream I can remember, as soon as I wake up. The ones that might possibly come from my past, I put on that wall over there."

She pointed.

Two or three hundred index cards were tacked to the wall.

"I wondered what those were."

"Last night was one of those dreams." Nicole tapped on the index card on the table and added, "Maybe it was true and maybe it wasn't. My mind likes to play tricks on me."

"Can I read it?"

"Sure."

Nicole waited for the woman to finish and said, "For a long time, I've had a feeling that something from my past was very, very wrong. That's pretty clear from the fact that

I was hitchhiking through Florida at age fourteen all by myself. I always had a feeling that I was trying to escape from something. If this dream's true, I was already in some kind of trouble by the time I was seven or eight. What I wonder is whether someone is still after me or whether all this has faded into obscurity."

Fallon asked, "So, do you think the girl you were playing with was a sister, maybe?"

Nicole exhaled.

"I have no idea. Maybe it was a sister or cousin or something like that or maybe it was just a playmate."

"I know this is stupid," Fallon said, "but have you ever, you know, felt the presence of someone who might be related to you?"

"No." Nicole shrugged and added, "I think if I had anyone left, a sister or mother or whatnot, that person would have been with me when I was heading for New York. No one was with me. I was alone. I think that, for some reason, everyone else was dead."

"Maybe someone was waiting for you in New York," Fallon said. "Maybe you were going there to meet up with someone. Maybe they had some kind of safe refuge set up for you or something."

"It's a theory, I suppose. Anyway, as you can probably guess, the couple that picked me up later formally adopted me. The lawyer, Logan Stone, got into politics and moved all the way up to where he is now, the Governor of Florida. He and Naya put me through college. I went into law enforcement. They said my face and body were built for vice, so I ended up spending years there undercover and just recently got upgraded to homicide."

Nicole scraped eggs out of a pan and onto a plate.

She took a bite. It was a lot better than the cold cereal she usually had for breakfast.

"Enough about me. Your neighbor's security cameras," she said. "That's the first thing I want to run down this morning. Then I want to get to headquarters and see if I can get some manpower. I'm proceeding at this point as if your friend Danica is alive. I'm not deviating from that course unless I get concrete proof to the contrary, and even then I might not."

"Thank you."

5

Fallon had the key to her neighbor's house, plus permission to enter, to water the plants and keep an eye on the place while the couple took a jaunt down to Key West. There were four security cameras in all, one on each side of the house, meaning that one pointed at Fallon's residence. It also turned out that the cameras weren't just live streams but actually recorded.

Camera 2, that was the one that pointed at Fallon's house.

Nicole pulled up the events of last night on a flat-screen monitor and watched with Fallon at her side. At approximately 9:50 p.m. last night, before the power grid got knocked out, a vehicle pulled into Fallon's driveway and the headlights turned off. The storm was thick and intense and the image was anything but clear. The vehicle was the size and general shape of an SUV. Right now, Nicole couldn't tell what kind it was but the lab should be able to figure it out later. No one came out of the vehicle for a full two minutes.

Then the interior lights of the vehicle turned on as the black silhouette of a man stepped out. He was visible only for a second or two, between the time the dome lights went on and the time they went off, when he closed the door. He was nothing more than a brief, black, blurred shape. He never looked at the camera. His face was always pointed the other way.

When the door shut, he all but disappeared.

Because of the storm and the fact that there were no close streetlights, there was virtually no light where he was.

Minute after minute passed and the screen was almost pitch black with rain.

At approximately 10:10 p.m., which was 20 minutes from the time the vehicle first arrived, lightning flashed and the camera saw a man walking briskly to the vehicle, almost there in fact, with a naked woman slung over his shoulder. The man wore all things black—black shoes, black pants, a black hoodie and worst of all, a black ski-mask. At the back of the vehicle, as lightning continued to flash, almost like gunshots—bam, bam, bam, bam—he threw the woman into the back of the vehicle, roughly, as if she was a old tire, and then slammed the hatch shut. Strangely, the interior lights of the vehicle should have come on while the hatch was opened, but they didn't. The next flash showed him at the driver's door about to get in, but hesitating for a second to focus at something in the street, no doubt the jogger.

The headlights came on.

The vehicle moved towards the street and out of the range of the camera.

Nicole hit the pause button and said, "This is good."

Fallon shook her head and said, "Not to me it's not. You can't see a thing."

"It's the timing," Nicole said. "It was 20 minutes from the time he left the car until the time he returned to it with Danica. That's consistent with the syringe having a knock-out drug as opposed to a poison."

Fallon wrinkled her face. "I don't follow—"

"All right," Nicole said, "you see all these shows on TV where the bad guy injects a woman with a needle and she immediately collapses to the ground."

"Yeah."

"Well, that's not the way it works in real life," Nicole said. "In real life, a knock-out drug is going to take time to work, especially if it's injected into a muscle group like the buttocks or an arm, as opposed to directly into a vein through an IV. Opiates take time to work. So do tranquilizers. The fact that the guy was inside the house for so long is possibly—hopefully—because he was waiting for the injection to take full effect before he brought the woman outside."

"So what did he do while he was waiting?"

Nicole shrugged.

"I didn't see that much of a struggle or a whole lot of smearing of the blood on the sheets. He might have pinned her down and held a knife to her face and threatened her to just stay calm. Who knows?"

"He would have seen her face then," Fallon said. "He would have known it wasn't me. That means he was definitely after her."

Nicole exhaled, not sure if she should say what she was about to say, but concluding that Fallon deserved the truth.

"I don't want to sound like doom and gloom but I don't think we can conclude that at this point. We don't know how much light there was in the room, or even if her face was up. He might have been holding her face down into the pillow. Even if he knew it wasn't you, he was committed at that point. He might have figured he needed to stay there until the drug took effect, then take her with him because she was a witness, then come back for you later."

"Wow, you're a real bottle of sunshine," Fallon said.

Nicole shrugged.

"We need to keep watching your back until everything sorts itself out. That's all I'm saying. Nothing's for sure yet, one way or the other." She paused and added, "You know what? I never asked you where you were last night while all this was happening. Why weren't you home? It was late, your friend Danica came all the way to Miami to see you and had only been in town a couple of days—"

"It's really not important."

The words landed like a two-by-four to the side of Nicole's head. Why was she getting resistance to such a simple question?

"Well, indulge me anyway."

"If I do, you need to promise to keep it on the down low."

"I can't promise that," she said, which was true.

Fallon hesitated, deciding, and then said, "Let's just say I have a friend on the side."

"A friend of the male persuasion?"

The woman nodded.

"Yes. If you could keep it out of your report, that would be peachy."

"Does he have a name, this friend?"

"He does," Fallon said. "But he's married and he's prominent and I'm really not at liberty to name names."

"Does your husband know about him?"

"No."

"The reason I ask is, he could have hired someone to take you and teach you a lesson. That someone then took Danica by mistake."

Fallon laughed at the thought.

"That's not his thing," she said. "He's an aerospace engineer. He bleeds formulas and equations and chalkboard scribbles. Plus, he doesn't know what's going on. I'm positive of it."

Nicole wrinkled her forehead and said, "All I'm saying is, if I was a husband and wanted to hire someone to teach my cheating wife a lesson, do you know when I'd do it?"

"No."

"When I was a million miles away in Tokyo with a beer in my hand and an ironclad alibi in my pocket."

"You're wasting your brain cells on him."

"Then I should be careful," Nicole said. "I've only got ten or eleven to start with, and that's on a good day." She got serious and added, "As long as we're talking about relationships, do you have one with Danica as well? Physical, I mean—"

Fallon looked in the distance.

Then she focused on Nicole and said, "At times, yes."

The answer made Nicole wonder. Did they have a fight? Did Fallon hire someone to take Danica, out of revenge or hate or whatever? Was Fallon's apparent concern for Danica all just a big ruse?

Good questions; she'd think about them more later when she had time.

Right now, she cued up the footage of a second camera, the one on the front of the neighbor's house. It showed the SUV coming down the street, and then pulling into Fallon's driveway at 9:50. It also showed the jogger at 10:10, as she looked to the right when the lightning flashed. It showed the vehicle coming out the drive just after the jogger passed and then heading in the opposite direction of the jogger, meaning that the jogger's call to 911 last night was a hundred percent accurate.

The driver's face never came into view.

Nor did the license plate number. It was always at a severe angle to the lens, not to mention totally obscured by the rain. No amount of enhancement or digital manipulation could bring to life what wasn't there.

"Let's head down to homicide."

6

Nicole walked into homicide and wove through the desks and dividers and mess towards the 38-year-old head of the bureau, Nick Trane, whose wandering green eyes were already studying her curves and the way she walked and her smooth mocha skin and her thick black ponytail. At age 28, Nicole's body was strong, her movement had purpose and her face was something men could get lost in; women too, for that matter. She didn't mind that Trane played this game, and stared right back as she approached. The way he looked at her made her feel like a tropical lagoon on a warm summer day; and Trane, he was a wanderer with rum in his gut and a need for shelter. In a different time and place, she might let him take that shelter. But in this time and this place, he was her boss and they were at work, and that's probably the way it would stay for the rest of their lives, barring a drunken party at some point in the future and someone betting Trane that he couldn't bounce a quarter off Nicole's ass and hit the ceiling. But that night, if ever, was still a long, long ways off.

The man took a sip of coffee as Nicole slipped into one of the worn mismatched chairs in front of his desk.

He said, "I heard you got yourself a little busy last night."

She nodded.

"A little."

With that, she filled him in on everything and at the end said, "Fallon Bow is in room two, waiting for someone to take her formal statement. I think you should do it."

"Why?"

"Because she's keeping something from me," Nicole said. "I can feel it. Maybe you can figure out what it is." She paused and added, "Just be careful. She's your type."

Trane raised an eyebrow.

"My type?"

Nicole stood up.

"Don't look straight into her eyes, Nick. You'll be ruined." She pulled a quarter from her purse and pushed it across the table to him. "Put that in your wallet. You never know when you'll need it."

He wrinkled his brow.

"I don't get it," he said.

"Private joke. Just trust me and keep it handy."

She headed upstairs to the crime lab to see if Paul Penn had stumbled on anything interesting while processing the scene last night. The man wrinkled his half-Korean face, from his mother's side, and said, "Maybe something a little interesting. The victim's purse was in the living room. Guess what was in it?"

Nicole shrugged.

"I don't know. An elephant?"

"Close enough," the man said. "A Sig subcompact 9mm."

"Seriously?"

He nodded. "With a loaded clip and one in the hole."

"Is it registered to her?"

"Don't know, don't care," he said. "That's your job. Guess what else was in there?"

"I don't know. Another elephant?"

He smiled. "There can't be another elephant if the first one wasn't in there. Next time guess, an envelope full of hundred-dollar bills. Twenty grand plus a few extra for good measure, to be precise."

Wow.

That was interesting.

All she could think to say was, "The girl knows how to party."

"Yes she does. Oh, and one more thing," Penn said. "Her cell phone was also in that very same purse that had no elephants in it. I made two backups." He tapped on a phone sitting on his desk and pushed it towards her. "This is it, for you—a present. Like I said, it's a backup so if you accidently delete something or mess something up, life will go on."

She looked at it.

"Anything good in there?"

"Messages, mail, phone calls, photos, Safari history, and some blah, and blah and blah. Other than that, nothing; except a truckload of iTune songs, and a calculator, if you ever wanted to figure out what the square root of 303 is."

She picked it up and gave the man a kiss on the cheek.

"Thanks. This is gold."

"Remember where you got it from, pretty lady. Oh, and I had the syringe delivered to the lab; the bloody sheets, too. I'll let you know what type of an ETA they give me."

While Trance interviewed Fallon, Nicole found an empty conference room, poured a long hot cup of coffee, rounded up a notepad and a #2 pencil, and kick-started the phone, which wasn't password protected.

Danica Rose, it turned out, was living a life of chaos.

For starters, she was juggling three love interests.

One of her lovers was the director of The Shoals, the internationally acclaimed Adam Montrachet himself; who liked to get naked pictures of Danica by way of personal messages, and, in return, send her pictures of his privates. It wasn't clear why, because they weren't anything to brag about, getting to about half-mast at best. It was possible that the 20 large in the envelope in Danica's purse came from him, as he wasn't a natural selection for her sexual favors, in spite of his posture in the film industry. At 53-years-old, he was 30 years older than her and, although he wasn't exactly ugly, he wasn't exactly the opposite, either. Danica was way out of his league. The more Nicole thought about it, the more convinced she became that he was in fact the source of the money.

Another of Danica's lovers was a female cast member of The Shoals named Maria Sanchez, an exotic Latino beauty with super-straight black hair that hung halfway down her back. They were each other's equals in every way, except on different ends of the color spectrum.

The third of Danica's lovers was Ethan Blue, the drummer of Rude, an athletic guy about the same age as Danica, in his early twenties, with a big white smile and shaggy surfer hair. Pictures of him were usually on the beach with a surfboard near by.

In addition to juggling three lovers, Danica's schedule for the last umpteen months had mostly been consumed in the Caribbean with intense filming of The Shoals.

Ethan Blue, the drummer, was pressuring Danica to join back up and get Rude going again, but so far she was resisting him, leaving the band in limbo.

Her agent, a man named Lance Fox, was getting a lot of interest in Danica from other directors, now that the word about her extraordinary talents was leaking out. Fox was busy reviewing screenplays and trying to determine which roles might best launch Danica to the next level. So far he'd suggested two auditions, each for killer roles in high-budget productions, but she'd hadn't yet committed to doing either of them, in spite of daily pressure from Fox.

Something dark was going on in Danica's life and Ethan Blue, the drummer, was the one who knew about it. He was the one who Danica approached four months ago, during the middle of the The Shoals filming, about wanting a gun. He recommended a Sig subcompact 9mm and encouraged her to purchase a new one legally from a licensed dealer, rather than a used one from Craigslist or a gun show or whatever. That would avoid any legal issues. After filming, when Danica returned to L.A., the two of them both bought identical Sigs from a licensed dealer. On several occasions over the last few months, they rented a 20-foot Boston Whaler, took it offshore to where no one was around, and practiced shooting at plastic bottles they set afloat on the water. Danica's photo folder had lots of snaps from out there on the waves.

The trailer for The Shoals hadn't yet been released to the public but Danica had an advance copy of it on her phone, and it was fantastic. The 30-second clip showed an intense, artfully filmed thriller set under a sizzling Caribbean sun.

She was a star in the making.

There was no doubt about it.

Interestingly, Danica had absolutely no presence on social media. She wasn't on Facebook, Twitter, or anything else. Nor did she have a blog or website.

Nicole found it all interesting but couldn't yet see any solid connection to the events of last night. It was still possible that the man who took her simply came across her somewhere and picked her out. Or, equally likely, he picked out Fallon Bow and ended up taking Danica by mistake.

The conference door opened and Trane walked in with a cup of coffee in his left hand. He slipped into a chair across the table from Nicole, took a long slurp and said, "I have a theory. It might be way off, but at least it's something to chew on."

"I'm hungry enough for a bite," Nicole said.

"Okay. When I started to ask Fallon Bow where she was last night when Danica got taken, all she would tell me is that she was with a man who was married and prominent and she couldn't tell me his name. I pressed but she said you told her that she could end the interview if that happened."

Nicole nodded.

"It was that or not have her come down at all," she said.

"I get it and you made the right move," he said. "So here's my theory. We have this prominent guy. Let's say some third person really wants him to do something that he's in a unique position to do. Mr. Third Person abducts Fallon Bow and holds her for ransom until Mister Prominent Guy does as he's told. He ends up taking Danica by mistake." Nicole felt Trane's eyes on hers, waiting for a response.

"It's possible, I guess."

Trane raked his thick brown hair back with his fingers. It immediately flopped back down over his forehead. "I wouldn't mind figuring out who Mister Prominent Guy is."

"How?"

"Get into Fallon Bow's cell phone," he said.

"You mean on the sly?"

"Yes."

The words tasted sour.

"She's sort of my friend," she said.

Trane nodded.

"If that's true then do what it takes to save her because there's a good chance she's next. She's waiting for you down in the conference room. Take her out to lunch or something and get a look at her phone."

7

Nicole dropped Fallon off back at the loft and said, "If you get bored, go down to the studio. Tell Juicy you're my friend. He'll let you hang out. Just be warned they have a stripper pole in there. He'll want you to take a test ride. Don't feel obligated."

Fallon shook her head in déjà vu and said, "I probably shouldn't tell you this, but I'm not a total stranger to those things."

Nicole focused on the woman to see if she was messing with her.

She wasn't.

"Seriously?"

"I danced at Bottoms Up for two years," she said. "That's where I met Conway. He was there at a bachelor party, way out of his element. Just for grins I went over and straddled his lap. The rest as they say is history."

"What about this guy you're seeing on the side?" Nicole said. "Is that where you met him? At Bottoms Up?"

Fallon laughed softly at the idea.

"No. He can't go to places like that." She took a sip of coffee and added, "He'd like to, don't get me wrong, and does when he's in Vegas, but here in town it's really not an option."

"So he's somebody I'd know, then—"

Fallon nodded.

"Oh, yeah."

"Where's he go in Vegas?"

"The Rhino, usually." She smiled and added, "Men will be men."

"You don't mind?"

"Mind, honey, I go with him. We have a blast." She took a sip of coffee, looked at Nicole over the top of the cup, and said, "So what's with you and Mr. Yummy?"

"Who?"

"The Yum-Yum man, Nick Trane—are you guys doing it or what?"

Nicole chuckled.

"He's my boss."

"Yeah, I know, but that's not what I asked, is it?"

Nicole rolled her eyes.

"You are a wild one, aren't you?"

Nicole checked her watch to find it was already mid-morning. She didn't have time for chitchat. She needed to get to the big questions. "I wanted to ask about your husband, Conway," she said. "You said he's an aerospace engineer at Martin Marietta."

"Right."

"How long has he been with them?"

"Eleven years, actually. They snatched him up right after he graduated from Harvard."

"Does he have a high security clearance?"

"I think so. Why?"

Nicole said, "Maybe someone wanted to take you to blackmail him into doing something; you know, access some confidential information or whatnot."

Fallon chewed on it.

Then she said, "It's possible, in theory, but I haven't detected any stress in Conway, other than the normal work-related kind. I think if he was under a pressure like that I'd see it."

"Maybe he wasn't under the pressure yet," Nicole said. "Maybe the plan was to snatch you out of the blue and then contact him. *We got your wife. Now here's what you're going to do to get her back.*"

Fallon shrugged.

"I guess it's possible. It would all come down to what he has access to and who would want it bad enough to get that crazy. I know he has a lot of clearance to sensitive stuff, but what it is exactly, I don't know."

"Was he working on anything like weapons? You know, nuclear bomb triggers; or surveillance satellites, or something like that?"

"I don't know. He's under a confidentiality clause that he takes pretty seriously. He doesn't tell me much. I know that whatever it is he's doing, it's leading edge, but I don't know anything about any of the specifics."

"How about this mystery man that you have on the side?" Nicole said. "Is there any chance someone tried to take you to force him to do something?"

"If he saw anything like that coming—something that could even remotely drag me into danger—he'd tell me about it and he'd also have a couple of guys hanging in the shadows to watch my back. He wouldn't be taking it lying down. That's not his style. I haven't seen any guys in the shadows and he's never said anything to suggest that I could be in danger. I think that what you have are the bones of a theory but those bones will never get up and walk."

"Okay."

"Plus," Fallon added, "before someone could use me as leverage against him, they would have to know that him and me are a thing. There aren't too many people in the world that fit that description. In fact, from my end, there aren't any. I never even told Danica who he is."

"And I take it you're still not going to tell me?"

Fallon patted Nicole's hand and said, "Can't, baby, sorry."

Time was precious and it was evaporating fast.

Nicole had to run.

She gave Fallon a quick kiss on the cheek and said, "Hang with Juicy."

Then she was gone.

Outside, Nicole took Penny Lane to Fallon's street and knocked on one neighbor's door after another to see if anyone had seen a white or silver SUV canvassing the area, or seen anyone on Fallon Bow's property (even if they looked like a utility worker or whatnot), or seen anything at all unusual in the neighborhood at any time over, say, the last week.

No one had anything to report until Nicole knocked on a door several houses down and got greeted by an overweight middle-aged woman in a bathrobe named Linda Monroe, who had both a mouthful of words and the time to spit them out.

"Yeah, I seen a white 4Runner around here a couple of times," she said. "I used to have a 4Runner so I know them when I see them. Best vehicle I ever owned; had 197,000 miles on it when I sold it and still ran like it was new. Never put a nickel into it except for maintenance. It never stranded me, not once."

"I'm jealous," Nicole said. "I have a old Porsche and it's like having a second mortgage. Tell me about the 4Runner."

"Well, I know it's not from this little enclave because I've been here for 26 years and I know which cars live here and which don't," she said. "This isn't exactly a cross-through street, either, so it was a little bit strange that I kept seeing it."

"Which was how many times?"

The woman retreated in thought.

"Well, not that many, really, now that I think about it,

maybe three or four over the last couple of weeks," she said. "The only reason I remember it is because the driver always had his arm hanging out the window with a cigarette dangling from his fingers. I hate cigarettes. Those companies get kids hooked and kill them just to put a few dollars in their pockets. They ought to be shot if you ask me."

"So he smoked?"

"Yeah, but the cigarette's not the thing that got my attention so much as it was the tattoos."

"He had tattoos?"

The woman rolled her eyes.

"All over his arm," she said. "They were crawling all over him like thieves. I never could understand how someone could do something like that to their body. No one will hire you if you look like that. Yeah, some liquor store or gas station maybe, but no one good."

Nicole disagreed but kept it to herself. Instead she said, "Describe the guy as best you can. What race was he?"

"Oh, white; definitely white. Not tanned, either. White. White as in, Casper. Do you know what I mean when I say Casper?"

"The Ghost, I assume."

"Right. He was white like that."

"Okay. What color was his hair?"

"I couldn't tell. He was wearing a red baseball cap and big black wraparound sunglasses," she said. "I really couldn't tell much about his head or his face. And he never really looked in my direction. Most of the times, I was in the house just looking out when I happened to see him driving past. It was only one time when I was outside the house and saw him. I was watering the flowers. He never looked my way."

"Okay."

"Sorry. I wish I'd seen him better."

"You're doing good," Nicole said. "How old was he? Could

you tell?"

"Not really. Thirties, maybe? I don't know—"

"What about his size? Was he big, small, fat, skinny?"

"He definitely wasn't skinny," the woman said. "Anything but. His arm had a lot of muscle to it. Now I remember something. He was wearing a T-shirt but he had a cigarette pack rolled up in the sleeve, back like they used to do in the '50s. That's why I was able to see so many muscles."

"What about the 4Runner? Were there any signs on it or dents or anything else other than just a normal factory vehicle?"

"Not really," she said. "It didn't look that old. It was nice and clean. Even the tires were shiny."

Maybe a rental, Nicole thought.

Suddenly Nicole's phone rang and Trane's voice came through.

"Where are you?" he said.

"Fallon Bow's street, knocking on doors."

"Get back to the office."

"Why, what's up?"

"I'll tell you when you get here. Leave now—and watch your back."

"Watch my back?"

"Just do it. Do you have your weapon with you?"

"Yes."

"Keep it close."

The line died.

Nicole thanked the woman, Linda Monroe, then made her way to Penny Lane and said, "Start." When she cranked over the key, the engine fired right over, which it usually did after it had been run a time or two earlier in the day. She said, "Good girl," did a 180 and headed up the street.

Then something strange happened.

A ways up the road, a vehicle was parked at the curb. A

man's arm hung outside the driver's side window. It looked like the hand on that arm could be dangling a cigarette. The vehicle wasn't a white 4Runner, it was a blue sedan of some sort, but still— As she approached, heavy tattoos showed, as did a cigarette. The arm was muscular.

Nicole brought Penny Lane across the centerline to nose in to the front end of the car. As she approached, the arm swung inside, bringing the cigarette with it, and the vehicle's daytime running lights turned on, meaning the engine had been started.

She got out and held her badge up as she approached on foot.

Suddenly the vehicle backed up violently, spun around and burned rubber as it raced away down the street.

Nicole never got a look at the man's face.

She could tell what kind of vehicle it was, though.

It was a Mustang, a blue Mustang.

She reflected on the fact that the man never flicked the cigarette or dropped it. He brought it back in with him in spite of the sudden movement.

You didn't hang onto it because you were going to finish smoking it, Nicole thought. *You brought it in because you didn't want to leave any DNA behind.*

You're a clever little bastard, aren't you?

8

Danica Rose woke from a deep dark sleep to a throbbing head and a stiff achy body, indicating that she had been passed out in the same position for a long, long time.

She wasn't in her bed.

She was on an air mattress, under a simple gray blanket.

She threw the blanket to the side and pushed up into a sitting position to find that she was inside an old, wrecked airplane that looked like it crashed eons ago. At this point it was nothing more than a gutted, rusty shell. Sunlight spilled in from the far end where the fuselage had torn apart. Beyond that opening were tall grasses and rolling nature without any hint of civilization. At the other end of the plane, behind her, was a cockpit that had been picked clean of wires and gauges decades ago. She guessed that it was some kind of WWII plane that went down way out in the middle of nowhere and then got forgotten by time.

Around her left ankle was a handcuff, fastened tight enough that she'd never be able to pull it off, but not so tight as to bite into her flesh. The other end of the cuff was secured to a thick steel chain that wrapped around part of the interior structure and was secured by a shiny new padlock.

Okay, don't panic.

Stay focused.

She stood up, thankfully having a couple feet of clearance above her head, and stretched the chain as far as it would go towards the open end. It turned out to be about 20 feet long and allowed her to go within five feet of the opening, give or take.

From this vantage point, she was able to see something out there in the grasses that she couldn't see before, namely a small, plastic cage of some type, about the size and shape of a 20-gallon aquarium. Inside that cage was a large rattlesnake; no, wait, two rattlesnakes.

Her chest pounded.

She scrambled back to the mattress, got under the blanket and curled up into a ball.

A couple of minutes later she spotted something that made her come out of the ball, namely a large plastic bin hidden under a blanket. She dragged it to the far end by the opening where the light was better and found goodies galore—canned goods, fruits, granola bars and snacks, water, plastic cups, a flashlight, toilet paper, soap, hand wipes, garbage bags, napkins, a hairbrush, a mirror, a pen and notepad, Tylenol, a small first-aid kit, a razor and, perhaps most surprising of all, three paperbacks—Cannery Row by John Steinbeck, Along Came a Spider by James Patterson, and Hawaii by James A. Michener. Plus there were magazines—People, Vanity Fair, Time, Fitness and Architectural Digest.

She also found a folded piece of paper that had been printed from a computer:

RULES

Do not call out for help.

Do not scream or try to get anyone's attention.

If someone should come around, stay quiet and hidden.

When I return for you, do not look at me.

Always address me as Master.
Obey all of my commands completely and promptly.
Failure to follow these rules shall result in serious
punishment.

She wadded the paper up and threw it out the opening where
it bounced off a rock.

9

When Nicole got to homicide, Trane pulled her into a conference room and closed the door. "Wait a minute," he said, then left and returned sixty seconds later with two cups of coffee, one of which he placed in front of her. "Okay, did I ever tell you about my friend Dr. Leigh Fielder?"

"No."

"Well, she's an FBI profiler in Quantico," he said. "I've had the pleasure—and she's had the displeasure—of working a couple of cases together."

Nicole smiled.

"Okay."

"Over the years I've tapped her as a resource, which she allows me to do on the promise that I'll take her out and get her drunk if she ever makes her way back to Miami again."

"That's a pretty lopsided deal."

Trane nodded.

"It is, it is indeed," he said. He wrinkled his face and said, "Lopsided which way?"

"Your way."

"You mean, I'm getting the best of it—"

She nodded.

"Right."

"That's what I thought you meant." He took a sip of coffee. "I had a little chat with her this morning."

"Regarding my case?"

He nodded.

"That jar that the guy left on Fallon Bow's kitchen counter, it's obviously some kind of signature move, so I thought I'd email a few pictures of it to Leigh and see if she had any cases in her database where the same move was used. It turns out that she did."

The words felt like the sun coming out. There were other cases to cross-reference to. There should be happiness on Trane's face but there wasn't.

"What's wrong?" Nicole said.

"Well, a couple of things, actually," he said. "They call the guy Hollywood."

"Hollywood?"

"Right."

"Why?"

"It's where he first struck. Here's the thing. The guy's hit eight times so far that the FBI knows of, meaning there are probably more than eight. The victims are always women, pretty women. They've ranged in age so far from 19 to 33. He always takes them from their house, usually after they go to sleep. He likes to do it on stormy nights. In each case, he injects them with a sedative made from a combination of opiates and a veterinary tranquilizer. He waits for them to pass out then carries him out to his car and drives off."

"That's exactly what happened here," Nicole said.

Trane nodded.

"The spinner on top of the bottle is always divided into 6 pie-shaped wedges labeled 2, 4, 6, 2, 4, 6. According to the FBI's theory, Hollywood spins it before he leaves. Wherever the pointer lands, that's how many days his victim gets to live." Trane looked at Nicole sideways. "You flicked the spinner, right?"

Nicole exhaled.

"Yes, twice."

"Okay, so here's the big question," Trane said. "Do you remember what number it was on before you flicked it?"

Nicole swallowed.

"I saw the bottle there on the counter and picked it up to get a better look at it," she said. "When I did that, the pointer moved. I never saw where it was before I picked it up. It could have been anywhere."

Trane nodded.

That's what he thought.

"Okay, so we don't know if she has 2, 4 or 6 days to live."

"God, I feel terrible," Nicole said, which was true.

"What's done is done," Trane said. "Things won't get better by kicking ourselves. We'll have a heart-to-heart later about not contaminating a scene, but I'm not really interested in that right now." He took a long sip of coffee. "The thing that's inside the bottle, that's the way the victim is going to die. So in this case, we have a rattlesnake head. Hollywood is going to kill her with a rattlesnake; maybe more than one, maybe a pit full."

Nicole pictured it.

A cold shiver ran up her spine and speared directly into her brain.

"This can't be happening—"

"Hollywood has been morphing over the years," Trane said. "His first known case had a bullet in the jar and the victim was shot in the back of the head. His second known case had a knife in the jar; the victim was killed from multiple stabs to her spine. Then he started to get a little more creative. One bottle contained acid, another contained a piece of electrical wire—the victim was electrocuted, and another contained a piece of rope—the victim was hung."

"This is crazy,"

"I'm glad you said that because we're going to talk about that in a second," Trane said. "Of the eight known abductions, six of the women have been found, killed in the exact way as indicated by the jar. In two cases, the women have never been found. One involved a bottle with a couple inches of dirt in it; the assumption is that the victim was buried alive, which explains why she was never found. In the other case, the bottle had a shark tooth inside. The assumption is that the victim was boated out to sea and chum was used to draw in sharks and whip them into a feeding frenzy. Then the victim was pushed in."

Nicole laid her head on the table and closed her eyes.

Her hands trembled.

She was scared.

She didn't want Trane to see it but there was no way to hide.

"We're only half done with the story," Trane said.

Nicole raised her head and locked eyes with him.

"What's the rest?"

"The rest is the scary part," Trane said. "Taking a pretty woman and killing her in some kind of weird beat-the-clock way isn't Hollywood's endgame. It's just the start of a bigger fun, which is between him and the detective trying to catch him. His endgame is to kill the detective before the detective saves the victim. He's killed five detectives so far. In the other three instances, the detectives managed to stay alive until the victim died. That spares them. If they can last that long they get to live."

Nicole processed the words.

"Are you saying he's going to kill me?"

"No, because I'm taking you off the case effective immediately," Trane said. "I'm in charge of it now. If this guy's going to kill someone, it's going to be me."

Nicole processed the words and knew she should be

appreciative and relived but she wasn't.

"Nick, this is my case," she said.

"Was your case—"

"Is my case," she said. "I've earned the right to do my job. I've earned the right to be treated just like everyone else. Get it out of your brain that my father is the Governor."

Trane exhaled.

"Here's the thing," he said. "I'd rather have you alive and pissed at me than dead and loving me. You're off the case and that's final. You're not to talk to anyone about it, you're not to do anything on it unless I ask you to, and you're not to go out of the office during working time." He checked his watch and then stood up. "They're waiting for me down at Channel 8. I'm going on the news, technically seeking information for the public regarding anyone who may have seen anything about the abduction last night, but actually putting my face out there as the detective in charge of the case. With any luck, Hollywood isn't aware of your involvement yet."

Nicole tapped her fingers on the table, remembering the headlights outside her loft last night.

Then she looked Trane in the eyes and said, "It's too late for that. I just showed him my badge not more than an hour ago. He's driving a blue Mustang."

Nicole filled Trane in.

Trane let her tell the story without interruption.

At the end, he wasn't impressed. "All you have is an arm hanging out and a tattoo and a cigarette," he said. "I could drive around Miami and see that exact scene at least a hundred times today."

"But he didn't flick the cigarette," Nicole said. "He didn't want to leave any DNA behind. The guy was Hollywood. I'm telling you."

"Or, cigarettes are expensive so you don't just throw them away," Trane said. "Look, I appreciate that he took off when you walked towards him with your badge, but that doesn't mean he's the one who took Danica. It might mean nothing more than he had an outstanding warrant; or he had a bag of goodies under the seat; or any number of a hundred other things. That's a rich neighborhood. He could have been there waiting to do a drug deal."

Nicole wasn't convinced.

"I think he was the one."

"You think, but you don't know and neither do I," Trane said. "The bottom line is this, we're not going to take any chances and you're off the case. I have to head down to the TV station now but I'll be back in an hour or two and we'll talk about this some more. You'll still get to help, it will just be from the sidelines. In the meantime, you're not to leave this office. Do we understand each other?"

Nicole nodded.

Trane stood up and gave her a sideways look when he paused at the door.

He said, "I'm serious, Nicole."

Then he was gone.

Ten seconds later he was back.

"I'm sorry about this, Nicole. You're a good detective. That's not what this is about."

Then he was gone, again.

10

Nicole stayed in the conference room so long that when she finally reached down to take a sip of coffee it was cold. Her thoughts weren't on her loss of the case, but on Danica Rose. So far, of eight victims taken, six had been found dead and two had disappeared permanently; one buried alive and the other fed to the sharks, presumably. Of the eight little pretties that had been abducted, there had been no survivors so far, not a one.

Nicole didn't care if she had the case or Trane had it or someone from the FBI came in and took it over or whatever. She didn't care if some freak-show called Hollywood was hunched in the shadows with demons in his head and waiting for Nicole to walk past.

But she did care about whether Danica Rose made it home alive. And she did care whether the guy might come after Fallon, if she was the target all along.

Maybe Trane was the best hope for a happy ending and a long scrolling list of credits. He did, after all, have a gazillion hours of experience compared to Nicole's zero.

Still, the old adage played in her head:

Two men fight. Their bodies are identical. Their training is identical. One has blond hair and one has black hair. Which one wins?

I don't know.

The one who's the maddest—

Right now, that was Nicole. She was the maddest. Having broken the case, and having spent the long stormy hours last night with Fallon in her bed, it had all moved into her blood. It wasn't abstract. It was pumping through her veins and beating in her heart, and that was worth something. She wasn't useless. She needed to be involved in the case one way or another, and not just as some we'll-call-you-if-we-need-you lump of clay sitting behind a desk where it was all safe and sound.

No, no way.

She was going to be in the case in a meaningful way whether anyone liked it or not.

If she ended up fired, then that would just have to be the price; no tears, no regrets.

At least she'd be able to look at herself in the mirror without seeing Danica's dead eyes staring back at her.

There was one other important thing at play, as far as she was concerned. From what she knew of Trane, he was a catch rather than a kill kind of detective.

Nicole, if given a half a justification, would put a bullet in Hollywood's face and send his soul screaming in a fireball down into eternal damnation where it belonged. That would be a better ending than the one Trane had planned.

She knew she could do it, too.

She was pretty sure she'd done it before; killed a man, that is.

She didn't remember when or who or why, but it had come to her in a dream and she'd written it down on one of her index cards and tacked it to the wall. That meant she'd done it before the coma, before she was fourteen. If she could do it at that young of an age then she could do it now, assuming of course, that the man gave her half a reason. She couldn't and wouldn't execute him in cold blood. But it wouldn't take much of a justification and certainly a lot less than Trane would need.

From homicide, Nicole took Penny Lane back to Fallon's house, where she parked in the street under the shade of a palm tree. Yellow crime scene tape still sealed the front door, as it should. She sat down on the front steps and let her eyes wander over the neighbors' houses. Everything was normal, perfectly Leave it to Beaver.

So, where was Danica Rose right now?

Hollywood would have had to take her somewhere secluded. He'd be spending the next two days, at least, hunting Nicole or Trane or whoever it was he ended up believing was the prime detective on the case. That meant he'd have to leave Danica alone, which in turn meant she'd have to be isolated enough that no one could hear her screaming for help. Even if the man drugged her, there was always a possibility she could wake up and start screaming. She'd need to be remote.

So where'd you stash her?

A farm?

A shack out in the everglades?

An old abandoned warehouse?

A car drove up the street. Nicole looked up to see if it was a blue Mustang or a tattooed arm. It wasn't. It was a way-too-pretty trophy wife in a drop-top Audi. The woman flicked a cigarette out into the world and gave Nicole a cold sideways glance as she passed.

Unless Hollywood was from Miami, which he probably wasn't, it would take time to find a good location to stash his little victim. He might have opted for something abandoned, but that brought the risk of someone stumbling into the place. It would be safer to rent a place; that would give him control. But renting a place would take time.

How long have you been hanging around in town?

A week?

Two?

Nicole dialed Fallon who actually answered with a live voice. "It's me, Nicole. Got a question for you. I've been assuming that Danica flew to Miami, but is that true?"

"Actually, no. She drove."

"I didn't know that. When, exactly?"

"It was spur of the moment thing," Fallon said. "She called me and said she needed to get out of Dodge and asked if I wanted a roommate for a week or two. I said fine. She rented a car in L.A. and drove out."

"So, before she called you, no one knew she was coming to Miami, not even her, right?"

"That's true as far as I know," Fallon said. "You don't sound so good. Is something wrong?"

Nicole exhaled.

"I came across some information after you left," Nicole said. "The guy who took Danica has done this kind of thing before, at least eight times. The FBI even has a name for him—Hollywood."

"Hollywood?"

"Yeah," she said. "Here's the important thing as far as you're concerned. Hollywood likes to kill the detective in charge of the case. That means that I could be a target, which in turn means that I can't have you hanging around. You're going to need to make arrangements to stay somewhere else."

Silence.

Then Fallon said, "I know how to use a gun. I'll see you back at your place later."

The line went dead.

Nicole almost dialed the woman back but didn't feel like arguing about it right now. Right now, the timeline was the thing. Okay, Hollywood could have picked Danica out in L.A. He could have followed her to Miami. He would have had three days to find a secure location to stash her. That might have been enough. So, Danica might have been the intended victim all along.

Danica arrived Friday night, meaning Hollywood would have too. He most likely got a hotel room that night. He might have rented an SUV, either that day or Saturday or Sunday or even Monday.

Suddenly a TV van pulled up in front of the house and, just like that, an attractive well-dressed woman holding a microphone headed towards Nicole at a brisk pace, followed by a barrel-chested man with a giant camera perched on his shoulder, struggling to keep up.

"Excuse me," the woman said. "Is this the house where the abduction took place?"

Nicole hesitated, because she wasn't supposed to be on the case, and then said, "Yes."

"Are you a friend?"

"No, I'm a homicide detective."

"You're a detective on the case?"

"Yes, Nicole Stone, Miami-Dade homicide."

"Perfect. I'd like to ask you a few questions if you don't mind," the woman said. The camera was already rolling. The woman turned to face it so that both she and Nicole were in the frame and said, "I'm here on Hibiscus Island, talking to Miami-Dade Homicide Detective Nicole Stone on a story that is just now breaking." She turned to Nicole and said, "Detective Stone, can you give us a report on what exactly is going on?"

The microphone went to Nicole's mouth.

She swallowed, unsure whether to run or talk, and said, "We're looking into the possible abduction of a woman from this residence last night."

"Can you give us a name?"

"Yes, I suppose so. Danica Rose."

"Can you tell us what happened?"

"About all I can tell you at this time is that it's an ongoing investigation and we're in the very early hours of it." A pause, then, "Hold on." Nicole pulled a picture of Danica up on her phone and held it still for the camera to zoom in on. Then she said, "This is Danica Rose. If anyone knows where she is or has seen her since last night, please call us at Miami homicide."

The reporter said, "Thank you," then turned to the camera and said, "That was Miami-Dade Homicide Detective Nicole Stone, asking for your help if you have any information as to the whereabouts of Danica Rose. We'll be sure to keep you updated as this story develops."

The camera dropped.

The woman let the smile and energy fall from her face and handed Nicole her business card. "Would you mind emailing me that photo? We'll get it up on the evening news for you."

Nicole saw no harm.

"Sure."

The woman wrinkled a brow and said, "Are you that detective who is the daughter of Governor Stone?"

"Yes."

"I thought so. I never forget a face. I voted for him, by the way. I guess that makes us blood sisters or something."

Nicole smiled.

Then the smile dropped off.

Up the street, parked under the shade of a tree, was a vehicle that hadn't been there before. The driver had an arm hanging out the window. The car wasn't a blue Mustang; it was something white, but still, it could be the same guy as before. He could have switched cars.

Nicole leaned in and said, "Do me a favor. Drive by that white car up the street and see if you can get any footage of it, especially the driver's face, and a license plate number if you can. Don't slow down or anything. Just do it on the sly as you're passing by. Can you do that?"

"Yes, but first, let's do this." Then to the cameraman, "Sean, I want you to frame up that camera like you're focusing on me and Detective Stone, as if we're doing more interviews. What I want you to do is actually zoom in on that white car down the street. Try to get the license plate number and the driver's face and whatever else you can get."

The man shrugged.

"Sure. Is he the bad guy?"

"I don't know." Then to Nicole, "Is he?"

"Time will tell. Thank you for this. I really appreciate it."

The cameraman did as well as he could, but the car took off ten seconds into the shoot. The license place couldn't be read because it was smeared with mud. The rear window reflected the sky and blocked all visibility of anything inside the car, including the driver's head.

In the end, all they got was a fairly good shot of the man's arm as it hung out the window. It was muscular and covered in tattoos. A cigarette dangled from the man's hand.

The reporter looked at Nicole and said, "A clean car but a muddy license plate. That's a little weird."

Nicole nodded.

"My thought exactly."

11

When the reporter and cameraman crew left, Nicole sat back down on the front steps of Fallon Bow's house and waited to see if the white car would make a pass down the street. If she saw it coming, she was going to run into the street waving her badge and shouting for the guy to stop. If the man didn't, Nicole was going to blow the tires to smithereens, so long as there were no innocent bystanders nearby.

Come on.

I'm waiting for you.

A minute passed, then another, and the vehicle didn't show. The more Nicole thought about her plan, the crazier it got. If she ran towards the car, each step would bring her closer to being a target. The window could come down, a gun could suddenly rise up and … Bam! Bam! Bam! The last thing she'd ever hear would be the dull thump of her own body hitting the ground and the simultaneous squealing of getaway rubber.

A vehicle came down the street.

It wasn't the white car. It was the trophy wife in the drop-top Audi, taking a long drag from a cigarette as she passed.

Nice life.

I'll take a plateful of that, maybe with some fries on the side.

Hell, throw in a shot of Tequila, too.

So, how exactly did Hollywood follow Danica from La La Land to Miami, assuming he did? He wouldn't have had time to rent a car. He would have had to use his own. That meant that when he got to Miami, he was driving a car that had California plates.

As for the white car down the street, the TV cameraman hadn't been able to capture a lot, but did get enough to show that the vehicle was a white Dodge Challenger; and, although the license plate was muddy and couldn't be read, it was definitely a Florida plate, not a California one.

So, was it a rental?

Could she figure out who Hollywood was by simply running down the list of people who rented a white Challenger in the last day or two or three?

Her phone rang.

The display indicated it was Nick Trane.

She hesitated, deciding, because she wasn't supposed to be working the case, and then let it go to voicemail. A minute later it beeped, indicating she had a message. She didn't pull it up. She could already feel the anger through the plastic. Right now, at this second, she needed clarity, not conflict.

It was already 1:15 in the afternoon.

In approximately nine hours, one full day will have passed since Danica had been abducted. There might be as little as one day left after that.

She knew what she needed to do.

She needed to get on the web and get the phone number of every car rental company in the Miami area. Then, starting with the largest ones, she needed to call those numbers, identify herself as a Miami homicide detective, and find out who rented a white Challenger in the last two or three days, especially if that person was from California. If she did it at the office, she'd have to confront Trane, so she decided to go home and do the work there, which would also give her a chance to check on the place and make sure nothing funny was going on.

On the ride home, she checked Penny Lane's rearview mirror every ten seconds.

No Hollywoods showed their faces.

The miles clicked off without any phantoms of death or flying bullets coming her way.

Penny Lane, bless her little heart, made it all back to the loft without breaking down, earning herself a little pat on the dash. The parking lot was full, meaning Jay-J had a serious recording session in progress. Nicole walked all the way up the fire escape and reached in her purse before remembering that she gave her one and only key to Fallon this morning. She turned the doorknob anyway, on the chance Fallon was inside and hadn't locked the door behind her.

To her surprise, the door opened.

Inside, there was no visible sign of Fallon, although she could have been behind the curtain taking care of business.

"Hey, Fallon, are you here?"

No one answered.

"Hello?"

Only silence greeted her.

She stood there, just inside the door where she could run out if she needed to, and let her eyes fall here and there, looking for anything amiss or disturbed or missing. Everything was normal, visually, but something felt off.

"Fallon?"

More silence came her way.

She got her gun in hand and stepped inside, one careful motion at a time. Everything was perfectly normal. She went back to the door lock to see if it had been jimmied. It didn't look like it had been tampered with.

She locked the door behind her.

It was then that she noticed something wrong.

One of the 12 x 12 panes of glass on the south wall was broken. Jagged glass was on the floor. Further inside, under a dresser, she found a rock. That wasn't totally unusual, it had happened before, with some of Juicy's visitors getting high and being stupid.

Still, it was weird.

Whatever had happened, Nicole didn't have time to give it any more thought. She fired up her iPad at the kitchen table and got busy contacting rental car companies, pleading her case for any information on white Challengers that had been rented out in the last two or three days, and in most cases getting a promise that they'd look into it and call her back as soon as they could.

In the middle of it, Trane called again, and Nicole let it go to voicemail again.

Then the return calls from the rental companies started coming in.

"No, no white Challengers were rented out in the last three days. In fact, I don't even see that we have any white ones in our inventory. Only red and black ones are showing up."

"Okay, thanks."

Then came a very interesting call.

"Yes, we did rent a white Challenger out. Got a pencil?"

She did.

She did indeed.

Elliot Drake of Cleveland, Ohio, he was the one who rented the Challenger, just after 11:00 a.m. yesterday morning, from the MIA location.

Bingo!

It all fit, except for the fact that the man was from Ohio instead of California. Still, it was possible that he recently moved from Ohio to L.A. and still had his Ohio driver's license. Or, he could have driven from Ohio to California simply to search out his next victim. After all, you couldn't keep killing people in your own backyard. Sooner of later someone would say, "Hey! Maybe he lives around here!"

Nicole called Trane.

She didn't let him talk.

"Just listen," she said. "I might have a lead. Hollywood might be someone from Cleveland, Ohio named Elliot Drake. I'm coming down to the office. I'll be there in ten minutes. See what you can find out on this guy before I get there. Elliot Drake!"

She hung up.

Then she was out the door and bounding down the fire escape, two steps at a time. At ground level she realized that she left her weapon upstairs on the kitchen table. For a second she contemplated leaving it there, then ran back up to get it.

The door was locked.

She kicked it, then bounded back down, slamming her body into Penny Lane and warning her, Start!

She turned the key.

A click came.

She turned the key back to the home position, then back to the right again.

Click.

Come on, baby. Not now.

Click.

Click.

Click.

That's it. You're history.

She punched the steering wheel.

Then she turned the key one last time.

Instead of a click, the engine sputtered asthmatically and then suddenly sprang to full life. She gunned it twice and popped the clutch, so fast that she stalled out.

She turned the key again.

Click.

12

The minute Nicole busted into homicide, Trane grabbed her by the elbow and escorted her down the hall to a private conference room where he sat her in a chair and said, "Nicole, I love you to death, you know I do, but you're totally out of control. Before I put you on suspension, tell me why you think someone named Elliott Drake from Cleveland, Ohio is Hollywood."

She filled him in, about how the tattooed arm was hanging out of a white Challenger down the street from the crime scene, how the license plate had been mudded out, how she theorized that the car had been rented, how she called around to rental agencies and learned that a white Challenger had in fact been rented at the airport to one Elliott Drake from Cleveland, Ohio.

Trane listened with an impatient face, then pulled up a Facebook page on his cell phone and said, "Meet Elliott Drake from Cleveland, Ohio." The man was a five-two stick figure with black coke-bottle glasses and two spaghetti arms, neither of which had a shred of ink. There was no way in this world or any other world that he would have been able to hoist a full-grown woman over a shoulder and throw her like a sack of potatoes into the back of an SUV.

"He's a real estate agent," Trane added. "Age 68. You want

to buy a house?"

Ouch.

"Are you sure that's him?"

"With your explanation, yes," Trane said. "Hell, he's posting right here about flying to Miami for his sister's wedding, her third. I suppose that's why the rental happened at the airport."

Nicole's body went limp.

She looked at Trane, defeated, and said, "I was so sure. Yeah, I would have been more sure if he'd been from California, but there was enough to get excited about."

Trane frowned.

"Which brings us to you," he said. "You're not supposed to be getting excited. You're supposed to be sitting at your desk bored out of your mind—no, not bored out of your mind, working on other cases—until all this blows over. I'm not going to see you dead and that's all there is to it. So, help me out here. Tell me what I have to do to get you to listen to very simple and very direct instructions."

She exhaled.

Then she said, "You could rip my soul out. That might be a good start."

"Nicole, come on—"

She locked eyes with him.

"If that's what you think my job is—to not do my job, to just sit on my hands—well, then we have different opinions." She paused and added, "I talked to a TV reporter an hour ago. I made it very clear I was a detective on the case. Do you know why? Because I am. It'll be on the evening news."

The words hit Trane hard.

"That was dumb," he said. "Beyond dumb."

"He's already after me, Nick. I can feel him trying to suck the breath out of my lungs. He's drinking my blood from the inside."

"Exactly," Trane said. "That proves my point. You

absolutely have to stay off the grid."

She stood up.

Then she put her hands on the table, looked the man in the eyes and said, "Trane, I'm the bait; repeat, the bait. At this point, your job is to figure out how to use that to our advantage so we can get this guy off the streets once and for all. Call me when you turn yourself into a man with a plan."

Then she was gone.

She wasn't just gone, she was gone fast, down the hall and around the corner, before the man could catch up and shout at the back of her head, You're fired!

Then she stopped.

Against her better judgment, she turned and went back. "I got to admit, I'm a little disappointed," she said. "I'd heard a million good things about you. There are a lot of people around here who think you walk on water. Frankly, between you and me, I'm not seeing it."

Then she was gone, again.

She dared not go back to her desk. The next words that got said between her and Trane would be final and non-retractable. The whole building was a big toxic mess. She headed down to Penny Lane, said Start, and turned the key. The engine fired, obediently, as if it had never done anything but.

Now what?

Her phone rang.

The display indicated it was Salter Shade, the closest anyone in homicide came to actually being Nicole's partner. In both appearance and mannerisms, he was the twin of Clark Kent, without the Superman powers of course, and with two other slight differences; his face was black instead of white, and the glasses on that face were white instead of black. Other than that, the two of them came from the same egg.

She answered, "Lois Lane here."

"Not funny, Nicole. What the hell is going on with you and Trane?"

She told him, namely that Trane had taken her off the case in an effort to have Hollywood go after him instead of her. But Hollywood was already coming for her and she wasn't about to hide her head in the sand while the hourglass on Danica Rose was running dry.

Salter exhaled.

"Look," he said. "Did Trane tell you about the FBI agent, John Pantage?"

"No."

"He's the point guy at the FBI for all the Hollywood cases," Salter said. "He's flying in to give us all the information. He's set to be at the office at 4:00. Didn't Trane tell you?"

"No. Is this guy Pantage taking over the investigation?"

"I don't know. All I know is that the party's at four in case you decide to crash it."

"Thanks."

She hung up.

The thought of being back in the same room as Trane felt like a sucker punch to the gut. But the thought of missing out on critical information that might help her find Danica Rose was even worse; it was more like a chainsaw to the throat.

She checked her watch.

It was 2:10.

She had two hours between now and the meeting.

That would give her time to run down something that had been nagging her. From headquarters, she headed into the heart of downtown Miami. She kept a close eye in the rearview mirror, looking especially for a blue Mustang or a white Challenger, but open to anything else that looked suspicious or hung behind there for too long.

She recalled her theory that Hollywood may have followed Danica into Miami on Friday and may have checked into a hotel. The problem with that theory is that there were hundreds of hotels. Contacting them all and getting a list of everyone that checked in, even if she could get that information cooperatively without a warrant, would take seven million years. And, at the end, all she would have would be a list, thousands or pages long.

Her theory that Hollywood rented a Challenger was also unraveling the more she pecked at it. He might have driven to California from another state and then followed Danica to Miami. Once here, he could easily have stolen some Florida license plates and stuck them on his car. Or, he might have driven straight to Miami and happened to spot Danica after he got here. So, maybe he never even followed her here at all.

None of her theories were holding up.

Worse, they were almost impossible to prove or disprove one way or the other, even if someone put in the time, which itself wasn't possible.

The best deal she had going for her so far was the bait thing.

That was the key.

She was the bait.

That was the thing she had to capitalize on somehow.

There was one other good thing she had in her favor, too. Hollywood would have no way to know that she knew about him. He didn't know that she knew he would be coming for her.

Following her was a FedEx truck, and tucked behind that was a black sedan with heavily tinted windows. It seemed like it had been there for a time.

Okay, let's see.

Are you real or are you Memorex?

She turned right at the next intersection, which was a four-lane road with two lanes in each direction, and stayed in the right lane.

Blackie-bear also turned right.

There were no FedEx trucks between them now.

There was only broad daylight.

Nicole did the speed limit, which for Miami, meant she was going at least ten miles an hour too slow. The left lane next to her was open. Blackie-bear, rather than swinging into it and getting his groove on, hung back in the right lane and copied Nicole's speed. Right now, he was the only person in Miami not tailgating.

Hollywood?

Is that you?

Her chest pounded.

You're actually making your move, aren't you?

All right, you go for it, you little bitch.

She debated whether to call Salter Shade and see if he could dispatch a couple of black-and-whites. No, that wouldn't be good, not if this turned out to be nothing more than a false alarm. Her standing was already in jeopardy. The last thing she needed at this point were jokes around the office about the wolf who cried boy.

She hung straight for several blocks and then turned right at a residential side street and pulled to the curb.

To her shock, Blackie-bear pulled up right beside her and stopped.

The passenger window came down.

The man behind the wheel was dark and rugged. She couldn't tell if he was a Mexican, an Indian or just a really dark white man. A scar ran down the right side of his face, from the corner of his eye to his jaw. Thick black hair showcased piercing eyes. He was tall, even sitting down, and his body belonged to Tarzan.

He smiled at her.

White teeth showed.

She smiled back.

The man said, "See that little girl across the street on the bike?"

Nicole looked in that direction.

A girl, five or six, was getting off a small bike with training wheels to pick a dandelion. No adults were around. She must be in front of her own house.

The man raised a gun off the seat just far enough for Nicole to tell what it was.

He said, "Don't scream or do anything stupid. Don't touch your purse, don't go for your gun. Get out of your car, slowly, and get into mine. Do it now, without any drama, or I'll shoot that little girl right where she is and then I'll shoot you."

Nicole's eyes fell on the girl.

Then she got out of her car and climbed into the other one.

"Close the door," the man said.

She complied.

The vehicle took off.

Without looking over, the man said, "Do you know who I am?"

"Hollywood," Nicole said.

The man grunted.

Then he said, "This is going to be fun."

13

As the car rolled down the street, Nicole was struck at how the world outside was so amazingly normal and unaware. A woman watered flowers. Two teenagers sat on a porch, one strumming an acoustic guitar. Birds flew and dogs barked. In a driveway, three young girls jumped rope. It was all in such stark contrast to the infinite emptiness in Nicole's soul, knowing that Hollywood had her by the throat.

She needed to do something, quick.

Do what?

Jerk the wheel?

Open the door and jump out?

Slam a fist into the side of Hollywood's head?

Plead for mercy?

Tell him she was pregnant?

Suddenly the man pointed the gun at Nicole's face, as if deciding whether to pull the trigger now or later. He gave her a hard twisted look, and then, for some mysterious reason, lowered the weapon and put it on the dash.

At the next street he took a hard left.

The gun slid across the dash to Nicole's side.

She grabbed it with a lightning fast hand and pointed it at his face.

The man smiled, almost as if catching Nicole in a lie, and said, "You don't have the guts."

Nicole swallowed.

"Where's Danica Rose?"

The man smiled.

"I don't know."

She said, "Wrong answer."

Then she pulled the trigger.

14

When Nicole pulled the trigger, something happened that she wouldn't have expected in a million years, namely, the weapon didn't fire. Rather, the hammer fell with an empty click. She pulled it a second time and got another click, then a third and a fourth. The man snatched the weapon from her hand, set it on the dash for the second time and drove in silence. To Nicole's astonishment, they ended up back at Penny Lane where the man looked at her hard and said, "Get out."

Nicole didn't know what was going on but wasn't about to ask. She didn't want to do anything or say anything that might make him change his mind.

She got out.

The little girl across the street looked as Nicole shut the door.

The car immediately took off.

She stood there watching it leave, not having the presence of mind to focus on the license plate until it was too late.

She was alive.

She was unharmed.

The question was, why?

Why did Hollywood bring her to the brink of death and then let her go?

It made no sense.

She got into Penny Lane.

Thankfully, the key was still in the ignition and her purse was still sitting uneventfully on the passenger seat. She said, Start, and turned the key. The engine fired up without a sputter or burp. She said, Good girl, gunned it twice and took off, alive, wonderfully alive, with no hint of the black car in her rearview mirror.

Suddenly her phone rang.

It was Fallon who said, "I'm at your place, just so you know."

"Be sure the door's locked. I'm swinging over. I'll be there in ten minutes."

"You sound weird—"

"Stuff's going on. Ten minutes."

When Nicole got to the loft ten minutes later, she climbed the fire escape to find the door locked and a note taped to it—"Down at the studio." From the landing, four floors up, Nicole surveyed the area to see if Blackie-bear was lurking in a shadow.

It wasn't.

Everything was normal.

The switchyard was slowly clanging and banging and doing its dirty dusty thing. The parking lot for the studio was full. Beyond it, between here and the normal world, the topography was a mismatch of old dilapidated warehouses and empty shells of industrial buildings that had been thrown away like old lovers who could no longer get it up.

Hollywood wasn't in view.

Whatever he was doing, he was done with it for the time being.

Nicole headed down the fire escape to the studio, walked through the reception area, which was unmanned, as always, and into the striper-pole room where a half dozen men, mostly black, and eight or ten well-proportioned women—half and half, race wise, were in the process of playing pool, drinking and sucking on joints. Rap spilled out of high quality speakers embedded in the ceiling.

Fallon wasn't there.

Nicole pushed through a thick soundproof door at the back of the room, walked down a short hallway, and then went through a second soundproof door into the recording area. There in the booth, with Jay-J and a half dozen other people, was Fallon, in the process of watching a black girl laying down a Jamaican reggae dancehall rap into a microphone behind the glass.

Jay-J Juicy wasn't hard to miss; at six-seven, and wearing a well-televised face that had seen almost twenty years of professional basketball play, including eight years with the Heat, he was a landmark in Miami and, in fact, most of the country. His former jump-shot body had given way to more of a relaxed refrigerator-shaped build, but, at 45, he was entitled to it. He looked up when Nicole walked in and tapped a finger against his check. She kissed it. As long as her ass was so close, Juicy gave it a little smack.

"Nicole the Stone," he said. "You looking good, girl."

"You too, Juicy."

He smiled.

Then he said, "Once you go Juicy, you'll never want Loosy."

Nicole rolled her eyes.

"Is that new?"

"Yeah, I've been working at it. Does it get you hot?"

"Like a 4-alarm fire."

"I thought so. Don't touch any paper. I don't want anything going up in flames." He tapped his cheek again, got another kiss, and said, "Gotta work, Ms. Stone. You hang around as long as you want." His eyes and concentration were already fixed back on the island girl.

Nicole grabbed Fallon by the hand and said, "Come with me."

Three minutes later they were up in the loft with the door locked behind them, where Nicole told the woman about her encounter with Hollywood, and especially the fact that the man had mysteriously let her go, even after she tried to shoot him in the face.

"I don't get it," she said.

Fallon reflected.

Then she said, "Unless he's already killed Danica. That would explain it."

"How?"

"His game is that he has to kill you before he kills Danica, right? So, if Danica's already dead, Hollywood doesn't get to kill you. You won. Maybe he took you just for a flash to shake you up before he split town."

"Yeah, but Danica would have at least two days to live," Nicole said.

"Presumably, but something may have gone wrong." Fallon went over to the kitchen table where her purse was and pulled a .357 Magnum out.

Nicole looked at it, then at Fallon, then at her watch.

It was a quarter to four.

"I've got to get to a meeting," she said. "Where do you want to be while I'm gone?"

"Probably back down with Juicy."

"Fine," Nicole said. "I'll walk you down. If they break up before I get back, get someone to escort you back up here. Deal?"

"Deal."

"Don't assume this is over just because Hollywood let me go. Promise me—"

Fallon held her pinky out.

"I promise."

They pinky shook.

Then Nicole was out of there.

At exactly four o'clock, she busted into homicide to find it empty, then headed down the hall to the large conference room where the big meetings were held.

What she saw she could hardly believe.

This couldn't be real.

No way.

She pulled her gun out and screamed, "Everybody down!"

15

Everybody down!

Bodies dove for the floor and scrambled behind chairs and behind one another, almost as one, in a mass panic, as if a bomb had just gone off. They were the bodies of Nicole's superiors and colleagues and friends and people she was trying to make her friends and some others she'd never even seen before.

Only two people didn't drop.

One was Hollywood, who was standing at a whiteboard at the front of the room with his Tarzan body and his thick black hair and his scar that went from the corner of his eye down to his jaw. He just stared at Nicole with a grin on his face as if daring her to shoot.

The other person still standing was Trane, who shouted, "Nobody shoot! Nobody do nothing!"

Nicole didn't listen.

She brought the gun into a two-hand hold and pointed it directly at Hollywood's chest.

"That's Hollywood!"

"No, it's not!"

"Yes it is, I know!"

"Nicole, don't move. Do you hear me? Don't move." Trane approached as he talked, getting closer step by step, then holding his hand out and saying, "Give me the gun, Nicole. That's not Hollywood. That's Special Agent John Pantage. He's with the FBI."

Nicole kept her grip tight on the weapon.

"No, that's Hollywood."

"It's not, Nicole," Trane said. "Give me the gun."

She looked into Trane's eyes, saw no lies, and let him pry the weapon out of her fingers.

Then she turned and ran out of the room.

She didn't make it to the end of the hall before Trane's powerful arms grabbed her around the waist and swung her into a wall. His face was close to hers. His eyes were wild. "That was my idea," he said. "Having you snatched. It was my idea."

Nicole shook her head in disbelief.

"What?"

"The guy who took you wasn't Hollywood," he said. "He was Agent Pantage."

"I don't get it—"

"You kept talking about being bait," Trane said. "I wanted to show you exactly what that meant. I wanted to show you how easy it would be for someone to get you even when you were on your highest guard and even in broad daylight."

"It was all a trick?"

Trane grabbed her by the shoulders and shook her.

"A trick? No, it wasn't a trick. It was a wakeup call that this is serious, serious stuff. This isn't a game, Nicole." He hugged her and said, "No more talk about bait. Come on, let's go back to the meeting."

She pictured everyone's eyes on her.

She pictured the muted words behind her back.

"Nick, I'm too embarrassed."

He pulled Nicole's gun from his waistband, handed it to her and said, "Don't be. I'll explain to everyone what just happened. It'll all be history in two minutes."

She exhaled.

Then she let him escort her to the back of the room.

Trane, as promised, explained what happened. Faces turned in Nicole's direction occasionally but none looked at her as if she was crazy; if anything, there might have been some admiration. When Trane was done and back in his seat, Agent Pantage took his place back at the whiteboard, looked at Nicole and said, "Nice to see you again, Detective Stone."

She nodded.

"Likewise."

Then the man focused on the group and started to talk.

With all faces now pointed forward, Nicole slipped her phone out and texted Fallon: Danica's not dead. Hollywood is still on the loose. Don't let your guard down.

Then she directed her attention to the man at the front of the room.

It became very clear very fast that Pantage wasn't anything like all the other men who were constantly trying to pry their way into Nicole's life. His face, the more Nicole stared at it, belonged to a rock-star, irrespective of the scar, which was actually starting to grow on her. His body had to be every inch of six-four and belonged to a warrior. His words had purpose and came out easily, depicting an intelligence and confidence that couldn't be ignored. His black hair was thick and healthy. He was a modern-day Tarzan with skyscrapers instead of trees and highways instead of rivers and Hollywoods instead of sharp-toothed tigers. Even Trane, compared to Pantage, seemed ordinary, which was something Nicole never expected to see in this lifetime.

It was clear she needed to be careful of the man.

He could get to her.

He could reach her if he set his mind to it.

He'd be able to do it fast, too.

Regarding the case at hand, Pantage had a lot to say that Nicole didn't know.

First, Hollywood had no discernible stalking routine or timeframe prior to taking his victims. In some cases, there were indications the man had stalked his prey for months. In other cases, he may have made his move literally within 24-hours. The latter gave some credence to a theory that some of his kills may have actually been hits. Phrased differently, Hollywood may be indulging his dark desires, but he might on occasional be indulging his bank account. It was unknown how anyone would have located Hollywood to hire him; possibly through the dark web, but the FBI had not yet traced anything concrete to him.

The detectives that Hollywood killed were taken in many different ways with no consistent pattern. Two were killed by way of a long distance sniper shot.

One was strangled.

One had a screwdriver shoved into her brain through her eardrum. Her partner was with her at the time and he was killed too, shot to death.

One was shot at fairly close range while driving. The vehicle ran over a 7-year-old girl and her mother before finally smashing to a stop against a building. The mother lived; the child didn't.

And one was beaten to death with a pipe.

In two of the cases the detective in charge stayed hidden off the grid until the victim was killed. In both of those cases, Hollywood never came back for the detective. They're both still alive to this day. Both of them later got out of law enforcement and went into other fields in other states.

It wasn't sure how Hollywood got around.

Each of the eight known cases was done in a different state, stretching as far as Los Angeles to the west and Atlantic City to the east. It wasn't known if Hollywood flew to his locations or drove or took a bus or a train or some combination thereof. The one unifying factor was that each case was located in a large city.

It wasn't certain where Hollywood lived but Pantage speculated that it might be New York because it was big enough and weird enough to hide him.

Hollywood was probably a single white male between 25 and 40 with a disturbed childhood that most likely included broken or abusive homes or an orphanage.

He was highly, highly intelligent.

He might have a background in law enforcement or the military.

Prior to developing the current game where he left a bottle behind indicating the way the victim would be killed and how long the victim would be allowed to live before that happened, Hollywood likely had a whole set of additional murders that had no such MO. Eight murders was the lowest number to credit, but it could be as high as twenty or thirty.

Because so many of Hollywood's victims were detectives, and because he killed his victims in such horrible ways, he was currently No. 1 on the FBI's most wanted list, and had been in that position for over three years.

He was not a man to screw with.

He was the demon in the dark.

He was the snake at your feet.

He was the reaper silently dropping down out of the sky.

Then Trane took over and said, "I want to feel my hands wrapped around this guy's throat. Are we all clear on that?"

"Yes." The word was a chorus, twenty voices strong.

"Okay," Trane said. "Here's how we're going to catch him. Detective Nicole Stone has a theory that Hollywood may have followed his victim Danica Rose from L.A. to Miami by car and would have likely checked into a hotel the night he arrived. I think that's a solid lead worth running down. So, we're going to contact every single hotel within an hour of Miami and build a database of every single person who checked in that night, meaning Friday, September 9th."

Voices agreed.

"Also," Trane said, "we're going to contact everyone in L.A. who has been in Danica Rose's life in any significant way in the last six months. That means her friends, her lovers, the people she was shooting the movie with, and everyone else we can put a name to. We're going to interview them. Some of you are going to be flying out to L.A. We're going to find out why she recently bought a handgun and what she was scared of. We're going to find out what TV shows she watched and what kind of toothpaste she used. Somehow, Hollywood came into her life. I want to know where, when, how and why."

Heads nodded.

"Now, there's a completely different theory that Hollywood never came into Danica's life, instead, he came into Fallon Bow's life and ended up taking Danica by mistake. So, everything that I just said about Danica, we're going to do the same thing with respect to Fallon Bow. If Hollywood came into her life, I want to know where, when, how and why."

"Done," someone said.

"Danica got thrown into a late model white 4Runner," Trane said. "We need to know about rentals and also need to find out if any have been reported stolen. The same goes for stolen license plates, no matter what kind of car they came from. Get locations and locate security cameras."

Trane had more ideas, lots of them.

When the meeting was finished, something happened that Nicole didn't expect, namely Pantage walked his six-four frame over to her and said, "Want to get a beer?"

16

Nicole and Pantage ended up in a dive bar sandwiched between a Thai restaurant called Duck Fat and a hole-in-the-wall tattoo shop called Ink, Inc. The place was dim and the bar was already loitered with lost souls who must have been there for hours based on their malfunctioning volume controls. They took a booth in the back, safe from most of the chaos, and sat there for a few moments before they realized there was no waitress. Pantage fetched two drafts from the bar, brought them over and slid the one with the cleanest glass to Nicole.

He took a long swallow, half the glass in fact and leaned across the table.

"All that stuff that Trane's handing out," he said. "It's all busy work. I'm not putting him down; don't get me wrong. I don't have any brighter ideas than what he did, except for the obvious one."

Nicole knew what he was talking about.

She took a sip of beer, held the man's eyes and said, "Use the bait."

Pantage nodded.

"That's why I did what I did, with Trane's permission," he said. "You need to understand in no uncertain terms that if we dangle you out there, there's a serious chance you're going to end up dead."

"You're a real box of kittens. Anyone ever tell you that?" Pantage smiled.

"Also, you need to control your emotions."

"Huh?"

"When you thought I was Hollywood, you put the gun to my face and pulled the trigger. That was emotions."

"And?"

"And, that's certainly one way to go," Pantage said. "But keep in mind that the guy has Danica holed-up somewhere. If you kill him, we'll never find her—not in time. She'll rot wherever she is and it will be a long ugly process. So, I guess what I'm saying is, next time shoot him in the leg instead of the face."

Nicole chewed on it.

"If we bring him in alive, do you really think he'll tell us anything?"

"Probably not, which is why we won't bring him in, at least not right away." Nicole studied the man to see if he was really saying what she thought he was saying. Pantage tilted his head and said, "That's between you and me."

The thought bothered her, but less than the thought of Danica dying some horrific death all alone.

She exhaled and said, "Maybe we could draw him in close enough to spot him, then follow him back to where he has Danica. He's staying with her when he's not out chasing me, don't you think?"

"I'd guess, yes. He has to check on her, give her food and water and make sure she hasn't escaped and all that good stuff."

"Good. So we follow him back to her. Maybe we could figure out what he's driving and slap a GPS on it."

He nodded.

"Can you round some up?"

"Yes."

The man took a long swig of beer and said, "You're clearly not afraid to get a little dirt on your fingernails. What's your background? Who are you, exactly?"

She told him about her past, about how she was hitchhiking through Florida and ended up in an accident and then a coma and, even now over a decade later, still couldn't remember anything from her past, so she wrote down her dreams on cards because some of them might actually be based on subconscious memory.

"No one could ever figure out who I was," she said.

"You're part Latino," Pantage said. "That's pretty obvious. Not a lot, but some."

Nicole nodded.

"I've always thought that one of my parents was half Latino which would put me at 1/4th," she said. "Plus, I speak both Spanish and English. From what I was told, back when I was fourteen, after I came out of the coma, I spoke both languages about equally well. Since then, of course, I've mostly spoken English so I'm a lot better at that language now. But I'm still pretty good at Spanish. I can watch TV shows in Spanish, read books, and the like. That's one of the reasons I was able to get a job so fast in vice, because of my Spanish."

Pantage tilted his head.

"So what's your theory?"

"On who I am?"

"Yeah."

"My theory? I have hundreds of them. It's all I think about half the time. But if I had to limit myself to just one, I'd say that growing up I spent some on my years in Mexico and some in the United States," she said. "That's why, by fourteen, I could speak both languages."

It was then, on the flat-screen TV above the bar, that

Nicole's face came on the evening news. She pointed. There was no sound but her face was clear.

"That was for Hollywood," she said. "I wanted to be sure he knew who to come after."

"Trust me, he already knew."

"Yeah, I know."

Nicole's phone rang. The display indicated "number unavailable" but she answered anyway. A man's voice came through, filtered through some kind of creepy distortive oscillator.

"Hello, Nicole. Do you know who this is?"

She was almost afraid to utter the word, but did.

"Hollywood?"

"That's not a bad name, don't you think? I was afraid it was going to be Nightman or something stupid, like something out of a Marvel comic; you know, something they hadn't given much thought to. But, Hollywood? Hollywood's nice. I wouldn't mind Vertigo, either. U2 made a song by that name. Did you know that?"

"Yes."

"Do you like it? The song?"

"Yes. Do you?

"Love it, actually. I'm playing it in my head right now." The man exhaled, suddenly more serious, and said, "The reason I'm calling, Nicole, is I wanted to apologize for throwing that rock through your window. I'm sorry about that."

"You're sorry?"

"Yes."

"Well, make it up to me. Buy me a beer and we'll call it even."

The man chuckled softly.

Then he said, "I'm half tempted. I like your voice, I must say. It's almost as sexy as you are. I really wouldn't mind having you sit on my face for an hour and read me lines from Robert Frost. Do that and I'll die a happy man."

"I don't like poetry. Wimps write that crap. They write it for other wimps."

The man chuckled.

"You can't press my buttons, Nicole. You don't know me that well yet. You will, but not yet. Your voice really is extraordinary. It reminds me a little of Sharon Stone when she was in that movie with Michael Douglas, way back. What was the name of it?"

"Basic Instinct."

"Right, right, that's it, Basic Instinct. God, every line that sultry little seductress let pass through her lips just oozed with sex. You could almost feel your tongue on her nipples. You're sort of like that, Nicole. It's a gift. You should be proud."

"Glad you approve," Nicole said. "Where's Danica?"

"That's really not important. What's important is that the guy you're drinking beer with, the treetop lover or whatever he fashions himself to be—he won't be able to save you. In fact, I think this time I'll kill him too just for the hell of it. Go ahead and tell him. It's only fair that he knows."

"I'll tell him," Nicole said. "In the meantime I have an idea. Why don't you trade Danica for me? An even swap; I'll whisper sweet nothings in your ear all night long. You can suck them into your brain and beat your cock to them. Or I'll beat it. Whatever you want, master. What do you say? Me for Danica—"

"Be careful what you wish for, Nicole."

The line died.

17

When the line died, Nicole immediately told Pantage, "That was Hollywood. He said the guy I'm drinking beer with wouldn't be able to save me." She sucked her breath in and said, "He's got eyes on us."

Pantage jumped up, ran through the bar so fast that he knocked two guys over, and screeched to a halt outside on the sidewalk as he swung his vision to the left and right. Nicole caught up to him just a few seconds later.

Pantage shouted, "Take that way!"

Nicole snatched her gun from her purse and ran south, past the dives and the debris, searching frantically for anyone who might be Hollywood.

Come on!

Show up!

I got sexy words for you!

A block up the street she came to a payphone.

The receiver was hanging down.

Which way?

Which way?

Which way?

Across the street was a thin alley that ran between two brick buildings. Nicole darted through buses and cars and trucks and ran in, not slowing, weaving around blind spots created by dumpsters and stacks of crates. The alley came to a dead end at a second perpendicular alley that went both right and left. She swung to the right, around the corner, and wham! A long piece of wood swung out from behind a garbage can and hit her smack in the gut. She screamed and went down so fast that she couldn't get her arms out fast enough to break the fall.

Her head bounced.

Her gun flew out of her hand.

Colors exploded inside her brain.

She screamed, Stop!

Then the wood came down with a lightning force onto her upper back. The pain was a thousand demons. She tried to turn her head up to get a look at her attacker but all she could see were colors.

Then a gun fired.

18

When Nicole gained consciousness everything was blurry and it took her a few moments to realize that she was lying in an alley. Pantage was with her.

"Just stay still," he said. "An ambulance is on the way."

Nicole could actually hear the sirens.

She struggled to her feet, spotted her gun on the ground and picked it up. "I don't want an ambulance." She looked down the alley, almost surprised to not see Hollywood, and said, "I never got a look at him."

"That's okay."

"Why didn't he kill me?"

Pantage pointed up to a third story window and said, "A guy up there heard the commotion. He fired down and Hollywood took off."

"Did he hit him?"

"I don't think so but we'll check for blood."

"How about a visual? Did he get a look?"

"Not really."

Nicole exhaled. There at her feet, in the dirt, was a broken two-by-four. She nudged it with her foot and said, "After we print it, I'm going to take it home and mount it on the wall."

Pantage smiled.

"You're back. I like that."

She winced at the pain in her gut and pressed in with a hand to get a feel for the damage. It wasn't as bad as it should be. Nothing felt like it was ruptured or bleeding.

She said, "Do me one favor in the future, will you?"

Pantage nodded.

"Sure."

"Next time you tell me to take that way, point in the direction that the guy didn't go, not the way he went. Would that be so hard?"

Pantage grinned.

Then he got serious and said, "I should have never sent you on your own. That was stupid."

Nicole shoved him in the chest.

"Stop it; you sound like Trane."

The next hour involved a lot of forensic motion, but whether that motion was forwards, backwards, or sideways, only time would tell. The alley was cordoned off as a crime scene and worked by a unit, which unfortunately only located blood where Nicole had been attacked and not farther down the alley, meaning the bullet from above probably hadn't hit the asshole.

The guy from the third floor who fired down at Hollywood turned out to be a feisty old Bangkok man named Channarong who, coincidentally, had just gotten off work at Duck Fat. He didn't have any visual recollection of the man he shot at other than he was wearing a red baseball cap; he saved Nicole's life but otherwise wasn't of much use, which was fine—they'd still count his little guardian angel act as a positive, and the fact that his gun was unregistered would be overlooked.

The payphone receiver was physically cut from its housing and rushed to the lab for fingerprinting and DNA testing in case Hollywood was kind enough to leave behind a little gift of saliva or sweat; same for the broken two-by-four.

Every public or private surveillance camera for blocks was being located and examined in hopes that Hollywood and his red baseball cap showed up on at least one of them; and on and on and on.

By the time things got under control, it was already seven in the evening. Nicole had hardly slept at all last night and had been going a hundred miles an hour all day. The exhaustion that she'd been pushing off for the last umpteen hours suddenly had her by the throat.

She needed to close her eyes, if only for a little.

They headed to the loft and climbed the fire escape to find that the door was unlocked but Fallon wasn't inside. Pantage drew his weapon and checked the space only to find everything secure.

Nicole fell backwards onto the mattress and closed her eyes. The darkness felt like cold water after a day in the desert.

"Just give me a minute," she said.

Then she felt Pantage unlacing her shoes and slipping them off. He massaged her feet and covered her with a sheet.

She held her arm up, for Pantage to hold her hand.

Then she told him, "Wake me half an hour."

"Okay."

"Pinky swear."

The man chuckled, then complied.

"Sleep," he said.

Nicole dropped her hand and curled up and was almost out but forced herself back into enough consciousness to say, "There's a music studio down on the first level. Do me a favor and make sure Fallon is there and that she's all right. Bring her up here."

Pantage hesitated, not wanting to leave Nicole alone and unguarded.

She read his mind and said, "Please and thank you. I'll be all right."

Pantage said, "Okay and you're welcome," but Nicole didn't hear him.

She was already out.

19

When Nicole woke up it was almost dark, in fact 9:16, meaning Pantage didn't keep his pinky-swear promise to wake her in thirty minutes. She forgave him though because even now with two hours of brain-out heaven under her belt she was still a class-A zombie. She needed at least what she got to be functional tonight. Pantage and Fallon were at the kitchen table eating pizza and talking; it seemed like Pantage was extracting information. The smell of pepperoni wove through the air like a beckoning hand and reminded Nicole that her tank had long been on empty.

She muscled her way off the mattress and headed over to the table, relieved to see three large pizza boxes piled on one another, meaning there was plenty left.

Outside, black-bellied clouds swept across a dull watercolor sky.

Weather was coming; not good weather, the other kind.

"Morning, glory," Pantage said.

Nicole nodded at him, gave Fallon a kiss on the cheek, and pulled a piece of pizza from the box as she said, "In an hour, Danica will have been gone a full day. We may be down to 24 hours left. Do we have a plan?"

"That depends," Pantage said.

Nicole chewed what she had in her mouth and said, "On

what?”

"On you."

She swallowed, tore off another mouthful and looked at him sideways.

"Go on."

"Okay," Pantage said, "here's the deal. As soon as it's dark, we'll have men moving into position. We're going to have a sniper up on the roof of this building, a second one on the roof of one of those abandoned buildings across the way, and a third behind a boxcar over in the rail yard. We'll have two undercover vans in the backstreets. Each one will have four or five men in them. We'll also have half a dozen black-and-whites stationed out of sight within a mile. We'll have someone walking inside your place, pretending to be you. We'll get a Porsche like yours and put it in the parking lot."

Nicole frowned.

"You don't think Hollywood will notice any of that?"

"Actually, I think he will."

"So why do it?"

"Because I found a GPS attached to the underside of your Porsche," Pantage said. "That's how Hollywood has been tracking you. That's how he found us at the bar. What we can do tonight is drive somewhere in your car, a bar or restaurant or something. Hollywood will think we're setting a trap for him here at your place while you've secretly moved someplace else, someplace you think is safe. With any luck, he'll show up to your car and he'll find us. What he doesn't know is that we'll be waiting for him."

"And by we, who do you mean?"

"You and me."

"Just the two of us?"

Pantage shrugged.

"It's risky but the more people we surround you with the more likely he'll spot them. Like you said, Danica might only have another 24-hours to live. Whatever happens tonight might be Hollywood's final attempt. He might just go back to Danica, wait for the clock to run out and then do his thing." He paused and added, "It's your call. We can certainly get two or three guys to shadow us if you want."

"If it's my call, then it's just us," Nicole said. "We'll dangle the bait as perfectly as we can."

Fallon shook her head negative, pulled the pizza slice out of Nicole's hand and said, "And me, too."

Pantage cut her off fast.

"Sorry, Charlie. No civilians."

"Think about it," Fallon said. "It's the civilian—me—that will convince Hollywood that you're not on to him. He knows you wouldn't set a trap with a civilian at risk. He'll be a lot more likely to try to close in and make his move if I'm with you guys."

Nicole thought about it.

It made sense, perfect sense, actually.

But still, what if Fallon got killed?

Fallon must have read her mind because she said, "I'm a big girl. Danica's my friend. I should have the right to help." She added, "Plus, we still don't know if Hollywood was after Danica or me. So I'm already at risk. In fact, I might be better bait than you."

Nicole chewed on it.

She looked at Pantage and said, "She has a point. I mean, if Hollywood really is after her, what's to say he won't roll back into town in a month or two when you and me aren't around to protect her anymore? She needs him off the streets as much as we do."

Pantage stressed his face.

Then he looked Fallon in the eyes, hard, and said, "I'm going to go to hell for this."

They waited for dark, hung around for another half hour while the snipers and black-and-whites and decoys crept into position, then squeezed into Penny Lane and drove off into the night. They headed south and then west. Within thirty minutes they were at their destination—Bottoms Up—and pulled into a shadowy parking lot, which was full except for a corner space all the way in the back. At this hour, the world was largely dark and unoccupied for miles in each direction, except for the strip club.

Bottoms Up was the perfect place for a number of reasons.

They needed a place with a lot of people so Hollywood would have enough human camouflage to feel comfortable getting out of his car and heading inside. It was two-for Tuesday tonight, meaning the place would be packed.

Having danced there for over two years, Fallon knew the management and the bouncers. She'd have muscle on demand if she needed it, especially if she gave them advance notice.

They could hang out in there for hours. At some point, even if Hollywood was reluctant to get out of his car, he'd get bored out of his mind and would head in.

Based on the comments Hollywood made to Nicole about her voice being so sexy, the man came off as a horny little toad. Bottoms Up was more than likely his kind of place. He'd rather be inside than out.

When they squeezed out of Penny Lane, the air was moist and the wind was kicking up.

A storm was brewing in typical southern Florida style.

They wove through the parked vehicles to the front entrance, between the bouncers, and inside where a blond with an easy white smile up top and lots of cleavage down below charged them ten dollars apiece for the pleasure of going through that glass door to their left. Pantage tipped her ten, bought a pocket full of ones, and then, just like that, they weren't in Kansas anymore.

20

Inside, the club was in full-tilt maniac mode, and Nicole no longer felt weird dressed in a white bustier, miniskirt and strap stilettos. Bodies were everywhere, at the stages, at the bar, circling like vultures and going crazy on the dance floor, where most of the women had their shirts off and their tits bouncing like Lynyrd Skynyrd free birds. The place was huge. There had to be at least eight stages, all packed like sardines, with most being worked by two or three dancers at a time. And, for the ladies, over in the far corner, those were the male gods, busy dragging holler-back women up on stage and putting them into positions that their husbands didn't even know existed. Smoke, perfume and lust charged the air; and the music, it pounded right into your soul.

To Nicole, it was perfect.

Hollywood would feel totally invisible.

Within an hour, she would be in the same room as him, and that was the first step to getting Danica back home alive. In the meantime, she had to be careful about the man walking past with a knife cupped in his hand and sticking it in her back. No one would see it. By the time she dropped to the floor, he would already be lost in the crowd. By the time someone saw the blood and screamed, he would be out the door. Bottom line, she needed to keep her guard up.

Thanks to Fallon twerking it up against a manager she knew from back in the day, they ended up in a VIP roped-off area at the end of the bar near stage one, with bottles of Vodka and Tequila and soda mixes and ice buckets and squeaky-clean glasses sitting on the table, and a good view of all the sin and decadence that was running rampant.

Drinks got poured.

A little Asian stripper dressed in Sailor Moon garb came over, looked at Tarzan, then at Nicole and said, "Is he yours?"

Nicole shook her head.

"Negative."

The woman straddled Pantage's lap and wiggled as she whispered something in his ear, something he liked, judging by the look on his face.

Nicole's instinct was to jerk the little creep off and stomp on her face. Instead, she took a long swallow of Tequila and checked out the crowd, hoping to see a red baseball cap or a muscular arm with a full-sleeve tattoo or a black T-shirt that said in white lettering, Here I am, Nicole.

No such person appeared, not in a minute, not in five, and not in ten.

The Tequila played with her brain and told her to go ahead and have a little more. She didn't see the harm. She was safe. Pantage was at her side, even if he was parked under a hundred pounds of gyrating Sailor Moon.

She poured a jigger and slammed it back.

It felt good in her gut.

It was supposed to be there.

Yeah, that was it.

Songs played.

She gave in to the beat and the chatter and the bodies and the nipples and the gyrations and the motion and the three or four other strippers that had joined the group and were now hitting on Fallon, who was offering no resistance.

Then she realized they'd been there for over an hour. If Hollywood was coming he should be here pretty soon. He'd had more than enough time to follow the GPS to the location, to make a couple of passes up and down the street, to park in some safe place with the front bumper pointing out, and to linger in the shadows as he decided whether he wanted to be stupid enough to actually go in.

Nicole closed her eyes.

The room spun.

The Tequila had her worse than she thought.

She opened her eyes.

The spinning slowed and then stopped.

She smiled.

No worries.

You're still in control, girl.

You screwed up, maybe; a little bit, but that's all, just a little, not too much. Hell, you can even have another jigger if you want. You're pacing yourself. You're doing good, considering. Pantage's had twice as much as you. And Fallon, well, let's just say you'll be holding her hair back before the night's over.

She reached in her purse to check her phone and felt the cold steel of the gun.

Don't shoot inside the club no matter what. Kill a bystander and you're history, especially after you've been drinking. Your life will be a not-so-fun series of lawyers and other equally evil creatures.

She told Pantage, "Ladies room," and headed through the crowd towards the far side of the dance floor over by the DJ box. Bodies brushed against her. They felt good. Her feet wobbled but not enough to bring her down. Inside the WC, she didn't head straight for a stall but paused to look at herself in the mirror. A slightly drunk but seriously sexy woman stared back. She winked at herself, did her business and left.

Then something unexpected happened.

Over at the far right, near the men's room, was an exit door propped open with a rock. She headed over and took a peek outside. The air felt like rain but none was actually falling yet. She wondered if she should head out and check the parking lot to see if she could spot a white 4Runner or a blue Mustang or a white Challenger.

Suddenly a voice came from behind her.

It was a man.

"Hey, baby," he said.

She turned.

The voice belonged to a rock-star with thick, shoulder-length blond hair, combed straight back. He was tall and fit and as soon as she saw him she wanted his face down between her thighs. He smiled at her reaction with amusement, then took her hand and said, "Come on, I'll buy you a drink."

They ended up at a stage.

The man laid a five down in front of himself, one in front of Nicole, and flagged down a waitress as she passed. "Tequila for me," he said.

Nicole nodded.

"Yeah, me too."

Suddenly one of the dancers was crawling across the stage seductively up to her. The woman threw the five to the middle of the stage, put her legs on Nicole's shoulders and scooted up. She wiggled her G-string insanely close to Nicole's lips, back and forth and up and down, as she bumped her thighs against the sides of Nicole's head. Then, just like that, she pressed in and made contact.

Nicole could have pulled her head back but didn't.

She left it there.

She let it happen.

When the woman finally pulled away, the blond-god came back into view. His shirtsleeve had inched up ever so slightly.

Under that shirtsleeve were a lot of tattoos; maybe leading up into a full sleeve.

Hollywood?

Is that you?

She looked him in the eyes.

Then, slowly, she brought her hand to his face and let the back of her fingers trace down his cheek.

The man couldn't look away.

Nicole's mind raced.

Get his glass.

His fingerprints are on it.

So is his DNA.

21

Nicole picked up her shot glass and dropped it in her purse, then did the same with the man's and said, "Souvenirs." She tapped a finger on the tattoos and said, "Can I see?"

"Sure."

The man pulled his sleeve up.

His arm was muscular.

The tattoos ran all the way up it. It could very well be the arm that was hanging out of the blue Mustang or the white Challenger, the arm that had been dangling the cigarettes.

"Nice." She reached in her purse as if searching for something that wasn't there and then said, "You don't have a cigarette on you by any chance, do you?"

He pulled a pack out of his pants pocket, tapped two out and lit them up. He brought one up to Nicole's mouth, let her open her lips and laid it in.

"Thanks," she said.

"You're welcome."

She took a drag, didn't inhale, and blew it out. It tasted like an old ashtray but she didn't let it show on her face.

"What's your name?" she asked.

"Ash."

"I'm Nicole— "

"Nicole," he said. "I like that. It fits you." He looked around, almost as if he was searching for a Hollywood, and said, "Let's go upstairs. I have something you might like."

"Such as, what?"

He took her hand and pulled her out of the chair.

"You'll see."

Upstairs was the nude room where fully naked women worked a runway and crawled down onto men's laps. Other women danced naked in cages; and sofas were everywhere, filled with men getting twerked and grinded on. Ash led Nicole to a small unisex restroom at the far end of the floor past the bar, locked the door behind them and lit up a joint. He took a long drag and then passed it to Nicole.

She knew she shouldn't.

This, on top of all the Tequila, would put her way over the edge; but saying no wasn't an option. She needed to know if the man was Hollywood.

She took a deep drag into her lungs and held it there for as long as she could before blowing out. The smoke immediately went to her brain. Her blood tingled. Her heart pounded.

The man picked her up and set her on the sink.

He stood before her, looking deep into her eyes. He must have found what he was searching for because he put a hand on each of Nicole's knees and spread her legs apart.

Then he kissed her, deep and hard.

She let him.

His tongue went into her mouth.

She let it.

Then, just like that, it was suddenly all too much. She pushed him off and ran out. She was all the way across the floor and down the stairs when her phone rang.

When she answered, a voice came through, filtered through the same eerie oscillator as before.

"Nicole, darling—"

It was Hollywood.

"What do you want?"

"Wow, right to the point, huh? I'm starting to think that maybe all that Tequila isn't agreeing with you."

"You're here?"

"Of course I'm here," he said. "That's what you wanted, isn't it? I just wanted to let you know that I'm actually thinking about that offer you made, to trade you for Danica. I'm intrigued about all those sweet nothings you were talking about. Anyway, I've had enough fun for the night. I'm going home. I'll call you later, kiss, kiss."

The line died.

Nicole ran back upstairs to the restroom to find it empty and no Ash in sight. She scrambled back to the stairs, ran down two at a time and caught a heel, sending her spiraling into two men who were coming up. If she was injured she had no time for it. She forced her way back upright, pushed hard through the bodies and got to Pantage. "Hollywood just called me! He's here somewhere in the club but he's leaving!"

"Right now?"

"Yes!"

Pantage was up immediately, sending Sailor Moon flying into Fallon's lap, then bulldozing his way to the front entrance and through the doors and into the night.

Nicole forced herself to keep up.

Outside, Pantage looked wildly from side to side, then he shouted, "Stay here," and sprinted at full pace to the right.

Nicole stood there for a minute as her head spun, then pulled her gun out of her purse and ran after him as fast as her stilettos would let her.

"Pantage!"

22

By the time Nicole caught up to Pantage, the man was already in a deadly fistfight in the shadows across the street with none other than the blond-god himself, Ash, whose shirt was off and whose powerful ripped muscles were coiled like a python. It was clear that neither man would go down without first inflicting a lot of damage on the other.

Fists flew.

Awful red blood splattered.

Then Nicole saw something she didn't expect.

She looked harder to be sure she was right.

She was right.

She was definitely right!

The tattoo was on Ash's right arm, not his left; his left arm was totally natural without an ounce of ink. If he was sitting in a driver's seat with his arm out the window, that would be his left arm sticking out, his natural Tone.

She screamed, "Pantage! Back off!"

The man ignored her and instead swung a deadly hook at Ash's face, fast, but not fast enough, succeeding in only brushing his fist off the side of the man's ducking head.

Suddenly headlights turned on from farther back in the shadows and a car charged wildly toward the street with squealing tires. They dived, all three of them. Nicole's face slammed into the asphalt and her body compressed with the impact. She ignored the pain and brought her head up just in time to see blinding red taillights squeal to the right and fishtail away at a terrible speed.

"Pantage! Back off! This isn't Hollywood! Look at his tattoo, it's on the wrong arm. Hollywood just took off!"

Pantage stood there for a moment, contemplating it.

Then he kicked the side of a car.

Ash picked his shirt off the ground, looked at Nicole and said, "This is quite a first date."

She smiled.

Then she said, "Wait 'till you see the second one."

The man pulled car keys out of his pants pocket and pressed the opener. The car next to them—the one that Pantage just kicked—responded with a beep and a quick flash of lights. It was a Corvette convertible that couldn't have been more than a year old. The driver's door was seriously smashed from Pantage's foot.

"I'll get it fixed for you," Pantage said.

"Don't worry about it."

The man got in, started the engine and rolled down the window. He handed Nicole a business card and said, "Call me when you're ready for that second date. Deal?"

She nodded.

"Sure, deal."

"Good. I'll be waiting."

Then he was gone.

Nicole looked at the card.

Ash J. Colt, Esq.

Attorney-at-Law.

Half an hour later, right around two in the morning, Nicole was home at the loft with Fallon, getting ready for bed and starting to come down from the buzz of the Tequila and pot.

Pantage came in only to do a quick search and then retreated to the roof with his gun and an armful of blankets to spend the night, opining that Hollywood was probably done for the night but it was better to err on the safe side. Two black-and-whites would also stay close all night.

Ash.

Ash.

Ash J. Colt, Esq.

Attorney-at-Law.

Nicole wanted to think about him and his face and his body and his smile and the way he pushed her knees apart on the bathroom counter and what would have happened if she hadn't run out, but she didn't have the time; not right now.

She needed to get some sleep while the sleep was there to get.

She also needed to figure out what she'd do if Hollywood really did offer to trade Danica for her. If she were honest with herself she'd have to admit that the thought scared her to death. It wasn't protocol, not by any means. No one would criticize her if she didn't go through with it. In fact, everyone would tell her not to do it. She could play off that if she needed to.

When she came out of the bathroom, Fallon was already on the mattress, under the covers.

Nicole climbed in.

Fallon eased over and spooned into her. Then she said, "Sleep tight."

"You too."

Nicole closed her eyes.

She felt Fallon's lips give her a soft kiss on the back of the neck.

The room spun, but it was more like gentle rolling waves than a typhoon.

It was a motion she could handle.

Five seconds later, riding up a cresting wave, everything

dropped down.

DAY THREE

September 17
Wednesday

23

At the first rays of dawn, Nicole pulled herself out of sleep and, with no dreams to record, headed straight to the shower to wash away all the Tequila and pot and smoke and sweat and sins and disappointment and frustrations of last night. Thankfully, she hadn't wrecked herself as bad as she thought. She'd be able to function today, albeit it at something less than a hundred percent.

She toweled her hair to the point where it was no longer dripping wet and then fluffed it out with her fingers to dry on its own. She didn't have time for a hair dryer, or makeup for that matter.

Today would bring the 48-hour mark.

If the spinner had landed on the 2, that meant that Danica would die at 10:00 tonight.

Every second was crucial.

She slipped into jeans and a T, gave Fallon a kiss on the shoulder soft enough to not wake her, then headed out the door, making sure it was locked tight behind her.

She took the fire escape up to the roof to find Pantage propped against the parapet with his head bent to the side, sound asleep. She nudged him with her foot, dropped the loft key in his lap as he opened his eyes and said, "I'm heading down to headquarters. Fallon's still conked out. Take a shower, make coffee, eat breakfast—whatever. I'll see you down at headquarters when you get there."

He wrinkled his face.

Then he said, "Do I know you?"

She turned and left, saying over her shoulder, "Did I say thanks for watching over me last night?"

He got to his feet, stretched and said, "Actually, no."

"Well, I will," she said. "Don't lose that key. It's the only one I got."

Thirty seconds later she was all the way down the fire escape and behind the wheel of Penny Lane, who was alone in the parking lot. She put the key in, crossed her chest and said, You know what to do.

Then she turned the key.

Penny Lane, it turned out, was still fast asleep and not enthusiastic that someone was trying to wake her up. She blew oily gray smoke and made ghastly noises in protest, but in the end they did no good. She gave up and turned over. Nicole looked through the windshield for signs of killers, found none, and popped the clutch.

Pantage.

Pantage.

Pantage.

Nicole had to admit, deep down, that she wouldn't mind a full-time diet of the man. He had the looks and the body. More than that, though, he was solid enough to keep her interest. He was stable enough to build something with—kids, even. He was tough enough to fight off the demons of the world and he could get through those moments when she turned into one of those demons, which only happened when a perfect storm of ugliness descended on her, but still happened on occasion nonetheless.

Pantage.

Pantage.

Pantage.

Yes, Pantage; he was a distinct possibility. She needed to get in closer for a better look. The geography was an issue; she lived in Miami, he didn't. But that was the kind of thing that could be overcome if there was enough motivation.

And then there was Ash.

Ash J. Colt, Esq.

Attorney-at-Law.

He was still largely a mystery, but one thing Nicole did know about him so far—he was the kind of man who could put his hands on her knees and spread her legs apart. That was worth something, right there. Plus, he spanned the spectrum; on the one hand, he was stable and professional enough to function as a lawyer, and a pretty good one at that, judging by his wheels. On the other hand, he had long hair, a full sleeve and knew had to blow smoke in a public place. Plus, he had that ability to look into your eyes. Someone might ask her in ten years how she and Ash met. Her answer would be, "He saw me. And I saw him."

Just as telling was his reaction after Pantage got in his face and ended up kicking his car. Instead of going the drama route, he just blew it off.

"Don't worry about it."

Ash Colt, yeah.

When Nicole arrived at homicide fifteen minutes later, no one was there yet. She brought the fluorescents to life, kick-started the coffee and then dialed the CSI guy, Paul Penn, on his cell phone, knowing full well she'd be waking him up. She said, "What time are you coming in this morning?"

Sleep was in the man's voice.

His words were sluggish and unfocused.

"Let me guess," he said. "Now?"

"Good answer. I appreciate it."

She hung up.

When the man arrived 45 minutes later, Nicole gave him her cell phone and said, "Hollywood called me twice last night. The last two calls are from him. I already know this is a dead end, but what I need to know is where he was calling from."

"Should be easy."

"Should be easy," she repeated. "My three favorite words, after, of course, eat that chocolate."

She was at her desk in homicide ten minutes later when Penn walked in and said, "Both calls to you came from a burner phone, the same one, not two different ones. It was initially sold from the service provider to a place called Jiggy's Little Shop. Where it went from there is anyone's guess."

"Thanks. I owe you one."

"One? What kind of math are you using?"

As the man left, Nicole said, "I'm staring at your swing in case you're wondering."

He turned and smiled.

"Then we're even."

Jiggy's Little Shop.

Nicole knew the place well, and vice versa. There was no love lost going in either direction. Jiggy's catered to the local gangs and other degenerative elements and was well known for its policy of not keeping records and having no surveillance videos, except of course, for when the store got robbed. Then the cameras magically worked, but that was the only time. How that happened was as big a mystery as a David Lynch film; Mulholland Drive, for example; or Lost Highway.

Jiggy's would fly to hell on the back of a bat before it would help Nicole or anyone like her, so, from the department's anonymous landline, she dialed Princess, one of her CI's, and pulled up an image of a girl in a pink Mohawk who had probably been stunning once upon a time, back before she spent the last two years packing on a decade of wear and tear. Nicole got dumped into voicemail as she knew she would. She left no message and dialed again. After doing that six times, the little Princess finally answered. She had more sleep in her voice than Penn.

"What the hell?"

"Princess, it's me," Nicole said.

"Aw, man—"

"Listen up, girl. I need a solid."

"So—"

"Do it and you'll get a lot of love coming your way the next time you need it," Nicole said. "I promise you."

The woman exhaled and said, "Go ahead. Talk."

Nicole did just that. Someone bought a burner phone that initially started at Jiggy's. Nicole needed to know who the man was that bought the phone. He was someone big and strong. Most importantly, he's probably from out of town. He also probably bought it sometime in the last couple of days, although it might have been earlier. He probably bought more than one. He might have bought a whole box. Nicole need to get everything she could on the man as soon as possible; his name, where he was staying, what he was driving, anything and everything.

Princess listened and said, "Nylons, Nylons, Nylons."

"Huh?"

"Nylons. She's a friend of mine who got picked up last night for some stupid stuff. Get her out of jail with no possibility of return. Tell her to call me when she gets out. Once I get that call, I'll start working on your little issue. No promises on results, though. You know how it goes—"

That was fine with Nicole.

"What's Nylons' real name?"

Princess groaned.

"How should I know?"
The line died.

24

At her desk in homicide after getting Nylons released, Nicole tried to think of one last way to catch Hollywood by using herself as bait. Obviously, Pantage could no longer be by her side or even in the vicinity. At this point, Pantage spelled trap and Hollywood knew it.

So, Pantage was out.

For the same reason, Trane was out. He'd put his face on TV as a detective on the case. He spelled the same four-letter word as Pantage.

The only realistic option would be to lure Hollywood in alone. More importantly, he'd have to know that she was alone. She'd have to entice him somewhere where he could be confident that no one was lurking around in the shadows.

So, where?

Down in the Keys, maybe?

Or an orange grove?

She could get there before him, plant a gun behind a bush, then slowly strip down to her underwear to prove she wasn't hiding anything. While he was busy getting his brain lost in her curves, she could dive for the gun.

There was also another option, potentially.

Maybe he'd call her at some point today.

If he did, she could let him pick the place.

That was a lot riskier but at least she'd be able to get in the same part of the universe as him. She'd at least have a chance of bringing him down.

Nicole's phone rang and Pantage's voice came through. "That guy from last night, what was his name again?"

"Ash Colt."

"Right, Ash Colt. He gave you his card, right?"

"Yeah, why?"

"Because I can't shake the feeling that he might be Hollywood," Pantage said.

Nicole chuckled at the thought.

"No, definitely not. His tattoo, remember? Wrong arm—"

"That doesn't mean anything," Pantage said. "First, we don't know if the guy in the Mustang or the one in the Challenger is really Hollywood. So the guy we're looking for may or may not have a tattoo on his left arm. Second, I wouldn't put it past Hollywood to draw tattoos on his arm and then wipe them off later. That's his alibi: *You saw someone with tattoos on their left arm, right? Well, mine are on the other one.*"

Nicole soured her face.

She tried to make the thought fit but it wouldn't.

Ash was too nice of a guy.

"Sorry, Pantage, I can't get my brain around it."

"Think about it, Nicole. One thing we know about Hollywood is that he's a serious game player. What better game would there be for him to play than to seduce the very detective who's trying to catch him? Plus, remember, right after he called you and basically said he was leaving, low and behold, who did we find leaving? Was that just a big fat coincidence? I kind of doubt it."

"Pantage, man—"

"Also, there was nothing nice in the way he treated you,"

Pantage added. "He basically just bought you a drink and then almost immediately took you upstairs and tried to screw you. There was no respect. He was basically treating you like a piece of meat. That's exactly how I would expect Hollywood to act."

Nicole exhaled.

"It was mutual."

"Mutual or not, are you still willing to be bait?"

"Yes."

"Good," Pantage said. "Then here's what I suggest. Call your little friend Ash Colt and see if he'll meet you for lunch. Be sure it's someplace public and crowded where he wouldn't dare make a move. Then take a good look at him. Look at him from the angle that he might be Hollywood. Maybe you'll see something." He paused and added, "I'm going to head down to Bottom's Up and see if they have any security cameras. I'll see you when I finish up."

She hung up and thought about it.

It wasn't a good idea.

She had better things to do.

Trane busted into homicide ten minutes later, headed straight for the coffee, then joined Nicole at her desk.

He wasn't busting with sunshine.

To prove it he said, "We're getting a few things but not anywhere near as much as we need or as quickly as we need. I feel like I've got us all mucked up in busy work. The one good thing is the interviews that Shalifa Tacher's been doing out in L.A. Yesterday she talked to Danica's friend, Ethan Blue, who's the drummer in that group that Danica sang in, Rule."

"Rude," Nicole said. "With a d."

Trane took a sip of coffee.

"Right, Rude. I was seeing if you were awake."

She smiled.

"Thanks for checking."

"No problem," he said. "Anyway, according to this guy Ethan Blue, Danica was scared to death of something, which is why he got a gun for her and took her out on the boat to shoot it. He had a feeling she was about to bolt, and I'm not talking about just coming to Miami for a week to visit a friend; I'm talking about disappearing forever."

"Because of Hollywood?"

"The guy didn't know," Trane said. "For some reason Danica wasn't giving him any details. But if I had ten cents in my pocket to bet, that's where I'd put my money—on Hollywood He must have been stalking her out there in California, and I'm not talking about from a distance. He must have gotten close enough to get under her skin."

"Like what? Calling her?"

"Unknown," Trane said, "But I'm guessing something like that—calling her, slipping things under her door, tailgating her with his brights on, whatever. In any event, we know for sure that she had a lot of roots there. It hurts like hell to cut roots like that off and just disappear. You have to be seriously motivated. If you ask me, she believed she was about to die unless she made a move and did it quickly. Oh, and here's the real kicker. Two weeks ago she opened up a bank account in the Caymans and transferred almost all of her money there."

Nicole exhaled.

"That's the pudding right there," she said. "The woman was definitely on the run. What about the boyfriend? Was he invited?"

"He wasn't her boyfriend, he was just a friend," Trane said.

"I had the impression he was a boyfriend—"

"Not according to him. They hung out a lot, and he was trying to talk her into coming back into Rule—"

"—Rude—"

"—right, Rude, with a d, listen to what I mean, not to what I say. Anyway, he wasn't sleeping with her. He has his own little surfer-girl, someone named Nadie or Natalie or something like that." Trane looked at his watch and then said, "We're having a task force meeting at 8:30. I'm going to grab some quiet time and prepare for it. Be there."

She nodded. "I will."

Nicole poured herself another cup of coffee and paced next to the windows.

Her watch said 7:40.

Danica might only have fifteen hours to live.

Come on, girl.

Get a plan.

She pulled Ash Colt's business card out of her purse, gave it a hard look while deciding, then dialed the man's number, got his office voicemail as she expected and left a message: "Hey, Ash, this is Nicole, from last night. I wanted to apologize for all the drama. Maybe I could take you out to lunch as a way to say sorry. Anyway, I'm free today if you're interested. Here's my number—"

She hung up.

The minute she did, she had buyer's remorse. She suddenly didn't think she had the time to blow one of her fifteen hours on such a long shot. Well, too bad, because she'd already made the call. All she could do now was play it by ear when the man called back; worst-case scenario, she'd apologize like crazy and reschedule.

Okay, now what?

Nicole's phone rang and Fallon's voice came through, sounding like she just stepped off a roller coaster. "I'm up on the roof!"

"And ...?"

Suddenly gunfire exploded,

Bam!

Bam!
Bam!
Then the line died.

25

Nicole exploded out of her chair and bounded down the stairs two at a time, down to Penny Lane, who must have known that this wasn't the time to play games and fired right up. She slammed into traffic, pushed the pedal to the floor and hardly got anything. The puny little four-banger wasn't about to be rushed.

Come on!

Come on!

Come on!

Weaving through traffic, she reached into her purse for her phone to call for backup and realized she'd left it sitting on her desk. She pictured it there, dutifully weighing down papers, and smashed a fist on the dash.

Ten minutes later she squealed to a stop in her parking lot, which was empty. No one was around that she could see; no one good, no one bad, no one at all, except for three crows flying overhead like omens of evil. She pulled her gun from her purse and sprinted up the fire escape, ready to shoot anyone who wasn't Fallon. Four floors up she paused briefly at her loft door, just to try it, and found it locked. Then she slowed down, caught her breath, and headed carefully up to the roof one step at a time, with the barrel of her weapon pointing the way. Getting her head up above roofline, she saw nothing.

She went all the way up and still found nothing.

She remained quiet and headed across, swinging around rusty metal ductwork and air conditioning units with her finger on the trigger. She found no one.

Suddenly, she felt a presence behind her.

She twisted with a lightning speed.

There was Fallon.

The woman screamed, "Don't shoot!"

Nicole almost pulled the trigger—she was moving that fast—but managed to interrupt the command and not squeeze all the way in. She lowered the gun and felt her lip quiver with the realization of how close she'd come. Fallon came over and pulled Nicole into a hug.

Then Fallon said, "So I came up here to the roof to have a look around the grounds and see if anyone was lurking around. I brought my gun with me, just in case. There was a rattlesnake right over there."

She pointed.

Nicole followed the finger to a spot next to a rooftop fan.

"A rattlesnake?"

"Yes."

"You're sure it was a rattler? Did you actually see the rattle?"

"Yeah," Fallon said. "It wasn't a bullsnake. It had a rattle. I couldn't believe I was seeing it. My first thought was that someone put it up here last night to kill Pantage. That's when I called you. Then, right after you answered, it started going around behind that thing right there, whatever it is. I sort of followed and when I came around to see where it went it was right there. It sprang at me and I fired at it."

"Did you hit it?"

"No," Fallon said. "It got freaked out and took off and then slithered down that pipe right there."

Nicole went over and checked it out.

Then she said, "That's part of the HVAC ductwork. That's not good."

"Why not?"

"Because wherever there's an air vent, it could come out," Nicole said. "Now I have to worry about it dropping down out of the ceiling or whatever." She paused in thought and added, "We need to go close everything off."

Over the next twenty minutes, they retrieved a number of cardboard boxes out of the trash dumpster, then cut them up into panels and taped those panels over every single duct opening in Nicole's loft. They were all up at the ceiling, meaning they had to get up on ladders to get the job done.

In the end, Nicole felt better but still worried.

She wasn't sure the tape would hold.

A lot of the surfaces they taped to were dusty. She didn't doubt that if the reptile got its full weight on the cardboard, it could possibly break loose and come crashing down. In fact, the more she thought about it, she wondered if the cardboard actually made things worse. If the cardboard wasn't there, and the snake came to an opening that emptied down into a fall, it might avoid it. But if it came to cardboard, it might think it had a solid surface to crawl across. Then, boom! If Nicole were sleeping, she probably wouldn't even hear the thing hitting the floor.

Fallon walked over to the wall that had all the 3x5 index cards and tapped on the one and only photograph, of a woman. "I was wondering, who's this?"

Nicole pulled the photo off, took one last look at it and tossed it in the trash.

"No one," she said. "Just someone a little crazy."

"So why is she here on your wall?"

Nicole checked her watch.

It was already mid-morning.

She needed to go.

"That lady saw me once and thought I was her long lost sister," she said.

"Why?"

"It's a long story but let me tell you how it ends," she said. "I actually accommodated her and did a bona fide laboratory DNA test. It turned out we weren't related, not even a trace."

"It doesn't surprise me," Fallon said. "You don't even remotely look the same."

"Tell me about it. Like I said; crazy lady, wasted time. I got to run. Follow up on that camera idea. Oh, and do me a favor. Give Juicy a heads-up on the whole thing. Also, if you get a chance, can you get a couple of spare keys made for my door?"

"Sure."

"That way we can both come and go."

She gave Fallon a hug and then she was gone.

Back at homicide, she called Pantage and told him how a rattlesnake had shown up on the roof, no doubt compliments of Hollywood, meaning he had more guts than they were giving him credit for. "I don't understand why he just didn't shoot you in your sleep."

"Because he's addicted to the game. He's always figuring out how to amp it up."

"Well he should stop, because that's how we'll end up catching him," Nicole said. "In any event, a crime unit's on the way over there to process the scene. What's your plan? You want to meet them there, or come here, or what?"

"I'll be there in ten minutes," he said. "I want to meet with you and Trane. Oh, and by the way, Bottoms Up has a lot of cameras but they're live only. They don't record."

"That's what I figured," Nicole said. "The girls there are pretty touchy. The last thing the place needs is to be creating evidence for a vice raid. See you in ten. Watch your back."

Suddenly Trane bounded into the room, headed over to Nicole with excitement all over his face and said, "Big news!"

26

Nicole had seen Trane excited before, but never anything like this. He said. "Out in L.A., Shalifa managed to get a search warrant this morning for Danica Rose's apartment, thanks to a lot of help from our counterparts out there. One of the things she found was a creepy piece of paper. Someone had cut letters and words out of a magazine and pasted them on, just like in one of those old stupid TV movies. Guess what the words said?"

Nicole shrugged.

"I don't know," she said. "Get your kicks on Route 66?"

Trane smiled and said, "Not exactly, but close. It said, *I killed Laura Palmer.*"

Nicole soured her face.

It didn't compute.

"Who's Laura Palmer?"

"She was the murder victim on Twin Peaks," Trane added. "The TV show, David Lynch, One Eyed Jacks—"

"Never watched it."

"Dana Scully, redhead, great big . . . personalities?"

"I still never watched it," Nicole said.

"Well, Laura Palmer was the murder victim on the show," he said. "But that's not what he was referring to. One of the detectives that Hollywood killed was a woman by the name of

Laura Wickliffe."

"And?"

"And," Trane said, "Laura Wickliffe was married to Mr. Wickliffe. But she wasn't always married. Before she got married, she was single; and guess what her maiden name was before she took those sacred little vows with Mr. Wickliffe?"

Suddenly it computed.

"Laura Palmer."

Trane nodded.

"Laura Palmer," he said. "Only Hollywood would get the joke. Everyone else in the world would think he was making some kind of obscure but creepy reference to Twin Peaks."

"So Hollywood was definitely the one freaking Danica out," Nicole said.

Trane nodded.

"He likes his games, doesn't he?"

"So, how do we use this?"

Trane tilted his head and said, "Coffee first."

He got one for himself and one for Nicole, sat down in front of her desk and took a noisy slurp. "The most immediate thing this means is that Hollywood must have followed Danica when she rented the car and made the drive from L.A. to Miami. That brings us right back to your initial theory that he probably stayed in a hotel when he arrived that night, which was Friday. We're already way down the road in computing a master list of those persons. With any luck, Hollywood's name is on that list somewhere, or will be soon."

"How long is the list?"

Trane frowned.

"Think, to the sun and back." He took a sip of coffee and added, "Oh, I almost forgot to tell you. There was another piece of paper with pasted letters. It said,

Swallow the Sun."

Nicole didn't get it.

"Not computing," she said.

"This one is a lot more subtle," Trane said. "Swallow the Sun is actually a metal band from Finland. In 2005 they put out an album called Ghosts of Loss. One of the tracks on that album is called Ghost of Laura Palmer."

Nicole considered it.

"So he's tying himself again to the detective he murdered, Laura Palmer."

Trane nodded.

"Once again, only he'd get the joke. Danica only got a piece of paper that no doubt gave her the creeps because she had no idea what it meant, other than an indicator than she'd gotten herself on the radar screen of some freak who was marching to his own strange drummer."

Nicole swallowed.

"This guy's smarter than I thought," she said. "This kind of stuff just doesn't fall out of the sky and land on your head. You have to work at it. He's weaving clues in all over the place. I bet if we took a hard look at all his other cases, we'd find a ton more just like this."

"Yeah, if we had the time," Trane said. "Except it's really not much of a clue other than to tell us that Hollywood is definitely the one who took Danica Rose and that he stalked her and taunted her first."

Nicole exhaled.

"He's a confident little prick, isn't he?"

"Alpha-male," Trane said. "Alpha-male from fangs to tail."

He smiled and added, "Hey, I'm a poet and don't know it."

Nicole winced.

Trane added, "I can make a rhyme any old time."

"I get it, Trane."

"Just give me a word, I'll say something absurd."

She punched his arm.

Then her phone rang and the voice of the lawyer, Ash J.

Colt, Esq., came through: "I just picked up your message about that lunch thing. Still want to do it?"

She paused, considering.

She really didn't have the time, but she had more than enough desire. She'd make it quick.

"Sure," she said. "Can I pick the place?"

"Absolutely."

"Be warned," she said. "I don't look as good through sunshine as I do through liquor."

27

Nicole got herself into the heart of Miami's financial district, Wall Street South, and looked around to find that the golden-boy Ash Colt wasn't at the appointed place yet. She parked her posterior on the ledge of a contemporary fountain and waited. People buzzed around her—suits, teenagers with skateboards, clumps of homeless guys, secretaries loose from their prisons, and all the rest of it, walking and strutting and smoking and hustling and scratching and doing whatever it was they needed to get done before the lunch hour ticked off and the grind sucked them back in.

The sunshine went straight into Nicole's blood as she recalled the mission:

> Call your little friend Ash Colt and see if he'll meet you for lunch. Be sure it's someplace public and crowded where he wouldn't dare make a move. Then take a good look at him. Look at him from the angle that he might be Hollywood. Maybe you'll see something.

To the east, over the ocean, clouds were building, but right now, here in the center of the city, it couldn't have been more perfect. A kid walked by with a radio tuned in to an old Cure song:

> I don't care if Monday's black
> Tuesday, Wednesday, heart attack
> Thursday never looking back
> It's Friday I'm in love

Then it happened.

Heading this way as if he owned Brickell Avenue was none other than Ash Colt himself. Damn it, the man looked good, all polished up in a suit and a tie. Nicole was suddenly underdressed in jeans and a simple T. Thankfully, by the look on Ash's face as he approached, he didn't care.

He came in close and said, "Sorry, but I've been dreaming about those lips all night." Then he kissed her, stood back to check her out and said, "That's a relief."

"What is?"

"There's an old joke among drunk guys," he said. "It goes, I never went to bed with an ugly woman but I sure woke up with a few. That doesn't apply to you; hence, the relief I just mentioned."

"I'm not ugly, is what you're saying."

He nodded.

"Bingo."

"Good to know."

He smiled.

"Just for your information, I know that someone took the word ugly out of the dictionary and that no one's allowed to actually use it anymore. So that joke, it's just between you and me."

Nicole considered it.

"Our first secret," she said.

"Yeah. Maybe I'll ask you about it in ten years and see if you remember it."

Lunch, since Nicole got to choose, turned out to be sausage dogs smothered under mountains of kraut and honey mustard from a street vendor, to eat right there at the fountain, and wash down with cans of diet Pepsi.

"So you're a lawyer—"

"That's what they tell me," Ash said. "Entertainment law."

"Really? What kind, music?"

"The firm I'm in—White & Stafford, LLC—does a lot of music entertainment law but I don't personally get involved in too much of it. My practice leans more towards the motion picture industry side of things."

"In Miami?"

"Miami's my home office," he said. "The firm also has offices in Atlantic City, Denver, Los Angeles, Chicago and Dallas. They hop me around to whatever the next fire needs to be put out."

Los Angeles.

That's where Danica was from.

Miami.

That's where Danica ended up.

"So what do you do, exactly?"

"Most of my clients are motion picture producers," he said. "We do all their contracts with the actors, the venues they film at, the directors, the suppliers and whatnot, plus make sure they end up with all the worldwide intellectual rights to the work, and things like that. I'm not going to drop names but any movie you've gone to see in a theater in the last year, it was probably produced by one of my clients."

Nicole took a big bite of the sausage.

The fatty juice was heaven in her mouth.

"So you're a big shot."

He shrugged.

"I'm just a guy out there in the world, looking around," he said.

"Looking around for what, exactly?"

"I don't know yet. You, maybe—"

Nicole rolled her eyes.

"I've met particles of light that move slower than you."

He tilted his head.

"Let me ask you something. Do you believe in fate?"

"No."

"Well I do," he said. "I'm thirty. I haven't been to a strip club since I was twenty-five. Yet I went to one last night and still don't know why. All I know is that I ended up seeing you and I haven't been able to look away since."

"And you think that's because of fate?"

He shrugged.

"Why not?"

Nicole's phone rang and Trane's voice came through: "Where are you?"

"Grabbing lunch."

"Well, there were fingerprints on both of those pieces of paper that we retrieved from Danica's apartment. Unfortunately, they all belonged to Danica."

"None were Hollywood's?"

"No."

"I'll be back in ten."

Danica.

Danica.

Danica.

Her time was running out and Nicole was out here in the sunshine eating sausage and getting flirted on. That was wrong on every level.

She was done looking at Ash as if he might be Hollywood.

He clearly wasn't.

She popped the last of the sausage in her mouth, stood up and said, "I got to run." Against her better judgment, she bent down and gave Ash a quick kiss on the lips, then headed off before either of them could say anything. She could feel his eyes on her body as she walked.

It felt nice.

It felt like sunshine in her blood.

But she didn't have time for it right now.

She needed to give all her time to Danica.

As she left, Ash's words echoed in her gray matter:

> Most of my clients are motion picture producers. We do all their contracts with the actors, the venues they film at, the directors, the suppliers and whatnot, plus make sure they end up with all the worldwide rights to the work, and things like that.

After thirty steps, she turned.

The man was nowhere in sight. She headed back at a trot and caught up with him a block down.

"Hey, Ash, hold on a moment," she said.

The man turned, at first surprised and then glad.

His face lit up.

"Hey!"

"Hey, back. Let me ask you something," Nicole said. "There's a picture being made right now called The Shoals. Have you ever heard of it?"

"The Shoals? Sure."

"Did you do any work on it?"

"Yes. How do you know about it?"

"I'll tell you in a second," she said. "So you represented the producer in connection with that film?"

"Right. Paradyme Pictures out of L.A. They've been a client of mine for, how long? I guess it's going on three years now —"

"Did you do the contracts between Paradyme and the actors?"

"Of course."

"How about an actress named Danica Rose?"

Confusion washed over the man's face.

"Danica Rose, Danica Rose— It's not ringing a bell," he said. "Who was her agent?"

Good question.

Nicole racked her brain and said, "Lance Fox?"

"Lance Fox?"

"Right, Lance Fox."

"Yeah, I did a contract with Lance," Ash said. "Okay, it's coming back. He was representing some new face, some young girl who was getting a really good part."

"That was Danica Rose," Nicole said. "She was blond, athletic, super pretty."

"Bingo," Ash said. "I remember her now. Lance actually brought her to the office to sign the papers. I remember because her contract called for nude scenes and she wanted to be sure that everything was legit."

"So you actually met her?"

He nodded.

"I did."

"You know I'm a homicide detective, right?"

He nodded.

"You told me last night after the fight."

"Danica Rose came to Miami recently and disappeared. Did you know that?"

Ash shook his head.

"No. When you say disappeared, what do you mean?"

"It's complicated."

"Is she dead?"

"Not yet, I'm pretty sure, but she could be soon," Nicole instinctively looked at her watch, then back at Ash and said, "Maybe you can help."

He nodded.

"Sure, anything. I can't see how, but yeah, whatever you want. Count me in a hundred percent."

28

Back at homicide, Nicole pulled Trane and Pantage into a conference room and told them about her discovery that Ash had a connection to Danica Rose.

Ash did a lot of work at his firm's office in L.A., where Danica lived.

Ash represented the producer of The Shoals.

Ash drafted Danica's contract for The Shoals.

Ash actually met Danica when she came to the office to sign the contract.

And last night, low and behold, who should magically appear at Bottoms Up and make a move on Nicole? None other than the man of the hour, Ash Colt himself.

Pantage slammed his hand on the table.

"That son-of-a-bitch! Danica's in his office signing a contract and thinking she has a wonderful life in front of her and all the time this sick little bitch-waffle is picking her out as his next victim. You know what? I'll bet he actually went to some of the shoots and watched her."

"Maybe."

Pantage shook his head in disgust. "Hell, what was the name of that group that Danica sang in?"

"Rule," Trane said.

He looked at Nicole with a smile, waiting for her to correct him.

She rolled her eyes and said nothing.

"Right, Rule," Pantage said. "I wouldn't doubt it a bit if our little friend was out there in the crowd even back then, working up a perverted little fantasy where Danica played the starring role."

Nicole shrugged.

It was possible.

But it didn't resonate down in her gut.

Trane frowned and said, "Here's the problem. It's all smoke—good solid smoke, don't get me wrong, but smoke as opposed to fire. From an evidentiary standpoint, right now there isn't enough probable cause to get a warrant for anything, not a wiretap, not a search, not a bug, not a tracker, not a nothing, and certainly not an arrest warrant."

Pantage nodded.

That was true.

They had a connection but they didn't have Ash doing a single thing illegal.

"The other problem is, we can't afford to bend the rules," Trane added. "We can't afford to get dirty. When we finally get this guy, we need to have every duck in a row. We can't afford to have some slimy defense lawyer wiggling him off; so, nothing illegal. Agreed?"

"Agreed," Pantage said.

The two men looked at Nicole.

She wondered if she should say what was on her mind, then decided to just go for it. "Look," she said. "I know there's a lot of smoke coming from Ash's direction. I've spent some time with him, not a lot, granted, but I just don't think he's our guy."

"Your judgment's clouded, Nicole," Trane said. "Hell, no offense, but you were in the bathroom spreading your legs for him."

She nodded and said, "That's true. But that doesn't mean I'm wrong. My gut says he's not our guy."

"In that case, put some coffee in your gut. Then you'll have at least one thing in there that you can trust." He paused and added, "Here's what we do. We get eyes on him and follow his every move. We get all the information on him that we can within the bounds of the law, meaning background, properties, cars, friends, social media, the whole big fat thing. We hope he leads us to Danica."

Pantage nodded.

"Remember," Trane said. "This isn't about him, not yet. This is still about Danica. Our goal is to bring her back alive. That means we need our friend alive and comfortable enough to lead us to her."

Nicole looked into Trane's eyes and said, "What about me? Should I try to squeeze more info out of him?"

She already knew the answer.

No.

No.

No.

No, it was too dangerous.

They'd take it from here.

Trane's eyes retreated, then they focused and he said, "No."

Nicole's shoulders sagged.

Trane looked at her hard.

"Stay away from him from this point on. That's an order. If he calls, you can talk to him just enough that he doesn't get spooked and think we're on to him; be normal, be smart. But under no circumstances are you to meet with him again." Trane patted her hand and said, "You're exhausted. Why don't you head home and get a couple of hours sleep? We all need to be at full capacity tonight."

"If you're serious—"

"I am. Go."

She went.

But it wasn't to sleep.

It was anything but.

Trane was wrong.

Ash wasn't their man.

Down in Penny Lane, she called Princess to see if the woman was making any progress in identifying the person who ended up with the burner phone initially sold from Jiggy's.

Princess didn't answer.

Nicole hung up and called again.

She got more of the same.

On the third try, Princess answered: "What!"

"This is Nicole. Where we at?"

"Oh, shit—"

"Tell me you're working on it."

"I'm starting right now," Princess said. Her voice sounded like a hundred years of sleep slowly getting beaten away with a stick. She'd had the project for over five hours and hadn't yet done a thing.

"Princess, do not go back to sleep, do you hear me?"

"I'm up, I'm up. You don't have to yell."

"I'm not yelling. This is important. I need you on it right now."

"What about Nylons?"

"We cut her loose a long time ago. She should have called you."

"Well, she didn't."

The line died.

Punching off, Nicole noticed that she had a phone update in her Settings. It turned out to be for a phone tracker app whose icon had been buried in an obscure file. She took it up to Paul Penn for his evaluation.

"This is the latest spyware," he said. "It's a GPS tracker. They can pull up your current GPS at any time and also a history of locations. Someone put it on your phone two months ago, July 13 at 2:25 a.m., to be precise."

2:25 a.m.

That was the middle of the night.

"What did they do, hack it in somehow?"

Penn shook his head.

"No. They have to physically have the phone in hand to install the app," he said.

"How can that be?"

"I don't know," he said. "Somehow they had it."

"Can we find out who's tracking me?"

"No, this is one directional only," he said.

"Can we turn it around and track them back?"

"No. Do you want me to uninstall it?"

Nicole considered it.

Then she said, "No. Let's play it out."

Two minutes later she had Trane and Pantage in a small conference room, showing them the tracker.

"Two months ago," she said. "That's when someone put it on. You know what this says to me? It says we've been looking at this Hollywood thing all wrong."

Trane raised an eyebrow.

"What do you mean?"

"We've been thinking from day one that Hollywood chooses his victim and then hunts down whatever random detective gets assigned to the case," Nicole said. "I think it's the opposite way around. I think Hollywood chooses his detective first, not his victim."

Pantage soured his face and tapped a finger on the table.

He clearly didn't get it.

Neither did Trane.

"Okay," Nicole said. "Here's what I'm saying. Hollywood chose me two months ago as the detective to kill. After he did that, he picked out a victim somewhere in my jurisdiction. Then he waited until he knew I was the detective on duty for the night. Then he takes his victim and I respond."

Trane wasn't impressed.

"That's a stretch," he said.

"Is it? Of the other eight cases, how many of the detectives were female?"

Pantage said, "Five."

"Does that seem proportionate to you?"

Pantage shook his head, getting it, and said, "That always bothered me."

"This whole thing has been in play for over two months," Nicole said. "And here's the freaky thing. He had to have the phone physically in hand to install the app. It was installed in the middle of the night; at 2:25 in the morning. I think he somehow has a key to my loft. I think he actually came in while I was sleeping. I think he knew I'd eventually figure it out and that's all just another part of the game he's playing. It's his way of telling me that I'm not safe even in my loft with the door locked."

She got up to leave.

"Where you going?"

She said over her shoulder, "To check something out."

29

Nicole understood all too well that she would likely be fired for what she was about to do. She also understood that if she was making a mistake of judgment, it was Danica Rose, not her, who might end up paying the ultimate price. That said, she decided to proceed anyway, and, to do that, drove from homicide to the financial district and pushed through the revolving doors of Ash's building.

Inside, she walked across the expansive, multi-story lobby.

Art deco punctuated the walls, looking as if a sports car filled with gallon buckets of neon paint had crashed into it at full speed. She took the elevator to the 35th floor, walked down a short stylish corridor to a contemporary lobby and pushed through the glass doors.

A too-cute receptionist wearing a thin wireless headset looked up as she talked into a receiver and held a finger up, indicating she'd be right with her. Behind her, in red lettering on a gray textured wall, were the words:

White & Stafford, LLC
Miami
Atlantic City
Denver

Los Angeles
Chicago
Dallas

"I'm here to see Ash Colt," Nicole said. "I don't have an appointment. My name is Nicole Stone." Less than a minute later she was being escorted down a spacious corridor decorated with beach-themed oil paintings and into a spacious glass corner office, where Ash waved her in as he talked into a phone. A bank of floor-to-ceiling windows showcased Miami below and the aqua waters of the ocean to the east. Three pinball machines hugged the opposite wall. In the corner on a stand was an old bicycle with a big wire basket over the front tire.

The man eyed Nicole as he hung up and said, "Let's play."

He fired up the middle pinball machine, a King Kong vintage, jiggled the flippers to get a feel for the action, and put a ball in motion.

"Winner gets whatever they want," he said.

Nicole tilted her head.

"That's pretty high stakes."

"Are you afraid?"

"You know the machine, I don't. You need to spot me," she said.

"How much?"

"You need to double me to win," she said.

"Fair enough."

Nicole won.

They played two out of three.

She won again.

Ash put a look of sweet defeat on his face, walked dangerously close to her and whispered in her ear, "It looks like you get whatever you want. I wonder what it will be."

She ran a finger down his chest.

Then she whispered in his ear, "That's going to depend on what happens in the next few minutes."

"Interesting," Ash said.

"Isn't it?" She dropped back, walked to the windows and looked down. People were dots. A toy bus took off, marking its departure with a plume of black smoke. Nicole refocused on Ash and said, "Where were you Monday night at around 10:00 p.m.?"

"Why?"

"Because," Nicole said, "at the risk of getting right to the point, some women have been getting murdered. There are some people I work with who are wondering if you might be the one who's been doing it."

The man put shock on his face.

"Does that include you? Because if it does—"

Nicole held a hand up to cut him off.

"No, it doesn't include me," she said. "That's why I'm here. In fact, that's why I'm risking my job right now at this very moment, because I know that you didn't do it." She kissed him and said, "Indulge me. Monday night, ten."

Ash retreated in thought.

"I was home, sleeping."

"Was anyone with you?"

He hesitated and then said, "Yes."

"Who?"

"It's a little tricky—"

"Why?"

"Well, because she sort of works here."

"Who is she?"

"I'll tell you on one condition," Ash said. "I have a condo at the Bluetone. It's where I live. I'll call security over there and tell them to release anything they might have on me to you. They'll have video of the parking garage and the elevator, plus key-card usage data. It'll show the lady and me getting there about eight. She left the next morning, about six. I left an hour later. What I'd like is for you to get all that information first. Hopefully it will satisfy you. If it doesn't then you can talk to the lady, but not before. Deal?"

Nicole nodded.

"Sure, I'll play. What's her name?"

"Kennedy. She's the receptionist."

"The one I just met five minutes ago?"

"Yes."

"Well, she's cute, I'll give you that much."

"We're not serious."

"That's none of my business."

"I was actually hoping it was," Ash said. "I met her three years ago. It was hot and heavy for awhile but now we're just occasional booty-call friends. I got her the job here. If anyone finds out we see each other off the grid so to speak, she won't last long. That's something I don't want to see happen, for her sake, not mine. Are you good with that?"

"No worries," Nicole said. "Let me shift gears a little bit. You go to the Atlantic City office sometimes, right?"

"Of course. Often, actually."

"A woman was murdered in Atlantic City in September of last year," Nicole said. "September 8th to be precise. Her name was Necha. She was a smoking hot little Puerto Rican girl who was working as a waitress at a bar called the Blackbird Ordinary. Have you ever been there, the Blackbird Ordinary?"

"Actually, yes. It's near Smuggler's Cove."

"That's right."

Nicole pulled a picture up on her phone.

It showed an exotic mocha beauty, about 20.

"This is her, Necha," she said. "Do you recognize her?"

The man looked, then harder, and finally nodded.

"Yeah, I've seen her, but I didn't kill her."

Nicole walked over to the bike, ran a finger across the seat and said, "What's with this?"

"It was my first job," he said. "Paperboy."

"Congratulations."

"Not really, it sucked," he said. "No one ever paid when you knocked on the door to collect. They always said to come back next week. Then, when next week came, they would say the same thing again. I didn't make much money but I sure started learning about life."

"So why is it here in your office?"

"To remind me where the bottom is," he said. "We're always just one epic misstep from falling back down into it. It's my reminder to keep my footing, be nice to my clients, count my blessings, and all that crap."

Nicole looked at the floor.

Then she looked up into the man's eyes and said, "I want to see your alibi. I want to know—not just in my gut, but in my brain—that it exists."

"My alibi—"

"Right. For September 8th of last year. Convince me that you weren't in Atlantic City on that day. Give me the solid irrefutable proof that you're not Hollywood."

"And if I do?"

"And if you do, then I'm going to cash in my winnings for that pinball game."

The man tilted his head.

"When?"

Nicole unbuckled her belt, pulled it off and set it on the man's desk. Then she said, "Immediately."

30

Nicole got back to the loft to find Fallon hanging out down in Juicy's studio. She pulled the woman into the bathroom, locked the door and said, "Trane and Pantage are pointing all their time and energy at the lawyer, Ash Colt. They're convinced he's Hollywood, but they're wrong."

"How do you know?"

"Because, Ash sort of has an alibi for Monday, although I still have to check it out. More importantly, before Hollywood came to Miami, his last victim was a Puerto Rican girl in Atlantic City named Necha," she said. "She got taken in the afternoon of September 8th of last year. Ash was in San Francisco giving a presentation at a law conference on that day. When a lawyer in his firm incurs expenses that the firm is supposed to reimburse, the lawyer submits the physical papers to the firm, which are then digitally scanned for tax purposes. So, everything related to that trip was preserved. He had copies of his plane tickets, hotel reservations, car rental, restaurant charges, and all that stuff, not just for September 8th but for the day before that and the day after it as well."

"That's pretty solid."

"Not just that; take a look at this." On her phone, Nicole pulled up a YouTube video of Ash Colt speaking at a conference. "This was him talking on September 8th in San Francisco right after the lunch break, meaning the exact same time Necha was being abducted in Atlantic City."

"So Ash is definitely not Hollywood."

"That's right," Nicole said. "But here's the problem. I can't tell Trane because he ordered me point blank to not contact Ash. If he finds out I did, there will be trouble."

"So what are you going to do?"

Nicole exhaled.

Then she said, "I have a plan. Don't freak out but I just found out that Hollywood put a tracker app on my phone two months ago. He actually had to come into the loft while I was sleeping to do it. I think he got a key somehow. But here's what's worse. I'm betting that he put spy cameras in there as well. I remember seeing something weird up by the water pipes in the ceiling but never checked it out. In hindsight I think he's been watching me shower, eat, sleep and everything else for at least two months—maybe longer, who knows?"

"That means me too," Fallon said.

"Yes, sorry about that," Nicole said. "But I figured out a way to use it to my advantage. You and I will go up to the loft and we'll have a conversation. I'll say that Trane has ordered me to leave town and lay low somewhere until everything quiets down. I'll tell you that I'm going to go down to Key Largo and get a room there. If I'm right that the loft is bugged, Hollywood will know where I'm going. And if the room isn't bugged, he'll still be able to find me because of the tracker on my phone, plus the GPS under my car—although, I'll be honest, I don't know what kind of range that has. He'll think I'll be laying low. What he won't know is that I'll be waiting for him."

"So you're back to the bait idea again."

"Right; except this time, it's going to work."

Fallon said, "I'm going with you."

"No, absolutely not."

"Yes I am." She slapped Nicole on the ass and said, "Get it in gear, girl."

Fifteen minutes later, with suitcases in the trunk, they were cruising out of Miami south, one more sardine in the can of sardines all crushed together and heading to wherever it was they were all heading at such maniac speeds. Nicole hated this stretch of congested hell and always had and always would. It pretty much sucked for miles. A thousand people could be tailing them and she wouldn't know about even one of them.

Thirty minutes into the drive, the clouds opened and sunshine poured down.

The traffic thinned.

She could breathe again.

Her brain could think about things other than how to keep from getting hit by the crazies.

Penny Lane wasn't making any strange warning sounds.

It was all good.

She could still feel Ash Colt between her legs as she cashed in her pinball winnings. If life ended right now, at least she had that.

Traffic stayed manageable and then thinned even more as they got closer to the Keys. She felt like she'd just been released from prison. An old red F-150 pickup truck passed them early on, but after that traffic both in front and behind faded off to almost zero. If someone was following her, they were either doing a really bad job or a really good one.

The miles clicked off.

It was almost five o'clock now.

The air was hot.

Her stomach was running on fumes.

Suddenly something happened that she didn't expect. Up ahead, the old F-150 was pulled over to the side of the road. The tailgate was down and the hood was up. Penny Lane had been in that exact same position about five million times. Two figures were out. As the gap closed, the figures appeared to be Hispanic, a male and a female. Nicole made a mental calculation as to whether Penny Lane could carry the extra weight.

The woman was now at the side of the road waving her arms for help.

Fallon looked over and said, "You going to stop?"

"Got to," Nicole said. "I got Karma to repay."

She pulled in behind the truck and considered briefly whether she should leave the engine running. Penny Lane had too long a history of being a bitch at the absolute worst time and not starting out here would be the kind of thing she'd like to add to her list. Nicole said, Start when I come back, bitch, I mean it. She killed the engine, and she and Fallon stepped out into the beating sun.

The woman looked fine.

She was in her prime, about 22, strong and pretty, dressed in cutoff jeans and a white sleeveless blouse, with sandals down below and a cowboy hat up top. She actually looked like someone Nicole could be friends with, if they were a little closer in age.

The man, though, was downright creepy.

He was a lot older than the woman; double her age, forty or thereabouts.

He wasn't overly big, at about five-eight, and was on the skinny side, but had the jaw cut of a boxer who'd taken more punches than he'd given. His eyes were too far apart and his nose was cocked to the side. A long black ponytail hung down his back. He had a lot of gross black tattoos.

The pungent odor of burnt antifreeze hung heavy in the air.

"Troubles?" Nicole said.

The man said, "Radiator," and pointed to a puddle of green liquid spewed in the dirt under the engine compartment. "A hose broke." He reached into his back pocket and pulled out a wallet. "If you could give us a lift, I'd be happy to pay you."

Nicole waved it off.

"No need," she said. "How far you heading?"

"To Key Largo."

"Same as us," she said.

The man shook her hand and said, "Gracias. I'm Thiago. This is my wife, Juana del Carmen."

Wife.

It seemed improbable.

The woman was too young.

She was too pretty.

She wore no wedding ring.

It was then that Nicole noticed a yellow Prestone antifreeze container in the dirt on the other side of the car, as if it had been deliberately emptied under the truck.

Suddenly the man looked up and down the road, saw no cars and pulled a gun from behind his back. His mouth grinned at the surprise. Then his face turned to demons.

With a lightning speed, he swung the weapon into the side of Fallon's head.

She immediately crumpled to the ground with a dull thud.

She didn't move.

She was either unconscious or dead.

"Fallon!"

The so-called wife quickly pressed a knife to the side of Nicole's stomach.

"Move and I slit you." Then she pushed the blade in to where it almost drew blood. "Do you understand?"

"Yes."

"Say it again!"

"Yes!"

31

As Nicole watched in horror, the man pulled Fallon's limp body from the ground, dragged it around to the passenger side of the pickup and threw it into the cab where it landed on the floorboard with a thud. Then he quickly tied Nicole's hands behind her back with rope, shoved her into the bench seat where she ended up between the man and the woman, and took off as fast as the old wheels would go.

No cars came during any of it.

No one saw anything.

Nicole's purse—with her cell phone and gun—stayed behind in the backseat of Penny Lane.

She pulled at the ropes binding her wrists, hoping for play but finding none.

They were tighter than her own true love.

The man slapped his hand on Nicole's leg, happy as hell and widening his mouth with a grin to prove it.

"Good, huh?"

He tossed the gun up on the dash. Nicole had no way to get it and they both knew it. Having it there so close and in plain sight was his way of telling Nicole how helpless she was.

The woman tapped two cigarettes out of a pack, lit them both and passed one to the man. Her feet were resting comfortably on Fallon's body; so were Nicole's, although she tried to minimize the pressure as much as her leg muscles would let her.

No one talked.

Then the woman said, "Up here on the right."

"Yeah, I know."

A hundred yards later, slightly past a dilapidated sign that was too faded to read, the man turned right on an old dirt road. It was choked with weeds and looked like it hadn't been used in decades. Almost immediately, the topography rose and then dropped, to where they were no longer in sight of the road. The man stopped, got out and went to each of the front wheels, locking them into four-wheel drive. Then they were back in motion, driving deeper and deeper into the middle of nowhere.

No one was out there and probably hadn't been in years.

The vehicle bounced and rocked as it crept along, jiggling Fallon's body underneath Nicole's shoes.

"Where are we going?" she said.

The man punched her leg.

"Shut up, bitch!"

The woman chuckled.

Nicole said nothing through the pain.

She didn't move.

Her legs weren't tied but there was nothing good to kick. At best, she could get a blow from her left foot to the man's shin or foot. That might be enough to bring his foot down on the accelerator. But it would be brief and it wouldn't be much. It probably wouldn't be enough to cause a crash.

The woman had her knife out, in her hands.

It was clear that if Nicole did anything, that knife was going to come down into the top of her leg.

She didn't move.

Sooner or later they'd stop.

When that happened, maybe she'd be able to make a break

for it. She had to admit, though, that the chances weren't good. The man was skinny but he looked fast. So did the woman; in fact, she looked faster than the man. Nicole would be slow with her arms locked behind her back. She wouldn't be able to pump. Worst of all, she wouldn't be able to outrun a bullet. Plus there'd be nowhere to run. They were already a good distance into the topography. Nicole could run fast for short periods but wasn't built for distance. Her lungs weren't made for it.

They continued on.

Then, up ahead, the burned remnants of an old structure appeared. Eight or ten feet of an old brick fireplace stuck up above the weeds. Even now—no doubt years later—the bricks were still covered in black soot, refusing to be washed off by the weather.

The man brought the vehicle to a stop and killed the engine.

Then he tied a 20-foot length of rope around Nicole's neck, pulled her outside and tied the other end to the truck's bumper, like a leash.

All hopes of making a break for it vanished.

She was stuck.

The sun beat down.

The woman stayed close with her blade in hand, seemingly eager for a reason to push it into Nicole's flesh.

The man watched the sky.

Thirty minutes passed and then Nicole figured out why.

A helicopter was approaching.

It was flying low, as if to avoid radar.

The rumble grew more and more pronounced as it approached.

Nicole couldn't breath.

He legs wobbled.

It was now obvious that whatever was going on wasn't just the brainchild of two crazies. Someone with money was involved; and the plan had definitely been in the making for some time.

Who was behind it?

Hollywood?

Could he possibly be this complex?

The man was waving at the helicopter, indicating it was safe to land.

Suddenly a gunshot rang out and the man's back pushed forward. Blood splattered and he dropped to the ground. Nicole turned to see Fallon with a gun in hand, the gun that had been on the dash. She fired at the helicopter, again and again and again, seeming to hit it but not causing any damage. Then, just like that, black smoke erupted from the fuselage. The aircraft twisted violently and flew off.

Fallon trained the weapon on the woman, who was running off and already a good distance away.

She fired.

Bam!

Bam!

The woman didn't go down.

Fallon fired one more and then the clip was empty.

Nicole shouted, "Untie me!"

Then, as soon as she was free, she ran at full speed after the woman, who at this point had good head start but was in sandals. It took a long time and every ounce of Nicole's strength but she finally closed the gap and brought the woman down with a diving tackle.

The knife flew out of the woman's hand.

Nicole scrambled for it and almost had it when a foot kicked into her face. Dirt flew into her eyes and grinded in like sandpaper to where she could barely see.

Then the woman was on her.

Nicole got a hand to the woman's wrist just as she was bringing the knife down. She wrestled it away, got the woman on her back and straddled her chest.

She raised the knife.

Then she looked into the woman's eyes.

They were young.

They were terrified.

They were enough to make the world stop.

Then she got to her feet, dropped the knife to the ground and walked away. The woman shouted from behind her, "It will never stop! Do yourself a favor and just give up!" When Nicole turned, the woman was walking off in the opposite direction, taking one last look back.

Their eyes briefly locked.

The woman raised a hand in a gesture, timidly, almost as if waving goodbye to a friend she'd never see again. Then she turned and headed off.

The knife was still on the ground.

Suddenly in the far distance a giant orange fireball erupted in the sky and the helicopter plummeted straight down in a thick shroud of black smoke.

32

Nicole made her way back to the truck to find Fallon sitting in the dirt on the shady side, with her back propped up against the rear wheel and her head hanging to the side, either sleeping or passed out or dead. She shook the woman, who opened her eyes but took a few seconds to focus.

It was clear she was in bad shape.

The blood had caked in Fallon's hair so it was hard to get a good look at the wound, but from what Nicole could see there was a gap that would need several stitches. Plus there was a distinct possibility of a concussion or even a cracked skull.

"We need to get you to a doctor."

Fallon forced a smile onto her face and said, "You're cute when you're all worried."

"Well, you're cute when you're all bloody so we're even." She got serious and added, "I have to ask you something. Is there anything in your past that would make cops want to stick it to you if they had a chance."

"I don't understand—"

Nicole sat down next to the woman in the dirt.

It felt good to be out of the sun.

"If we report this, shooting that guy over there, that won't be a problem," Nicole said. "It was justified. We were fighting for our lives. Shooting the helicopter, though, is a little messier."

"Why?"

"Because they never shot down at us," Nicole said. "Don't get me wrong, it's clear they were part of the whole deal. They were part of a conspiracy at the least. They were coming to further our abduction. We were justified in protecting ourselves."

"Right."

"Yeah, right, but, the investigation could drag on," Nicole said. "It won't be pleasant because it hangs over you even if you're pretty sure it's going to end up good." She didn't say, Maybe somebody hijacked the helicopter. Maybe the pilot wasn't in on it; maybe he turned out to just be another victim. Maybe he had kids. Maybe someone wants to see some justice for him. She squeezed Fallon's hand and said, "Just so I know, if there's anything in your past that might make the cops want to screw you over, if they had a chance, we should talk about that now before we decide whether to call them or not."

Fallon exhaled.

"I did one thing once," she said. "It was a couple of years ago and in a different state. Nobody knows about it."

"Did anyone get hurt?"

Fallon shook her head.

"No. I didn't hurt anyone. It wasn't anything violent. Like I said, nobody knows about it."

"What about your husband?"

"Well, yeah, he knows, obviously; and one other person. That's it."

"Who's the other person?"

Fallon hesitated, deciding, and then said, "Danica Rose, actually."

"Danica. Interesting."

Nicole rose to her feet and walked over to the dead man to

see who he was. Inside his wallet was a crude Texas driver's license for one Thiago Cruz; it might not have been fake to the average person but to Nicole's trained eye it clearly was. There were no credit cards or anything else with the man's name on it. He was carrying a lot of cash, upwards of $5,000 in US currency plus a lot of high-value Mexican bills. That was it for the wallet, except for a condom and a folded piece of paper with the handwritten name Alejandra, followed by a phone number.

In his front pants pocket was a cell phone.

It didn't take long for Nicole to figure out that it was the cell phone that was tied into the app on her phone, meaning it was this man, not Hollywood, who had come into her loft in the middle of the night and installed the tracker on her phone.

The Photo file was jammed with videos of Nicole taken from inside her loft—showering, walking around in panties, sleeping, pleasuring herself, and all the rest. They went back at least two months and based on the angles of the shots, there must be at least three different hidden cameras involved.

The Phone file was disappointingly empty; same thing for the files of favorites, contacts and voicemails, there was absolutely nothing there. Clearly the man had a strict policy of wiping his phone tracks clean as soon as they were made.

As for Google searches, the history had also been cleared.

Nicole slipped the phone back into the man's pants and then checked the glove box of the truck. Registration papers showed that it belonged to one Robert Adams of Belle Glade, Florida, which was north of Miami, plus inland.

So, the truck had probably been stolen.

A pack of cigarettes was on the dash.

Surprisingly, there was no purse anywhere inside the cab; the woman must have traveled with just a wallet.

The only other thing of relevance inside the cab was a box of bullets under the seat.

Nicole grabbed a pen from the glove box, pulled the man's wallet back out and checked the folded piece of paper again. Then she pulled down her sock and on the top of her foot wrote Alejandra, plus the phone number. Just to be sure, she also repeated the number inside her head several times, trying to memorize it.

Then she had an even better idea.

She pulled the truck registration out of the glove box and used the envelope to write the same thing, Alejandra, followed by the phone number.

The registration stayed in the truck but the envelope went into her back pocket.

Okay.

Now what?

If she reported the scene to the police, she'd be tied up for hours.

She needed those hours to trap Hollywood.

Once those hours disappeared they'd never come back.

Plus, the whole thing would put her off track.

She needed to stay focused.

Okay, then; we'll report it tomorrow or the next day, not now. See you later, dead guy. It was nice meeting you.

She helped Fallon off the ground and into the cab of the truck.

"Doctor time, girlfriend."

33

Nicole maneuvered the truck back to the road, then down that road to Penny Lane, who was standing there like an unmolested virgin, waiting for someone to ask her to step onto the dance floor. No one had tried to kiss her or feel her up; the key was still in the ignition and both purses were sitting calmly in the back seat. Nicole's gun, her wallet, her stuff, it was all there, intact. She helped Fallon get from the truck to Penny Lane and then went back to the truck, not exactly sure why. As long as she was there, she turned it around so it was in the exact position it had been initially, with the engine bay above the antifreeze in the dirt. She raised the hood, got a rag from Penny Lane's trunk, and then she wiped their fingerprints clean of all surfaces, plus she scrubbed up Fallon's blood from the floor mat as good as she could. A few vehicles swept by but no overly-curious faces turned their way.

She took one last look at the scene.

Then she got the hell out of there.

The next two hours consisted of a drive back to Miami, getting Fallon set up with stitches and an x-ray and a concussion examination, which turned out negative, then heading back south in hopes of getting checked into a hotel before dark.

Strangely, when they passed by where the truck should

be, it wasn't there. Since it had been stolen, maybe the police found it and took possession. Then again, the key was in the ignition, so it could just as easily be the opposite.

Either way, it made Nicole feel weird.

It was as if the reality of just a few short hours ago was already changing.

Farther up the way, they came to the point where the man had diverted the truck from the road into the open space. Without knowing she was about to do it, Nicole stopped and looked out into the land.

"What's going on?" Fallon said.

There was a cell phone out there that held embarrassing videos of her that she didn't need ending up on YouTube for the next two or three eternities.

She looked at Fallon and said, "Wait here."

"Where you going?"

She was already out of the car.

"I'll be back," she said. "Keep your gun close. On second thought, it's probably not a good idea for you to be sitting here alone just in case Hollywood actually is tracking us. Do me a favor; get into the brush far enough to hide and wait until I get back. Keep your gun with you. Will you do that for me?"

"Sure."

"If Hollywood shows up, don't engage him. Just stay hidden. If he stumbles on you, shoot to kill. Oh, and put your phone on vibrate in case I have to call you."

She headed into the terrain at a trot, one she could hopefully sustain all the way. The topography soon crested and she lost sight of the road.

The shadows were long.

Twilight was here and the clouds were setting up to bring the darkness in even sooner.

Her body was tired but the movement still felt good.

It made her feel free.

The air was empty and quiet.

The only signs of life consisted of small white butterflies, geckos and distant crows. The more she thought about the helicopter, the more she didn't feel sorry for it. It had a hundred opportunities to set down safely. It took the risk to keep flying.

She was half an hour into the trek, almost to her destination, when something came into view that made her heart pound, namely the old red pickup. There it was up ahead, squatting motionless in the weeds where the body went down, in front of the charred fireplace.

She ducked down behind a large bush.

There was human motion behind the truck. It looked as two people were digging a hole. One of the people was the woman, the one with the knife, the one that Nicole let walk off. The other was a large athletic man who had his shirt off. His skin was brown and his muscles were thick. His head was shaved and glistened with sweat. Nicole watched as the two dug for five more minutes and then kicked the dead man's body into the hole with their feet. It took them hardly any time to fill the hole up. They tossed two shovels into the bed of the pickup and got in.

The engine fired.

Then the truck turned around and started heading in Nicole's direction.

She laid flat on the ground and called Fallon.

No one answered.

She dialed again.

No one answered again but this time she let it go to voicemail and said, "Fallon! Get out of there! The pickup's coming! Get out of there, now!"

She hung up and called again.

As before, she got no human voice.

Damn it!

The truck swept past her, not more than fifty feet away.

Then it kept going.

Thirty yards later it skidded to a stop.

Nicole's heart pounded.

She couldn't breathe.

Did they see her?

She didn't think so but then she realized that they probably had the dead man's cell phone, which tracked to hers. Maybe they connected and saw that she was right there with them. She powered her phone off, left it on the ground and crawled backwards, staying out of sight as best she could.

The man was out of the truck now, walking towards her direction with a gun in his grip.

She got her weapon in hand, got to her feet and ran.

Gunfire exploded from behind her.

Bam!

Bam!

Bam!

Then she heard the woman scream, "No! We need her alive!"

She twisted as she ran, just enough to see behind her. The man and the woman were both running after her. They were catching up.

Nicole brought her knees up into a full sprint.

This was it.

Within a few minutes they'd have her.

She should have never let the woman go.

She should have shoved the knife into her face when she had the chance.

Go!

Go!

Go!

She ran with every pore of strength in her body. The two

were closer now, a lot closer. She heard the woman scream, "Shoot her in the legs!"

Nicole dived to the right, into the ground, just as a gunshot exploded from behind.

She twisted around and fired.

The bullet hit the man's right arm.

Blood splattered and his gun dropped to the dirt.

"Bitch!"

He picked it up with his left hand and fired.

The bullet passed so close to Nicole's head that her hair actually moved. Before the man could pull the trigger again, Nicole fired, once and again and again. Blood splattered from the man's chest and his stomach and his face. His body stayed upright for a second and then fell to the ground.

It twitched violently.

Then it stopped moving altogether.

Nicole looked up to find the woman a mere five steps away, stopped dead in her tracks, with a gun in her hands pointed directly at Nicole's chest.

They locked eyes.

The woman stood there, breathing heavily, for a long time. Suddenly she lowered her weapon and said, "We're even. Next time I don't owe you anything."

Then she turned and walked back towards the truck.

Nicole stood there, watching her about to drive off.

Then she shouted, "Hey!"

The woman turned.

"What?"

"Can you give me a ride to the road?"

The woman narrowed her eyes. Then she pulled a pack of cigarettes out of her back pocket, lit one and said, "I'll make you a deal."

34

The deal was a simple one: the woman would give Nicole a ride back to the road if Nicole first helped her bury the dead guy. Work-wise, Nicole would get the worst of the deal but that wasn't her concern. Her concern was figuring out why they were after her in the first place and how to make it stop.

So she agreed.

She'd do whatever it was that she needed to do to spend time with the woman.

They uncovered the first body because the dirt was already loose, then dumped the new body in and covered them both back up. The second man, like the first, had a wallet with cash, a fake driver's license and nothing else. Unlike the first, he didn't have a cell phone.

They split things up.

The woman got all the money.

Nicole got the first man's cell phone—the one with the compromising videos of her—plus they stopped long enough for her to claim her own phone from where she'd dropped it in the dirt.

Ten minutes later they were almost back to the road.

So far, the woman hadn't said anything of relevance; but when they got to within a hundred yards of the road she braked to a stop and said, "Those two men. They're scum. The world's a better place. Don't cry for them. I hired them. Next time I'll get better ones."

"Next time?"

The woman nodded.

"It's not over," she said. "My job is to bring you in alive."

"In to who? Why?"

"Why? Because they have my daughter and I don't get her back until I bring you in."

"Who? Who has you daughter?"

Fear etched onto the woman's face.

"That's not for you to know."

"I'll help you get her back," Nicole said.

The woman hardened her face.

"That's impossible," she said. "Just your trying will get her killed. I'm only telling you this so that you appreciate what I just did for you. I could have shot you in the leg. I could have gotten my daughter back. You'll never get another break like that again, not from me, not from anyone—and there are others like me out there hunting for you. I'm not the only one, be aware of that. Like I said before, now we're even. You let me live, and now I've let you live. We're back to square one. It's time for you to go. Get out."

Nicole slid out, shut the door and took one last look through the window.

"Bye," she said.

The woman gave her the finger.

Then she was gone.

By the time Nicole walked the last hundred yards to the road, it was almost dark. Penny Lane was sitting there, just as before. Fallon was nowhere in sight though.

"Fallon!"

No one answered.

"Fallon! Where are you?"

No one answered.

Nicole searched, all around, for a good ten minutes. She called Fallon's number, heard no rings, and got dumped into voicemail.

Then she got in Penny Lane.

The key was in the ignition, as before.

She turned it.

The starter didn't engage.

The engine didn't fire.

All she got was a clicking noise.

Where are you Fallon?

Did Hollywood get you?

35

Penny Lane might have her share of evil little tricks, but Nicole had seen them all. She popped the hood, twisted the battery cable back and forth on the terminal to get a better connection and tried the key again.

This time the engine fired.

She revved it twice and headed south towards the Keys with the headlights on, keeping an eye out for Fallon but losing hope as the miles ticked off.

Then drizzle came, slow and steady and foggy and full of creepy reflections.

Penny Lane's wimpy little headlights could hardly punch through it and the rubber of the wipers was hard and twitchy, never quite cleaning the windshield but only scraping clear spots here and there. A long ways down the road, stationary lights appeared up ahead and got bigger and bigger as they increasingly turned into Key Largo.

Nicole cruised the area and eventually decided that the Blue Heron Hotel, nestled right against the lapping waves of the Atlantic, was her best option to trap and kill Hollywood. It was a two-story deal built on hurricane posts, with parking underneath. All the rooms were located on the second floor. They were accessed from an outside landing that ran the length of the structure, with an external stairway at each end. The other side of the hotel was a mirror image. If Hollywood came after her, he'd have no option but to go up one of the stairways.

To the south of the hotel was a dark, boarded-up gas station. No one was spending precious money keeping the property lit or free of rats or weeds. On the other side of the hotel to the north was an empty lot a block long that eventually dumped into a Sunoco, no doubt the new gas station that killed the boarded-up one.

Across the street was a long eerie building with multiple truck docks, looking as if it had might have once served in some type of warehouse capacity but was now better equipped to star in a horror film.

Trane had called and texted a number of times over the last few hours, as had Pantage. They deserved a reply so she gave them one: I'm OK. Laying low out of town for the night. See you AM.

Just as she punched off, the phone rang and Fallon's voice came through.

"Nicole!"

"Damn it, girl. Are you okay?"

"Yeah, yeah—"

"Where are you?"

"Key Largo."

"Where in Key Largo?"

"At a payphone, in a gas station."

"Which station?"

"I don't know . . . a Sunoco."

"Stay there. I'm two minutes away."

Fallon turned out to be a stray cat out alone in a stray night if there ever was one. She was drenched, exhausted and at her road's end. In her right hand was a stale gas station donut, half eaten. Nicole got her into Penny Lane, drove her down to a place called Cali's Kitchen, and pumped them both full of burgers and fries and coffee.

Fallon's story was simple.

She got Nicole's voicemail to get the hell out of there. Then her phone battery died. She couldn't get Penny Lane started and headed off on foot, sneaking into the shadows whenever headlights approached in case they belonged to Hollywood, and only throwing her thumb out for a ride when the headlights clearly belonged to an 18-wheeler.

"Do you still want to help me get Hollywood?" Nicole said.

"Yes."

"I have a plan," Nicole said. "But it's going to be dangerous."

Fallon took a sip of coffee.

"Tell me," she said.

36

Nicole left Fallon alone in a booth at Cali's, drove down to the Blue Heron and deflected come-on's served from the fat lips of a tatted up, big-gut scumbag in the office who eventually realized he wasn't going to get any and handed her the key to room 203 for four twenties and a ten. It was the only room being rented tonight on the non-ocean side of the hotel.

He pointed a bottle of whiskey at her as she walked out and said, "If you get lonesome—"

"Good to know."

Then she was out.

She parked Penny Lane directly under room 203, hauled both suitcases up slippery metal stairs, unlocked her door and stepped in. The room was bigger than she suspected but just as cheap and worn. At auction, everything in there would be lucky to fetch a hundred dollars, if you threw in a bus ticket to Toledo. The one good thing was the window covering, which was a medium-weight curtain that didn't have too many holes in it. From the outside, you'd be able to see the shape of a person moving around inside but wouldn't be able to see any details. It looked like there used to be a pull shade too, now gone the way of the Dodo bird.

There were two beds.

She pulled the mattress off one of them and got it situated on the floor behind the other one, where a bullet through the window wouldn't be able to get to it.

As for the other bed, she put cushions under the covers to mimic a sleeping person.

There.

Good enough for now.

Suddenly her phone rang and Ash Colt's voice came though.

"Nicole, you still up?"

"Yeah."

"I'm not going to beat around the bush," he said. "This is a booty call."

Nicole smiled.

She could hear partying in the background.

"Where are you?"

"Some fancy bar in South Beach," he said. "At a beauty pageant."

"Seriously?"

"No, no, not that kind," he said. "The law firm kind; we're wining and dining some prospective clients; show 'em how beautiful we are and why we're the best lawyers for them and all that crap."

"Got it," she said.

"We get 'em drunk and get 'em laid. That's how you get the billable hours down the road."

"I'm getting the picture."

"Anyway, I've been thinking of you."

"Meaning my booty—"

He laughed.

"True, but not just that, all of you. Every single little chewable morsel," he said. "So how about it? I'll swing over when I'm done here, an hour or so—"

Nicole turned off the lights and plopped down on the bed.

She closed her eyes.

"Tell me I'm pretty," she said.

"Baby," he said, "I'd crawl across a field of broken glass just to kiss your feet. That's how pretty you are."

Fifteen minutes later, Nicole was replaying those words in her head as she hid behind an old rusty 55-gallon barrel over at the boarded-up gas station. From there she had a good view of the Blue Heron. The only lights on this side of the structure came from room 203. Inside that room, the light of a TV flickered and a shadow occasionally brushed past the window. From the outside, it looked like a person in motion. In reality, it was Fallon, lying on the floor and manipulating a pillow, just in case a bullet decided to come flying through the glass.

The drizzle had strengthened into a rain, a light rain, but still more than enough to soak Nicole to the core and keep her that way.

The cold steel of her gun was in hand.

A bullet was in the chamber and a lot more were lined up behind it.

So far there was no sign of Hollywood.

He might not come for hours.

He might not come at all.

The prospect was daunting.

Nicole was already exhausted.

Whatever was going to happen, she needed it to happen within the next ten minutes.

I'd crawl across a field of broken glass just to kiss your feet. That's how pretty you are to me.

Umm—

It was getting way after dark now.

Key Largo wasn't built for the dark. It was built for the light. It was built for showing off the surf and for selling shelter and food to weary travelers. Right now all the weary travelers were already working on that weariness in a bed somewhere. The place rolled over in its sleep occasionally but that was about it. That was good. If Hollywood showed up he'd stick out like a blinking neon sign.

Hollywood on.

Hollywood off.

Hollywood on.

Hollywood off.

He'd probably sweep through to get eyes on Penny Lane. He'd see the room light on. He'd pee his pants at how easy this was going to be. He'd bide his time and pass by a couple of more times, maybe on foot, just to be sure it wasn't a trap. Then he'd make his move.

Ten minutes clicked off and nothing happened; then half an hour.

A full hour came and went.

Hollywood wasn't coming.

Nicole's eyes were heavy. The only thing she wanted in the whole world was to close them, just for a few minutes, just to give them a little rest. She closed them for ten seconds then forced them back open. No harm done and it felt like wine in her blood. Okay, one more time, just once more. She shut her eyes and let the pain subside. Okay, open them now—but she didn't. Just a couple more seconds, then she'd open them; just a few more seconds—

At some point later she got pulled out of an uneasy sleep by the sound of a vehicle pulling into the gravel parking lot of the creepy warehouse building across the street.

The headlights immediately went out.

A man got out, looked quickly around, and then jogged across the street directly towards Nicole.

She brought her body off the ground and realized that the gun was no longer in her hand. It took her only a frantic second to find it and get her finger on the trigger.

The rain hadn't let up.

Every fiber of her clothing was soaked. She couldn't have been more wet if she'd just swum up from the depths of the ocean. Her body was stiff and achy from being on the ground so long. Running was out of the question.

She wiped the water out of her eyes.

Things came into better focus.

The man kept approaching.

He came closer and closer and closer, directly at her, making her finger tighten on the trigger. Then he suddenly stopped directly on the other side of the 55-gallon drum, not more than five feet away.

Nicole held her breath and got every pore of her body quiet.

She was standing upright against the building, looking directly at him, ready to shoot.

If the man turned and looked hard enough, his eyes would look directly into hers. Right now, though, he kept those eyes pointed at the room light on the second floor of the hotel.

Nicole's chest pounded like a hundred maniac drums.

If he turns, pull the trigger!

Don't hesitate!

Don't let him get his hands on you!

Suddenly the man darted towards the hotel, across the gravel parking lot, past Penny Lane, to the exterior metal stairs, and up, two steps at a time. At the second-floor landing he stopped and looked around, then walked on slow cat feet to the lighted room, 203 — *Nicole's room.* He stopped at the door, put his ear to it, and listened. After a moment he tried to look in the window. The curtain must have completely blocked his view because he didn't try for long.

He walked quietly past the window to the next door down the landing, room 202.

He removed something from his pocket and worked at the lock for some time, a full minute or longer, but finally got it jimmied open.

He took a final look around him, then stepped in and closed the door behind him.

No lights turned on.

Hollywood.

What's your game?

Are you holing up until you're positive it's not a trap?

Are you looking out the window, making sure no one's coming?

What then?

Do you have a silencer on your gun?

Are you going to swing over to my room, shot the lock to hell and then bust in? Do you have some special words saved up? Are you going to say something clever right before you shoot me?

Hey, baby.

How's your day going so far?

Bam!

Bam!

Bam!

Nicole didn't move, not an inch. The rain was too thick for her to see into the dark room. She couldn't tell if the man's eyes were peeking out from the edge of the curtain, or what.

Her chest tightened.

A minute passed.

She focused on the curtain. It was white and picked up the faintest of light. If it moved, Nicole might be able to detect the motion.

She saw none.

She stared harder and longer and still saw none.

Suddenly, before she even realized she was doing it, she swung around to the back of the gas station, made a wide circle around the hotel's parking lot, and approached the structure from the ocean side.

At the stairwell she paused.

Remember what Pantage said.

Control your emotions.

Don't kill him.

Go for a leg.

She climbed the slippery steel stairwell one careful step at a time and then, wham! Her foot came out from under her, just like that, with a lightning speed, shooting her backwards down the stairs. The first impact came to her right shoulder, hard, with her full body weight landing on it, followed immediately by a out-of-control tumble. She tried not to scream but sounds came out of her mouth, especially when she landed at the bottom on the asphalt. The gun was no longer in her hand.

Find it!

She got to her feet, fighting through the pain of her body, and frantically searched the area, finding the weapon within a few feet of where she landed. She gripped it hard and swung the barrel to the top of the stairway.

Hollywood wasn't there.

No one was coming for her.

The rain must have masked the whole thing.

She tested her body and felt strains but didn't think anything was broken.

She went back up the stairway, this time with a hand on the railing. At the top, no one was on the landing. She walked slowly down it with the gun in a double-grip, leading the way. She came to the lighted room — her room, 203 — and listened at the door. Inside, a TV was on.

She took a deep breath and walked to the next door, 202.

She kept her weapon in her right hand and gently turned the doorknob with her left.

It was locked.

She put her ear to the door.

Inside, there was some kind of quiet movement.

The window curtain was fully closed, leaving no gaps at the edges. But there was enough transparency to show that a flashlight was on somewhere near the back of the room.

Hollywood, you bastard.

Your ass is mine.

She positioned her body at the door and took three deep breaths.

Ash.

I wish you were here.

She pointed the barrel at the door lock, closed her eyes and pulled the trigger.

37

The lock shattered with a violent explosion and Nicole catapulted into the room. A man at the back wall swung around. He was in his thirties, his face—eerily lit by his flashlight—was taut and mean and already seemed to be looking for a way to kill her.

"Don't move!" Nicole shouted.

The man stood there, at first staring at her, then letting his eyes fall to the right, to a gun sitting on a table.

"Don't!"

The man shrugged, suddenly composed, as if the whole thing was no big deal.

"No worries," he said. "What's this about?"

"Shut up! Turn around and put your hands on the wall."

The man stood still.

"Do it!"

He shrugged.

"Sure. Whatever." He slowly turned, raised his hands, and then moved them to the wall. "There. We happy?"

"Face the wall and don't move!"

The man complied.

Then he said, "Why don't we take a deep breath and talk this through."

"Shut up!"

Nicole approached, quietly and slowly, with the weapon pointed directly at the man's back and ready to pull the trigger if he gave her even half a reason. She made her way to the far end of the table and pulled it towards her. The man's gun was supposed to stay on it and get out of his range. Instead, it slid off and dropped to the floor by his foot.

"Kick it away," she said.

Instead of complying, the man raised his hands and slowly turned around. "If you're going to shoot me you're going to have to do it to my face." Then his eyes fell to the door and he said, "Friend of yours?"

Nicole turned, just for a split second, but it was long enough for the man to lunge at her.

She fired.

The man hit her just as she pulled the trigger.

She fell to the floor but didn't let go of the gun. The man froze, not knowing whether he could get to her before she could train it on him, then sprang for the door. Nicole was already on her feet and directly behind him.

She fired into the air.

"Stop!"

The man froze.

He was standing in front of the lighted window, the window for room 203 — Nicole's room.

"Don't move!" Nicole said.

She approached, almost as if charging.

"Get down! Now!"

The man dropped to his stomach.

Just as he did, a weapon exploded somewhere in the distance behind them and the window shattered into a thousand shards of glass as the bullet blasted it to hell.

From inside the room, Fallon screamed.

Nicole shouted to the man, "Don't move!" Then she was

at the door, the locked door. She shot it open and busted in. Fallon had made her way to the bathroom. Panic owned her face but her body wasn't bloody.

"Are you okay?" Nicole said.

"Yes."

"Get in the bathtub and lay down."

"Okay."

The whole exchange took only a few seconds, but when Nicole got back out to the landing the man—Hollywood—was up and running.

"Stop!"

The man looked back but didn't slow down. Nicole trained the gun on his leg and pulled the trigger. The bullet missed but hit the railing next to him with such a violent ricochet that the man pictured the next one in his back and slid to a stop with his hands up.

"Don't shoot."

Nicole was on him in a flash, getting him face down on the landing, straddling his back and pressing the gun into his head.

"Where's Danica!"

"I don't know any Danica."

She punched the side of his head.

"Where is she?"

"I don't know. I don't know what you're talking about."

"Last time. Where is she?"

"I have no idea what's going on. I'm a private investigator."

"Bullshit!"

"Check my wallet." Nicole hesitated and the man said, "Go on. Do it. It's in my pants pocket."

Nicole didn't check.

She could care less what a piece of paper said.

She pressed the gun harder into the back of the man's head and said, "Did someone hire you to kill me?"

"No. I don't even know who you are."

"What were you doing in that room?"

"Spying."

"On who?"

"The man in the next room."

"There is no man in the next room."

"No, I'm not talking about this side of the hotel, I'm talking about the other side. The back wall of the room I was in is the same back wall for the room on the other side of the hotel. He's in that room. I was drilling a hole in the wall to slip a camera through."

Sirens approached, no doubt responding to the gunfire. They were still a good distance off but definitely coming.

The man wiggled.

"Look," he said. "Just let me get out of here. If the cops find out I broke into a hotel room I'll lose my license. I have a wife. I have two daughters. I can't afford to lose my job."

The sirens were getting louder.

"Please!"

Nicole didn't move.

The man said, "If I'm going down then you are too. I'll file a criminal complaint. You shot at me. You tried to kill me."

Nicole ran the scenarios.

They were ugly.

She got off.

Then the man was on his feet, to the landing, bounding down the stairs two at a time. Nicole remembered that the man's gun was still on the floor in the room. The cops would be able to trace it to him.

She shouted, "Your gun!"

The man stopped as he processed the implication. It must have registered because he ran to the room and then back out, now with a gun in one hand and a small black bag in the other.

"Thanks," he said as he passed.

"Go."

Nicole's stomach churned as the man disappeared into the weather.

It had all happened too fast.

The man might actually be Hollywood.

She might have just done the dumbest thing in her life.

The sirens were closing in.

Nicole scrambled into room 202 and checked the back wall for drill marks.

There were none.

The wall was in perfect shape.

She ran into her room, 203, and shouted at Fallon, "Grab your stuff. We're out of here!"

DAY
FOUR

September 18
Thursday

38

Nicole woke Thursday morning in her loft, on her mattress, naked, with Fallon at her side, equally naked and so deep in sleep that she almost looked dead. The faint rays of morning washed in like a watercolor through the higher windows above the curtains. Nicole wiggled out from under the sheets, muscled to her feet and pulled a window covering to the side just far enough to check outside. The sun was up but not by much. Last night's thunderclouds were already fading to vapor. The puddles would be dry within a couple of hours. The parking lot was empty except for Penny Lane.

The two-day mark of Danica's abduction came and went at 10:00 p.m. last night. If the needle of the jar had landed on the two, then Danica was dead right now and Nicole was no longer a target.

If Hollywood killed Danica last night, would he call and say goodbye?

Game over, baby.

Big congrats to you on still being alive.

Catch you next time.

Kiss, kiss, lick my lips.

She headed over to the shower, giving Fallon a kiss on the forehead as she passed, and got the water up to temperature.

Then she stepped in, lathered up and let her mind drift.

She wasn't sure how much trouble she'd gotten into yesterday and didn't want to think about it. Luckily, the office letch at the Blue Heron never asked Nicole her name or made her sign a register since she paid cash. Her fingerprints and DNA were all over the place, sure, but there were no dead bodies or evidence of an injury to anyone. The things that were evident—the shot room locks, the shot window—were property damages. They probably wouldn't warrant fingerprinting the scene, much less DNA collection.

So, who put the bullet through the window?

Most likely it was Hollywood, either thinking that Nicole was inside the room and shooting in, or knowing that she was actually on the landing and taking a shot while he had one. That scenario was actually a comforting one because the shot came well after 10:00, meaning the game was still on as of that time, meaning that Danica hadn't been killed at the two-day mark.

But Hollywood wasn't the only one who could have pulled that trigger.

It could have been someone from Nicole's past, trying to wound her and take her in.

Or, if the man from 202 really was a private investigator, the shot may have been meant for him. A guy like that could get pissed at from a hundred different people for a thousand different reasons.

Or, if the man from 202 was actually Hollywood, he too might have an enemy who was trying to take him out. How would that enemy find Hollywood? Simple, by following the target that Hollywood was following, namely Nicole.

Over cereal and coffee—while Fallon was still sleeping—Nicole took a few moments to weigh the pros and cons of keeping the wallet of the man with the red pickup truck who tried to abduct her, Thiago Cruz, according to his fake driver's license.

The cons were that it tied her to the scene, the scene where Fallon shot him in the back, to be precise. So, indirectly, it also implicated Fallon. It was evidence they were there and were in a position to end up with the man's wallet.

The pros were that it would corroborate her story of what happened—namely abduction and self-preservation—if it ever came to pass that she would have to tell that story to someone.

Inside that wallet, as before, was a condom and a folded piece of paper with the handwritten name Alejandra, followed by a phone number.

Nicole left the condom where it was.

As for the piece of paper, she pulled it out and Googled the phone number to find that it belonged a bar in Juarez, Mexico called El Hoyo—The Hole.

Alejandra, who are you, baby?

Do you own the place?

Are you a hooker?

Do you sell drugs there?

What do you know about what's going on?

Do you know who I am?

Do you know what my real name is?

Do you know who's trying to collect me?

Or why?

Nicole's heart pounded as she dialed the number.

The phone rang and rang and rang some more and was obviously ready to continue in that mode for as long as it took to outlast any human who was stupid enough to play. Nicole hung up, dialed again, and got more of the same.

Okay.

Juarez was two hours behind Miami.

So call back tonight when the place is open.

She put the paper back where it came from and then tossed

the wallet on top of a kitchen cabinet. That would be good enough for now. Once the cameras were all found and removed she'd find a better place to hide it; maybe put it in a waterproof container and bury it out on the grounds somewhere. There'd be plenty of time to figure it out.

She put a note on the table for Fallon.

Went to work.

Call me when you get up.

She was almost out the door when a groggy voice said from behind her, "Hey, princess."

Nicole turned to find Fallon fighting her way out of sleep and trying to wiggle out of bed into a standing position.

"Is there any news on that helicopter? I've had nightmares about it all night—"

Nicole headed over, gave the woman a hug and said, "According to the news, a helicopter crashed yesterday afternoon and the NTSB has sent a team in to investigate. That's about it."

"What about bodies?"

"No word yet. Look, I got to get to work. Hang out down at the studio today where you'll be safe." She pointed to the ceiling at the far end of the loft where one of the cardboards they had taped to the ductwork was hanging down. "I don't know if that just came loose on its own accord or whether our little friend of the poisonous persuasion fell through it. Keep your eyes peeled. Don't stick your hands anywhere you can't see." She paused and added, "I can't believe you wake up looking this pretty. Did I say that out loud?"

Fallon smiled.

They hugged.

Then Nicole was gone.

39

anica Rose woke Thursday morning at the first rays of dawn, realizing that she'd somehow survived another night in the guts of the wreck without any sharp yellow fangs pouncing through the opening to gobble her up. She fired up the flashlight and checked the interior to be sure no rats or snakes had slithered in during the darkness.

None had.

She was alone.

There was no evidence that her captor had visited her last night while she was asleep.

Her body ached. It had been without substantial movement or exercise for too many days and hours. If she could be free anywhere in the world right now, she'd be on a beach where she'd run and run and run until every muscle in her body imploded with exhaustion and she had nothing left to do except drop to the edge of the surf under her own weight. That would feel so damn good. She'd just lay there with a stupid grin on her face and let the foamy saltwater wash over her body.

The captivity was wearing on her brain.

With every passing minute another piece of sanity peeled off and vaporized.

Poof.

Gone.

Welcome to crazier.

How's it feel?

Outside, one of the rattlesnakes uncoiled and raised its creepy little head until it bumped against the top of the cage. It was hungry. It was approaching the limits of its tolerance. It was ready to sink its fangs into anything that came along.

She wondered what her captor looked like.

In the vision she'd formed in her head, he was the human equivalent of the snake.

When would he come for her?

In ten minutes?

What if he got injured or killed and never came for her at all?

Have fun rotting to death.

She slapped her face.

Don't do this!

Don't you dare!

Stay focused.

The feeling she had now wasn't anything new. She'd had it before, surfing, when a massive rogue wave scraped her across the bottom until every last molecule of oxygen in her lungs was gone. She'd had it cliff climbing at Big Sur, when she went out alone to test her limits and got stuck high on a ledge that wouldn't let her go up or get back down. She'd had it at the 7th Grade dance, when she was hugging the wall and waiting for someone, anyone, to look over and notice that she was alive.

You lived through that.

You'll live through this.

But you have to stay calm. You have to stay focused.

She called out for the hundredth time, "Hello! Is anyone there?"

Her voice sounded puny.

It sounded like the call of an ant floating on a stick in the middle of the ocean.

40

The first one to the office Thursday morning, Nicole fired up the fluorescents, kick-started the coffee machine and munched on a day-old chocolate donut as she took a minute to check the web to see if there was any more news on the helicopter crash.

There was.

The aircraft, according to the latest NTSB update, was registered to El Paso Helicopter Services, Inc.

El Paso?

Wow, that was weird.

El Paso, Texas, was right across the Rio Grande from Juarez, Mexico, where El Hoyo—The Hole—was located.

El Paso Helicopter Services, Inc. had a website.

It showed that the company was a bona fide business with helicopters available for film, video and aerial photography; charter; real estate site inspection; and utility, power line and pipeline services. It had two helicopters, both of which were Aerospatiale TwinStar AS355 F1s, which had a five-passenger capacity. Surprisingly, to Nicole at least, it didn't operate out of the El Paso International Airport. Rather, it was stationed at a hanger on private land fifteen miles east of town.

Ownership-wise, the website of the Texas Secretary of State showed that El Paso Helicopter Services, Inc. was a

Texas corporation that was in turn owned 100% by a second corporation which in turn was 100% owned by yet a third corporation which in turn was 100% owned by an actual human being, namely someone named Mia Notaro.

Mia Notaro.

Behind all the smoke and mirrors, she was the one in ultimate control of the helicopter.

She was also a lawyer.

In particular, she was a 30-year-old associate attorney in Steel & Hawkes, P.C., one of the largest and more prominent law firms in El Paso, with offices in the prestigious Anson Mills Building, plus smaller satellite branches in Houston and Dallas. According to the firm's bio page, she headed up the employment law division. Interestingly, she was also the owner of the land that housed the hanger that the helicopter operated out of. That property was quite substantial, exceeding five thousand acres, which was a lot to own for a 30-year-old.

She was pretty, in a tough way, with long black hair and high cheekbones and golden-brown skin.

Suddenly Pantage pushed his way into the room, glanced at her sideways without saying anything, then poured a cup of black coffee and headed her way. He sat on the edge of her desk in a position of dominance, took a loud noisy sip of the black stuff as he studied her over the edge of the cup, and said, "You're alive, I see. How about the other guy?"

Nicole frowned.

"The trap didn't work."

"Don't fret over it. It was a long shot. The main thing is, you're okay."

The man's presence filled the room. Nicole had forgotten how much of a force he was. She pictured herself on her back in bed with her legs forced wide open and him above her thrusting away with a primal frenzy that most men didn't even know existed.

He said, "Have you talked to Trane lately?"

"No. Why?"

"He's getting more and more convinced that Ash Colt is Hollywood. He has evidence that the man was in L.A.—Danica's town—on three separate occasions in the last two months. Plus he does a lot of legal work in Atlantic City, where another one of the crimes occurred, although Trane hasn't tied him there yet expressly on the date of the abduction."

Nicole soured her face.

"Ash isn't Hollywood. I already know about the Atlantic City connection. The victim's name was Necha. She was taken on September 8th. Ash was three thousand miles away at the time, in San Francisco, giving a speech at a law convention. It's documented beyond belief. It's even on YouTube."

"Well, if you tell Trane, be careful," Pantage said. "At this point he may well kill the messenger."

She let her eyes fall across the room, unfocused, then looked hard at Pantage and said, "We need a plan. I hope you have something because I'm empty."

Pantage shrugged.

"Maybe we could get on the news and say something to make Hollywood want to contact us," he said.

"Like what?"

"I don't know," he said. "But if we could get a dialogue going, it couldn't hurt."

Nicole's heart raced.

She knew where Pantage was heading.

If they got a dialogue going with Hollywood, he might re-kindle his old idea of trading Danica for Nicole. Just the thought of it felt like a spider climbing up her spine. She'd do it—make the trade—probably, if she could gather the courage and if a solid realistic opportunity actually came up; they'd need to dial it in perfectly, though, so that Danica definitely ended up released and safe.

She said, "So, what do we say to draw him out?"

"I'll chew on it." The man stood up and said, "I'll touch base with you later."

"Where you going?"

"To check out a gut feeling."

When Pantage left, the whole world felt empty. Deep down, Nicole had to admit that maybe she wasn't cut out for this job. She was taking too many risks and they were coming too close together. Sooner or later one of them was bound to bite her.

She called Fallon and said, "You've got a little spending money, right?"

"Sure. For what?"

"That helicopter had a lot of smoke and mirrors around it but I was able to find out that it's owned and controlled by a 30-year-old lawyer down in El Paso, Texas; someone named Mia Notaro."

"Was she the one flying it?"

"I don't know," Nicole said. "What I need you to do is to find a private investigator down in El Paso. Be sure he's someone reputable. Have him dig up everything he can on our new lawyer friend. I want to know who she is, who she's connected to and why her helicopter was over here in Florida trying to snatch me."

"Done."

"One more thing and this is important," Nicole said. "Don't give the PI your real name." She thought about it further and said, "You know what, forget everything I just said. I don't want you to get connected to that helicopter. It was here for me, so I'm already connected. I'll hire the investigator. I'll make the call, not you."

"You sure?"

"Yes. I just might need a little help with the money."

"Give me your bank digits," Fallon said. "I'll transfer ten grand over. That ought to be enough to get us started." She paused. "You know what? If I were you I wouldn't mention anything about the helicopter to the investigator."

"Why not?"

"Because you're not supposed to know about it."

Jeeze.

Fallon was right.

"Good catch," Nicole said. "Don't wire the money. I don't want a banking connection. Just get cash and I'll deposit it into my account."

"Done."

"Thanks. Any sign of that snake?"

"Not yet."

"Well, keep a watch out for it."

Ten minutes later Nicole was on the phone with a man named Conek, one of the more reputable El Paso private investigators, explaining the assignment.

"Mia Notaro?" the man said.

"Correct. She's a lawyer there."

"Yes, yes, I know who she is." After a long pause the man added, "I'm sorry but that's a case I cannot take."

"Why not?"

"Have you ever been to El Paso?"

"No."

"Well, most of it is very nice, very safe. But it's also in the shadows of Juarez. You don't want to wander into those shadows. You learn where they are and you stay away from them, because if you ever see something in there, it sees you back. Take these words to heart; and please, don't ever tell anyone we spoke. This conversation never took place."

The connection died.

Suddenly her boss, Nick Trane, burst into the room and

headed past the coffee and straight for her. He was mad about something. It was all over his face and in the force of his movement.

Nicole braced herself.

Whatever was about to happen, it wouldn't be pretty.

41

Trane said, "I just spoke to Pantage. He said you told him that Ash Colt has an alibi for when that victim in Atlantic City got taken."

Nicole swallowed.

"That's true. He has an alibi for Monday night, too."

"How would you know he has an alibi? Did you talk to him?"

She hesitated, not wanting to officially commit to what she'd done, but knowing that she had to tell the truth, not just because Trane would eventually get to it if she lied, but because she didn't want to start a history of lying to him.

"Yes."

"I told you to stay away from him," Trane said.

She said nothing.

Trane shook his head in disappointment.

"Tell me about what you found out," he said.

"Sure."

She showed him the itinerary for the law conference, which was sponsored by the American Bar Association and still posted on the ABA website, set for September 7, 8 and 9 of last year. Ash Colt, Esq., was clearly identified as a speaker on September 8, the day when the Atlantic City victim, Necha, was taken. Ash was clearly in San Francisco at the time and date when he was supposed to be. In fact, his speech was even on YouTube.

Trane listened patiently, watched ten seconds of the YouTube video, then punched it off.

"You've known this, since when?"

"Yesterday."

"Yesterday," he echoed. "And you didn't tell me? You just let me spin my wheels?"

"I knew you'd get mad that I contacted Ash," Nicole said.

"You knew I'd get mad. So you protected yourself and let me waste time that I could have been using productively?"

"I thought you'd fire me," Nicole said. "I wanted to stay on the case. I can't do Danica any good being fired."

Trane hardened his face.

"We have two things going on here," he said. "First, you did something that I expressly told you not to do, not to mention something that could have gotten you killed if my theory had been correct. Second, you didn't come forward with information you had that would have exonerated a suspect and let us move on to other things. Quite frankly, neither one of those things is consistent with the way this office operates."

Nicole swallowed.

She could feel it coming.

"You have a lot of guts and a lot of drive," Trane said. "I'll give you that. But it's not channeled. You're not in control of it. I want you to go home, right now, and don't do anything on this case. You're officially on vacation. If you don't do that, I'm going to have no choice but to officially put you on administrative leave and I really don't want to do that until I think about it some more and get myself calmed down." He stood up, headed for the coffee machine and added over his shoulder, "I'd like to get you to a safe house until everything blows over."

Nicole didn't hesitate, "No."

"Do you at least want a black-and-white to sit outside your window?"

"No. I don't want anything."

"Fine," he said. "You can change your mind later. Don't be shy about it. I'm disappointed, but that doesn't mean I want to see you hurt."

"Nick—"

He held a hand up for her to stop.

"Go."

She stood up and walked towards the door.

There, she turned and said, "You're right. I acted selfishly. That was wrong."

Then she was gone.

Five seconds later she returned and said, "Just so there's no more secrets, you should probably know that I had sex with Ash in his office yesterday."

Then she was gone, again.

At the end of the hall she lingered, waiting for Trane to burst through the door and shout down the corridor, shout that she was fired, or shout that he'd changed his mind and was going to give her another chance, but to at least shout something.

But the door didn't burst open.

And no shouts came.

She felt like a fly that had been swatted hard and knocked to the floor but was still wiggling, not quite dead yet.

She by-passed the elevator and took the stairs down to the parking garage.

A tear slid out of her eye.

She wiped it off her face with the back of her hand.

Screw you, Trane.

Screw you and the horse you rode in on.

42

Officially off the case, Nicole drove the streets of Miami having nowhere to go and nothing to do. She couldn't go home. She didn't want Fallon to know that she'd failed. She didn't want to drop in at Ash's office and let him see her in this state. The only good thing was that she still had her badge and her gun. The more she thought about it, though, it might not be because Trane might keep her around in the end. It might be because he didn't want her to be unarmed while she was in danger. He might well have plans to permanently fire her after the whole Hollywood thing was over. He was just taking precautions to not get her blood on his hands. That's why he offered the safe house, and the black-and-white.

There'd be a task force meeting this morning.

She wouldn't be there.

Everyone would wonder where she was.

Even if Trane sugarcoated it—which he probably would— it would come out that she'd been removed from her position, at least temporarily. It would be hard to look anyone straight in the eye again. Her reputation was shattered.

She found herself on MacArthur Causeway not too far from Fallon's house, and decided to swing by. The neighborhood was bright and normal, in fact, alive with the motion of kids heading to school and people who hadn't been fired from their jobs going to them. Fallon's house, in contrast, was still and lifeless and had yellow crime scene tape across the front door. Nicole coasted to a stop in front of the structure and killed the engine.

Danica.

Was she alive or dead?

Fallon.

Was she Hollywood's intended victim?

Would she still be taken at some point?

Nicole headed around to the back of the house, found the back door locked and broke the glass with her elbow. Five seconds later she was inside, peering out from the edge of the broken window to see if anyone outside had taken notice.

No one had.

Why was she here?

She didn't know.

She really didn't care.

She had to be somewhere in the universe and right now this was as good of a place as any. It was the genesis of all the motion.

She made her way to the couch, laid back and stared at the ceiling.

You know what?

I'll say it again.

Screw you Trane.

If he decided that Ash Colt was guilty and decided to spend all his time proving it, then that was his problem. He set himself on that course of action, not Nicole. She had nothing to do with it. In fact, she told him right from the start that he was going down a rabbit hole. She wasn't put on earth to correct his mistakes or stop his misadventures. And as far as her talking with Ash after Trane told her not to, that was because she already knew him. What was she was supposed to do, abandon all sense of instinct and knowledge just because someone who actually had less information told her to?

Screw that.

Trane was jealous.

She was ahead of him on the case and he didn't like it.

That was the real problem, plain and simple.

Nicole closed her eyes.

Fallon was a great gal but there was still one thing about her that pissed Nicole off, namely that even though they'd gotten tight over the last however-many hours, the woman still wouldn't say who her secret lover was, the one she was with Monday night when Danica got taken.

He might be behind things, in some twisted kind of way.

Maybe if Nicole sniffed around, she'd find something to indicate who he was. There had to be a memento stashed around here somewhere—a secret gift of jewelry, a souvenir hotel key or restaurant napkin, a love letter, whatever. It would be somewhere hubby-face wouldn't stumble on it.

Nicole sprang off the couch and headed upstairs to the master bedroom, past the bed and dressers and nightstands and furniture, to the master walk-in closet. Above the clothes, from the rods to the ceiling, were two high rows of shelves that wrapped around the entire room, even above the door. They were jammed with boxes and junk and stuff. If a memento existed, it would either be stashed here or in some dark corner of the basement.

She pulled a box down from the top shelf near the back corner.

The top was dusty.

Inside was an eclectic collection of twenty or thirty old 45 records, all in mint condition and still in their paper sleeves.

Linda Scott—I've Told Every Little Star.

The Ronettes—Be My Baby.

The Hollies—Bus Stop.

Jan and Dean—Surf City.

Chuck Berry—Maybellene.

Phil Phillips—Sea of Love.

That last one reminded Nicole of the movie by the same name, Sea of Love, with Al Pachino and that blond with the crooked smile—what was her name again? Nicole couldn't remember. It would come to her later when she could care less. In any event, she reminded herself that she needed to watch that movie again. It was too good to not see at least twice.

Fallon was way too young for the 45s. She must have inherited them, or else the hubby was a collector. Nicole put the box back and pulled down another one.

As before, the top was dusty.

Inside were mementos of Fallon's high school and college days—photos, concert ticket stubs, diplomas, and the like. Underneath it all, at the very bottom, was something a little out of the norm. It was an Atlanta Journal-Constitution newspaper from two years ago.

What's with you?

Do you have a story on Fallon?

Nicole spread it out on the bed and flipped through the pages one by one. It was the usual news—weather, politics, editorials, classifieds, entertainment, world news and assorted local stories; a teenager attacked by a pack of dogs, a bank robbery, a woman who gave birth to quintuplets, and the like. None of the articles were circled, marked or cut out. As far as Nicole could tell, none of them were about Fallon, either under her current married name, Fallon Bow, or her old high school name, Fallon Parks. None of the obituaries were about anyone with the last name Bow or Parks.

Nicole put the paper back at the bottom and sifted through the photos. In most, Danica was with her. Both of the women were stunners, even back then, and the assortment of boys they went through was impressive.

She clearly knew how to party.

In hindsight, it wasn't surprising that she hadn't let marriage get in the way of her appetite.

Suddenly her phone rang and the voice of a woman came through, a voice Nicole didn't recognize.

"Nicole Stone?"

"Yes."

"My name is Sophia Brown," the woman said. "I'm a private investigator in El Paso, Texas. I just received a call from a colleague of mine by the name of Conek. He said you're looking for help."

"I am," Nicole said.

"He said it concerns Mia Notaro."

"It does. Conek told me to drop it."

"That's actually good advice," the woman said. "In fact, it's the best advice that you'll ever get. Have you ever heard of a man named Jafet el Perro?"

"No."

"Jafet el Perro is the head of the second biggest drug cartel in Mexico, and he's in the middle of a bloody turf war right now. He's a vicious, violent man with an endless army of ruthless sickos and a reputation for torturing his enemies," the woman said. "I believe that Mia Notaro may have some type of connection to him."

"What kind of connection, exactly?"

"I don't know. It's just a theory I've developed after having my ear to the ground for so long down here. But digging into her could be dangerous. That's why Conek told you to stay away."

Nicole considered it.

Then she said, "Mia Notaro owns a helicopter under the guise of El Paso Helicopter Services. It recently crashed here in Florida, west of Miami. I want to know who chartered it and who was flying it. Based on what you just told me, plus some other things I know, it may have been someone working on Jafet el Perro's behalf. But I need to know for certain."

"What's your interest in this helicopter? Why do you care?"

"That's not something I'm at liberty to divulge," Nicole said. "The NTSB is investigating the crash so if you decide to take this assignment, you'd need to be real careful not to drop any breadcrumbs that could lead them to you or to me. You'd need to stay totally invisible."

"This could be very dangerous for me," the woman said.

She meant it.

Nicole could hear it in her voice.

"You knew that before you called me," Nicole said. "So why'd you call?"

"Money, honey. That's why everyone does everything."

Two minutes later, Nicole's phone rang again.

This time it was Ash Colt.

"I need to talk to you," he said.

Something was wrong.

His voice was tense.

"Why? What's happening?"

"Are you at home?" he said.

"No."

"Can you meet me there?"

"Sure, I suppose."

"It's about Hollywood," he said.

43

Nicole found Ash already there when she arrived at the loft. He pulled her tight, gave her a big kiss and said, "Hollywood called me." The words landed on Nicole like a rock to the side of her skull.

"My Hollywood? The one we're hunting?"

"Yes."

Why would Hollywood call Ash?

In fact, how did Hollywood even know Ash existed?

"What'd he say?"

Ash's eyes fell to the distance as if seeing a strange distorted world. Then he focused on Nicole and said, "Let's take a walk."

"Okay."

She followed as he led over to the rail yard, through rusty tracks and strings of motionless cars lined up like cattle waiting for slaughter. On the far side of the yard a red switcher dragged three flatbeds loaded with shiny new yellow bulldozers. Ash pointed to a standalone boxcar at the end of a line and said, "Let's climb up. You want to?"

"Sure."

They made their way up a rusty ladder to the top where the view was custom-made for hungry eyes. The surface was surprisingly clean, no doubt from all the recent rain.

They sat down and Nicole said, "What did Hollywood

say?"

"Well, I don't remember it exactly because it was long and rambling, and he was talking through some kind of a scrambler so it was hard to understand," he said. "But it was something like this:

Hey there, mister lawyer guy. We have a friend in common; her name is Nicole Stone.

Who is this?

Who is this—right, as if you don't know. She's a great sport, that little Nicole. She tried to draw me into a trap down in Key Largo last night. Did you know that?

You want to pick on somebody? Why don't you pick on me?

Sure, no problem. Consider your name on the list. That took some guts on Nicole's part, setting up a trap like that. I actually had to admire her. If she's wondering whether I'm a bad shot, tell her I'm not. Tell her I missed on purpose.

What do you mean?

She'll know. But tell her I didn't do it for her. Tell her I did it for me. At the last second I decided that I didn't want the game to end. I wanted it to go on for just a little longer. It's still going to end—don't get me wrong. It just didn't end last night."

"That's it," Ash said. "Then he hung up. Weird, huh?"

"Dangerous is more like it. You need to watch your ass. Take every breath as if he's right around the corner because he probably is."

Nicole looked around, wondering if Hollywood was out there in the sneaky little shadows watching them even as they spoke. Over by a rail switch, two lucky crows tore away at a dead squirrel. If Hollywood was out there, Nicole didn't see him.

"When did this happen?" she said.

"Just this morning. Right before I called you."

"Have you told anyone else besides me?"

"No."

"Do me a favor for the time being and keep it that way."

He wrinkled his face in confusion.

"Sure. Any particular reason?"

"Because it's true what Hollywood said, that he took a shot at me last night. He ended up breaking a hotel window. I don't want anyone connecting him to that hotel because then they'll connect me to it."

"So?"

"So, I did a few things there I shouldn't have," she said. "I discharged my weapon a number of times and even shot at an innocent man. I can't afford anyone finding out, at least not right now."

Ash eased backwards until he was flat on his back and closed his eyes. Nicole laid back next to him and stared up at the way the yellow morning sun wove its magic into the clouds. She squeezed his hand and said, "It sounds like Hollywood's getting sweet on me. Maybe we can use that to our advantage."

"How?"

"I don't know yet. Maybe I'll ask him out on a date." She got to her feet on top of the boxcar, pulled up her top and flashed her breasts in all directions. "There, Hollywood. If you're watching, that's for you. Give me a call."

44

An hour later, with eyes pointed straight ahead, Nicole walked down Brickell Avenue in the heart of downtown Miami as the buzz of the city washed around her. The plan was simple, namely zigzag past every security camera she knew, go back and get the footage later and see if she could spot anyone following her. As she walked she let her thoughts turn to the Mexican connection.

Jafet el Perro.

Was he the one after Nicole?

All things pointed that way. First and foremost, it looked like he had ties to Mia Notaro, whose helicopter in turn was used in the attempt to abduct Nicole. Also, the woman who came to Miami to do the deed—Juana del Carmen—said she was being forced to act because someone took her child. Jafet el Perro would have both the power and the ruthlessness to do something like that. Also, the woman was being funded with a blank check to hire men and get the job done. Money like that would be nothing to a man like Jafet el Perro. Yes, his plan had been to have her snatched in Miami, flown to El Paso and then brought to him in Mexico.

Why?

What possible interest could a man like that have in her?

Whatever she did or didn't do in her youth that she could no longer remember, she'd been a child at the time, no more than fourteen at the most. Now she was twenty-eight. Her life had been absolutely normal for the last fourteen years. She'd done nothing wrong. She'd had no connections to Mexico. She'd been nothing but a girl growing up and going to college and getting a job.

She wasn't a threat to Jafet el Perro, or anyone like him.

So what was his interest in her?

Was it revenge?

Had she done something in her youth so terrible that the man was still seeking his revenge more than a decade later? Was that the dream she had?

It didn't make sense.

No one can hold onto hate that long, especially against a child.

But still, it was real; and if he really was the one after her, he'd get her sooner or later, unless she disappeared—maybe she should go to Paris, get a new name and look, learn the language and open a bistro or something.

Jafet el Perro.

Jafet the Dog.

Nicole pictured herself in a concrete room, stripped naked with her wrists chained above her head and her toes barely able to touch the ground. A blinding light was in her eyes. Behind that light sat a man in a chair, patiently studying her as he smoked a cigar—relishing in the anticipation.

He leaned forward and his eyes came into view.

They were eyes that had seen both the beauties and the horrors of the world. They were eyes that trusted no one and could no longer be tricked or made to hesitate. They were eyes that knew what they wanted and took it.

He stood up and brought his face to hers, close, then circled around, flicked her hair and licked her neck. Then he whispered in her ear, Your death will be slow. You'll beg me a million times to kill you before I do. Shall we get started?

She shook the image off and kept walking without turning around or trying to play the windows as mirrors. If Hollywood was following her, she didn't want to spook him. Downtown was alive with bodies in motion, old men playing checkers, fountains squirting and street vendors selling hot dogs underneath colored umbrellas.

Up ahead a teenage girl sat on the sidewalk with her legs stretched out and her back resting against a building. Next to her on the cement was a dirty backpack. Her blouse was too big and her hair was tangled. She couldn't have been more than fifteen.

Nicole looked at the girl's eyes as she passed.

The girl didn't look back.

At the intersection, the light was red and a crowd five deep had already built up. Nicole turned and looked back. The girl hadn't moved. Instead of crossing when the light changed, Nicole bought hot dogs and chips from a street cart, went back to the girl and sat down next to her in the same position, with her legs out and her back against the building. She handed the girl the bag and said, "Hot dogs."

The girl looked at her, then in the bag.

"You a cop?"

"Yeah, sort of, my name's Nicole Stone, I'm a homicide detective here in Miami. But once I was just a fifteen-year-old girl, same as you. I'm assuming you're fifteen. Am I right?"

"Close, fourteen."

"Ah, fourteen. You're mature for your age."

"Thanks."

The girl took a bite of the dog, popped the lid of the can of diet Pepsi, and washed it down. The sleeve of her blouse pulled up just far enough for Nicole to see needle tracks on the girl's arm.

"Do you have a name?" Nicole said.

The girl nodded.

"Diamond."

"Diamond, that's nice. Do you see that man across the street in the red shirt staring at us?"

"Yes."

"Do you know him?"

"No."

"I think you do," Nicole said.

"I'm not supposed to talk about him."

"Did he give you that name, Diamond?"

"I'm not supposed to say."

"What's your real name, the name your parents gave you?"

"I only had a mom."

"You never had a dad?"

"No."

"Where's your mom?"

"She's not here anymore."

Nicole exhaled.

"I'm going to help you," she said. "I'm going to be straight with you. It's not going to be easy. You're going to have to go through rehab, you're going to have to meet new people and you're going to have to get off the streets and back in school. I'll be with you every step of the way if you want me to, I promise. I need you to talk to me, though. That man in the red shirt across the street, has he ever hurt you?"

A tear dripped out of the girl's eyes.

"I'm not supposed to say."

"Does he make you have sex with men?"

"I'm not supposed to say."

Nicole squeezed the girl's hand.

"He won't be able to hurt you ever again," she said. "I promise. You'll be safe."

The girl looked into her eyes.

"You promise?"

Nicole nodded.

"Cross my heart."

The girl's lips trembled.

"And hope to die?"

"And hope to die. Go ahead and tell me. Has he ever hurt you?"

"Yes."

"Does he give you drugs?"

"Yes."

"Does he make you have sex with men?"

"Yes."

"Does he make you have sex with him?"

"Yes. You said you're a homicide detective, right?"

"That's right."

"I think he might have killed someone," the girl said.

"Who?"

"A girl named Amber. She was keeping money from him and they had a big fight. I haven't seen her since that happened and he talks about her like she's dead. He says I'm next if I ever do something stupid like that."

"When did they have the fight?"

"Three nights ago. Monday night."

Nicole patted the girl's knee.

"What's your name, your real one?"

"Jamie."

"Jamie what?"

"Jamie Lake."

"Stay right where you are, Jamie Lake. Don't move, okay?"

"Okay."

With that, Nicole got up slowly as if walking away, and then suddenly turned and raced across the street at the man in the red shirt with her weapon drawn.

"Down on the ground, now!"

The man hesitated, deciding, and then ran.

People were around.

Shoot or not?

Shoot or not?

Shoot or not?

Nicole took aim, almost positive she could get him in the back, but changed her mind at the last second and fired a warning shot into the sky instead.

The explosion ripped through the air.

People screamed and ran.

The man didn't stop.

He didn't slow down or look back.

He raced away with every frantic molecule of strength he had.

Nicole chased him as hard as she could but the gap continued to get bigger and he finally disappeared around a corner.

When Nicole got back, Jamie Lake was gone.

A half-eaten hotdog was on the sidewalk where she'd been.

People were filming Nicole with their cell phones.

From down the street, a news crew was already racing her way.

45

The girl, Jamie Lake, was gone. Nicole ran down Brickell Avenue through the crowd, ignoring the startled looks and clipping the bodies that got in her way, needing to find the girl before she disappeared forever.

Damn it!

If the girl ended up dead, it would be Nicole's fault.

She should have just gotten the girl to safety and worried about the guy later. She should never have attempted an arrest that had a hundred ways of going wrong.

The girl wasn't in sight yet.

Nicole ran on.

She ran more and then more and then more.

It did no good.

The girl had been swallowed by the buildings and the buses and the crowds and the motion and the heat.

Nicole called dispatch and got a BOLO going, both on the girl and the red-shirt guy, although she didn't have much of a description for the guy, other than his size and clothes, hat and sunglasses. She'd never gotten a good look at his face and wouldn't be able to pick him out of a lineup.

Then she called Manny Roundhouse, the head of the sex crimes unit, who knew as much as anyone in Miami about the exploitation and trafficking of minors. She explained what just happened and asked, "Do you know anything about these girls? Do you know who they are or where I can find them?"

The man grunted.

"No," he said. "By way of background, most minors are being booked by way of the web nowadays, not in person. The pimps used to use terms like fresh. Now they're using emojis like a growing heart or a teddy bear, which are a lot harder for us to find by robo search. Plus they're changing the signals all the time. I have files on the top thirty or forty likely perps currently working the area and you're welcome to come down and go through them if you'd like. We concentrate more on the pimps than their girls, so right now names like Diamond and Jamie Lake and Amber don't mean anything to me. I haven't heard rumors of anyone being murdered, either, but that certainly doesn't mean it didn't happen. I'll ask around."

"If this guy finds her, she's dead," Nicole said.

Roundhouse said. "I'll tell you what I'll do. I'll get a team pulling the security cameras where he was. We'll see if we can get a shot of his face."

"Thanks," Nicole said. "Keep me posted?"

"I will."

"Oh, get a picture of the girl too, if you can. You'll see me with her on the sidewalk. I want pictures of both of them on the five o'clock news if we can."

"Of course. I'll Google her and check missing persons too. You never know—"

"No, you don't."

Hanging up, Nicole wasn't satisfied. She'd gotten as much as she could expect, more even, but didn't have time for a system to work. She needed more and she needed it now. Her fear was that sooner or later the girl would need a fix. If she didn't have the funds or connections to get it on her own, she'd make a trip to the red shirt. She'd have no choice. He'd be her last resort but in the end, when every other option was exhausted, the devil in her veins would make her take her chances with him.

Nicole pounded the streets for another half hour, talking to every group of homeless kids she could spot, and finding that most of the girls get approached by at least one sleazebag pimp a week. The pitches were always the same.

Get you a good safe place to crash where you don't have to worry.

Get you some food and some cool clothes. We'll go shopping.

Get you some pot and liquor.

Get you some good spending money.

Get you a lot of good friends and a lot of good parties.

Get you into modeling—you're pretty enough, did anyone ever tell you that?

The descriptions of the guys were all different—white, black, skinny, fat. The red shirt clearly wasn't the only wolf working the herd, not even close. Then, finally, she got some words from a young black girl that she could actually use.

"Most of the guys are by themselves when they try to get us to work for them," she said. "But one guy had a girl with him. I guess she's supposed to make you feel more comfortable."

"Did she have a name?"

The girl nodded.

"Yeah, but I don't remember what it was."

"Was it Diamond?"

"No."

"How about Amber?"

The girl lit up.

"Yeah, that's it. How'd you know?"

"Beginner's luck," Nicole said. "How about the guy? Did he have a name?"

"Yeah, but I don't remember it."

"When did you talk to him?"

"I don't know—it was pretty early in the spring, I guess. It was still getting a little cold out at night—"

"So, April, maybe?"

The girl shrugged.

"Could be."

"Several months ago—"

"Right. It wasn't last year. It was this year."

"Where were you when he approached you?"

"I don't remember."

"Think, please," Nicole said. "This is important."

"Okay, yeah, it was over at Brickell Key Park. Me and a friend were killing time watching the cruise ships."

"Okay. Did you ever see him again?"

"Yeah, now that you mention it."

"Where?"

"Same place, actually."

"Was the girl with him, Amber?"

"No. He was alone."

"How long ago was this?"

"Just a couple of days ago. Did he kill Amber?"

"What makes you say that?"

"I'm not stupid. Did he?"

"I don't know. You stay away from him. Tell your friends, too." Nicole pulled a card out of her purse, plus all the money she had, which was $120, and handed it all to the girl. "Get yourself some food. This isn't for wine or pot or anything like that. Can you do me a favor?"

"Sure."

"My number's on that card," Nicole said. "If you ever see the guy again, I'd like it if you'd call me immediately. Get to a payphone and call me. If I don't answer, please leave a message. Let me know where you saw the guy and when. Can you do that?"

"Sure."
Nicole gave her a hug.
Then her phone rang.

46

Nicole answered the phone with an abrupt, "Yeah?," not having the time or patience for an interruption at this exact wrong moment in time. Detective Salter Shade was on the line, with an edge that wasn't normally present in his typical Clark Kent demeanor.

"There's a nasty rumor going around that you're getting fired," he said.

"It's a work-in-progress but to be honest I really don't have time for it right now," she said. "Did you go to the meeting this morning?"

"Yeah. Your chair was empty."

"Are there any leads?"

"No, nothing."

"What about all that work that Trane has everyone doing—checking hotels and rental cars and crisscrossing this and that?"

"It's all crash and burn. We aren't getting anything."

"Okay," Nicole said. "Can you break free and do me a favor?"

"Sure, anything."

She explained the situation. "I've been walking around Brickell. I'll give you the route in a minute. What I need you to do is pull every surveillance camera that could have shined on me and see if anyone was following."

"You mean Hollywood?"

"Exactly," she said. "It's a chance we could actually get some footage of him. I was going to do it myself but I'm running out of time."

"No, that's okay, I'll do it. What are you going to do while I'm doing all the work—repeat, all the work?"

Nicole smiled, appreciating the many hours of labor involved, and said, "I don't know yet. Do me a favor and call me first if you get anything useful, will you?"

"Sure—"

"I want Hollywood alive," Nicole added. "There are a lot of people who would kill him just to have the bag."

Ten minutes later she was back on Brickell with her thoughts off Diamond and back on Danica, trying to come up with some brilliant plan.

Nothing was coming.

Was this it?

Had she run out of moves?

Come on, think!

Get your freaking brain in gear.

We don't have time for you to be stupid right now.

Did you hear me?

Think!

She huffed down the street, weaving relentlessly past strangers as if she could harness the sheer power of her frustration if she just tried hard enough. Then out of the blue she came across something she didn't expect, something that brought her movement to a breakneck stop. It was a movie poster in a window, advertising an upcoming movie called The Shoals. There, right before her eyes, was Danica, in a dramatic chase scene set in the tranquil beauty of a white-sand lagoon. Danica had a look of terror on her face as she ran for her life at the surf's edge. Tight in her fist was a leather bag, something important enough that she wasn't about to let go even to save her own life. Behind her, closing fast, were three strong shirtless rogues who wanted nothing more in the world than to get her.

The power of the scene went straight to Nicole's blood.

Danica was running.

She was running for all she had.

She was not giving up, even now, in what were obviously her final seconds.

Suddenly Nicole's phone rang and Ash's voice came through: "Where are you?"

"Brickell, two blocks south of your office, in fact. Why?"

"Stay there," he said. "I'll be there in ten minutes. I need to talk to you."

"Ash, I'm seriously busy—"

"It's about Hollywood," he said. "I think I know who he is."

47

It's about Hollywood. *I think I know who he is.* Nicole paced, not because she believed that Ash knew who Hollywood was—he couldn't. No, she paced because time was running out. It was running out for Danica. It was running out for Jamie Lake. It was even running out for Nicole herself. And Nicole, in return, had no good plan for any of it.

Ash showed up in ten minutes and got right to the point. "When Hollywood called me this morning, he used a scrambler," he said. "It was effective. There was no way to even tell if the caller was a male or a female. Still, though, it all seemed familiar somehow. I've been thinking about it all morning and now I know what had me on edge. It was the spacing of the words, by which I mean the tempo of the words and the length of time between them, and how that time sometimes speeds up and sometimes slows down. I know I'd heard that tempo before and it finally came to me. I think it belongs to your FBI friend, John Pantage."

"Pantage? That's your theory?"

"Yes."

"You think Pantage is Hollywood?"

"Yes."

Nicole tried to hide her disappointment but could feel it taking over her face.

"I can guarantee you he's not Pantage," she said. She looked at her watch. "Look, Ash, I got to go. We'll pick this up later, okay?"

"Hear me out first," he said. "There's more. For starters, he's big enough and strong enough to pick someone like Danica up and throw her into the back of an SUV. He fits the physical profile. But the big reason is, if he's Hollywood, and if he's also in the FBI, wouldn't it be nifty to work himself into being the top person in charge of the Hollywood investigations? He might have positioned himself in the organization so that he could protect himself. He'd know if anyone was closing in on him. He'd have the opportunity to manipulate files and misdirect investigations. He'd be the fox in charge of the hen house."

"Nothing personal, Ash, but that's crazy. The world doesn't work like that."

"Think about it, Nicole. How did he get the top job on the task force? I'll bet dollars to donuts that it's because he was constantly coming up with more clues and evidence than any of his other FBI cohorts. It became more and more apparent that he was the best hunter on the squad and deserved to be the top dog. Now ask yourself, how did he magically come up with all those elusive clues and evidence?"

"Because he was there at the crime scenes—"

"Exactly."

"Look, Ash," Nicole said. "I understand the reasoning. I get the logic, I really do. But—"

"Hold on. There's the rattlesnake, too," Ash said. "When Pantage spent the night on your roof, ostensibly watching over you in case Hollywood showed up, the rattlesnake was on the roof the next morning. Now ask yourself, who had the perfect opportunity to put it there?"

"Pantage himself."

"Bingo," Ash said. "He kept it in a cage for the night and

let it go in the morning. He was never in any danger. He put it there to suggest that there was a real Hollywood out there in the world who was out to kill him. It was a sneaky diversion. He was laying in evidence that he couldn't possibly be Hollywood, in case you or anyone else ever started considering the option."

"No. Not true."

Ash was undaunted.

He said, "Plus, just being up there, close to you all night, it's all part of his game. He's the last person on earth you'd suspect. Every time you look at him like he's on your side, he gets a little tingle down in his cock."

"Ash, he's not Hollywood," Nicole said.

"I think he is," Ash said. "I can feel it down in my gut. He's going to kill you and you'll never see it coming. That's his plan. That's exactly his plan."

"No."

"He already knows how he's going to do it," Ash said. "He's already figured out a way to do it so no one would ever suspect him, not in a million years."

Nicole squeezed Ash's hand.

"You're sort of sexy when you're looking out for me," she said. "Here's the bottom line, though. Pantage's been with me right by my side on more than one occasion when Hollywood has called me."

Confusion washed over Ash's face.

"He has?"

"Yes."

"I didn't know that."

"Well, now you do."

She put her arms around his waist and pulled him in tight. "I know you two hate each other but you don't have to be jealous of him. Trust me, you really don't."

To the left, a motion caught Nicole's peripheral vision.

When she looked right at it she couldn't believe what she

saw.

48

The motion in Nicole's peripheral vision was none other than the mysterious man from Key Largo, the one who was in the hotel room 202 next to hers, the one who said he was a private investigator tailing someone on the other side of the back wall, the one who Nicole shot at, the one she let go because he said he had a wife and kids. Her instinct was to run over and confront him—ask him point-blank what the hell he was doing here—but Ash was present. He didn't know anything about the situation and it was better that it stay that way.

Nicole got rid of Ash but it took time.

The next time she looked over, the man was long gone.

With a pounding heart, she hunted for him up and down the hot concrete but got nothing.

Are you Hollywood?

Did I have you right there, square in my sights, and you tricked me into letting you go?

Am I that stupid?

Although conceptually it made sense—the man could actually be Hollywood—Nicole's gut deep down wasn't convinced, not by a long shot. He was someone, clearly, up to something, but the chances were slim that he was Hollywood. He didn't have physical prowess. He might be able to throw someone into the back of an SUV if he really set his mind to it, but he looked more likely to drag them over, lift them up with both arms and wiggle them in. Maybe he really was an investigator like he said and it just so happened that his office was around here somewhere.

Let him go, at least for now.

Don't let him become a distraction.

Don't let him suck away time that you don't have.

Stay focused.

She took the ten-minute walk over to Brickell Key Park, which was one of the no-doubt many places that the red shirt hunted down the innocent little souls that happened to drift through Miami, hoping to see either the red shirt himself, or Jamie Lake. Neither one of them was there, of course. Nicole took a seat on the ledge by the water, in the shade, and stared at the expanse of sun-drenched water before her.

A minute later she turned and looked behind her.

Fifty yards away, a man leaned against a tree. He was staring right at Nicole and didn't turn away when she looked at him. His face was hidden under a baseball cap and sunglasses. His left arm was heavily tattooed. He pulled his right hand up to his mouth, took a long drag from a cigarette, and blew it at Nicole.

Are you the guy from the white Challenger?

Nicole couldn't actually tell if the man was looking at her or not, so she waved at him.

He smiled and waved back.

Hollywood?

Is that you?

Nicole reached into her back jeans pocket for her phone, to pretend she was taking a call when she would actually be sneaking a picture of him.

When she looked back up, the man was gone.

Suddenly her phone rang and a voice came through,

scrambled. It was Hollywood. "We should meet," he said.

Her blood raced.

"Sure," she said. "Why not?"

"Good. I'm going to give you some GPS coordinates to write down. Now, listen carefully because this is very important: come alone. I'm going to repeat that—come alone, just you, only you, no one else. Am I clear?"

"Yes."

"And don't tell anyone. If you do, I'll know. Everything will be off and you'll never get this opportunity again. Do you understand?"

"Yes. Is Danica alive?"

"You'll find out soon enough."

49

As Nicole slipped the phone into her back pocket, she kept the fear off her face in case Hollywood was actually studying her from a distance, as if she was some type of bizarre insect project. She walked calmly off. En route her phone rang. It was mister boss-man, Trane.

"Are the rumors true that you shot your weapon over at Wall Street South?"

Nicole's brain raced.

Should she tell him about how Hollywood just called her to meet?

Should she change her whole strategy of going it alone, and instead bring an army with her?

No, no army.

Hollywood would detect it.

He'd kill Danica.

He'd escape.

He wasn't stupid.

"Nicole, are you there?"

"Yes."

"Did you shoot your weapon?"

"Yes."

"You need to get down here right now and fill out a discharge report."

She shook her head.

"Now's not good," she said. "I'll come in later this afternoon."

"No, now," Trane said. "We got TV stations down here talking about reckless endangerment. We need to get into a position to defuse it."

"Nick, I can't right now, I'm sorry."

She hung up.

The phone rang.

It was him.

She didn't answer.

Thirty seconds later a text landed from Trane: "Come to headquarters immediately to file a weapon discharge report. Failure to do so will be considered insubordination and handled accordingly."

Nicole shoved the phone in her back pocket, got squished into a crowd as she crossed a street, then made her way down the concrete at a trot two blocks north to Penny Lane, who was waiting patiently on sizzling asphalt in front of an expired meter. She pulled a ticket off the windshield, unlocked the door and threw the ticket in the back seat as she hopped in.

The heat of hell greeted her.

She rolled down both windows, put the key in the ignition and said, "Start, bitch. I'm dead serious."

The engine immediately fired, as if it never did anything but.

She patted the dashboard and then, with Hollywood's GPS coordinates guiding her, wound out of the thick of Miami, farther and farther from the heart of downtown, to where the buildings got shorter and the traffic got thinner and the jagged edges of life got less jagged. Then she kept going, pointing ever west, past the farms and the water towers and the railroad tracks and the telephone poles and ever deeper into the uncivilized contours of no-man's land.

Now the GPS coordinates were roughly five miles farther up ahead.

She cruised toward them down a cracked, warped stretch of desolate road that hadn't seen a repair crew in decades and probably hadn't seen a single traveler all day. She was alone in the universe. No one else was around. Where was Hollywood, waiting for her up ahead, or closing in from behind? She checked her cell phone. The signal was strong, the battery was 12% charged.

It wasn't too late to call for backup.

Should she?

The resolve she had when she first told Hollywood she'd meet him was long gone. In its place was a black cloak of dread, whispering dark things in her ear. The only thing that kept her going was the possibility that Hollywood would exchange her for Danica. If that happened, it would all be worth it. Deep down, though, she had to admit that Danica might already be dead, or that Hollywood would simply kill them both, one after the other, and the game would be officially over. Either way, at least she'd be able to meet him. She'd be able to look him straight in the eyes and tell him what a sick little freak he was. She'd also have a chance to kill him, even if it was only one in a million.

In hindsight, it was a good thing she didn't tell Trane where she was going. This part of the universe was too open. Backup would have been spotted a mile away.

You're doing good.

Just keep going.

Don't turn and run no matter how much you want to.

The seconds clicked off, one after another, like a slow countdown from the throat of the grim reaper. Then it was time to stop. She was as far as she could go by car.

She pulled Penny Lane off the road into the weeds and killed the engine.

Just like that, everything was silent.

The whipping of the wind through the windows was gone.

The whining of the tires was gone.

The squeaking of the suspension from the torture of the road was gone.

Everything was gone.

She got her gun in hand and stepped out.

The sun immediately beat down on her face and wedged its way into her eyes.

According to the GPS, the meeting point was off the road, into the wild yucca and sage and grasses, over a curvature.

She looked that way.

This is your last chance, girl.

Change your mind now, if you're going to do it.

Overhead, way up on a thermal, two hawks circled on outstretched wings.

Nicole swallowed.

What do you see up there?

Do you see my flesh rotting in the sun?

You want to eat me?

Is that it?

50

With her gun in her hand and a knife in her back pocket and a pounding in her chest, Nicole took one last look down the road in both directions, didn't see anyone coming, and headed into the terrain one step at a time, trying to keep her feet from landing on a lizard or a rock. Given that no car was in the vicinity, she was pretty sure Hollywood hadn't arrived yet. That would give her time to check the place out—whatever it was—assuming she'd written the GPS coordinates down correctly.

She already knew what she was going to find.

She was going to find her own grave.

It would be there, already dug, grimly waiting for her. Hollywood would make her kneel next to it. He'd utter some smug words—"Hey, baby, can I have this dance?"—and then shoot her in the back of the head. Her brains would splatter and his voice would be the last thing she'd ever hear. The hawks would tighten their circle and point their eyes down. Hollywood would kick her lifeless body into the hole. Maybe he'd cover her up or maybe he'd just leave her exposed for the coyotes and birds and bugs. Either way, it wouldn't matter to her anymore. Someone would eventually find her and she'd go down in the books as the dumbest detective in the history of mankind, the one who voluntarily walked right to her own grave.

Her fingers tightened on the gun.

No, no way.

She wouldn't go down like that.

She'd go down fighting.

Screw you, Hollywood.

Screw you to hell and back.

She crested a rise, saw nothing of interest up ahead, and kept her feet moving, probably not more than two hundred yards now from where she was headed.

A few minutes later she saw something strange.

It was some kind of interruption; just like everything else around it but not exactly. As she got closer it looked like an old airplane fuselage. Over time, the terrain had closed in on it and at this point almost had it buried.

She stopped.

A butterfly flew past on silent wings.

She pointed her gun at the fuselage.

Come on, Hollywood, step out.

I'm here.

Make your grand entrance.

She turned to see if he was behind her.

Nothing was there, not a Hollywood or anything else.

She took a step forward, then another and another, working her way to the side of the wreck, to see that it was open at the back. She focused on that opening, looking for any sense of movement inside.

All was still.

On the ground outside was a rifle.

Nicole kept moving, saying nothing, as silent as the air.

She got to a point where she could see inside.

What she saw she couldn't believe.

Inside was a man, lying flat on his stomach as still as death. Blood was everywhere. His pants were off. His big old fat ass was right there on full display.

Hollywood?

Nicole trained her weapon on the man's back and approached.

"Don't move!"

No reaction came. Nicole kicked the man's foot and got no reflex. She swept down, quickly pressed the barrel of her weapon into the man's back and took a closer look at his face. His throat had been slit, deeply. His eyes were open, staring at nothing. He was clearly dead and apparently had been for some time, including the time Nicole had last spoken to Hollywood, meaning this wasn't him.

This was somebody else.

Danica wasn't there but it looked like she had been.

There was food, books, a small port-o-potty, magazines and the like. Most telling was the chain affixed to the inner structure of the fuselage, with an ankle bracelet on the other end, no doubt having kept Danica a prisoner.

Nicole checked the dead man's back pocket and found a wallet.

Inside was a driver's license for one Bobby-James Flagger, age 42. Also inside was a photo that had been partially cut off. What remained was Bobby-James and a girl, about nine or ten, probably his daughter. If Nicole had to guess what got cut off and thrown away, it would be an ex wife. The man had no wedding ring on his finger.

Nicole pictured it.

Okay, you're out here walking around with your rifle and killing innocent little things with big manly bullets, rabbits or birds or whatever, and suddenly, just like that, you hit the freaking lottery. Right there in front you of you suddenly find a beautiful woman, oh so wonderfully alone, all chained up with nowhere to go.

She has no gun.

She has no knife.

All she has is words, but stupid things like that aren't going to stop someone like you now, are they? You decide to show her what she's been missing for all her life, but things didn't end like you planned, did they?

So who got you?

Was it Danica, with the top of a can that had been cut off?

Or, was it Hollywood?

Did he somehow show up at the exact wrong second, grab your hair from behind and jerk your head back as he ripped a knife across your throat?

Chock on your blood, asshole!

Nicole looked around for the object that inflicted the wound. If it was there, it wasn't jumping up at her in flashing neon.

Nicole stepped outside to see if Hollywood was approaching.

He wasn't, at least not yet.

The only thing out there was nature, quiet, calm and, under other circumstances, beautiful. The hot Florida sun squinted into her eyes and beaded sweat on her forehead. She wiped it off with the back of her hand. Above her the hawks circled, except now there were three of them instead of two.

Come on, Hollywood.

Show up.

I'm saving a dance for you.

51

Nicole checked out the scene as much as she could without disturbing it as she waited for Hollywood to show up, but he didn't; not in ten minutes, not in thirty, not in an hour. During that time, she didn't call Trane or Pantage to tell them about the scene because she didn't want Hollywood scared off. It was clear now though that he wasn't coming so she made the call. Maybe Hollywood had changed his mind, maybe he never intended to show up, who knew? A long time later, Pantage, Trane and a whole squad of forensic robots in white suits showed up. Nicole met them at the road and led them in. Walking through the terrain next to Nicole, Trane wasn't happy.

"What you did was beyond stupid," he said. "You could be dead right now. You know that, right?"

"I took a chance," she said. "We ended up ahead."

Trane looked at her in disbelief.

"I don't ever want you going rogue like that again. We need to be absolutely, one hundred percent clear on that. Are we?"

Nicole said nothing.

Trane grabbed her by the arm, jerked her to a stop and let the seriousness of his words tighten his face. "You're not to play games with this guy. I'm dead serious, Nicole. I need you to look me in the eyes and tell me you won't. And I need you to mean it."

She looked at the ground.

She said nothing.

"Nicole—"

"I can't promise anything," she said. "All I can do is take things as they come."

Trane exhaled.

"You got me in a corner. I'm taking you off the case," he said. "I have to. You're really not leaving me any options."

The words landed like a rock to the forehead.

Nicole tried to show no reaction.

"Fine," she said.

He held his hand out and said, "Give me your badge and your weapon. You're on a two-week suspension for insubordination starting right now."

Nicole didn't see that coming, at least not this fast.

Two weeks.

Danica would be long dead by then.

"Nick, please—"

"Do it!"

She complied, slowly, handing over the weapon first, then the badge.

"You can have these back right now," he said. "All you have to do is promise me you won't play any more games with Hollywood. If he ever calls you again, you call me immediately. You don't do a damn thing until and unless I tell you to."

Nicole weighed it.

Then she turned and walked back towards the road.

"Nicole, stop being your own worst enemy!"

She didn't turn.

She just kept walking.

A tear rolled out of her eye.

She wasn't cut out for this job.

It was just that simple.

She got in Penny Lane and started the long trek back, calling Salter Shade on the way to see if he was having any luck getting footage of someone following her this morning.

"Not yet," he said. "The day's early, though."

"Call me either way."

"Will do."

She hung up without telling him she'd been fired, in case he might decide to question what he was supposed to do.

Then something happened that she didn't expect.

A white vehicle appeared a half-mile back in her rearview mirror, going the same direction as her and keeping the gap steady, not getting any closer and not falling any farther behind. It was too far back to identify but it could be a Challenger. It could be the guy who'd been lingering around since day one, the guy with the tattooed left arm and the dangling cigarette.

Hollywood?

Is that you?

She crested a rise in the road. It wasn't high but it was enough to get her out of line of sight for at least a time. There she jerked to a stop, sprang to the trunk and pulled her own private weapon out from under a towel, a 9mm Glock. She checked the clip and found it full, as it should be. One was in the chamber.

She squatted behind Penny Lane and took aim at the road behind her, waiting.

Come on.

Be Hollywood.

Let's do this.

52

As the white vehicle approached, it took shape as a pickup truck with one person inside—a male, wearing a black cowboy hat. He was tanned and range-strong, about forty birthdays long, give or take. She lowered the gun and waited for the vehicle to pass. Instead, it pulled up behind her and the man got out, grinning, possibly thinking he just won the lottery, it was too early to tell.

"You okay, lady?"

The guy was bigger than Nicole first envisioned; stronger, too.

He had a chiseled, manly face with a Kurt Douglas dimple in the chin, the kind of face that they used on all the old Marlboro commercials, back before the powers that be snuffed out all cigarette advertising.

"Yeah, I'm fine," Nicole said.

"You're not broke down or anything?"

"No, I just pulled over for a second."

The man took his hat off and raked his hair back with his fingers. It was thick and wet from the confinement.

"Well, okay," he said. "You have a nice day now, you hear?"

"I will. You too."

"Thanks. That's mighty kind of you."

Mighty kind.

Those were words Hollywood would never use.

Hollywood was more urban, more sophisticated, more inclined to impress.

So this man here, he wasn't Hollywood.

"Hey, wait a minute," Nicole said. "Do you live around here?"

"More or less."

"Back there in the open space there's an old crashed airplane," Nicole said. "Do you know it?"

The man nodded.

"I've been there once or twice, back when I was a kid. We all have. You had to spend a night there alone without getting killed. It was kind of an initiation."

"Have you seen any cars parked in that vicinity lately? You know, someone who may have pulled over to pay it a visit?"

The man scratched his chin.

"You know, maybe," he said.

"Maybe, like how?"

"Two days ago, Tuesday, I was driving back, going the opposite way of what I'm going now, and there was a car right around here. He wasn't pulled over and stopped or anything like that, but he was going real slow, almost as if he was about to pull over but then changed his mind when he saw my car."

Nicole's chest pounded.

"Did you see him?"

"No."

"No?"

"No. He was going one way and I was going the other way," the man said. "He sort of had his hand in front of his face, like he was scratching his nose or something."

"So you didn't see him at all?"

The man shrugged.

"Not really. Not his face."

"What about the car? What do you remember about the car

he was driving?"

"It was white," the man said. "It was something new. It looked fast."

"Was it a Dodge Challenger?"

"I don't know. I don't know what they look like. I'm more of a truck guy. I don't pay all that much attention to cars, to tell you the truth."

"Hold on."

Nicole pulled out her phone, Googled *Dodge Challenger*, and pulled up an image.

"Is this what you saw?"

"Maybe. It could be."

"Okay. What time did this happen?"

"I'm guessing three or four; mid-afternoon, for sure. What's going on back at the plane? Another murder?"

"What do you mean by another?"

"That plane," he said. "It's cursed. I should have blown it up twenty years ago, that and the other one too."

Nicole wrinkled her brow.

"There's another one?"

"Yeah, it's just as cursed as this one, maybe even more."

Nicole's chest pounded.

Whoever knew about this plane may well know about the other one. If Danica got moved, maybe that's where she got moved to.

"Can you show me where it's at?"

"I haven't been to it in decades."

"But you know where it is, right?"

"Yeah, roughly."

"Can you take me there?"

"It's not close," he said. "It's west of here, and you got to hike in over a mile from the road."

"I don't care," Nicole said. "I want to see it." She paused and added, "I'm a homicide detective from Miami. It may relate to a case I'm working on."

"We're a long way from Miami," the man said.

"Tell me about it. What's your name, by the way?"

"Daniel."

Nicole extended her hand.

"I'm Nicole," she said. "Nicole Stone. You got a last name?"

"I do," he said. "Flagger. Daniel Flagger."

Flagger.

Flagger.

Flagger.

Nicole swallowed and tried to not show her alarm at the name.

The dead man in the plane had the same last name.

He was Bobby-James Flagger.

The man pulled a pack of cigarettes out of his shirt pocket, tapped two loose and tilted the pack towards Nicole.

"No thanks," she said.

The man nodded.

"You mind?"

"No, you go ahead."

The man lit up, took a deep drag and dangled the butt from his fingers.

"You still want to see that plane?"

Nicole nodded.

"Sure."

"Okay, but be warned, it's cursed," he said. "Maddie Fitt got murdered there back in the day. She was only in eighth grade at the time. Once you go to a place like that you can't get rid of it. It's with you for the rest of your life. It's like something you breathe down into your lungs and it never comes out."

53

Nicole followed Daniel Flagger's white pickup truck down crappy old roads, mile after mile after hot dusty mile, while a twisty storm churned in her gut. She might actually be closing in on Hollywood. He might have feared that someone would come looking for Mister Dead Man, Bobby-James Flagger, sooner or later, and stumble on Danica. He figured it would be best to relocate her while he had the chance. Since he somehow knew about the first plane he might equally know about the second one. So, that's where he might have taken her.

If Danica was there and was still alive, Nicole would kill Hollywood as quickly as she could.

She wouldn't try to capture him.

She'd have to make her first shot count because it would be a battle to the death after that and it probably wouldn't last long.

Don't think.

Just shoot.

Go for the chest.

Hit him somewhere and then when he goes down, shoot him again.

Keep shooting him until he's definitely dead.

They passed no gas stations and Penny Lane at this point

was running on fumes. Then, just like that, the pickup suddenly pulled to the side of the road and Flagger stepped out, taking off his cowboy hat and running his fingers through his hair.

He pointed north and said, "It's about a mile that way."

Nicole looked into the rolling terrain.

It was a place abandoned to nature since the dinosaur days, stuffed with centuries of dirt and bushes and tall grasses and rocks and whatever else would fit. There were no tire tracks mashing anything down.

She turned to see that Flagger had a gun in his hand.

"It's best, in a place like that," he said.

Nicole realized just how alone she was, way out here off the grid with a man she didn't know, a man who had the same DNA as the one who pulled his pants down for Danica's entertainment.

She forced herself to keep her face calm and her smile easy.

"I need to go alone," she said.

The man shook his head.

"You'll never find it. I'll go with you."

"Thanks but no." She wiped sweat off her brow with the back of her hand. "I'm out of gas. Will you be here when I get back?"

"If you want. I'd rather just come with you though. There's a crap-load of coyotes out there and a lot of them are rabid. They're not like the one's you're used to. They don't care if you're a human or not. They'll attack."

"I'll keep a lookout. Can you do me a favor?"

"Sure."

"If any cars come by here, get their license plate numbers. Don't engage them though. They could be dangerous."

The man smiled.

"I've been known to be dangerous myself."

Nicole swallowed and then made sure she had her cell phone. She checked her gun and headed into the terrain.

She could feel Flagger's eyes on her as she walked.

She'd have to keep a lookout for him.

He might decide to surprise her out there.

She went a hundred yards and turned to look back. Flagger was leaning against his truck, smoking with his lungs and watching with his eyes.

She waved.

He clearly saw it but didn't wave back.

Why?

Was he mired in dark thoughts about what he was going to do to her?

She kept going.

Let it go.

Get to the plane.

Her throat was as dry as sandpaper and would only get worse as the footsteps clicked off.

It's about a mile that way.

She was beginning to realize just how far a mile was out here in a place like this. She hated to admit it but Flagger was right; she might never find it on her own. She stopped and got her bearings, taking note of the position of the sun and the angle of the shadows. The last thing she needed was to get turned around out here and not even be able to make it back to the road. Would Flagger call for rescue or just say screw the crazy bitch and head for home?

She kept going, on and on and on.

The wind picked up, powerful enough to make just about everything around her dance.

Then, it happened; she spotted it—the plane—way off to her right and slightly behind her. If she hadn't taken that last awkward head swing she would have walked right past it.

She stopped, got her gun in hand and zeroed in on the wreckage. Nothing moved. There was no sign of Hollywood or Danica or anyone else. No sounds came her way—no coughs or talking or screams for help. From here it looked as abandoned as abandoned could be.

She headed in, one careful step at a time, but moving as fast as she quietly could so as to get close enough for a clean shot if Hollywood's head suddenly popped up.

Ten steps away, she stopped.

The wreckage was different than the other one.

This one was an older plane, dating back possibly to the thirties or forties or fifties, with two props, laying upside down on its broken wings. It looked like it tried to land, caught the nose on something and flipped over forward. The metal supports for the wheels stuck straight up in the air. The rubber tires were long gone. All the metal was rusty brown. Hardly any paint remained. Tall weeds had invaded it, both from around and under.

Nicole made her way closer.

The sides of the fuselage had no glass or openings. A hinged cargo door was still shut.

She made her way to the front of the aircraft.

The cockpit window was close to the ground. The glass was gone. The weeds in front of it had been pulled away and were shorter in comparison to everything else around.

Nicole bent down and looked inside.

A few rays of sunlight filtered in through holes and cracks in the fuselage, but basically everything was dark.

She heard nothing.

She saw nothing.

There was no way Hollywood would be in there.

Danica might, but not Hollywood.

"Danica, are you there?"

No one answered.

"Danica!"

Before going in, she looked around one last time.

To get in, she had to get down on her belly in the weeds

and rocks and crawl forward with her forearms. She got her head inside, panicked for several seconds, then got control of herself and continued. Once inside she was able to get up into a sitting position.

It was stifling hot in there; well over a hundred.

No one could live in there for long.

"Danica, are you in here?"

Her voice was weak and timid.

It was too freaky that she had only one way to get out. If someone suddenly snuck up and blocked it, she'd be in a coffin.

Get out now.

Just leave.

Get back to Miami.

Suddenly, to her right, she spotted something she didn't expect, namely a flashlight.

It actually worked when she turned it on.

She pointed the beam into the darkness.

Then she screamed.

54

At the back of the plane was a man's decapitated head; no body, just a head. He was a white man in his mid-thirties with a seriously busted nose that had flowed blood down into his mouth and chin. The horror of his death was still etched on his face. His eyes were wide open, staring at nothing. Tons of ants crawled on his decaying flesh. He hadn't been dead long; maybe just a few days or a week. It was hard to tell given the heat.

That wasn't the only weird thing.

There was lots of writing in black magic marker on the inside walls of the plane. There were smears, too, of what looked to be blood.

Something that looked like a foldout restaurant menu ten feet in caught Nicole's eye. Her instinct was to leave, now, this second, before the maker of all the horror returned, but the menu wouldn't let her go.

It was too out of place.

She crept towards it then flipped it over, being careful not to touch anything but the edge. Sure enough, it was a menu from a restaurant—one called Blackbird Ordinary.

Blackbird Ordinary . . .

Blackbird Ordinary . . .

For some reason the words seemed familiar. She looked

closer to see that the restaurant's address was in Atlantic City, New Jersey. Then it hit her. The Blackbird Ordinary was a restaurant where one of Hollywood's victims worked. Yeah, that was it. Her name was Necha. She was a smoking hot little Puerto Rican girl who was working as a waitress. She disappeared right after work on September 8th of last year.

Only one person in the world could have put this here—Hollywood.

So, Hollywood had definitely been here.

But why would he leave a mark like this behind?

What was his game?

Nicole shined the flashlight back on the decapitated face.

Hollywood killed you, didn't he?

Why?

What'd you do to him?

Were you a detective investigating one of his cases?

Is this how I'm going to die?

Suddenly she couldn't breathe. The space was too confined and the air was too putrid.

Out!

Out!

Out!

Get out!

She clawed her way frantically through the cockpit windshield, not caring about the scrapes to her elbows or the bangs to her head.

Then she was out; out where the world was normal.

The sky was blue.

The sun was in her eyes and never felt so good.

She would never go back in there; not ever, even if she had a full crime unit with her and a thousand friendly faces all around. Danica wasn't there and that's all she really wanted to know.

Her hair blew.

The wind had picked up even more than before.

Then she got a whiff.

She knew right away what it was, a whiff of death.

She looked around to be sure Hollywood wasn't lurking out there somewhere — which he wasn't, at least that she could see — and then picked her way through the terrain ever closer to the smell. It turned out to be farther than she thought, a good quarter-mile or so past the plane.

There she found a pit.

A number of dead bodies had been dumped in there, possibly going back years based on the stages of decay. All of them were women except the one on top.

That one belonged to a man.

He had no head.

The head had been cut off.

She suddenly got a weird feeling that someone was watching her. She turned her head wildly and cast her eyes in every direction but saw no one.

Someone was out there though.

She was sure of it.

She could feel sick little eyes worming their sick little way into her bones.

Her fingers tightened hard on the weapon.

Come on, Hollywood.

Come and get me.

It's time.

55

Nicole waited for Hollywood at the body pit, looking around this way and that, but he wasn't coming for her, not yet. She took her focus off the inevitable confrontation long enough to pull her cell phone out, only to find the battery dead, meaning she couldn't take any pictures of the gruesome grave or get the GPS coordinates of its location or let Trane know about it.

It also meant she couldn't call for help if she needed to.

Her breath quickened.

It was time to leave; now, not in ten seconds.

She picked her way back to the road to find Penny Lane right where she should be, but that was it. Daniel Flagger and his pickup truck were gone.

Why'd he leave?

Was he the one responsible for all the mess back there?

Was he on the run now?

Was he Hollywood?

She slipped into Penny Lane, crossed her heart and said, "Don't do me wrong."

Penny Lane fired right up.

She even went a full mile down the road, good girl that she was, with no problem. Then she gasped and coughed and sputtered as the last gas fume sucked its way into her carburetor.

She died a silent death as Nicole steered her to the side of the road, turned off the key and put on the emergency brake.

Then she sat there, alone in the silence.

She had no phone.

She had no car.

The sun up above was a demon.

Her throat was sandpaper.

Miami was a million miles away.

She got out and headed up the road on foot. It probably made more sense to stay put and let someone stumble upon her, but there was a lot more traffic about ten miles back; her odds of encountering a human faster were at least double. She could be there in—what?—three hours? She was tired but she could last three hours unless her throat spontaneously burst into flames.

She walked for a mile, then another, and then another. An hour into it, she curled up under the shade of one of the only trees she'd encountered so far out here in the sun-infested hell.

She closed her eyes.

It felt so damn good.

It was a cold wet waterfall on her brain.

She let her thoughts drift.

Daniel Flagger—was he Hollywood?

In a way it made sense. He had the size and the strength. He knew about both plane wrecks, and Hollywood had unquestionably been to both of those places. If he were Hollywood, his brother—Bobby-James Flagger—probably would have known about it. Maybe that's how the brother knew about Danica; he didn't stumble on her by accident, Daniel had told him about her. Maybe Daniel was the one who killed Bobby-James, not Danica—for invading his space or whatever. Also, it was strange that he stumbled on Nicole by accident out here in the middle of nowhere. Maybe it wasn't so much of an accident after all.

But why would he tell her about the second plane if he was Hollywood?

Maybe it was part of the game. Maybe he'd planted the Blackbird Ordinary menu there and then told Nicole about the plane for no other reason than for her to find it.

It was all just a nasty plot to freak her out.

He could have killed her when she came back to the road; in fact, maybe that's exactly what he had planned. That's why he didn't wave back when she waved to him as she headed in.

He could have changed his mind, though, because killing her would have meant the end of the game and he wasn't ready for it to end; no, not yet.

He was having way too much fun.

Suddenly the sound of a vehicle crept into the air.

Nicole got to her feet, made her way to the middle of the road and flagged it down with waving arms. It turned out to be two girls in an old open-air Wrangler. The doors weren't there, the top wasn't there and the wheels were oversized. Both of the occupants were pretty and young; somewhere in their early twenties. Nicole made her way to the driver, who was wearing a white T and Daisy Dukes, and said, "I did something stupid. I got myself stranded out here."

The woman flicked ashes off the end of a cigarette, said, "Hop in," and took a long drag as Nicole climbed over the back tailgate and wedged her behind onto the hot metal floor next to two suitcases.

Then they were off, as bumpy and noisy as hell itself.

The Driver shouted back, "You got a name?"

"Nicole."

"I'm Mandy. That's Sunshine."

"Pleased to meet you."

"Likewise."

Nicole watched the scenery rewind as they headed up the road from the way she'd walked. Both the young woman had cell phones—that was inevitable—but Nicole suddenly wasn't so sure that borrowing one to call Trane was the right idea. Her supposition about Daniel Flagger being Hollywood was just that, supposition. There wasn't enough of anything concrete there to support a search warrant.

No, don't call Trane.

Find out where Flagger lives, sneak in, and see if Danica's there.

They passed Penny Lane, sitting there lonely and forgotten at the side of the road, and kept going for several miles where they came to a crossroads that had a couple of rickety old buildings. One of them was a general store that had a one-hose gas pump out front.

The driver, Mandy, put the hose in the Wrangler, and Nicole stayed with her as Sunshine went inside to search for snacks. It turned out that the girls were strippers coming home after working a two-week stint at a club in Miami. They'd both been born around these parts, "unfortunately." As for Daniel Flagger, neither of them knew him by name but by description thought that he might be the guy who lived at the end of the dirt road that teed-off three or four miles up ahead. No one ever went up that way. Word was, it wasn't safe.

Nicole drank a ton of water, bought a bunch of food, filled up a gallon jug with gas and got a ride back to Penny Lane, compliments of Mandy and Sunshine, who refused any payment.

"That road I was telling you about—I've heard it said that there's a helicopter that goes in and out of there sometimes," Mandy said. "Me myself, I've never seen it personally so I can't tell you if it's really true or not. Don't go there, if you're thinking about it. That's my advice."

"Why?"

"Because people tend to disappear around these parts." She smiled and added, "By the way, you busted me once. Do you remember?"

"No, not really."

"Think about it. Maybe it will come to you."

Then they were gone.

56

With a pounding heart, Nicole drove back to the one-pump where she gassed up Penny Lane and used the facilities. Then she went hunting for the dirt road that teed-off three or four miles up ahead, the one that may or may not lead to Daniel Flagger's place. She expected a well-worn graded road and almost missed it when it turned out to be a rutted jeep trail choked with weeds.

Penny Lane would never make it.

She'd bottom-out within a hundred yards.

Nicole sat there in the silence, deciding, then drove another half-mile around a bend and parked Penny Lane in the weeds, where she wasn't visible from the trail. Then she headed back on foot and started in, not knowing if the trek would be two hundred yards or five miles. So far, nothing was in sight. The air was quiet. If a car came from either direction, either heading in or leaving, she'd be able to hear it in plenty of time to hide.

The sun was even more of a demon than before, doing everything it could to own her.

A mile in, structures suddenly appeared up ahead, looking like an old ranch that was no longer being operated—a wooden house, several large barn-like structures, corals, and long stretches of wooden fence posts and curled barbwire. The rusty hulks of old tractors and dilapidated cars littered the grounds.

Nicole's first thought was that there'd be a million places to stash someone like Danica, and that wasn't even counting the underground chambers or concrete vaults that could have been added over the years.

No dogs barked.

Flagger's pickup truck wasn't in sight.

There was no indication that anyone was currently there.

Nicole picked up the pace, ever ready to dive into the weeds if she had to, and made her way to the rusty shell of an old tireless car squatting on cinderblocks. From there she surveyed the grounds for signs of life, particularly the front door of the house, which was closed.

Nothing moved.

Nothing made a noise.

No music played.

No sounds of work wove through the air.

Flagger's pickup truck, from this vantage point, still wasn't visible, nor was any other car except the useless rusted out hulks that actually seemed to be multiplying.

With her gun in hand, she quickly trotted through the open air to the house, put her ear to the front door and listened. No sounds or movements or vibrations came from within. She slowly tried the knob to find it locked. Then she made her way to one of the front windows, which was halfway up, and peered in from an angle to see something in the nature of a living room, with a couch, a number of chairs, lamps, an old rabbit-ears TV and the like. A shotgun sat silently on the coffee table in front of the couch, next to a pile of crumpled beer cans and a stack of girlie magazines. The pages of the top one fluttered from the wind of a floor fan, flipping a pair of oversized breasts in and out of view. She stuck her head all the way in the window and got more of the same, plus a glimpse into a kitchen that had an old yellow refrigerator.

She swallowed, deciding, and then said, "Hello? Is anyone

home?"

No one answered.

"Is anybody here?"

Only silence responded.

With that, she muscled her way up and through the window and dropped noisily down on the other side, inside the structure, where she held her breath and listened. No one came screaming or rushing at her. She was alone. Then with her gun in hand she called out, "Danica! Danica Rose! Are you here?"

No response came.

She shouted louder, "Danica! I'm a detective. I'm here to help!"

No answer came.

That didn't mean she wasn't here, though. She could be tied up and gagged, or deep in a crazy unconsciousness from being shot up with drugs.

Come on!

Be here!

She headed into the kitchen and found bills addressed to Daniel Flagger—good, she had the right place.

A narrow set of creaky stairs led to an upper level hallway with a bathroom at the end. If Flagger was Hollywood he might have a shrine. It would more than likely be up here.

One of the rooms was filled with junk, none of which looked like souvenirs from murders. Another was a bedroom with an unmade bed; nothing unusual there. The bathroom was normal with no prescriptions in the medicine cabinet for mental illness or the like.

There was one room left.

The door to it was closed.

Nicole turned the knob and stood back as she pushed the door open, in case it was booby-trapped. Inside on folding tables that covered most of the square footage were fifty or more glass aquariums of varying sizes. Inside those aquariums were snakes, all kinds of seriously freaky snakes, some of which had to be at least ten feet long. In the corner on the floor was a 55-gallon aquarium squirming with a hundred or more live mice and rats. A smaller aquarium next to it was filled with crickets and grasshoppers, all busy jumping on each other. A hand-made wooden box half the size of a coffin sat on the floor near the back wall under one of the folding tables. On top of it sat an old unplugged AM/FM radio covered with a decade of dust. It looked like that kind of thing you could buy at a flea market for a buck. Most of the snakes ignored Nicole's entry, but one—a thick boa constrictor—was now raising its head and flicking its tongue and staring at her with lifeless eyes. She had a brief vision of it sinking fangs into her face and then wrapping itself around her head and neck and staying exactly like that until it squeezed every last molecule of oxygen out of her lungs. It was vivid enough to make her get out, now, and pull the door closed securely behind her.

Danica was supposed to be killed by way of rattlesnake.

That's something Daniel Flagger had. He also had the ability to cut off a rattlesnake's head and put it in a jar on Danica's kitchen counter.

Nicole's pulse tightened.

Daniel Flagger was Hollywood.

She was almost positive of it.

That meant Danica could very well be here on the grounds somewhere, assuming she was still alive.

Nicole checked the basement, which turned out to be a damp creepy-crawly space with a low ceiling, exposed joists, and an eon's worth of boxes and crap and spider webs. Danica wasn't there, not behind the furnace, not under the stair crawlspace, not anywhere.

Upstairs, Nicole slipped out the back door and made her way down a dirt path to a barn-like structure in the back.

The large front doors were chained together and locked.

There was no getting in that way.

Nicole headed around to the right side and found a steel man-door, which was odd for a structure like this. The knob was locked, plus there was a second lock above it, no doubt for a dead bolt.

She kept going.

At the back end was a large, modern garage door, the kind you'd find in any normal neighborhood. The outside handle was locked. There was no way to get it up, not without the remote.

She continued around to the other side where she found a high window. She rolled a rusty 55-gallon drum under it, got up and busted the glass in with an old two-by-four, chipping away the jagged edges that remained in the wood. She threw an old tarp across the bottom edge, muscled her way through and dropped down on the other side.

She was in an extremely large dark space that smelled like stale wood.

The air was coffin-quiet.

She shouted, "Danica!"

57

Nicole knew in her heart that everything was about to end, one way or the other. She made her way carefully into the guts of the structure, one silent step at a time, barely able to see what was in front of her.

"Danica!"

No one answered.

At the back end, a faint line of sunlight showed at the bottom of the garage door. She headed over and ran her hands blindly along the sides of the door, looking for an opener, but found none. Nor could she find any kind of handle to unlatch.

As her eyes adjusted to the darkness she was able to pick out the walls, the dark silhouette of a tractor's old carcass, several high storage areas and, over in the corner, a large walled room, which would be the perfect kind of place to stash Danica. It turned out to have a locked steel door. She pounded on it and shouted, "Danica!"

Not a sound or vibration or sleepy moan or sense of movement came from inside.

Lying in the dirt by the wall, she found an old wooden ladder handmade out of two-by-fours and nails, which she muscled upright against one of the large storage areas and climbed up. There she found lots of dusty forgotten junk but no sign of Danica.

On her way down a rung suddenly snapped out from under her.

She dropped, trying to hang on as she fell, landing hard on the ground and bringing the ladder down on top of her. White-hot pain shot up her spine and stabbed into her brain. She tried to push the ladder off but couldn't, not from this position.

Then, like lightning, something happened.

The door at the side of the structure opened.

A man stepped inside, flicked on a flashlight and headed straight for the room in the corner.

Nicole didn't breathe.

She didn't move, not a single solitary muscle.

Her gun was no longer in her grip.

It had fallen somewhere.

She had no idea where.

The man walked right past without seeing her, unlocked the door to the room and pulled it open. The walls of the room were lined with vividly bright flat-screen monitors, displaying what appeared to be live streams from video cameras that must have been secretly placed at hidden locations; there were bedrooms, living rooms, pool areas, car interiors, and on and on, each with people present. Some of the monitors were black, meaning the cameras must be motion activated and there was no motion to detect for those cameras right now. Stacks and stacks of DVD recorders sat on the floor, flicking digital displays and being busy preserving it all. The man—now clearly visible as Daniel Flagger—cast his eyes over the monitors. Nicole expected him to focus on the one that showed a fat man spanking a stunning young blond on her bare behind, no doubt a prostitute or high-money escort. Instead, he focused on the monitor next to it— an elegant woman talking into a phone—and brought up the volume.

Nicole couldn't make out the specific words but the voice sounded familiar.

Where had she heard it before?

At a party?

On the TV?

Yeah, maybe it was that—the TV.

Suddenly one of the black screens jumped to life and Nicole couldn't believe what she saw. It was her loft; her loft, not some stranger's, *hers*. Fallon had just come through the door and was heading for the fridge. Nicole's heart pounded like a thousand maniac drums and she had to stifle the noises that were rising up in her throat.

Get out of here!

Get out!

Get out!

She felt around for her gun but couldn't locate it anywhere.

Flagger was kneeling down now, checking the DVD recorders and changing out some of the discs. A gun was tucked into the back of his belt.

Nicole used all her strength to muscle out from underneath the ladder. Flagger's back was still to her. He hadn't heard anything. He hadn't detected the motion. The outside door that he'd come in through was halfway open. Sunlight was squirting through it.

Get to it and get out!

Nicole stood up and made sure she had her balance.

She was in plain view.

All Flagger had to do was turn his body or his head ever so slightly, just enough to let his peripheral vision swing over. Nicole moved towards the door, one silent step at a time, praying that Flagger just kept doing what he was doing for just a little longer.

Ten more seconds; that's all she needed.

Ten little seconds.

58

Somehow, someway, Nicole made it all the way to the door without Flagger turning around, and immediately kept moving as fast as her broken body would take her, all the way down the side of the barn and then around the back corner, where she stopped and listened. No one was coming for her but that didn't mean she had much time. Flagger might see the ladder down, or the window broken, or the gun in the dirt.

What to do?

There was a shotgun in the house, on the table, but once Flagger finished up in the barn that would probably be exactly where he'd head.

She was in full sun.

It was already starting to heat her up and draw her energy.

Right or wrong, she headed over to the second barn, a smaller structure, even though she had to be in plain view most of the way. She slipped around the back, now firmly out of sight, and took her first real breath of calm air.

A door at the back pushed in easily.

Inside, the light was good, streaming in through broken planks in the roof and sides.

Danica wasn't there.

There were a couple of random storage sheds farther back

but the chance of Danica being in one of them was almost zero. Nicole checked them anyway. Danica wasn't in them.

Nicole knew what to do.

She needed to get the shotgun and force Flagger to tell her where the woman was. If he didn't, she'd blow him away; simple as that.

She made her way to where she could see the side of the first barn and was surprised to see that the steel man-door on the side was now fully shut.

Suddenly, the garage door at the back of the barn lifted up.

Flagger came out riding on a green Yamaha dirt bike and disappeared down a narrow path into the terrain as the door closed behind him.

Where are you going, bitch?

To check on Danica?

She waited until the noise of the engine faded off and then made her way back to the barn; the barn that had her gun somewhere inside. The side door was locked. Dropping through the window again might be too much for her body; plus there would be the problem of getting back out.

Forget it.

She broke back into the house and thankfully found the shotgun still sitting on the coffee table exactly where it should be. It was loaded but that only gave her two shots. She hunted around long enough to find a box of shells in a kitchen drawer. She grabbed them, put on a Marlins baseball cap, and took a long, long drink of water from the kitchen sink. Then she made her way to the dirt path and followed it into the terrain.

It wasn't hard to follow.

It had definitely been used a lot more than once.

She followed it for a full mile without anything yet appearing up ahead.

She kept going.

A second mile passed.

The sun beat down.

Her body had never been so hot.

Even with the three tons of water she'd stuffed into her gut, she was already thirsty again.

She kept going.

Forty-five minutes later she came to a road, as abandoned and desolate as all the other roads out here in this part of the universe. Nicole tried to gauge which direction Flagger would had gone but had no luck.

It didn't matter anyway.

He was gone.

Now what?

She guessed, for one, she could head back to Flagger's place and check it out better. Maybe there was some kind of paper trail that hinted as to where the man might have stashed Danica. Plus, that big wooden box in the snake room—what was in that? If there was something Flagger didn't want anyone to find—say glass jars with spinners on top—that would be the perfect stashing place. It would be worth the effort to find a hammer and pry it open. Just thinking about going back in that room, though, sent a creep up her spine.

It would also be worthwhile to get into that surveillance room in the barn.

How many DVDs did Flagger have recorded of Nicole?

Who were all the other people under surveillance, and why?

Her throat was sandpaper.

A hundred yards to the left, across the road, was an old shuttered pre-fabricated metal building, the kind used for machine shops, body shops and the like.

Maybe it had an outside water faucet.

She approached to find the entire building encased by a chain-link fence that had barbed wire at the top. On the front of the structure was a sign that said, Morgan Sign Company. Hanging in the window of the front door was paper sign that said, Closed. Below that, hand-written in black magic marker, were the words, Out of Business.

An old driveway and parking lot had once been asphalt.

Now hundreds of thistles and weeds sprouted up from the cracks and ruptures.

Lizards scampered everywhere, billions of them.

There was no sign of an outside faucet.

Suddenly Nicole had a strange thought.

Danica, are you in there?

Is this where Flagger went to check?

59

With the shotgun in her hand and panic in her blood, Nicole headed up the road towards the metal building as if it was the gate of hell itself, realizing full well that if Danica was in there so was Flagger.

If you see Danica, kill Flagger immediately.

He'll no longer be of any use.

Don't hesitate.

Blow his putrid head off.

Blow it as far as it will go.

She approached through the brush from the side of the building where there were no windows, scanning the eaves for surveillance cameras. If they were there, they weren't readily visible. The area behind the building was exactly as it should be, littered with rusty old drums, a broken ladder, a cracked toilet, old discarded signs and years and years of other junk.

Most importantly, Flagger's motorcycle wasn't there.

As Nicole circled the building, it wasn't anywhere else, either.

Her heart sunk.

She'd been wrong.

It was then that she noticed something unusual; the chain locking the front gates shut was rusty but the padlock looked like it was bought yesterday.

She shoved the shotgun under the fence to the dirt on the other side, took off her shirt, climbed up the chain-link and put the cloth over the top of the barbed wire. Slowly, she maneuvered her body over the barbs without ripping her flesh to shreds, and dropped down on the other side.

The front door was locked tight, so was the large overhead delivery door to the left. Nicole headed around back, broke a window with a rock and waited outside with the barrel of the shotgun pointed in.

Flagger didn't show his face.

He didn't come around a corner to see what the noise was, not in two seconds, not in a minute.

Nicole exhaled, hoping she wasn't being trapped, and climbed in.

What she found wasn't what she expected.

Instead of a filthy abandoned shop of some sort, she found a clean dry-walled interior with a kitchen, a shower, and a closet full of clothes that looked like Flagger's size, including three expensive suits, a half-dozen pressed white dress shirts, a number of silk ties and three pairs of very nice leather dress shoes, two black and one brown. Flagger's old clothes—the ones he'd been wearing when he left the barn on the dirt bike—were hanging over a chair. Dirty work boots sat below, with white cotton socks stuffed inside.

More important than the clothes, there was a large garage area big enough to hold two cars.

Flagger's green Yamaha dirt bike was in that space.

No car was there.

He must have changed clothes, swapped out the bike for a car and gone somewhere.

"Danica! Are you here?"

The woman was nowhere to be found, not inside, not outside, not in some secret hidden chamber.

Nicole paced.

Then, for whatever reason her brain made her do it, she pointed the shotgun at the dirt bike and blew it to hell.

60

Nicole made a sandwich, drank her fill of water and took up a place in hiding in the bushes and weeds across the road from the building, where she waited.

Sooner or later Flagger would return.

She'd be here when he did.

He would either tell her where Danica was or he'd get a taste of his own shotgun. It was that simple. She was done screwing around.

An hour passed.

That was okay.

If Flagger switched into a suit and took a nice car somewhere, it could very well be Miami. Just driving there and back would take hours in and of itself, on top of whatever meeting or adventure he had scheduled.

Be patient.

He'll be back sooner or later.

Another hour passed.

Her eyes got heavy from the relentless Florida heat. They wanted to close in the worst way. Her thoughts kept drifting to the cans of cold diet Pepsi in the fridge and the granola bars up in the cupboard.

Why didn't she grab them before she slipped out?

Should she head back?

It would be safe, except for the few brief minutes when she was getting over the fence, which she could do at the back. The chance of Flagger returning at that exact wrong moment was almost zero. It was basically safe if she wanted to expend the energy.

So, should she?

Give it a little more time.

Just a little more.

It'll still be there when you need it.

The air was quiet and peaceful.

An occasional grouping of crows flew by and, of course, there were the small white butterflies constantly darting here and there, and the shadows changed ever so slowly as the sun crept across the sky, but other than that the place could have been in a time capsule.

Nicole laid down on her back in the shade and closed her eyes.

It was the right thing to do.

It was exactly what her body and mind needed.

She'd be able to hear Flagger's car if it came.

It was okay to rest; in fact, it was actually a good idea.

Ash Colt.

What was he doing right now? He'd probably tried to call her and she hadn't called him back yet. Was he worried? Had he called three more times trying to get through?

Everything slowly softened.

It felt so damn good.

Just give in to it.

It's okay.

No one's going to blame you.

At some point later Nicole felt sun on her face and realized that she'd fallen asleep for so long that the sun had actually shifted in the sky. Something else was wrong though, beyond that. She could feel it.

Her watch said 5:30 p.m.

She'd been out a long time.

She got into a sitting position and checked the building across the road. It was exactly as the last time she'd seen it. Flagger hadn't come back yet.

No, wait.

The front gates were closed but the chain that had been holding them shut was now lying on the ground. Nicole got to her feet, shook herself awake and double-checked to make sure the shotgun was loaded.

Then she headed towards the building.

61

Nicole pushed through the gate, silently returned it to a closed position, and crept up to the front door of the building. It was locked as before. She swung around to the back and peered inside through the broken window.

She saw nothing.

Everything looked the same but somehow it was slightly different. She concentrated, desperate to figure it out. Then she realized what it was. There was a faint whiff of smoke in the air. Was Flagger in there somewhere sucking on a cigarette?

What to do?

Wait for him to come out, or climb in the back window and blast around the corner when he least suspected it?

She'd blast in.

She couldn't sit back and wait for him.

Her mind wasn't built for that anymore.

Carefully, as silently as she could, she maneuvered her body through the window, completely vulnerable during each and every one of those precious seconds. Then she was in, square on her feet with the shotgun firmly in hand.

She took a deep sigh of relief.

Okay, this is it.

If you see Danica, shoot Flagger in the head or chest. Kill him as dead as you can.

If you don't see her, shoot the bastard in the knees.

Do it on three.

One . . . two . . . three!

She swung around the corner, saw no one, and proceeded quickly down a short hall, past the kitchen, past the closet, past the shower, to the end.

The door there was closed.

On the other side of that closed door was the garage area.

That's where Flagger was.

It was the only place left.

Nicole thought about putting her ear to the door but didn't want to take a chance of getting knocked back if the man suddenly came swinging through.

She swallowed.

Okay, this is it.

Don't be afraid.

You can do it.

With the speed of lightning and with a tight finger on the trigger, she pulled the door open and charged in.

To her shock, Flagger wasn't there.

His motorcycle was there, exactly how she'd left it—blasted to hell—but Flagger wasn't there, nor was a car present as it should be if he returned to make the exchange. Also, strangely, the cigarette smell wasn't hanging in the air anymore, but that could be because she'd gotten used to it.

What the hell?

She double-checked every crack and crevice in the building just to be sure he wasn't there or hadn't returned and stuffed Danica somewhere.

No one was there.

Only her.

Confused, she climbed back out the window and made her way to the front fence. The chain was clearly on the ground;

the lock was lying there next to it, now that she took a second look.

The smell of smoke was back.

It was then that she saw something horrific. A black plume of fiery smoke was shooting high into the sky from the far distance, approximately where Flagger's house was.

Nicole's heart sank.

She immediately knew what happened.

He'd returned to the metal building—possibly with Danica—and saw the motorcycle shot to hell. He knew someone was hot on his trail and went home to see if someone had been there too. In the house, he found the shotgun missing. In the barn, he found the broken window, and the broken ladder, and possibly even Nicole's gun. He burned the whole crazy place to the ground and got the hell out of there while the going was good.

Nicole pictured the monitors and computers and discs melting to oblivion in the flames.

She pictured the snakes frantic in their cages as the fires of death relentlessly came for them.

If Danica were still alive, she wouldn't be for long. If Flagger had her with him, she'd be an anchor to his escape. He'd kill her quickly, if he hadn't done so already, and dump her body at the first reasonable place. If Flagger had her stashed somewhere, he might just leave her there and concentrate on getting away. She'd die a lonely agonizing death.

Nicole sank to the ground.

This was all her fault.

She should never have shot the motorcycle.

It felt good at the time but it was so stupid.

Flagger seeing it—that's what set everything in motion. Sure, he might have seen the broken window in the back, but probably not. He would definitely see the motorcycle when he returned, though. Shooting it was the stupidest thing in the world that anyone could have done.

Tears built up in Nicole's eyes.

She had time to wipe them but let them go.

They rolled down her face like rivers in the desert.

Danica, I'm sorry.

I failed you.

I did something stupid and you'll be the one who has to pay for it.

I'm sorry.

I'm so very, very sorry.

62

Nicole made it home just as the shadows of night swept over Miami to find that Fallon wasn't at the loft and hadn't left a note as to where she went or when she'd be back. She stuck her phone in the charger and found a considerable number of texts, missed calls and voice messages. She wanted to call Ash Colt, have him come over and hold her tighter than tight until the morning. Instead, she made the call she had to, the one to Trane, and said, "Can you come over? I have some stuff I need to tell you."

A pause, then, "Where have you been? I called you ten times today."

"I'll explain."

"There's not supposed to be anything to explain. I put you on two-week suspension, remember?"

"Come over and we'll talk. Do it now before I change my mind."

She hung up before the man could respond.

Then she grabbed a bottle of wine and headed up to the roof where she took a seat on the pulpit and dangled her legs over the edge of the building. She took a long swallow from the bottle. Almost immediately everything softened. All she had to do was lean forward into the darkness. Everything would be over in two seconds; two measly seconds—and, puff!—

wham, bam, thank you ma'am.

The headlights of Trane's pickup punched into the parking lot fifteen minutes later.

"Up here," she shouted.

He found her sitting on the edge and hesitated a moment, deciding, then said, "What the hell—," and joined her.

She handed him the bottle.

He took a long swig and said, "You okay?"

"Yeah, sure, why not?" she said. "Hollywood is a man named Daniel Flagger. I had him dead to rights. I was this close, Nick, this close, and I let him get away." She took a swig of wine and added, "I did a lot of stupid things today and that's why he got away. At first I wasn't going to tell anyone; not you, not Pantage, not anyone. I was going to keep my big mouth shut and keep my dumb-ass mistakes to myself and try to save my job and all that. But I have to tell you so you can get resources on Flagger's trail, just in case there's a one percent chance that Danica is still alive. I don't want her rotting to death chained up somewhere all alone if there's even one stinking chance in hell that we can find something at one of these scenes, no matter how small, that might point us to where she is."

Trane patted her knee.

"Okay, we're going to back up and start at the beginning, all right?"

"Sure."

With that, he asked her questions in that calm, professional way of his, and she answered them. When they were done, Trane knew it all—the second wrecked airplane, the severed head and the Blackbird Ordinary menu inside, the pit of bodies, the snake room, the surveillance room, Fallon on camera, the fat guy spanking the blonde, the dirt path, the metal building, the shot to hell motorcycle, the fence chain in the dirt, the fires that destroyed everything, the whole damn thing.

At the end Trane said, "I'll be honest with you. I like you, I really do, I think you know that. But if Danica ends up dead, everyone's going to make you the fall guy. They're going to second-guess everything you've done. You're job will be history. I won't be able to save you." He looked into the night, then at her and added, "Get some sleep. You're exhausted. Be at the station in the morning."

Then he was gone.

She called after him, "Hey, Nick."

He stopped at the fire escape.

"Yeah?"

"Would you have done something different? If all that stuff happened to you this afternoon?"

He considered it.

"Some things, yeah."

The words felt like a tire iron to the back of her head.

"Like what? Which things?"

"Remember when you went and used the bathroom at that one-pump place?"

"Yeah—"

"I would have used it standing up. Other than that, yeah, I probably would have done everything the same as you."

She smiled, ever so slightly.

Then she said, "See you in the morning."

"Right."

She stayed on the pulpit where she watched the man walk to his truck, flick the lights on and drive away. As the red of the taillights disappeared into the night, she sent a text to Fallon— Where are you?—and kept the phone in her hand as she waited for a response. Ten seconds later it rang. She answered without even looking at the number, expecting Fallon's voice.

It wasn't Fallon's voice though.

It was a different one.

"Miss Stone, this is Sophia Brown, the private investigator from El Paso. I'm sorry I'm calling so late. I hope I'm not waking you up."

The name, Sophia Brown, sent bark and bite into Nicole's brain; not because of the woman herself—no, she was fine, in fact she was on Nicole's side. It sent bark and bite because it reminded Nicole of the whole other horrific reality in her life, the reality that had mercifully suppressed itself during the many hours that Nicole had been chasing Hollywood. The floodgates were suddenly opening and it was all coming back like a sick disease that had never actually gone away.

"No, no, this is fine," Nicole said.

"Good," the woman said. "I know that I told you before that I had a suspicion that the lawyer who runs El Paso Helicopter Services, Mia Notaro, might have a connection to Jafet el Perro."

"Right—"

"Well, I've been digging into it," Sophia said. "I still don't have any concrete proof one way or the other but one thing is interesting. The law firm that Mia Notaro is in represents a number of banks on both sides of the border. It's possible that she could be moving Jafet's money around and getting it into seemingly bona fide accounts under various shell names."

"For what purpose?"

"To move money across the border, mostly, but also so the cartel can purchase things in the United States where it might need to use a legitimate check or credit card or line of credit," Sophia said. "Real estate, airline tickets, cell phones, whatever; anything where a bag of cash won't work. Mia Notaro has a ton of banking connections and may be using them to Jafet's advantage. The problem is, I doubt that I'll ever be able to get the details and prove the theory one way or the other. Banks are too confidential even when they're doing normal stuff. If they're actually bending the rules it will be even worse."

"Forget the proof," Nicole said. "The theory's good enough at this point. What about the El Paso Helicopter Service? Is she moving Jafet's money through it, too?"

"My guess?" Sophia said. "Probably not, there wouldn't be enough volume to make it worthwhile. My guess is that Jafet had the lawyer set up the helicopter as an escape measure, in case he really gets his back against the wall. I'm sure his money funded the whole thing."

"Makes sense," Nicole said. "At this point let's just assume that the lawyer's working for Jafet. See if you can find a way to get to her."

"As in what, dirt?"

"Dirt, weaknesses, fears, whatever. I want something to use as leverage against her. I want to force her mouth open and tell me what I want to know."

"She'd never talk against Jafet. It would be suicide; worse than suicide, actually."

"Maybe, but I'll never know until I get her between a rock and a hard place. Right now all I have is a hard place. Keep digging. Find the rock." Nicole paused and then added, "I'm pretty sure she knew that one of her helicopters was being used to snatch me over here in Miami and fly me down to El Paso. Hell, she might have even arranged the whole thing. See if you can get any proof of that. See if you can find out if she has any connections to a man who goes by the name of Thiago Cruz or a pretty woman called Juana; she might have a daughter that The Dog took to force her to do stuff. Are you getting all this?"

"Yeah, I'm writing it down—Thiago Cruz, Juana, daughter. Got it."

"See if you can find out who was flying the helicopter."

The woman moaned.

"Anything else? Where they buried Jimmy Hoffa's body or anything like that?"

Nicole smiled.

Then she said, "The guy, Thiago Cruz, might have a connection to someone named Alejandra, who might work in a bar in Juarez bar called El Hoyo."

"The Hole—"

"Do you know it?"

"Yeah. It's right across the river."

"Good. Find out what she knows."

"I'll go there tonight," Sophia said. "I'll call you in the morning and let you know how it went."

Nicole hung up, dialed Ash Colt and said, "Can you come over?"

"Where are you, home?"

"Yeah."

"Are you okay?"

"Yeah, mostly."

A beat, then he said, "I'm on my way."

63

Nicole got a fresh bottle of wine from the loft, plus two glasses and a Bluetooth speaker, and headed back up to the roof to wait for Ash. A soft patina of yellow light shimmered through the air from a rising moon. On her phone, she pulled up one of her favorite songs in the world, Devil Doll's sultry Bourbon in Your Eyes, set it on repeat and played it through the Bluetooth speaker. When Ash showed up she called him to the roof, said "Don't talk," and handed him a glass of wine as he sat on the pulpit.

Then she danced for him.

She danced slowly, with her hips swaying seductively and her arms raised, caught up in her own spell, as if there was nothing in the whole freaking world except this moment and this place and this song and this person who suddenly had his eyes busy trying to memorize her every move.

She could feel his intensity.

She could feel his needs.

She could feel his lust.

She could feel the blood in his veins getting hotter and crazier with every gyration of her body.

Call me Angel and take my hand,
Wishing you could be my man.
But I can't tell if it's truth or lies,

When you got bourbon in your eyes.

This dance wasn't for him; it was for her.

She knew that.

She needed someone to look at her and want her and not care about her flaws or what she did right or what she did wrong. She needed someone to look at her and actually see her. She didn't want to be invisible, not right now; tomorrow, fine, but not right now.

She pulled her hair loose and shook it.

Then she grabbed the bottom of her T-shirt and slowly raised it up, past her stomach, past her breasts, past her neck and then over he head. She swung it like a victory flag and tossed it at Ash.

He caught it.

He caught it good.

It was his now.

He didn't let it go.

> *Tell me something that I don't know,*
> *Then I dare you to prove it so.*
> *I'd ask you to try this on for size,*
> *But you got bourbon in your eyes.*

Her bra came off next.

Then her pants.

Then her panties.

The night air felt so damn good on her body.

She danced with her eyes closed, swaying, never ever wanting this moment to end. Then, suddenly, Ash was there with her, with his arms around her, and his body tight against hers, and every molecule of his body on fire.

DAY FIVE

September 19
Friday

64

Nicole rolled over in bed Friday morning to find that Ash wasn't there and the room was flooded with sunlight. The clock said ten, long past what it should. She had to use the facilities like crazy but instead first looked around to see if Ash had left a note. He had, on the kitchen table. She grabbed it, ran to the bathroom and read it as she went.

> *You're so sweet talking,*
> *And you're so fire walking,*
> *I know I shouldn't but I want some—*

She recognized the lyrics, from Devil Doll, and smiled.

Then she took a long hot shower, filled her gut with cereal and coffee and called Trane, who didn't answer. She tried Pantage second, who did answer.

"Where are you?" she asked.

"Right now, at the body pit. We're taking them out one by one. Most of them are young women. You can come out and join us if you want."

"We'll see. What about Daniel Flagger?"

"We have BOLOs out all over the state but there's no sign of him yet," Pantage said. "We're not sure what he's driving, plus we don't think that's his real name."

"Why not?"

"No digital trail, nothing."

"So he made it up—"

"That's my belief."

"What about Danica? Any sign of her?"

"Not yet, unfortunately."

"There has to be something—"

"We're questioning people that live in the area, trying to find out who Flagger is, what he does, where he goes, and all that. So far we're not getting much. The man kept to himself. People were a little bit afraid of him. They did their business and smiled but didn't ask questions."

"What about his house?"

"Actually, Trane and a team are up there as we speak. We're sifting through the ashes but don't have our hopes up for much. It turns out that Flagger had lots of gasoline stashed here and there. He did a lot of preparation to be sure everything got totally destroyed if the need ever arose. That goes for both the house and the barn."

"What about the second barn, the one farther back?"

"It's still standing but there's no indication he ever used it."

"Damn, Pantage, do you have anything good to say?"

"The hunt's still young, Nicole. Be patient. Do you still have Flagger's shotgun?"

"Yes."

"Take it down to headquarters and bag it into evidence; and don't forget, just because Flagger's on the run, that doesn't mean you're safe. Watch your back."

"My back's fine."

"I mean it, Nicole. Don't let your guard down for one second. We're not positive yet that Flagger is Hollywood."

"He is."

"Maybe yes, maybe no. Maybe the real Hollywood is still out there getting a kick out of the fact that we're so distracted. He could be within a hundred yards of you even as we speak.

Act like he is until we can get all of this sorted out."

Nicole called Fallon, got dumped into voicemail, then hung up and sent the woman a text, "Where are you?"

She did the dishes as she waited for a response.

None came, not in one minute, not in five.

Nicole told herself not to panic. Daniel Flagger was on the run and even if Fallon had been his intended victim all along, there was no indication he had her or had the time or opportunity to go after her.

Still, where was the woman?

Putting the last dish in the dishwasher, she suddenly remembered where she'd seen the blond before, the one who was on the Daniel Flagger's monitor in the barn, the one getting spanked by the fat man. She was a prostitute that Nicole actually busted two years ago when she was working vice.

What was her name again?

Pepper?

Pristine?

No, Poison.

That was it, Poison.

Why were you on Daniel Flagger's monitor, Poison?

What do you know about him that might help us?

65

Nicole rolled Penny Lane to a stop in front of a hooker bar called the Paradise Lounge, killed the engine and headed inside. It was as she remembered—dark, smoky, and sticky. Two hookers sipping warm beer at the bar briefly eyed her as she walked in. Two others cuddled in booths with customers. Dim music fell out of cheap ceiling speakers. Nicole had been here plenty of times before, back in her early days working vice, dressed like a slut, sipping beer at the bar and hauling in every slob who thought she'd be oh-so-happy to suck them off for the crumpled twenty in their pocket.

Not quite, baby.

Not quite.

Someone new was behind the bar—a guy in his thirties wearing a wife-beater shirt, with greasy hair and an ex-con vibe.

"I'm looking for Poison," Nicole said. The man looked her up and down like she was a lollipop dipped in sugar. Nicole cut him off before he said something that would piss her off. "I'm a cop," and said, "and I'm not in a particularly good mood. Poison—where can I find her?"

The man took a long drag on a cigarette, put his elbows on the counter and leaned in.

Nicole leaned in, playing along.

The man said, "She don't come around here no more."

"So where can I find her?"

"I don't know," he said. "I'm not good at finding things. I've been trying to find a fifty all morning and haven't had any luck."

Nicole pulled a twenty out of her purse and set it on the counter but still kept a finger on it.

"Where is she?"

The man grabbed the bill, briefly contemplated holding out for more, judging by the look on his face, and shoved it in his pocket. Then he blew smoke in Nicole's face and said, "Try Ladies en Secret." Nicole knew the place. It was mostly a high-end, ultra-chic escort service that scheduled meet-ups from the web, but it also had a physical location.

She took the man's cigarette from his lips, mashed it on the counter and said, "Those things will kill you. You're welcome."

Then she was gone.

Twenty minutes later she pulled into an industrial park on the edge of the city. The place had seen better days. Half the buildings were unoccupied and had the weeds and plywood to prove it. At the far end, all the way back by the railroad tracks, she pulled into a parking lot in front of a large windowless brick building. Over a dozen cars sat motionless in the sun, waiting. There she killed the engine and walked across the cracked asphalt, past a shiny new red Corvette with a license plate Dr Dan, to a pink steel door. Stenciled in black were the words, Ladies en Secret.

Inside, she was greeted by a busty young thing, not more than twenty, who didn't recognize her.

Nicole said, "Well, aren't you the yummy one?"

The girl smiled.

"Thanks."

"You're welcome. I'm looking for Poison."

The girl checked a monitor screen that was pointed out of Nicole's view.

"Do you have an appointment?"

"No."

"She's not here right at the moment but she's on call. You can have an hour slot, starting in about thirty minutes, if you're interested."

"That'll be fine."

"Awesome. That'll be three hundred fifty, and includes dancing," the girl said. "Gratuities are on top of that and will need to be paid directly to the dancer before the session begins. The house takes cash or credit card. Direct tips need to be paid in cash. If you need cash, we can forward you up to five hundred and add it to your credit card."

Nicole dug out her Visa and handed it over.

The girl said, "Your statement won't say Ladies en Secret. It'll say Charity Foundation. Are you good with that?"

"Yes."

"Do you want cash too?"

She considered it.

"Yeah, give me five."

The woman smiled and said, "You are in for one wild ride. You won't regret a dollar of it. What kind of room do you want? We have Bangkok Hotel, Classroom, Bar, New York Office, Bondage—"

"Bondage."

"Bondage it is."

"Hard or sensual?"

"Sensual."

"Good choice."

Two minutes later Nicole was walking down an elegant, dimly lit corridor with doors on either side painted in different colors. High-quality music filled the space, masking what little noise might be escaping from behind the doors. She put an

Aqua key into a matching colored door, stepped inside and closed the door behind her.

Soft music and equally soft lighting filled a classy spacious room.

There were a number of places to be tied down; a large bed with crisp fresh sheets, a large padded massage table and an x-frame against the wall, being the obvious ones. There were also chains hanging from the ceiling, plus a wall filled with spreader bars, gags, blindfolds, masks, lots of different-styled cuffs, ropes, and anything else you might need.

In the back, behind a maple door, was a nicely appointed, immaculately clean bathroom with a shower and jetted tub.

She had half an hour to kill.

What to do?

She took a seat on the bed, dialed Fallon and, as before and before and before, got no answer.

Come on, girl.

Stop it.

Then, suddenly, her phone rang and the voice of Sophia Brown came through from El Paso.

"Okay, I made it to El Hoyo last night," the woman said.

"And?"

"Our friend Alejandra pours the liquor there, her and a crazy tattooed guy named Carlos. I sat at the bar, bought us both enough shots to kill a donkey, and tipped her to the moon and back. She dared me to dance on the bar, which I was drunk enough to do, for a long time actually, and she did too. By the time the place closed, we were best friends, or so I thought. I was hoping she'd invite me back to her place where I could ask her questions without getting her in danger. Instead, she kissed me on the lips, said It's been nice, baby, and walked out the door like we'd never met. I've been wham-bammed before but never anything like that. Anyway, I hung back a little and then followed her as she headed down the street on foot. That's when two guys saw me."

"Two guys?"

"Yeah."

"Two guys from where, the bar?"

"I don't know."

"So, what happened?"

"Not what they wanted," the woman said "They grabbed me and started to drag me back into an alley but they were as drunk as I was. They had me on the ground and one of them let go for a minute to get his belt unfastened. That's when I managed to break loose and get to my feet. I ran into the night with everything I had. They came after me, hooting and hollering and all like they were chasing some kind of an animal, and they didn't stop and we ended up all the way down at the Rio Grande, where they had me trapped. I dived into the water and they came in after me. One of them got a fist in my hair and started to swim back to shore with me. I managed to reach down and squeeze his balls. He screamed something and his fingers came out of my hair and he went under the water and didn't come back up."

"He drowned?"

"I think so."

"What about the other guy?"

"I don't know," she said. "He came into the river at the same time as the first guy but he disappeared almost immediately. I don't know if he went under the water, or went back to shore, or what."

"Maybe he couldn't swim."

"I'm thinking that's right and the current grabbed him," Sophia said. "He was in the water before his drunk ass even realized it. It got real deep real fast right there. In any event, I'm monitoring the papers and the news to try to figure out who they were. So far I got nothing. I'm hoping that at least one of their bodies gets spotted and pulled out at some point today. With any luck, they're not with the police or a cartel and nobody is going to be out for revenge."

Nicole processed it.

Then she said, "This is way beyond what I ever envisioned. I think we should get you off the case."

Sophia grunted.

"No, no way. I'll call you when I have more information. If they turn out to be nobodies, I'm heading back to the bar tonight."

Then the connection died.

66

When Poison was almost due to arrive, Nicole put on a black mask, stripped down to her panties, and laid on her back on the bed with the five hundred dollars on her stomach. Two minutes later someone knocked on the door.

Nicole raised her arms above her head, wiggled slightly and said, "It's open."

The knob turned and a woman entered. She was blond, stunning and dressed in a short black dress with matching high heels. She took a long look at Nicole and said, "This is going to be fun." Then she locked the door behind her, approached, and ran a finger lightly on Nicole's stomach around the bills.

"Are all these pretty little things for me?" the woman said.

"That depends."

"On what?"

"On how friendly you're willing to get."

The woman slowly brought her mouth to Nicole's neck and gave it a teasing kiss. "I can get very, very friendly," she said.

"Tell me," Nicole said. "What are my options?"

"Unlimited. We can do whatever you want," the woman said. "I can be your slave, you can be mine, we can do whatever you got stored up in those hidden little thoughts of yours. I'm here to make your fantasies come true." She brought her mouth to Nicole's ear, licked it and whispered, "I haven't had a woman in here for awhile. Do you want to feel my tongue between your legs?"

"You'd do that?"

"Oh, yeah, I'll do it like you've never had it done before. I'll tie you up while I do it if you want. I'll make you beg for it."

Nicole moaned.

Then she said, "Why don't you take that all those green things off my stomach. They're yours."

The woman gave Nicole a deep wet kiss, softly picked the bills up and slipped them into a small purse. Then she seductively slipped out of her heels, her dress, her bra and panties, until she was totally naked.

Then Nicole said, "You know what? Let's do something first."

With that, she tied the woman up to the chains hanging from the ceiling, with her arms above her head, stretched so tight that she had to balance on the balls of her feet.

Then she took off the mask.

"Do you recognize me?"

"No."

"Think," Nicole said. "We met once. You weren't so high-society yet. You've come a long way since then. I'm actually impressed."

The woman focused, still unsure, then her eyes flicked.

"Are you that vice cop?"

Nicole smiled.

"Look at all those memory cells busting a move."

The woman struggled to see if she was really bound to the point of no escape.

"This is entrapment," she said.

"Actually, it isn't," Nicole said. "You offered sex for money and then took that money."

The woman hardened her eyes.

"What do you want?"

"Answers to some questions," Nicole said. "None of this, by the way, relates to you. I'm not here to get you or harm you in any way. And the stuff you tell me, I'll never tell anyone it came from you."

"If I talk," the woman said.

Nicole nodded.

"Right, if you talk. You don't have to, of course. We can play it the other way. But you should know that I'm trying to find a young lady by the name of Danica Rose who's been abducted and time really isn't on her side right now. If you help me, you're going to walk out of here a free woman in a few minutes and I'm going to be very grateful."

"I don't know anyone named Danica Rose."

Nicole got her face directly in front of Poison's and said, "How about Daniel Flagger? Do you know him?"

"No."

Nicole pulled up a picture of the man on her cell phone and said, "This is him. Do you know him?"

"Yes. I didn't know his last name. I only knew him as Daniel."

Nicole poked the woman's stomach.

"Yesterday afternoon, you were getting spanked by some fat guy. Am I right?"

"How do you know—"

"Just answer."

"Yes."

"Who was he?"

"This can't come back to me—"

"It won't," Nicole said. "Who was he?"

The woman hesitated, deciding, and then said, "He's a lawyer. His name is Lloyd Price."

"Okay, good," Nicole said. "Did you know that session was

being recorded by Daniel Flagger?"

"Yes."

"So you were working with him?"

"In a way."

"Tell me."

"Look, I don't really know what he's up to," the woman said. "All I know is that I had a spanking session with the lawyer two weeks ago. They're always at his house, the sessions. When it was over and I was heading out to my car, this man walks past me and quietly slips me a hundred dollar bill and says, Drive around the corner and park. I'd like to talk to you about a business proposition. It'll only take two minutes."

"Did you meet him?"

"Yes."

"And that was the first time you ever met him?

"Yes."

"Okay, what happened next?"

"He said he wanted to get a videotape of one of my sessions with the lawyer."

"Why?"

"He wouldn't tell me," the woman said. "What he did say is that I'd be paid ten thousand dollars in advance and he promised that it would never come back to bite me in any way. He said he'd get a miniature camera that looked like lipstick. All I had to do was set it on a table or chair next to my purse. To turn it on, all I'd have to do is push in the end. We met again later. He gave me the camera and the money. My next session with the lawyer was yesterday. I did what I was paid to do. That was it. I don't know anything about this Daniel guy other than what I just told you."

"Do you know what the whole thing was about? Why he wanted to tape the lawyer?"

"I don't have a clue."

"What about Daniel? Did he tell you anything personal about himself—where he lives or what he does or anything like that?"

"No, nothing."

"What about his car? Did you see what he was driving?"

"I did see it, the second time we met, when he gave me the camera and the money, but I really didn't pay that much attention to it. Plus, it was raining out."

"Take a guess."

"If I had to guess, I'd say it was a BMW."

"Something new?"

"Yeah, recent. Four doors."

"What color?"

"Something dark; black, or deep gray, maybe. Like I said, I'm not positive. It's a guess."

Nicole smiled, finally having something, even if it was no more than a guess, and then said, "I know you've looked at this whole thing as Daniel wanting to have video on the lawyer, but he may have actually been wanting it on you. Have you ever considered that?"

The woman shook her head at the idea.

"For ten thousand dollars? No way—"

"He plays games," Nicole said. "He likes to trick people. It would be a cool thing for him to make you think you two were working together and had some big important secret together. If I were you, honestly, I'd get out of town. You're the exact kind of pretty little thing he likes to play with."

67

Outside in the parking lot of Ladies en Secret, Nicole called Trane to let him know that Flagger might be driving a black or dark gray BMW, but he also might not—it was just somebody's guess. Then she headed back to the loft to see if Fallon had shown up yet, which she hadn't; nor did she answer her phone, yet again.

She grabbed a yogurt from the fridge and ran her eyes around the floor and the corners as she ate, a habit now, to make sure the rattlesnake wasn't lying there curled up and ready to strike, which it wasn't. Not spotting it should have given her comfort but it didn't. She'd heard too many stories about snakes living in houses and whatnot for years before anyone officially saw them. They were sneaky little bastards; sneaky little bastards with fangs.

Daniel Flagger's shotgun sat quietly on the kitchen table.

Nicole ran a finger down the barrel.

She was supposed to take it in for processing but she let it sit. It reminded her of how deadly the man was. It also gave her a chance to kill the man with his own weapon if he turned out to be stupid enough to come for her, which at this point would be fine with her.

She'd take it in for processing tomorrow, maybe, if Pantage pressed her.

Now what?

She ran information on the lawyer, Lloyd Price, the guy who liked to spank Poison's tight little ass with his big fat hands. He had no criminal record and from the outside, on paper, looked like a fine upstanding citizen. He turned out to be an uppity-up partner in Lennon & Snow, a large law firm with high offices in the heart of Miami's financial district. Interestingly, the firm had an entertainment law group, headed up by none other than the fat man himself.

So, he did the exact same kind of work as Ash Colt.

A coincidence?

Nicole's chest tightened.

Twenty minutes later she stepped into Lennon & Snow's fancy-schmancy reception area where she announced that she would like to see Lloyd Price if possible but didn't have an appointment. She got pointed to a blue leather chair where she sipped coffee and stared at oil paintings for ten minutes before she was escorted down a spacious corridor to a corner office at the end.

The fat man was behind his desk.

He didn't get up but smiled and waved her into a contemporary leather chair in front of his desk. She felt like Princess Leia in front of Jabba the Hutt. She waited for the door to close behind them and said, "My name's Nicole Stone. I'm a Miami homicide detective. I didn't tell that to the receptionist. I think she believes I'm a potential client. So no one knows you're talking to a cop right now except me and you."

Tension washed over the man's face.

"Okay. I assume someone's dead—"

Nicole nodded.

"I'm trying to locate a man named Daniel Flagger."

The man wrinkled his face and shook his head.

"Never heard of him—"

Nicole pulled Flagger's face up on her phone and said, "This is him."

"Never seen him."

"You're not working with him?"

"No."

"Has he ever made any threats against you?"

"No. Like I said, I've never seen him. I have no idea who he is."

"Do you have any enemies?"

"No more than I should."

"Is there anyone who would like to get dirt on you and blackmail you?"

"That would be a dangerous game," he said. "Should I be worried?"

"I don't know," Nicole said. "Do you know a lawyer by the name of Ash Colt? He does the same kind of work as you."

The man nodded.

"I know him. We chase some of the same clients. We've crossed swords a few times in the past."

"Are you two friends?"

The man laughed.

"No, not hardly."

"Enemies, then?"

The man shrugged.

"To a point I suppose; is he out to get me for some reason?"

"I don't know. What do you think?"

"There's no love lost between us, based on some things that have happened. I don't think he'd ever act, though. He's not that stupid."

"What kinds of things have happened?"

The man receded, then focused on Nicole and said, "We're starting to get into an area that's probably protected by the attorney-client privilege. Sorry, but I'm not at liberty—"

"Was Mr. Colt your client?"

"No."

"Were you his?"

"No, it's something totally different."

"A third person is involved—,' Nicole said.

"Yes. That's all I'm comfortable saying about it."

Nicole looked directly into the man's eyes and said, "What about a girl named Poison? Do you know who she is? Before you answer, I'd remind you that lying to me would be a serious offense. You could end up disbarred."

The man hardened his face.

Then he stood up and said, "I think we're done here."

Nicole nodded.

"Well, I'd like to say it's been nice talking to you," she said. "But I can't."

Then she was gone.

Leaving the building, the strangest thing happened; Nicole spotted the private investigator who'd been in the room next to hers at the Blue Heron Hotel, the man she tried to shoot because she thought he was Hollywood.

He was sitting at the edge of a fountain eating a hot dog.

His face was pointing in her direction but not directly at her.

What the hell?

Nicole headed for him.

Almost immediately, the man got up and walked briskly in the opposite direction, then disappeared around the corner of a building.

That's the third time we've crossed paths.

What's your game?

68

Walking back to Penny Lane, Nicole dialed Fallon yet again, who didn't answer yet again, and then drove over to the woman's house, chasing a long shot. At the front door, the knob was locked and the crime scene tape remained in position. Nicole headed around to the back door where she'd busted the glass before and entered there.

"Fallon? You here?"

No one answered.

Fallon had a mystery lover, a prominent man that she was with the night Danica got taken, someone that Nicole hadn't thought much about but maybe should have.

She'd looked for a lead to him the last time she was here, but she hadn't checked the basement very well and decided to give it another shot.

There she found several old art deco prints being stored in a cylindrical cardboard tube. She pulled them out and unrolled them to find a 9 x 11 clasp envelop inside. Hidden away in that envelope were two curious things.

The first was a bill to Fallon from an Atlanta lawyer by the name of Alex Foster, Esq., in the amount of $450, for 3 hours of "Consulting services," at $150 per hour. It was almost two years old. Hand-written in pencil were the words, "Paid in Cash."

The second was the printout of a Facebook profile for a man named Sean Seven. He looked to be in his mid-twenties and had a party vibe to him. For some reason, he looked familiar, but if Nicole knew him she couldn't place it. The date on the printout showed it was almost two years old, right around the same time as the lawyer's bill.

It was interesting to a point but not relevant. Sean Seven, whoever he was, clearly wasn't Fallon's mystery lover. He was too young plus too far in the past.

Nicole put everything back the way she found it.

Then her phone rang.

It was the El Paso investigator, Sophia Brown.

Her voice was laced with stress.

"It's worse than I thought," she said. "The whole other side of the Rio Grande is going crazy right now."

"Why? What happened?"

"Two bodies got pulled out of the river," she said. "One turned out to be Antonio Diaz, who's way the hell up high in Jafet el Perro's cartel. Some say he's even number two. They call him Chaquoquo, the little dog. The other was Cisco Martinez, who runs point on Jafet's assassinations and interrogations. It's all over the news. Everyone's afraid that a major bloodbath is on the way."

"Get out of El Paso," Nicole said. "Come to Miami and stay with me."

"Thanks, but no."

Nicole said. "Then at least stay off the case. Don't do anything to have Jafet looking your way."

"I'll be careful."

"Sophia, I'm serious. I appreciate your loyalty but it's gotten too dangerous. To be honest, I don't want your blood on my hands."

The woman exhaled and said, "Can I tell you something?"

"Sure."

"Something happened a couple of years ago," she said. "I ended up losing my license. Right now, I don't have a license to operate as a private investigator. I'm sorry I tricked you."

"What happened?"

"Nothing anyone can fix," the woman said. "I developed an alcohol problem, too. Most days are good, I don't touch the stuff; but I have a relapse every now and then. That's what happened when I went to El Hoyo last night. I told myself I'd have just one and stop. It's a lie I use on myself." She exhaled and added, "If I hadn't done that everything would be different right now."

"Look," Nicole said. "I don't care about the license and I don't care about the drinking, unless your lips get loose—"

"They don't."

"What I do care about is you getting in over your head."

"I'm okay," Sophia said. "I can't see a way that Jafet will be able to link the dead guys to me. He'll lay the blame on his enemies and kill them all if he has to. I'd like you to have enough faith in me to continue on. I'll be careful."

Nicole considered it.

Then she said, "Look, I appreciate your efforts, I really do. But I don't want you swept up into whatever violence ends up happening. So let's back off for now. We'll reevaluate everything in a month or two. If things have calmed down, maybe we'll fire it up again at that point. Okay?"

"Jafet's always dangerous," Sophia said. "You need to wrap your head around that and keep it wrapped around tight. He'll be crazier than normal and he'll start lashing out like a madman but he's already got his sights on you. We need to figure out why and how to stop it. If we don't, you probably won't be alive in a month or two, and neither will I." She cleared her throat and added, "There's one more thing I need to disclose to you. Going after Jafet is personal for me. I'd be going after him sooner or later even if I'd never heard your name. The truth is, this case actually gets you in my corner. Having this case actually makes me safer. Does that make any sense?"

"I don't know."

"Have faith. I'll be in touch."

69

Down in her bones, Nicole could feel Daniel Flagger—Hollywood—slipping farther and farther and farther and farther away. When she closed her eyes she could picture him clicking off the miles in a nice air-conditioned BMW, already in another state, smoking a cigarette with a cocky grin on his face, smug in his ability to escape every single time. No one would ever catch him. He knew that. He was too smart, too fast, too different, too strong. He was born for this shit and, for whatever reason, the stars had aligned to keep him doing it for as long as he wanted. Maybe someday he'd get bored and buy a marina down in Key West and go fishing every day. But that day was a long, long ways off. He had way too much to do between now and then. Right now, for instance, he had the next Danica to pick out, and the next detective to kill.

A chill went down Nicole's spine.

She could feel the case already getting cold.

She could look into the future and see the days passing, one by one, with no sign of Danica. The theory of rescue would be replaced by recovery. The insane adrenalin of everyone searching for her would drain away drop by drop until it was bone dry.

This is the way the world ends,

This is the way the world ends,
This is the way the world ends,
Not with a bang but a whimper.
Hollywood would win.
Nicole needed to keep him coming for her.
That was her only hope.

She went back to the loft, wanting Fallon to be there sipping coffee at the kitchen table, waiting for her, but not getting it. Nicole had never removed the camera, the one that flashed to life in Hollywood's surveillance room and showed Fallon entering the loft. She didn't know why until now. It was because it was one final desperate link to him.

With any luck, he'd be able to watch it on his cell phone. Maybe his phone even pinged to alert him that the camera had sprung to life.

She dragged her workout mats to the center of the space, where the camera had the best view, and stripped down to her panties. She stretched for ten minutes and then started into her floor exercise routine, being careful to never look directly at the camera.

Come on, Hollywood.

Get me in your blood.

Get addicted to me.

I'm the cure for your disease.

Want me more than life itself.

Half an hour later, she put the mats back against the wall, took a long cool shower, slipped into fresh jeans and a T, and headed down to Penny Lane. She tossed her phone into the passenger seat and stared at it with intensity, willing it to ring.

Come on, Hollywood.

Call me.

Do it!

Two minutes later, her phone rang.

It was Princess, the little pink-haired confidential informant, who was supposed to find out who ended up with the burner phone that started life at Jiggy's Little Shop and was being used by Hollywood. Nicole had forgotten all about her.

"Here's what I found out," Princess said. "Jiggy sold a box of burner phones to a 14-year-old kid who goes by the name of 99. You ever heard of him?"

99.

99.

"I don't think so—"

"He's a low level street thug trying to work his way into the Crips, talking about blood in and blood out and all that stupid stuff," Princess said. "He sold the phones on Craigslist at a markup."

"To who?"

Princess said, "Some white guy, big, with a rough edge to him. I had to give him a hundred bucks for that, plus let him squeeze my tits. I'm going to need reimbursement."

"Yeah, yeah, fine. Where can I find him?"

"99?"

"Yeah."

"I can't tell you," Princess said. "If anyone thinks he's talking to the cops, he's dead."

Nicole exhaled.

"Okay, look," she said. "I'm going to text you a picture of a guy. His name is Daniel Flagger. Show it to the kid. Ask him if that's the guy who bought the phones. Ask him if the name Daniel or Dan sounds familiar. The guy, Daniel Flagger, he might drive a dark BMW. Ask the kid if he saw anything like that. Pay him another hundred if you have to."

"I get reimbursed, right?"

"Of course, always."

"I'll need it up front, the money. I'm dry."

"Fine."

"Four hundred, total. That covers the tits, too."

Nicole's instinct was to negotiate the price, especially since she might not get reimbursed from work, but she bit her tongue instead. "Okay, fine, four hundred, but I need you to get on it right away."

Princess said, "I'm in SoBe by the Monument Hotel. You have fifteen minutes. Kiss kiss."

The line died.

Nicole checked her wallet to find three twenties and a couple of singles. Ten seconds later she was at her secret stash pulling out all she had left, about nine hundred. While she was there, she grabbed the only other private gun she had left—a Glock 19 GEN 4 9mm—and checked the clip.

It was full.

She threw it all in her purse.

Then she was outside, locking the loft door behind her and scrambling down the fire escape two steps at a time.

70

Nicole got to where she was supposed to meet Princess and pulled Penny Lane into the first opening she could, about half a block down from the hotel. She sat there for a few minutes but no little Princess walked over to fetch money. Nicole sent the woman a text that she was there. No reply came. She called and didn't get an answer. Then she stepped out into the blistering Miami sun and hoofed it to the hotel, exactly where she was supposed to be.

Come on, Princess.

I don't have time for this.

No Princess emerged from a shady spot and trotted over to greet her. Nor did she fall out of the sky and land at Nicole's feet. The only thing that happened was that guys strolled by and tried to talk her up.

She leaned against a post and fired up the web on her cell phone as she waited. It turned out that the Atlanta lawyer, Alex Foster, who billed Fallon $450 for consulting fees two years ago, specialized in criminal law. So, Fallon must have seen him about some criminal matter. As for the surfer guy, Sean Seven, his Facebook profile was long gone, and he hadn't popped up anywhere else. As far as the web was concerned, he didn't exist, and maybe never had.

Weird.

Fifteen minutes had passed.

She texted and called Princess again and got the same as before, nothing.

Come on, girl.

No drama.

Where are you?

She checked the lobby of the hotel and got a zero.

Then she paced outside back and forth so that Princess could see her from any angle. She couldn't see the woman in any direction, then headed back to the shade. She'd give the woman ten more minutes, then that was it.

The body dump, as she suspected, was already landing as big, big, huge national news.

Reporters and well-known talking heads from major stations were already descending from all over the country.

Although the crime scenes were secured and everyone was being kept at bay, including journalists, photos taken through long-distance lenses were starting to pop up. They showed a small army of white forensic suits moving slowly and carefully out in the Florida wilds, apparently working two separate but fairly close areas. One was a large open pit containing a number of bodies that had been dumped inside, possibly going back over a period of unknown years. So far, none of the victims had been identified and it wasn't even clear exactly how many there were or what sex they were or what their ages were.

The other crime scene was the wreckage of an old plane. Although it couldn't be yet confirmed, it was rumored through reliable sources that a man's severed head had been found inside.

A special agent with the FBI by the name of John Pantage would be holding a press conference at 5:45 p.m. Hopefully a lot of answers would be forthcoming at that time.

Pantage, you're in the major spotlight, dude.

Way to go.

Maybe I should come down there and crash the party.

It was my find, after all.

What do you think?

Nicole pictured it—the sea of reporters, the microphones, the rapid-fire questions, her face dead center in the middle of it all, right there for the whole country to see. It would come out that she was the Governor's daughter, this was her very first case, and on and on and on.

She wrinkled her brow and flicked the picture off.

She needed to stay focused on Danica.

Anything that was a diversion from that was just a mouthful of mud in disguise.

She looked up and down the street.

Princess was nowhere in view.

She called the woman one last time, then walked back to Penny Lane and turned the key.

The engine didn't fire.

The starter didn't grind.

She got a big, fat silence; that was it.

She titled her head to the side, calmly absorbing the situation and telling herself to stay even. Then the boil in her blood reached critical mass and she slammed her hand on the dash, so hard that the vinyl cracked.

It should have made her feel better.

It didn't.

Instead she felt like someone who had a car that wouldn't start, and now also had a car with a screwed up dash that she would either have to look at for the rest of her life, or get fixed by some greedy mechanic who'd want a wallet full of money that would be better spent on wine.

She turned the key again.

Nothing happened.

She opened the hood, jiggled the battery cables and tried it again. This time the engine responded as if nothing had happened. Just as she pulled into traffic, her phone rang. She continued with her shift into second and managed to answer just in time. A man's voice came through, one she didn't recognize.

"I like the way you exercise," he said.

Bingo!

It was Daniel Flagger, Hollywood, in his own voice.

He wasn't using the scrambler any more.

He didn't need to.

"It's nice to hear your voice," Nicole said. "I did that routine just for you, in case you were wondering."

"I know that. You're a tricky little thing—trying to lure me in by shaking your assets—but we both already know that, don't we?"

"Umm . . . You want more? I have plenty—"

"Sure, but instead dance next time; something sexy."

"Whatever you want," she said. "Do you have any favorite songs I should use?"

"Black Velvet. Do you know it?"

"I do," Nicole said.

> *Black velvet, with a little boy smile,*
> *Black velvet, with a smooth southern style,*
> *Black velvet, it will bring you to your knees,*
> *Black velvet, if you please.*

"Is that the one?"

"It is," he said. "You're wasting yourself as a detective. You're so much more than that. You have a damn good voice."

"Thanks," she said. "Do you know what else I have? I have your shotgun. I'm keeping it warm for you. You can stop by and pick it up whenever you want."

"I will, most definitely," he said. "I can't promise it will be right away, but you never know. Hell, maybe I'll even find myself with some free time tonight—"

The connection died.

Nicole looked up to find that the traffic had slowed almost to a complete stop in front of her, four thick behind a bus that had just pulled out from the curb. She powered her foot into the brake pedal with every ounce of strength she had.

Penny Lane locked her wheels and fishtailed.

Then she nudged into the vehicle in front of her, not hard, but with definite contact.

Nicole immediately got out and approached the other vehicle.

She had insurance.

The damage wasn't much.

Maybe the other driver wouldn't even need a police report.

Then something very strange happened.

The other car accelerated into the left lane and took off at a high rate of speed, swerving in and out of traffic as it went.

It was a fairly new black sedan of some sort.

Flagger, is that you?

Were you staring at me in your rearview mirror while we were talking?

Well then, come on, you sick little squirt!

No more games.

No more foreplay.

Come for me!

Do it!

Do it!

Do it!

71

Nicole drove around the city aimlessly, with her eyes in the rearview mirror and her gun within grabbing distance on the passenger seat, giving Hollywood more than a big fat opportunity to make his move. An hour into it, about to give up, she found herself cutting through the financial district, right past Ash Colt's building, and jerked into a parking lot on a spur-of-the-moment impulse.

She killed the engine.

As long as she was right here, maybe she should swing up and talk to Ash; find out what his dispute was with Lloyd Price, the lawyer who liked to spank Poison. It was so strange that Hollywood had Price under surveillance—and Price in turn coincidentally happened to be a mysterious enemy of Ash's, for reasons still unknown.

Was Hollywood working for Ash?

Is that why he had the lawyer under surveillance, because Ash asked him to?

Did Ash actually know who Hollywood was this whole time?

Hey, here's a crazy theory. Maybe Ash actually knows who Hollywood is but obtained that knowledge through an attorney-client relationship. Say, for example, Ash actually represented Hollywood at some point in the past, for some reason. Obviously Ash wasn't a criminal defense lawyer, so he wouldn't have represented Hollywood in a criminal matter, but maybe Hollywood hired Ash to represent him in an entertainment law capacity. Maybe Ash learned during that representation that his client had a criminal history. Maybe Ash learned that his client was in fact a crazed killer the FBI had nicknamed Hollywood. Hell, maybe Hollywood actually told Ash who he was point blank; he liked to play games, and maybe deep down he had some kind of weird need to brag to someone about how great he was. Who better to brag to than an attorney who wouldn't be able to repeat anything because it would violate the attorney-client privilege?

If Ash ever disclosed his client's secrets, he would be disbarred. Plus it wouldn't do any good; the police wouldn't be able to use the information in any capacity since it was illegally given, other than possibly a heads-up, but certainly not as any type of admissible evidence.

More to the point, though, maybe Ash couldn't talk because his client made it very clear that he would kill him if he did; and not just him, maybe someone he held dear, a sister or whatever.

Nicole shook her head.

Maybe.

Maybe.

Maybe.

You have too many maybe's going on, girl.

She knew it was all just a whole great big pile of crazy speculation, but still, she couldn't shake it out of her head.

Maybe—that's right, another maybe for the pile—maybe the night that Nicole met Ash down at the strip club, maybe he didn't bump into her by accident. Maybe he knew Hollywood was in play.

Maybe he followed Nicole there to protect her.

Wow.

Now that was a theory.

Save it for a romance novel, girl.

This is real life.

One thing was almost certainly true. If in fact Ash represented Hollywood at some point in the past, there would be a file. That was a given.

There would be a file.

It would really be nice to know if Ash had a file in his office for a client by the name of Daniel Flagger, and what was inside that file. That would be the nail in the coffin for Flagger, as far as Nicole was concerned. Maybe parts of the file were electronic as well. What would turn up if Nicole somehow got into Ash's computer and did a search for "Hollywood?"

Unfortunately, getting into the files would be almost impossible. She'd almost need to hide somewhere in the suites and wait until everybody left. Even in that scenario, she'd still have to get out somehow, not to mention that the file cabinets might be locked, and Ash's computer would probably be password protected.

Nicole shook her head, surprised at how far she'd let her thoughts drift. She couldn't break into an attorney's office to steal confidential information, even if that attorney was someone she was sleeping with.

Case closed.

Move on.

Put away the fantasies and concentrate on finding Danica.

Suddenly her phone rang.

The incoming number wasn't one she recognized. It was long distance, too, with an out of state area code.

She answered, curious.

"This is Nicole Stone."

"You don't know me," a woman said. "My name's Mia Notaro. I'm a lawyer in El Paso, Texas." Nicole recognized the name immediately. Mia Notaro owned the helicopter that was used to try to abduct her; the helicopter that Fallon shot down. She was more than likely doing the dirty work of Jafet el Perro. "I'm in Miami," the woman said. "Can you meet me? I think it's time for the two of us to have a little chat."

Nicole swallowed.

Then she said, "When?"

"Now."

"Where?"

"Look to your left."

Nicole obliged.

The passenger window of a white Lexus powered down to reveal an attractive, black-haired woman of obvious Hispanic heritage, sitting behind the wheel with her head turned directly at Nicole. The woman waved at her, almost gently, and then said into her phone, "Come on over and get in. We'll go for a drive and talk."

Nicole's blood raced.

This could well be the next attempt by Jafet to abduct her; do it with honey in a non-threatening way in broad daylight.

"Don't worry, you'll be safe," the woman added.

Nicole wasn't so sure about that, but she was pretty sure she'd rather deal with a lawyer in the middle of the day than get blindsided by whatever Jafet would throw at her next. She put her police parking badge on the dash, shoved the gun in her purse and walked step by step by step ever closer to whatever it was that was awaiting her.

72

Nicole approached the Lexus from the front angle where she could see the license plate and made a mental note of the numbers, J2283. She paused at the passenger door and looked in the window to make sure that no one was in the back seat. It was empty. Mia smiled, understanding the anxiety but dismissing it as unnecessary, and said, "Don't be afraid. You'll be fine. I promise."

Nicole got in, put her seatbelt on and felt the cool blow of the air conditioner as the woman behind the wheel powered up the passenger window. She was attired as if she was about to walk into a Fortune 500 boardroom, wearing an elegant sea foam green skirt, a crisp white blouse, and all the appropriate gold and diamond accessories, elegantly expensive without being flashy.

Nicole got comfort from it.

The woman clearly wasn't dressed to attack.

She looked like anything but a killer.

Still, under the calming exterior, there was a brutally strong body that could match Nicole's in a fight if it ever came to it.

"You work out," Nicole said.

The woman nodded.

"The workouts are easy. It's the eating right that's the hard part."

Nicole nodded.

"Chocolate. That's my weakness."

"Mine's almonds. I can eat them by the bag. Are you wearing a wire?"

"No. Are you?"

"No."

"Then I guess we're even."

"It looks that way."

The woman gave Nicole another smile, turned the radio on to 94.9, and merged into thick traffic. Saying nothing, the woman wove out of downtown and out into the county where the roads were narrower and the sky was bigger. To the east puffy white clouds were starting to build and swing over their heads. Nicole resisted the urge to ask where they were headed. The woman clearly had a plan and Nicole would find out soon enough. She'd checked the back often enough to confirm no one was following them, including Hollywood.

Her purse was on her lap.

Her gun was in it, locked and loaded.

She felt as safe as she could.

They drove for quite some time. Then up ahead a line of cottonwood trees sucked up to a small river or canal of some sort. There, the woman pulled right onto a dirt road and drove slowly up it, looking for a cool place to pull over, and eventually bringing the Lexus to a stop under the shade of a thick bank of trees.

She killed the engine.

Nicole looked around.

There were no other cars or signs of life.

They were alone.

The woman looked at Nicole, smiled and said, "This is as good a place as any. Do me a favor, will you? There's an envelope in the glove box. Can you grab it for me?"

Nicole opened the glove box.

Inside, she found a clasp envelope.

Mia was already out of the car, checking out the scenery.

Nicole grabbed her purse and joined the woman.

"I need to pat you down," the woman said. "What we're going to talk about is extremely confidential. I need to be one hundred and ten percent positive that we're not being recorded."

Nicole raised her arms and let the woman search to her satisfaction.

"Thanks," the woman said. "Do you have a cell phone in your purse?"

"Yes."

"I need to be sure it's not recording anything. Do you mind throwing it back into the car while we talk?"

"No."

Nicole obliged.

Then the woman said, "Let's take a walk."

They walked down to the banks of a shallow meandering river, no more than thirty feet across and a couple of feet deep. The sun danced on the water, bouncing playfully off the ripples. White butterflies were everywhere. The temperature, here in the shade by the water, was just about perfect.

The woman said, "Go ahead and open the envelope and take a look at what's inside."

73

Nicole opened the envelope to find two large photographs inside. The top one depicted a woman laying face up on the ground, grotesquely dead, with a bloody bullet hole in her forehead. The bottom one showed a young girl, no more than four or five, sitting in the dirt with her back leaning against a rusty chain-link fence. Her face wasn't happy and looked like it hadn't been for a long, long time.

The woman waited for Nicole to process the information and then said, "Do you recognize her?"

Nicole nodded.

The dead woman was Juana del Carmen, the woman who tried to abduct Nicole and Fallon, the woman who almost succeeded in getting them to the helicopter, the woman who said she'd be coming back for Nicole again, because that was the only way to get her daughter back.

Nicole said, "Did you do this? Did you shoot her?"

The woman shook her head.

"No. That's not my style. That's the work of Jafet el Perro."

"He did this?"

"Yes."

"By his own hand or through his men?"

"His own hand."

At that moment, Nicole's world shifted ever so slightly. She should have hated Juana del Carmen for trying to abduct her—and she did, to a point—but at the same time, deep down she respected the woman, and even liked her to a point, for doing whatever it took to protect her child.

Nicole had one thought and one thought only: Jafet would pay the price for doing this.

Nicole would see to it, personally.

"Her name," Mia Notaro said, "if you don't already know, is Juana del Carmen. Her assignment was to bring you back to Jafet. She failed in that assignment and this is the consequence. The child in the photo is her daughter. Her name is Olivia. She'll be six years old next week. Jafet's going to kill her too but you can save her."

But you can save her.

"How?"

"Turn yourself in, to me right here, right now," the woman said. "I have a plane waiting. I'll take you to Jafet. As soon as you're there, he'll let the girl go. I give you my personal promise that she won't be harmed. There are no tricks here. I also personally promise to make sure that she gets placed in a nice family where she'll flourish and be safe for the rest of her life." The woman added, "It's the best option, Nicole, trust me. If you don't do it this way, all that will happen is that Olivia will end shot in the face, and someone else will end up coming for you. They won't be as nice as me."

Nicole receded in thought, picturing herself in Jafet's control and, even then, still not knowing if the child would truly be released. Maybe Jafet would kill the girl right in front of her just to see the look on her face.

"Why does Jafet want me?" she asked.

The woman shrugged.

"I don't know."

The pressure built up in Nicole's blood and before she knew

it she had the gun out of her purse and was pointing it directly at the woman's face.

"I asked you a question! Why does he want me?"

The woman looked deep into Nicole's eyes. Then she headed for her car and said over her shoulder, "I'm going to take a drive and give you some quiet time to think about it. I'll be back in ten minutes. I'll need your answer then."

Nicole pointed the barrel at the woman's back as she walked.

She didn't pull the trigger, as much as she wanted to.

Instead, she watched the woman get in the car, turn around, and drive off. As if in a trance, she kept her eyes on the vehicle until the very last part of it disappeared over a crest in the road.

She was alone.

She had ten minutes to think.

She screamed in frustration.

Then she fired the gun into the river.

Bam!

Bam!

Bam!

74

Nicole wasn't sure whether the lawyer, Mia Notaro, would actually return or not, but sure enough the Lexus came into sight ten minutes later and pulled to a stop. A low plume of dust kicked up from the tires. The woman left the engine running and powered down the window. As Nicole walked over, the woman said, "Do you have an answer for me?"

"Maybe."

"There are no maybes," the woman said. "There is yes or there is no."

"Let me ask you a question," Nicole said. "Obviously you have a ton of money. Jafet is paying you well. But you don't strike me as someone who would do all this just for the money. So the question is, what does Jafet have on you?"

The woman smiled.

"Nothing."

"Nothing?"

"No. Like you said, he's paying me well. That's all there is to it."

Nicole shook her head.

"I don't believe you," she said. "Whatever it is, I'll help you. In return, you help me get the girl free."

"So, you want to be partners?"

"Yes."

"You make it sound so simple."

"Look, I know it won't be easy but—"

The woman held her hand up and cut Nicole off. "I came here to deliver Jafet's offer to you. My advice is to take it. But either way, the time is now. Tell me your decision."

"In that case, take a message back to Jafet for me."

"Which is, what?"

"Tell him I'm going to kill him for what he did to Juana del Carmen. And if he touches a hair on that girl's head, tell him that his death is going to be the slowest and most painful one in the history of mankind."

The woman chuckled.

"Stupid words," she said.

The window powered up.

Then the car took off.

Just like that, Nicole was alone, with the wisdom of her decision already gnawing at her gut. She reached for her cell phone only to realize it was still in the car.

It wasn't more than thirty seconds later when another car suddenly appeared on the horizon, racing in Nicole's direction as it threw up a wild rooster-tail of dust. At least two figures were in the front seat and possibly more in the back.

Get out!

She darted into the terrain, behind the cottonwoods where she couldn't be seen, and then into the naked treeless terrain, farther and farther and farther into the brush and weeds and rocks, where she finally dived to the ground at the very last second.

The vehicle fishtailed to a stop at the very spot by the river where Nicole had been meeting with Mia Notaro. A woman and two men jumped out with weapons drawn.

Even from this distance, which had to be a hundred yards,

Nicole recognized the woman. It was none other than Juana del Carmen, the same woman who was supposed to be shot in the forehead.

Stupid, that's what she was.

They'd tried to trick her into coming along peacefully.

That didn't work.

Now they'd moved on to plan B.

Either way, they were going to get her.

She'd been doomed from moment one.

Suddenly one of the men fired into the air.

Bam!

Bam!

Bam!

The woman shouted, "Don't make this hard, bitch!"

Nicole didn't respond.

The three figures checked the river and behind the jagged cottonwood trunks, finding nothing. Then they spread out and started to quickly pick their way out into the terrain, directly in Nicole's direction.

She already had her gun in hand.

Her heat beat like a thousand wild drums.

They'd be on her in minutes.

Do something!

Don't let them catch you!

Then just like that, before she could even process what she was doing, she was on her feet, running and running and running deeper into the terrain, not looking back, and zigzagging in wild pivots with all her might. Shots came from behind her, fast and furious, whizzing past her body and kicking up dirt and rocks all around her.

She kept going.

She didn't slow down.

She didn't think.

She just kept running with everything she had.

She ran a long way, until the firing behind her stopped, but finally slowed down enough to take a fast look back. No one was in sight. She dropped to the ground on her stomach in the shade of a large bush, now totally hidden from eyes and bullets, and carefully raised her head for a few seconds at a time until she'd checked everywhere.

Nothing moved that shouldn't move.

Nothing was there that shouldn't be.

She wasn't surprised.

She was faster than them and everyone knew it at this point. They couldn't catch her and the pain of the sun and the humidity was more and more unbearable with every passing step. More importantly, they'd probably run out of bullets.

Nicole flipped onto her back.

The shade felt so damn good.

It pulsed through her blood and washed her soul.

She closed her eyes, just for a second.

Nothing in the world had ever felt so good.

Ash Colt.

She'd spend the night with him tonight, at his place, safe.

They'd drink wine.

She'd dance for him until he couldn't keep his hands off her for one more second.

Later, at some point, a weird sound worked its way into Nicole's consciousness. She focused on it enough to realize that it was something from the real world pulling her out of a groggy state.

She opened her eyes.

A bright sky above forced them most of the way shut again.

She found herself on the ground, on her back, next to a large bush. Her face was in the shade but her legs were in the sun.

A stiffness in her neck pulsed with pain.

Her tongue was as dry as dirt.

Every pore in her body screamed for water.

She remembered why she was there.

She didn't move.

The sound was no longer there. She held her breath, listening as hard as she could. The world was coffin quiet.

Then it wasn't.

A lighter flicked.

Nicole moved her left fingers ever so slightly to see if the gun was by her hand.

She felt nothing, only weeds.

A mouth sucked in air and blew it out. The pungent odor of cigarette smoke wove through the air.

Nicole held her breath and didn't move a muscle.

75

Nicole laid as still as a rock. Maybe the guy truly hadn't seen her; but every pore in her body said he was looking down on her right now at this very second—a predator studying its prey—just waiting quietly with a sick grin to see the expression on her face when she finally looked up to see his eyes locked right on her.

Suddenly a voice in the distance shouted, "Hey, over here!"

A man grunted followed by heavy footsteps leading off.

Nicole moved just enough to locate her gun in the dirt and get it in hand.

Then she raised her head to see the back of a man trotting away.

Her fingers trembled.

Sweat rolled down her forehead.

What to do?

They'd passed her—so far; but if she stayed where she was, she wouldn't be so lucky a second time. She shouldn't have even been that lucky this time.

She waited where she was, minute after minute after minute, letting the sun move across the sky and giving her stalkers plenty of time to work farther into the terrain, past her. Then came the time when she could no longer see them, even when she stood full upright. That's when she ran back to the river.

The sedan was there but it was locked and the keys weren't visible anywhere inside. She smashed the window with a rock, anyway, and checked. Luck hated her, because the keys weren't there—not in the console, not under the seat, not in the ashtray, not up in the visor, not anywhere. Two bottles of water were on the passenger seat; she drank one and shoved the other in her purse. An open pack of cigarettes sat unceremoniously on the dash, waiting for someone to stick them in their lips. Nicole ripped them out of the pack and mashed them to smithereens in her fingers. Then she let the air out of all four tires, wrote Screw You in the dirt with a stick, and got the hell out of there.

76

Due to absolutely zero traffic out there in the sticks, Nicole had to walk for hours before she finally caught a ride, if you could call it that, because it was with a crazy old pirate-like guy with a gold tooth and an actual real-life eye patch, who kept talking about how he'd come up with a secret formula to beat the slot machines in Vegas. He was going to own that town, every last square inch of it. Nicole had him pull over at the first sign of a payphone and tipped him a hundred, never so glad to be out of a vehicle in her life.

"Seed money," she said.

The pirate looked at her sideways, shook his long black locks and handed the bills back. "I ain't splitting the pot with no one. I've been working on this for way too long—"

"No, I understand," she said. "Just take it."

"You're not looking for a cut?"

"No. No cut."

The man hesitated—looking for a trick—then snatched the bills out of her hand before she changed her mind, and gunned it so fast that Nicole had to jerk her arm back out the window to keep it from getting ripped off.

Okay, that was that.

Her plan at the phone was to call Ash Colt to see if he could come and get her, but now that she was here slipping coins in the slot, she thought better of it. She didn't want to be a burden, especially if he was throat deep in law stuff, which he probably was. More to the point, she wasn't pretty, not right now, not at this particular second in the universe. She felt more like a stray cat that had been doused in oil and dragged behind a car. Eventually she'd let him see her at her worst, but not now. Now, it was still too early in the relationship. She didn't want to look into his eyes and sense hesitation or rejection on his part. She didn't want to feel him comparing her to others and coming up short. She needed to be first every time the man looked at her, otherwise she'd explode.

So she called a cab.

It was supposed to be there in forty minutes.

It actually showed up two hours later, but at least it showed up.

Eventually, in exchange for a small fortune, it dropped her off at Penny Lane. From there she made a quick stop to buy a new cell phone, and then headed home through long twilight shadows. It was stupid, going home—instead of to a hotel—but she was too tired to care.

She needed wine.

And bottles of the stuff were up there, waiting for her.

Nothing else really mattered now, did it?

When she got to the loft and stepped out of Penny Lane, however, she found something she didn't expect. A man was sitting at the top of the fire escape, all the way up at her door in the dark, almost invisible, with his back leaning against it as if he'd been waiting there a long time. She didn't recognize him. If she were smart, she would get back in the car while she had the chance and drive away.

Instead she pulled her gun out of the purse and headed up.

On the way she shouted, "I have a gun in my hand, just so you know."

77

Nicole slowed as she got near the top of the fire escape, and checked the man out as best she could in the fading light. He looked like a bushy-bushy-blond surfer off a California beach, not more than twenty-five or thereabouts, seriously out of his element right now. His clothes were crumpled and eyes were stressed as if they hadn't closed in days.

"I'm looking for Fallon Bow," he said. "Do you know where she is?"

"No, not really—"

"Are you sure? This is really important."

"I don't know where she is."

The man processed the response, as if thinking about it hard enough could change it, and then slammed his hand against the door with a violent force and shouted, "Damn it!" He pushed past Nicole so hard that he almost knocked her down, and bounded down the steps. Nicole stood there for a second, dazed, and then raced in step behind him; it was too strange that Fallon had been missing for some time now and suddenly some stranger was here looking for her.

"Wait up!" she shouted. "What's going on with Fallon? Is she in trouble?"

The man jerked to a stop.

For a second it looked like he was about to say something, but then he turned and ran. Nicole tried to keep up but the pain of the day made her too slow. The guy got to a vehicle and squealed off before she could get a grip on him. She took aim at his tires but didn't squeeze the trigger.

Two minutes later, upstairs in the loft, she poured a healthy volume of Lindeman 50 into a tall glass of ice cubes, flicked on the TV to find a Marlins game in progress, and settled into the couch with her iPad to do a little sniffing around.

Bad news quickly followed.

It turned out that the license plate on Mia Notaro's Lexus— J2283—didn't belong to that vehicle. It belonged to a Nissan Juke registered to one La La Wine, who, according to her social media accounts, was a flight attendant for Frontier. The plates had probably been stolen out of a long-term parking lot at the airport. She probably didn't even know they were gone yet.

Even worse, the Mia Notaro who drove Nicole off the grid this afternoon wasn't the real Mia Notaro, not when compared to the woman's bio photo from the Steel & Hawkes, P.C., website. The two women were close in appearance but definitely different people. So, all those stray thoughts that Nicole had been having about bringing the lawyer down on some kind of charges like conspiracy or aiding and abetting were now gone.

She stood up, stripped to her panties, swallowed the last mouthful of wine and said, "Night, Daniel," at the surveillance camera.

Then she turned off the TV and the lights and flopped down onto the mattress.

Sleep grabbed her almost immediately.

At some point halfway through the night, strange lights

woke her up. They were coming from the headlights of a car sitting outside in the darkness, way back at the very end of the parking lot.

Nicole couldn't make out the details of the vehicle.

She threw on a top, grabbed Daniel Flagger's shotgun, as well as her pistol, and took the fire escape to the roof, locking the door to the loft behind her. From behind the parapet, she trained the shotgun at the front end of the vehicle.

Juana del Carmen, is that you?

Are you making your next move already?

Or how about you, Flagger?

Is that you?

Are you stopping by for a dance?

The vehicle wasn't a Corvette, that much she could tell. Whoever was sitting there, it wasn't Ash Colt.

Maybe it was the white Challenger; the guy with the full-sleeve tattoo on his left arm.

She'd actually forgotten all about him until now.

Let's find out who you are, yeah?

Nicole took a solid aim at the front end of the vehicle, steadied the barrel until it no longer shook or jiggled, and then slowly exhaled as she prepared to squeeze the trigger.

In one second the front end of the vehicle would explode.

The headlights would blow out.

Everything would get dark.

Whoever was in there wouldn't be able to get away.

She pictured it and then released her finger from the trigger. Her job was already on tenuous ground. A shot like this—without full information, and without provocation, and without imminent danger—would be the final blow to her career, especially if she took it with wine in her blood. What if it was nothing more than a lost cab driver at the wrong address?

Suddenly the headlights went out.

Whoever was in the driver's seat lit a cigarette.

It wasn't clear if they knew Nicole was up on the roof or not.

Screw it!

You want to play?

Let's play!

She bounded down the fire escape all the way to ground level and walked briskly at the vehicle through the dark with a weapon in each hand. Both barrels were pointed down at the ground but she could swing them up with the speed of a devil's bite.

Suddenly the headlights turned on with a blinding light.

Then tires squealed.

Nicole fired.

She didn't think.

She just fired.

As she did, she realized the vehicle was squealing away from her, not trying to run her over.

Bullets pierced metal.

The engine died as the vehicle rolled backwards and came to a stop. The pungent reek of antifreeze assaulted the air; and then, just like that, the headlights shorted out with a bright blue flash, and everything turned black.

A cigarette flicked through the driver's side window and hit the ground with a splash of sparks.

Then the door opened and a man stepped out.

78

The man briefly focused on the destruction to his vehicle, then turned his attention to Nicole and said, "I think something bad has happened." Nicole recognized the voice. It belonged to the bushy-bushy-blond surfer guy who'd stopped by earlier in the evening looking for Fallon.

"With Fallon?"

"Yes." The man shifted from one foot to another, a dark silhouette in an even darker night. "If I tell you, you can't ever tell anyone," he said. "You need to promise me that."

"Why? What are you going to tell me?"

"Promise me right now or I'm walking away," he said. "I can't blow it, not after everything that's happened. You need to promise me that whatever I tell you, you take it to the grave. You can never tell anyone, not tomorrow, not in ten years, not ever."

Nicole exhaled, considering it.

"I don't think I can—"

"Fuck!"

The man turned and ran.

The darkness swallowed him almost immediately.

Nicole stood there, alone in the night.

Then she shouted, "Okay!"

Thirty seconds later the man came back out of the cloak of night, suddenly there, breathing heavy. He said, "This can't be a trick. This has to be one hundred percent real."

"It's real," she said.

"Say the words."

"I promise," she said.

The man said nothing, weighing Nicole's sincerity. Then he said, "I need a beer. You got any?"

Nicole didn't know what the man was going to tell her but did know that she didn't want him to say it in front of Daniel Flagger's security camera—which she was still reluctant to smash, given that it was her only link to him—so they ended up on the roof, him with a Bud Lite and her with a fresh glass of wine. The shotgun and handgun sat next to her just in case someone decided that this was the perfect time to swing by and pay her a visit.

The guy's name was Ethan Blue.

Nicole recognized it from somewhere but couldn't place it, until he told her that he was from California; he was the drummer in Rude, which was the band that Danica Rose sang in. He was one of Danica's three lovers, who detective Shalifa Tacher flew out to interview when this whole thing started.

"Okay, it goes like this," he said. "Remember your promise—"

"I remember."

"Danica got herself in a truckload of trouble," he said.

"Danica? I thought this was about Fallon—"

"It's about both of them. Just hear me out. It was two years ago. Danica and Fallon were friends. They were up in Atlanta on a girl's thing, to get some R&R. Danica ended up meeting a guy named Sean Seven at a club."

Sean Seven.

Nicole recognized the name.

A printout of his Facebook page was hidden in some old art posters down in Fallon's basement. Shortly after that he disappeared from the face of the earth.

"What happened?" she said.

"Nothing good," the man said. "They spent the night together. In the morning, the guy wanted to swing by his bank and get some money out. They were in his car but Danica was driving because the guy was still a little hung over. Anyway, a few minutes go by, and suddenly the guy comes running out with a bag in his hand. He jumps in the passenger seat and says, Go!"

"He robbed it?"

"Yes," he said. "Danica had no idea it was going to happen but she took off like the guy told her. She was scared. She didn't know what to do. All of a sudden, she was like in the middle of this thing—"

"Okay."

"Anyway, within a block or two, a cop car is suddenly behind them, giving chase. All of a sudden, the guy has a gun and he's leaning out the side window, firing at the cops. He hits a tire and the cop car loses control and slams into a telephone pole. There were two cops in the car at the time. One of them was a guy named Andrew Ward. He was the one driving and didn't get a scratch. The other one was a female, named Alondra Bonilla, a four-year veteran and mother of two. She died in the crash."

"Are you serious?"

"Unfortunately, yes," the man said. "Right after the cop car crashed, Danica swung around the corner and slammed on the brakes. The car skidded to a stop and she got out and ran. Sean Seven slid over and got in the driver's seat and took off."

"Wow, I had no idea."

"No one does," the man said. "Danica flew back to California and acted as if nothing had happened. She hid in plain sight, just going about her normal life and not giving any indication to anyone that anything was wrong. All the while, inside, she was scared to death."

"She should have turned herself in," Nicole said. "She was a victim, not a criminal."

The man frowned.

"That's true but it's not so black and white," he said. "On Danica's behalf, Fallon went to see a criminal defense lawyer in Atlanta by the name of Alex Foster to get his opinion on things."

Nicole recognized the name.

That was the mysterious bill for $450 that was rolled up in the art posters in Fallon's basement.

Paid in Cash.

"According to this lawyer," the man said, "he expected that the police would go after Danica. A cop was dead. You don't participate in something like that in Georgia and then simply walk away from it. In his opinion, Danica would be charged and they would go after her hard. They'd argue that she was part of the plan from the start. She was the getaway driver going into it and she did her job. According to the lawyer, maybe she'd be able to convince a jury she was innocent; but probably not, and if she didn't, she'd go down for some serious time. It was all a big fat crapshoot. Maybe they'd even go for the death penalty."

"So when did you learn about all this?"

"From the start," he said. "I'm the one who suggested that Fallon go see a lawyer on Danica's behalf."

"And you agreed with the lawyer, for Danica to hide?"

He nodded.

"There are some things in Danica's past that could work against her if anyone ever found out about them. Anyway, the days were passing and no one was coming to arrest her and everything sort of defaulted back to normal. Then one day

Danica was out surfing and got spotted by a man named Adam Montrachet. It turned out that he was a director with Paradyme Pictures who was going to be filming a movie called *The Shoals*. He invited Danica to audition for a bit part. She ended up with an agent by the name of Lance Fox and by the time it was all said and done, she had a major role. The movie was filmed last year and now, pretty soon, it's going to be released. Danica's face is going to be everywhere. The cops in Atlanta already have some security footage of her. Once the movie comes out, someone's going to put her name to that face."

"They'd show up out of the blue one night and arrest her," Nicole said.

"Precisely," the man said. "That's why she needed to die."

79

That's why she needed to die.

Nicole said, "I don't follow."

"The plan was to fake her death," the man said. "Fallon found someone who would do the job."

"Who?"

"I don't know."

"How did she find him?"

"I don't know. All I know is that the guy knew about a serial killer called Hollywood, who had a real unique MO. The plan was to make it look like Danica got taken by Hollywood, and then never returned, meaning she was presumably dead."

"So it was going to be a copycat—"

"Yes, yes, a copycat. Danica came to Florida to stay with Fallon to set the stage. Then she was abducted out of Fallon's bed. All the clues left behind pointed to Hollywood. Really, though, this hired guy is the one who took her. He planted her in an old airplane wreck out in the middle of nowhere, just like something the real Hollywood would have done. He was supposed to release her Thursday morning to Fallon. Fallon was then going to hand her off to me and I was going to drive her to California. I had a boat set up to take us to Mexico, where we were going to hole up for a year or two or three. But Danica and Fallon never showed up and I haven't heard from either one of them. I've called Fallon a billion times. Something's gone way wrong. I keep picturing them dead."

The words were coming too fast for Nicole to process.

They were too opposite of everything she'd come to know.

"Alright, back up," she said. "So the man who carried Danica out of the house and threw her into an SUV, you're saying that it was this guy that Fallon hired."

"Yes. Exactly."

"And you don't know who he is?"

"No, I don't."

"You never met him?"

"No."

"And you don't know how Fallon found him?"

"No, I don't have a clue."

"Was it on the web?"

"No, I don't know. I think that maybe someone helped her."

"Who?"

"I don't know. Someone she trusted, obviously."

"When did she start looking for someone?"

The man receded in thought. Then he said, "I don't know, exactly. We've been talking about it for two or three weeks, at least."

"So she might have started looking for someone two or three weeks ago—"

"Right."

"Okay."

"I don't know who the guy is."

"I understand," Nicole said.

"If I did, I'd be talking to him right now, not you."

"I understand. In the last two or three weeks, did Fallon mention anyone's name to you? Someone who, in hindsight, might have been helping her find someone who would get involved in faking a death?"

"No. We hardly talked during that time to tell you the truth.

Fallon came to California and me and her and Danica came up with the general plan to fake Danica's death," the man said. "Fallon took the job to find someone and come up with a more definitive plan. That way Danica wouldn't have any direct connections to anyone, no phone records or any of that type of thing. Then later Fallon called and said she'd come up with a plan. She explained it to us, this Hollywood deal. At first Danica was scared to death and didn't want to do it, but it was her only option."

"Okay. The guy who was going to pretend to be Hollywood, I assume he was going to be paid—"

"Of course."

"Do you know how much?"

"Fallon gave him fifty thousand up front," the man said. "After the job was done he was supposed to get another one hundred fifty. All the money was going to come from Danica. It was her movie money. She gave all the money up front to Fallon in cash."

"Two hundred thousand—"

"Right, all of it," the man said. "Fallon passed fifty thousand cash onto the guy at the start."

"What about the other one fifty?"

"Fallon was supposed to pay it when the guy delivered Danica to her alive and well Thursday morning. Whether that happened or not, I don't know. Everything's gone dark. I have no idea what happened."

"I understand."

"Do you?"

"Maybe someone found out Fallon had all the cash on hand and killed her for it."

"I don't know—"

"Maybe Fallon never arrived to pick Danica up?"

"I don't know."

"Did you mention the cash to anyone?"

"No," the man said. "I knew about it. Danica knew about it. Fallon knew about it. That's all, to my knowledge. No one else."

"And the guy who was Hollywood," Nicole said. "He knew about it."

"Yeah, I suppose."

Nicole took a long swallow of wine and said, "Okay, let's shift gears for a second. There was a jogger who was running past Fallon's house the night that Danica got taken. She called 911. I think her name was Hannah Sonnen, a nurse. Was she in on all this, too?"

"No," the man said. "She was just a strange coincidence. The plan was for Fallon to come home and find Danica gone and call it in to the police. Fallon's neighbor was out of town and had a security system. The plan was that tape would eventually be uncovered and it would show the abduction, looking like the work of Hollywood."

"And where was Fallon that night? Who was the mystery lover she was with?"

"No one," the man said. "She made that up just so she had an excuse for not being home when Danica was taken. She was actually just killing time in her car."

"Where?"

"I don't know. I don't care. All I know is that this whole thing is screwed up."

Nicole exhaled.

Then she said, "Look, I don't mean to be rude or anything, but maybe they cut you out for some reason. Maybe they went to a plan B. Maybe Danica changed her mind about going to Mexico with you."

The man didn't hesitate.

"No way. No way."

"Are you sure?"

The man screwed up his face in disgust.

"We're in love," he said. "Do you even understand what that is?"

He threw the beer can.

It bounced off an HVAC duct with a loud clang.

"I knew I shouldn't have come here," he said. "I'm wasting my time."

Then he was gone.

DAY SIX

September 20
Saturday

80

Saturday morning Nicole got pulled awake by a loud knocking at the door. She slipped on a long-sleeve shirt, grabbed her gun and was able to get one button done by the time she got to the door. She cinched the rest of the shirt closed with a hand, unlocked the door and stepped to the side as it swung open, with the weapon pointed at whoever it was that was there.

It was Trane.

He looked into the barrel, then down at the exposed areas of Nicole's body, and said, "You okay?"

"Yeah, I suppose."

"You're not answering your phone," he said.

"Lost it. Got a new one."

"Did you call the new number in?"

"Not yet. Do you want some coffee?"

"No time," he said. "I just swung by to make sure you're okay. Call the new number in, okay?"

She nodded. "I will. Sorry about that. Any progress on Flagger?"

"No, nothing. He's still on the run. Probably in Mexico sipping Margaritas."

Then he was gone.

Two minutes later another knock came at the door.

It was Trane again.

"What happened to that car out there? It looks like someone blasted it with a shotgun."

"Yeah, well, guilty."

"You shot it?"

"Yeah, pretty much."

"Why?"

"I thought it was going to run me over," she said.

"Someone tried to kill you?"

"Actually, I was mistaken," she said. "I was in front of it and the tires squealed and I thought it was coming at me but it wasn't. It was backing up."

"Were you approaching the car?"

"Yeah. I was walking towards it I guess. It was last night, after dark. It was suspicious and I was checking it out. I thought it might be Flagger."

"And you had the shotgun in your hands at the time, when you were walking towards it?"

"Yeah."

"Who was inside?"

Nicole considered answering but needed to make sure she kept her promise to Ethan Blue.

"I can't get into it right now," she said.

"Was it Flagger?"

"No."

Trane tilted his head in disbelief. Then he said, "Did you file a discharge report?"

"No. Like I said, it happened last night. I didn't wake up until just now."

"Did you at least call it in last night after it happened?"

"No."

"How about that incident downtown? Did you file a discharge report on that yet?"

"I haven't had time."

Trane hardened his face.

"What weapon did you use on the car?"

"A shotgun, like you said."

"Is it licensed?"

"It's the one I got from Daniel Flagger's house."

"I thought Pantage told you to bring that down to the station and log it into evidence—"

"That's true."

"But you didn't do it?"

"Not exactly, not yet. Things have been a little crazy on my end, Trane, in case you haven't noticed. I'll get to it today, I promise."

Trane retreated in thought, then steadied his voice and said, "This isn't working out, Nicole. I hoped it would, I really did. I hoped putting you on that two-week suspension and giving you some time to collect your thoughts would do the trick." He looked back at the car, then into her eyes, and added, "You got me backed into a corner, yet again; there are too many things. I have to put you on an indefinite leave of absence pending a full evaluation. It'll be with pay, I can do that much for you; but don't hold yourself out as a homicide detective from this point forward. Do you still have Daniel Flagger's shotgun?"

Nicole swallowed.

"Yes. It's inside."

"Go get it for me, will you? Any ammo, too."

"Sure. You want to come in?"

"No. I'll wait here."

A tear came to Nicole's eye.

"I'm sorry, Trane," she said. "I honestly don't know how everything got so screwed up."

"It's okay," he said. "I'm probably partly to blame. I should have mentored you more. I don't think I really made you appreciate the importance of following protocols."

"No, you did fine," she said. "This is on me, not you."

Back inside, she kick-started the coffee pot and called Poison, who wouldn't recognize the new phone number but would hopefully answer anyway.

She did.

"Poison, this is Nicole Stone," she said. "Don't hang up. When you met with Daniel Flagger, and he gave you the money and the lipstick camera to film that lawyer—"

"—Lloyd Price—"

"—Right, Lloyd Price. Where did that exchange take place?"

"Let me think," the woman said. "Okay, it was at Ladies en Secret. I was working that night. He met me there between sessions. Why?"

"I'm trying to get a license plate number for his car," Nicole said. "Do they have any security cameras pointed out at the parking area?"

"Yeah, but I don't know if they record or anything."

"Meet me there," Nicole said.

"When?"

"Right now."

"Are you serious?"

"Dead serious. I'll owe you forever."

Twenty minutes later at Ladies en Secret, Nicole was in a room with Poison, fast-forwarding thorough security footage of the parking lot from Monday night, which is the night Daniel Flagger made his appearance. The weather was bad. It was raining like a madman. Suddenly, Poison stopped the footage, backed up, and played it at normal speed. It showed a woman bursting out of the club into the rain and running to a car in bare feet.

"That's me," Poison said. "I took my heels off."

"Okay."

She swung a car door open and got in. Two minutes later,

she came back out carrying a small bag, and ran through the puddles back to the building. The headlights of the vehicle came on and it pulled forward, swung to the left and headed back towards the street. It was clearly a BMW. They backed up the footage and played it again. When the vehicle got closest to the building, Nicole said, "Stop it there!"

Poison hit the button.

"Can you zoom in on the plate?"

"I think so—"

It took a little fiddling, but they finally got the plate in focus. It was DEP-X55. They also got the driver's face in focus, only for a watery second, but that was long enough.

The face clearly belonged to Daniel Flagger.

There was no question about it.

Then Nicole realized something; the meeting occurred at Monday at 10:00. *Monday night was when Danica got abducted.* From Ladies en Secret, it would have taken Flagger a good 45 to 60 minutes to get to Fallon's house. According to the jogger, the nurse—what was her name? Hannah Sonnen, yeah, that's it, Hannah Sonnen—Danica got thrown into the SUV around 10:10. That time was also consistent with the security camera from the neighbor's house.

So, Daniel Flagger definitely wasn't the one who took Danica.

He wasn't the one Fallon hired to be Hollywood.

"What's wrong?" Poison said.

"Monday night," Nicole said. "That's when you met with Daniel Flagger? Monday night?"

"Yeah, it was Monday. I already told you that before. Plus the date's on the tape. Why? What's wrong?"

"Nothing," Nicole said. "I'm just being double sure."

"It was Monday," Poison said. "I had just finished up a session at around, I don't know, 9:50 or thereabouts. I had another one coming up at 11:00. I met with Flagger between the two. I don't get what's wrong."

"What's wrong is that you just gave Daniel Flagger an alibi," Nicole said.

"For what?"

"For everything."

"I did?"

"Yes."

"Ouch," Poison said. "But you came here to get his license plate number—"

"Yeah, I know."

"And now you have it, right?"

"Right."

"Well in my books, they call that a win."

Nicole was almost all the way back to her loft when she realized she'd said something wrong. Daniel Flagger didn't have an alibi for "everything." He only had an alibi for the time that Danica was abducted. It was still possible that he ended up taking Danica later, plus Fallon too for that matter—both of them, probably together. Maybe he just stumbled on the two of them at the exact perfect time. Or maybe he was waiting in the shadows, waiting for them because he believed that Danica killed his brother; and he couldn't take her without taking Fallon too because they were together at that point.

She got home and immediately ran the plates, DEP-X55.

What she found, well, it figured, because that's the way her life worked; the plates didn't belong to a BMW, they belonged to a pickup truck registered to some stupid construction company called Shadow Reef Construction, Inc., meaning Flagger had stolen them.

Nicole called Pantage and gave him the numbers anyway.

He was grateful but not excited.

"Good work but I doubt it matters," he said. "I'm sure he ditched the BMW a long time ago. We'll find it in two weeks, abandoned at a Walmart."

"You're probably right."

"Hey, you still there?"

"Yeah."

"Trane called me. He said he fired you."

"He did."

"Well, Danica didn't fire you, and neither did I. Do you understand what I'm saying?"

"I do."

"Good. Stay in touch. Everything's important no matter how small. Remember that."

"Pantage—"

"Yeah?"

"I'm so tired of dead ends. They're wearing me out."

He chuckled.

Then he said, "When I lose something, do you know where I always find it?"

"No."

"In the very last place I look," he said

As Nicole smiled and said goodbye, a knock came from the door.

She froze at the sound.

A quick peek out the windows showed a small sea foam green scooter leaning on its kickstand near the bottom of the fire escape.

Nicole had never seen it before.

She grabbed her weapon and silently headed towards the loft door.

81

The person on the other side of the door turned out to be Princess, dressed in pink shorts down below and a matching pink Mohawk up above. Between the two was a black T, cinched in a knot to let a cute little bellybutton show.

"Kiss kiss," she said. "It's me."

Nicole wasn't amused, flashing back to the meet-up at South Beach, the meet-up that never happened.

"I waited for you. You didn't show."

"Life," Princess said. "It's a messed up thing. You still got the money?"

"I suppose. Come on in."

Inside, Nicole pulled $400 out of her purse. Princess grabbed it, shoved it in her bra and said, "I already earned it. I showed 99 the picture of that guy."

That guy.

She was referring to Daniel Flagger.

He was that guy.

"And?"

"That's not the guy 99 sold the burner phones to."

"Was he sure?"

"Yeah, he was sure." Princess gave Nicole a quick peck on the lips and said, "Got to run."

Then she was down the fire escape, kick-starting the scooter three times, and pulling away in a puff of blue smoke.

Nicole wasn't surprised. Flagger already had an alibi for the time when Danica was taken, complements of Poison; that alone showed he wasn't the "Hollywood" that Fallon hired. The fact, now, that he wasn't the one who bought the burner phones from 99, well, that was just more of the same. Flagger wasn't the person Fallon hired and that was that.

So if Flagger wasn't the one, who was?

She headed over to Fallon's house. Inside, upstairs in the master bedroom, the ominous creepy feeling of evil was gone. Everything was completely different now, knowing the whole abduction had been nothing more than an Oscar-worthy ruse.

In the master closet, she pulled down the box that had the old Atlanta Journal-Constitution newspaper. She spread it out on the bed and turned the pages. On page 4 she spotted an article, *Federal Reserve Bank of Atlanta Robbed, Officer Killed*. It was short and to the point—the bank got robbed by a male, he said he had a gun in his pocket, he made off with $10,520, he was whisked off in a getaway car being driven by a female, two officers pursued in a marked car, the suspects fired, hitting the officers' car and causing it to crash. Officer Alondra Bonillo died in the crash. The male suspect had not yet been identified but a security camera image of his face is shown. Anyone who recognizes the suspect should call authorities immediately.

Nicole recognized the face.

It belonged to Sean Seven.

None of this was new, but it was good collaboration of Ethan Blue's story. It was also interesting in that the article referred to a "getaway car," which is no doubt how the cops described the vehicle to the reporter. Nicole could picture Danica reading the article and getting scared to the ends of the world.

She put the paper back and checked the rest of the closet. She'd been through it once before but this time she was more thorough, looking in particular for the other $150,000 which, if present, meant that Fallon had never done the final meet-up with the person she hired.

If he were still owed his money, would he show up at Fallon's place to look for it?

He might.

And he'd probably know what was going on. He might even be able to say whether Flagger abducted the two women from him.

Maybe it would be worth the effort to set up a surveillance camera or two, if things didn't pan out here in the next hour. She'd have to fund it herself, or possibly get Pantage to help; Trane was out.

She continued the search—the search for anything that might shed a clue on who Fallon hired; a name, an address, a phone number, a meeting, anything that seemed even remotely out of the ordinary. She started with the dresser drawers, feeling every single article of clothing in case a piece of paper had been stuffed inside. She pulled the drawers all the way out and checked the bottoms and side and backs.

Nothing was there that shouldn't be.

She completed the rest of the upper level fairly quickly, not really expecting much, but checking all surface areas for signs of hidden compartments in walls or flooring or ceilings.

Then she headed downstairs.

She found bank statements, but there was nothing unusual. It didn't appear that Fallon had deposited any of the $200,000 cash that Danica had entrusted to her. Nor had she written any large checks to anyone. In fact, she'd hardly written any checks at all. Almost all of her transactions were credit card. None of them were suspicious.

The cell phone bills were summary in fashion. They didn't

contain call or text information.

She checked the basement, every square inch of it.

Nothing was there.

Nothing was anywhere.

There was only one place left—the garage.

The garage, it turned out, was filled with storage boxes, tools, cabinets, rafters, walls with exposed batten insulation, and the like, which made it the perfect place to hide cash. Nicole went through it all, inch by inch. Then she found something interesting. A piece of plywood was sitting on top of the rafters in the back corner. From the ground level, Nicole could see sprinkler system parts resting on it; PVC pipe, joints, old heads and the like. When she pulled a stepladder over and reached behind it all, she found a large envelope. Inside that envelope were rubber-banded bundles of $50 bills. She poured the contents out on a workbench and found that each bundle contained 100 bills, meaning $5,000 apiece. There were 30 bundles total, adding up to $150,000.

Okay. Now what?

Take it or put it back?

She paced, thinking it through, then decided to put it back, at least for now. That way, if the circumstances came to Fallon needing the money to make the final payment, she'd be able to do it. If she didn't have the money, things might not end up well for her.

On her way back to Penny Lane, Nicole passed by the mailbox in the front of the house. On a whim, she opened it. Inside were a number of mailings. One was the most recent statement from Fallon's bank.

Nicole tossed it into the passenger seat and shoved the rest back in the box.

A woman from across the street shouted, "Hey! What are you doing?"

Nicole waved at her as if everything was okay and then got

the hell out of there.

Just before she got back on MacArthur Causeway she pulled over to the curb and opened the bank statement. It showed some very, very, very interesting credit card items. One was a charge by United Airlines for a roundtrip ticket from Miami to Washington/Dulles International Airport, two weeks ago, in one day and returning the next. Another was a charge from Hertz for a rental car, also two weeks ago. A third was a charge from the Washington, D.C. Marriott for a room for one night, also two weeks ago. A fourth was a charge for almost $80 from a Washington, D.C. restaurant called Lagoon House.

She smiled.

This almost certainly related to the person Fallon hired.

So, the guy lives in D.C.

Fallon went there to personally check the guy out and deliver the fifty thousand dollars cash down payment.

Nicole racked her brain.

She couldn't remember Fallon every mentioning anyone from there.

The restaurant bill was interesting—almost $80.00.

That would be a lot for one person, if Fallon had been eating alone. It would probably be just about right for two people though, say, for supper.

That's where Fallon must have met up with the guy, at the restaurant.

Maybe the place had surveillance tapes.

Equally intriguing, the guy would have been the one to pick the place out, not Fallon. So, maybe he was a regular there.

Maybe someone knew his name.

She smiled.

Gotcha, you little bitch! I got your money, too.

You're going to talk to me.

You're going to talk to me and tell me what happened to

Danica.

82

On the drive home Nicole called the Lagoon House, identified herself as a Miami homicide detective, and got put through to the manager on duty, who turned out to be a guy named Richard. With a little work he was able to find the itemized bill in the restaurant's computer system. It showed that there were two customers. It also showed the waitress to be "32." Richard, however, would not divulge the waitress' name, address or phone number.

"Corporate policy," he explained.

Nicole slammed her hand on the dash.

"Come on, man," she said. "I don't have time for policy. I need to speak to this person, and I mean right now."

"I'd like to help, I really would, but I got to follow the rules," Richard said. "It's a matter of privacy and all that. If you want, I can give you the number of our corporate headquarters. Maybe they'll be able to help."

"I don't want corporate headquarters," Nicole said. "I want to talk to that waitress and I want to do it right now." She paused and added, "Is she there?"

"You mean, right now?"

"Yes."

"Yeah, I'm pretty sure."

"Do me a favor," Nicole said. "Just put her on the phone.

You don't have to tell me her name or address or anything else. All I need you to do is hand the phone to her and tell her someone wants to talk to her. There's no policy against that, is there?"

The man hesitated.

Then he said, "Hold on. I better not get in trouble for this."

"You won't."

Thirty seconds later, a female voice came through.

"Hello?"

"Hello," Nicole said. "Thanks for talking to me." She explained who she was. She explained that the woman didn't need to tell her what her name was or anything else. "All I'm trying to do is find out about the guy who was at the table; what he looks like, in particular."

The woman exhaled.

"I'm sorry. I really don't remember anything—."

"Think. Please—"

"This was two weeks ago," she said. "I get tons of people every day. They come and they go."

"I understand," Nicole said. "I couldn't even tell you what I had for breakfast this morning." She paused and added, "Let me do this. Let me send you a picture of the woman who was there. That might jog your memory. I can send it to the restaurant if you want."

"No, that's okay. You can send it straight to me. My name's Madison, by the way. Madison Paige. I suppose that if this is really important you're going to find out anyway. Here's my number—"

Nicole sent a picture.

Within seconds the woman said, "I remember them."

"You do?"

"Oh yeah. The guy was pretty unique. He was seriously rugged and he was really dark. He had a scar on the right side of his face, from the corner of his eye to his jaw. The most striking thing about him though was his body. It was straight out of a Tarzan movie. I had the feeling he was a football player or something like that, not one of the fat ones, one of the guys who runs down the field and catches the ball. Anyway, he kept giving me a look, sort of on the side. You know the kind I'm talking about, like he wanted to slam me against the wall and own me."

The words hit Nicole like a brick to the brain.

Pantage!

"His name's John Pantage," she said. "Did you ever see him in the restaurant at any other time?"

"No. That was it, it was just that once. Did he kill someone?"

"I don't know."

"Because to me, he looked like he could."

"Well, time will tell. Either way, you did good, Madison Paige, you did real good. Let's keep this conversation just between us girls, alright?"

"Sure, if you want."

She headed to MacArthur Causeway faster than she should have, trying to not get run over by one of the two million maniac cars around her. So, Pantage was the one Fallon hired to be Hollywood. That made sense in many ways, mostly because Pantage would be able to play the part to perfection, plus there really wasn't much risk to him because he would be investigating his own "crime," so to speak. It also explained why Fallon went to D.C. to meet with Pantage, because that's where the FBI offices were. It's where Pantage worked and lived.

It all made total sense.

One thing didn't make sense, though.

When Pantage was with Nicole the night they went to the strip club, she actually got a call from Hollywood. The caller clearly wasn't Pantage; he was sitting right next to her.

The same thing happened when she was with Pantage in that dive bar drinking a beer, when they ended up running out to catch Hollywood and she ended up on the ground in an alley, compliments of a two-by-four.

So, someone was helping Pantage perpetrate the ruse.

Who?

That was the big question.

Who?

Maybe it was Danica's boyfriend, Ethan Blue; he was one of the few people on earth who actually knew about the whole charade. Maybe Pantage recruited him, told him when to call and what to say.

Maybe, but deep down Nicole couldn't convince herself of it. Ethan came across as someone who simply wanted to wait in the shadows and let everything work itself out, then spend the rest of his perfect days playing on a sunny beach with the girl he loved.

No, Ethan didn't feel right as an accomplice.

But if it wasn't him, who was it?

There was another big thing that didn't add up, too. The payoff—$200,000—seemed like a lot of money when you viewed it in isolation all by itself, but it became chump change when you compared it to the consequences if things went wrong. Why would someone like Pantage risk his job, and more importantly, risk going to jail, for something that probably wasn't much more than a year's salary?

Also, why didn't he ever get the final payment?

Did Danica die in his custody?

Did Fallon blame him?

Was she threatening to go to the police?

Is that why she disappeared, because Pantage shut her up?

Five minutes from home Nicole sent Princess a picture of

Pantage and asked her to show it to 99 to see if he was the one who bought the burner phones. She already knew the answer but wanted to hear it anyway.

"I'll need more money."

"Of course. Can you meet me at the loft in ten minutes? I need the answer yesterday."

"Give me an hour."

"Fine, but show. Don't blow me off."

"Me?"

"I'm serious, Princess."

When Nicole got back to the loft, the parking lot was full, meaning they were recording down in Jay-J's studio. The cars were like friends. They were like soldiers guarding her from Juana del Carmen or whatever new crazy creep Jafet el Perro might be sending her way. No one would make a move on her with so much activity around.

She checked the loft door and found it locked, as it should be. Then she got her gun in hand, made sure a bullet was in the chamber, unlocked the door and swung it open as she hung to the side.

A quick survey showed nothing there alive, whether in human or rattlesnake form.

She went in and locked the door behind her.

She stood in front of the security camera Flagger had installed and said, "Flagger, do me a favor and call me. I have a new number." She gave him the digits and added, "I'd like to get the names of the people in that pit. I'd like to notify their families and get some closure going. I appreciate that you probably don't want to help me but if you do, that would be great. In fact, I'll do a long slow strip for you. Hope your day's going good. Watch out for pesky little things like bullets and stuff. Kiss, kiss, your voice I miss."

Then she got a ladder and killed the camera by unplugging

a wire in the back, breaking her link to the man.

It would be easy to reactivate later if she chose to.

Then she called Ash Colt and naturally got his voicemail instead of his voice. She left a message, "Hey Ash, it's me, Nicole. Can you come over? Call as soon as you get this, okay?"

Her stomach growled.

She checked her watch to find that the entire day had slipped by and it was already suppertime.

Outside, clouds were churning.

It looked like the devil was inside them trying to claw his way out.

83

Nicole was a balloon about to pop, a solo balloon, one without Trane—he'd fired her; and one without Pantage, he was the one trying to trick the world and had everything on the line. She was prepared for him to try to kill her if she cornered him.

Maybe that was the thing to do, corner him.

Why not?

It was better than sitting around on her ass.

Princess came over, then left with money in her pocket and a promise on her lips that she would try to track down 99 as soon as she could.

Nicole threw some fruit in a paper bag, grabbed a bottle of water and headed back to Fallon's house in hopes that Pantage would show up looking for his money. Parking two blocks away, she made her way as inconspicuous as possible back to the house. A couple of boats went past but as far as she could tell no one took an interest in her.

In the master bedroom, she sat on the floor next to the bed with her back against the wall and her legs stretched out and her weapon at her side. No window shined to where she was. No one could see her unless they entered the house first. If anyone did, she'd know it; she left the sliding glass doors open, too, so she'd be able to hear if anyone came sneaking around.

Outside, the sky was darkening and the wind had picked up considerably.

A storm was coming.

She anticipated sitting there and staring into space as she waited for Pantage's face to show, but suddenly she realized what had been bugging her since the moment she discovered that the license plates on Flagger's BMW had actually been stolen off a pickup truck registered to Shadow Reef Construction, Inc.

Nicole had heard that name before somewhere — Shadow Reef Construction, Inc.

She now remembered where.

Behind the old sign shop that Flagger had converted into a secret den, a number of old forgotten signs squatted in the weeds out back. One of those signs, rusty and ugly, was for Shadow Reef Construction, Inc.

So what the hell did that mean?

Anything?

Suddenly her phone rang and Ash Colt's voice came through. "Hey, just picked up your message," he said. "Sorry I'm getting back to you so late but I've been putting out non-stop fires all day. Do you still want me to come over?"

"Yes, definitely."

"I could finish up here and be there around, say, nine?"

"Perfect."

"Are you okay? You sound weird."

"I am weird. You should know that by now."

Outside, a strange hard noise rose above the sound of the wind.

Pantage?

She hung up with a quick *Got to Go* and crawled across the bedroom carpet on all fours towards the sliding glass doors. Down below by the swimming pool, two boys on bikes had pulled off the street for a little privacy. One lit a smoke, took a drag and passed it to the other one, who looked around one last nervous time before touching it. He took a drag and coughed.

Nicole crawled back to the wall, fired up Safari on her cell phone and searched for Shadow Reef Construction, Inc. It turned out to be a duly registered Florida corporation in good standing. The Articles of Incorporation had been filed five years ago by one D. Edward Flagget. The company was in good standing, meaning the Annual Report designating the Registered Agent for Service was up to date. Currently the Registered Agent was D. Edward Flagget. The address for service of process was a place out in the industrial fringes of the county.

Nicole's brain shook.

Clearly D. Edward Flagget was the same person as Daniel Flagger.

Flagget was Flagger ending in a "t" instead of an "r."

The "D" part of D. Edward Flagget clearly stood for "Daniel."

The conclusion was inescapable: Daniel Flagger incorporated Shadow Reef Construction, Inc., albeit under a slightly different alias.

It was his company.

So why was his name misspelled? No doubt so that a web search of Daniel Flagger would never turn up Shadow Reef Construction, Inc. He had the company hidden in plain sight. If it ever came to light to the Secretary of State's office that D. Edward Flagget didn't really exist, Flagger could merely apologize for the typo; "t" and "r" were right next to each other on the keyboard.

Sorry about that.

Outside, the wind picked up a light rain and was now

flinging it against the house.

The sky had darkened considerably.

The streetlights were almost ready to come on.

Nicole checked the time.

To her shock it was 8:30, long past when it should be.

Ash would be at the loft in thirty minutes. He was probably already en route.

She got to her feet and checked outside. The kids were long gone.

Suddenly her phone rang and Princess came through. "I showed 99 the picture of that guy," she said. *That* guy was Pantage. "He's the one."

"He bought the burner phones?"

"Yes."

"Are you positive about this?"

"It's what 99 told me," Princess said. "By the look on his face he was telling the truth."

"Okay, you done good. Thanks."

She hung up.

So, Pantage was without question the one Fallon hired. She went to D.C. to meet with him. Later, he came to Miami and bought burner phones for the project.

Nicole made her way outside, seeing no one. Ten seconds later on the sidewalk one of the kids from the backyard came riding up the street from the opposite way. Nicole flagged him down, pulled out her cell phone and pulled up a picture of Pantage.

"I saw you smoking before but I'm not going to tell anyone," she said. "Look at this picture and tell me if you've ever seen this guy round here."

The kid was a deer in headlights.

He focused on the picture, as if it was the only way to stay alive and said, "Yeah, I seen him."

"Where?"

The kid pointed at Fallon's place.

"At that house."

"How many times?"

"Just once."

"When?"

"Yesterday."

Nicole smiled. Pantage must have come over to search for the money. She squeezed the kid's hand and said, "What's you name?"

"Randy."

"Randy what?"

"Randy Jensen."

"Do me a favor, will you, Randy Jensen? Don't smoke any more. All right?"

"All right."

"It's not good for you."

"I know."

"It ruins your lungs. Your lungs are important."

"We only did it a couple of times."

"Well, now you know what it's like. You'll be fine as long as you stop now."

"I will."

"You promise?"

"Yes. You're not going to tell my mom though, right?"

"No. I'm not telling anybody. I'll see you later, Randy Jensen."

"Goodbye," the kid said. "I think you're pretty."

She ruffled his hair and said, "Back at you."

Then she was gone.

84

Back at the loft, Nicole was a caged animal pacing at the bars, back and forth, constantly looking out the windows for Ash who of all times was running late right now, no doubt because of the storm that had gone from mere weather to something wicked, but still, why now? She poured a glass of wine and drank it way, way too fast. Then she poured a second even though she knew she shouldn't. Finally at 9:30, a full half hour late, the man showed up.

Nicole immediately told him everything she'd found out, including her conclusion: "Pantage is definitely the one Fallon hired to play Hollywood. Whatever went wrong with Danica, Pantage knows about it. Hell, he may have even caused it. He might have done something that caused her to die and now he is actually covering it up."

Ash wasn't impressed.

His focus was deeper.

His focus was on Flagger.

"Give me that address for Shadow Reef Construction," he said. Then he pulled it up on Google Earth. It was a place way out on the fringes where the junkyards and metal plants and pollution factories tried to hide away from the world.

Ash hardened his face.

"How many guns do you have?"

"Just one."

"Then that will have to do. Come on!"

She grabbed her weapon and fell into step, but hesitantly. "I don't get it—"

He jerked the door open.

"I'll explain in the car."

Ten seconds later they were down the fire escape, in Ash's Corvette and cutting dangerously fast into the darkness of the storm with the wipers swishing at full speed.

Nicole wasn't sure about any of it.

"Where we going?"

"To Flagger's place, Shadow Reef."

"Why? I don't give a flying crap about Flagger right now. I need to figure out something with Pantage. He's the one who knows what's going on. If Danica's hurt or something—"

Ash grunted.

"Remember when I told you before about how I thought that Pantage was Hollywood, and you said he couldn't be, because he was sitting next to you in the strip club when Hollywood called?"

"Yes. Later at a bar, too."

"Well, I've been doing some research on him," Ash said. "It turns out that years back he was assigned to a cold case out here in Florida involving a girl who lived out in Daniel Flagger's neck of the woods. Her name was Maddie Fitt. She got murdered back in the day when she was only in 8th Grade. It happened in that airplane wreck, out in the fields where the body pit is."

"So what? Ash, we need to—"

"Hold on. That case caused Pantage and Daniel Flagger to meet. Their paths crossed."

"Who cares?"

"We do," Ash said. "I have a theory."

"Ash, we don't have time—"

"Hear me out," he said. "I think Flagger is the one who killed that girl Maddie Fitt but that's not the important part. The important part is that Pantage came to Florida to investigate the case and figured it out. He knew Flagger killed the girl, not just from the evidence, but he could see it in the man's eyes. He could see it because he had the same kinds of secrets in his own eyes. Instead of bringing Flagger in, however, Pantage ended up forming a sick alliance with the guy. They were two kindred souls and the universe had magically brought them together."

"Huh?"

"What I mean is that Flagger and Pantage, together, are Hollywood. They work together. Hollywood has two heads, one belongs to Flagger and one belongs to Pantage. They cover for each other. One of them will snatch someone while the other one has a perfectly public alibi. The next time, they split it the other way. In your case, one of them calls you while the other one's sitting next to you. It's all part of the cover. It's all part of their sick little game."

Nicole's brain recoiled.

It could actually be true.

It would explain a lot of things.

It also meant that when Fallon hired Pantage to play Hollywood, she was actually hiring the real Hollywood and didn't even know it. Danica never had a chance. For that matter, neither did Fallon. Once Pantage killed Danica, the trail leading from him back to Fallon would need to be erased.

Ash's prior argument about Pantage being Hollywood spun to the top of Nicole's brain:

"For starters, he's big enough and strong enough to pick someone like Danica up and throw her into the back on an SUV. He fits the physical profile. But the big reason is, if he's Hollywood, and if he's also in the FBI, wouldn't it be nifty to work himself into being the top person to be in charge of the Hollywood investigations? He might have positioned himself in the organization so that he could protect himself. He'd know if anyone was closing in on him. He'd have the opportunity to manipulate files and misdirect investigations. He'd be the fox in charge of the hen house."

"Nothing personal, Ash, but that's crazy."

"Think about it, Nicole. How did he get the top job on the task force? I'll bet dollars to donuts that it's because he was constantly coming up with more clues and evidence than any of his other FBI cohorts. It became more and more apparent that he was the best hunter on the squad and deserved to be the top dog. Now ask yourself, how did he magically come up with all those elusive clues and evidence?"

"Because he was there at the crime scenes—"

"Exactly."

"Look, Ash," Nicole said. "I understand the reasoning. I get the logic, I really do. But—"

"Hold on. There's the rattlesnake, too," Ash said. "When Pantage spent the night on your roof, ostensibly watching over you in case Hollywood showed up, the rattlesnake was on the roof the next morning. Now ask yourself, who had the perfect opportunity to put it there?"

"Pantage himself."

"Bingo," Ash said. "He kept it in a cage for the night and let it go in the morning. He was never in any danger. He put it there to suggest that there was a real Hollywood out there in the world who was out to kill him. It was a sneaky diversion. He was laying in evidence that he couldn't possibly be Hollywood, in case you or anyone else ever starting considering the option."

"No. Not true."

Ash was undaunted.

He said, "Plus, just being up there, close to you all night, it's all part of his game. He's the last person on earth you'd suspect. Every time you look at him like he's on your side, he gets a little tingle down in his cock."

The words, silly before, now hit with a force.

It could be true.

Pantage could be Hollywood; or, half of Hollywood, to be precise.

Plus, now, there was even more support. Pantage got himself hired by Fallon and bought burner phones. He'd stuck Danica in a wrecked plane. He'd been tricking Nicole and the rest of the world from the start. All of that in and of itself showed he was a man on the edge. He had no qualms about playing games—dangerous games—and engaging in obstruction of justice. He clearly wasn't the straight shooter he portrayed himself to be.

Also, Pantage ended up with a rattlesnake up on the roof of Nicole's building. Flagger had a lot of snakes. That's probably where Pantage got it from, Flagger.

Yeah, Pantage could be Hollywood.

"So what's the plan?" Nicole said.

"The plan? The plan is that Flagger set up Shadow Reef Construction to have a place off the grid," he said. "I'll bet everything I have that if Danica's still alive, she's there."

The rear wheels suddenly hydroplaned and spun out.

Ash jerked the steering wheel and got them back in line mere feet before the rear end slammed into a telephone pole.

Lightning split the sky.

Thunder exploded so fiercely that the vehicle actually shook.

They were getting farther and farther out of the city, sucked ever deeper into an eerie industrial zone. Flashes of lightning lit up crooked silhouettes of metal buildings and power lines and smokestacks.

The world was dark.

Streetlights no longer existed.

Other traffic no longer existed.

The headlights were no match against the darkness. It was hard to tell if they were even on the road.

A sign appeared on the right.

Jackson's Junk Yard.

The place was dark and abandoned.

Ash slammed on the brakes, turned onto a dark gravel access road and immediately killed the engine. The storm pounded down even louder now that it was no longer competing with the noise of the road.

"Flagger's place is right over there," Ash said.

Nicole looked.

She saw nothing.

There were no lights, not a single one, not in that direction or any other direction. It was as if the world had defaulted to a primitive time.

"Wait here," Ash said. "Keep your gun in your hand."

"Ash—"

"I'll be right back."

He muscled the door open against the wind, pushing it off as he squeezed out. Heavy rain immediately flew into everything. Then the door slammed shut.

Nicole was alone.

Everything was black.

The sky suddenly exploded with a flash of electricity. For the smallest fraction of a second the whole world lit up as if caught in one violent punch from a strobe light. Nicole could see Ash walking into the distance.

He was so small.

He was so alone.

The light punched off.

Darkness immediately swallowed everything.

Ash wasn't there anymore.

Nothing was there anymore.

Nicole grabbed the gun, opened the door and stepped out.

The storm assaulted her immediately.

She hunched against it and ran in the direction she'd last seen Ash.

85

Nicole caught up to Ash and together they worked their way into the night. At first the world was as dark as dark could be, filled with nothing but invisible black rain and horizontal demon winds, but then a light flicked up ahead in the far distance, maybe as far as a hundred yards away. It came from inside a large industrial structure, faint but definitely there, pulsing with an evil beat as the weather sucked it in and out of focus. Did it just turn on or had it been on the whole time?

Nicole's chest tightened.

Flagger?

Is that you?

Do you have Danica with you?

Her fingers tightened on the weapon as she silently pulled Ash to a stop to take a better look. There was no movement around the light to indicate someone was there. There were no darting shadows or shifting shapes. It was just a dull yellow glow, probably not more than a single bulb, burning alone in the universe. The rest of the building was dead and empty.

They crept closer, past abandoned hulks of machinery and piles of lumber and unknown things of bulk laying there like death in the night.

The ruts were deep and suffocated with water and mud.

Every square inch of Nicole's being was soaked and heavy.

Her clothes clung tight, fighting her every step.

Thirty steps away from the building, they stopped. The light appeared to be located in a small storage room tucked in the corner of the building. Nicole could make out rusty metal shelving filled with boxes and parts and tubing and other dust-soaked things of dubious purpose.

Suddenly something inside the room moved.

Nicole jumped.

It was a rat, scurrying across the top shelf. She caught her breath and realized that anyone inside the room would have seen it. The fact that no one threw anything at it or swore at it meant that no one was there. Since the rest of the building was dark, no one was there either.

Flagger wasn't here.

Nicole's chest pounded.

Her breathing got rapid.

What about Danica?

Was she holed up here somewhere in the dark?

The light brought some of the world immediately outside the building into focus. She could make out 55-gallon drums, broken 2x4s, a bin full of broken glass, waist-high weeds and an old engine sitting on cinderblocks. It looked like no one had been around since the dinosaur days. Most importantly, there were no vehicles.

There was no pickup truck.

There was no BMW.

The storage room had an exterior door. Nicole put her hand on the handle and twisted. She expected resistance but it actually turned.

"It's open," she whispered.

Ash muscled in front of her and said, "Stay behind me."

Then they entered.

Inside, with the door closed behind them, everything was suddenly quiet and calm and rational. The rat wasn't anywhere to be seen but Nicole suspected it was behind the red box at the end of the top shelf. Other than the rage of the storm, no sounds came from anywhere. There was no radio, no talking, no TV, no nothing. Dust was rampant. The room clearly hadn't been used for a functional purpose for a long time.

At the end of it was door.

Nicole slowly opened it.

On the other side was a small room that looked like it had once been an office. There were metal filing cabinets, a heavy wooden desk, a florescent ceiling fixture, and an old swivel chair leaning sideways on a broken caster.

Nicole tried the wall switch.

It didn't work.

No lights came on.

Maybe the bulbs were burnt out.

At the end of the room was another door.

Nicole opened it.

Behind it was a world of darkness. She couldn't tell if she was looking into a space twenty feet deep or a thousand. She felt around on the other side of the wall for a switch. All she got was a handful of grime.

Suddenly something happened.

The light in the storage room pulsed.

At first Nicole couldn't figure out the cause. When it happened again and then again, she realized what it was. Headlights were approaching the building. They were punching through the storm and bouncing up and down through the ruts.

They were coming fast.

Flagger!

86

Nicole was going to die. She could feel it coming and didn't care. It was going to happen sooner or later anyway. It might as well be right here, right now, with Ash at her side.

"Nicole!"

She jolted.

Ash had her by the hand, pulling through the office door and into the darkness beyond. They made a left, following along a concrete wall, until they bumped into some kind of a wooden obtrusion, where they dropped to the floor and waited in silence.

"It's got to be Flagger," Ash said.

"Yeah."

"You want me to kill him?"

"No."

"I will," Ash said. "I'll do it, I swear. I don't want him having a chance to get you."

"No."

"I'll do it," Ash said. "We'll get out of here and never come back. We'll never tell anyone. Just give me the gun."

"Ash, no. Just stay calm. We need him alive to find Danica."

They huddled silently in the dark as the storm raged against the building and a second ticked off followed by another and another and another. Then the door to the storeroom burst open and someone entered the building, muttering something incoherent, agitated to no end.

The door slammed shut.

Footsteps pounded across the office floor.

Then the second door swung open and a large menacing silhouette bounded in, picking his way into the darkness with the spray of a flashlight sweeping wildly back and forth across the floor in front of him. Ten steps in he pulled a gun and fired at the ceiling.

Bam!

Bam!

Bam!

Then he shouted, "Ladies, I'm home!"

Nicole recognized the voice. It belonged to Daniel Flagger. She trained her barrel at the man's back, trying to decide whether to call his name or just shoot him in the leg.

Then someone in the far distance screamed.

It was a female voice laced with terror.

Nicole looked in that direction but could see nothing. All she could see was the neurotic spray of Flagger's flashlight as it worked its way farther and farther into the darkness. She could now tell, however, that the building was cavernous, at least as big as a football field. The ceiling was way the hell up there. At the top were rails, no doubt for some type of overhead crane system. Hooks hung down from chains at several different locations. At ground level there was stuff everywhere; an old forklift, metal stairs, platforms, a stack of bulldozer wheels, piles of stuff everywhere.

The man was already too far away to shoot, even if Nicole could define his shape clearly, which she couldn't. If she fired she'd have a one in five chance of hitting him, at best.

It would be suicide.

He had the flashlight.

That was the big advantage, the flashlight.

He could hold it to the side, charge and light her up.

All she'd see would be a blinding sun.

He'd shoot her dead, then Ash. He'd bury them out in the north forty before the sun came up. He'd find Ash's car keys in his pocket. He'd locate the Corvette, move it somewhere and wipe it clean. Their bodies wouldn't be found for forty years, if even then.

Suddenly the flashlight stopped.

It raised and illuminated some type of large cage hanging from a wire rope.

Inside were two people, females.

Flagger was up on some type of platform now, four or five feet off the ground. There must have been some type of overhead controls there because the cage dropped down from the ceiling and moved over until it was in front of him, now swinging back and forth.

Nicole recognized one of the women.

It was Fallon.

The other was very similar in appearance, young and blond.

It had to be Danica.

Nicole was up now, on her feet and walking quickly through the darkness with Ash behind her. Thirty steps away, they ducked behind some type of metal object, possibly the bed of a pickup truck.

Nicole's blood boiled.

If she fired, she couldn't afford to miss. She absolutely, positively had to hit him. And the hit had to be good. It had to kill him, or at least wound him so badly that she'd be able to squeeze off another round. The women were only ten feet from him. If he got wounded, he might shoot them. He might do it for spite. At this range, Nicole had a one in two chance of hitting him.

Suddenly something weird happened.

Flagger was picking rats out of a container and tossing them into a pit below the cage.

What was he doing?

Feeding something?

What?

Alligators?

No sounds came from the pit; whatever was in there, if they were feeding, they were doing it in silence.

"The reaper is in the building!" Flagger shouted. He did something with the controls to make the cage drop a foot and jerk to a stop. "I can't lie," he said. "This is going to hurt."

The women screamed.

They were huddled in terror at the far corner of the cage with their arms around each other.

Suddenly lightning flashed, coming through windows high up on the walls, strong enough to bring the whole interior space into focus for one eerie second.

Nicole was more exposed than she realized.

Flagger's eyes turned and looked directly into hers.

Then he blinded her with his flashlight and shouted, "Drop the gun!"

She froze.

Flagger fired, not at her—at the women in the cage.

One of them screamed in pain.

He twisted the light over.

Fallon was flat on the floor, bleeding badly.

The light swung back to Nicole and the man shouted again, "Drop it!"

She couldn't think.

She couldn't breath.

"Drop it I said!"

She didn't know what to do.

"Do it!"

"Do it!"

"Do it!"

Her head spun.

Then she dropped the gun.

87

The next few seconds exploded so fast and so desperately that Nicole couldn't even process them. Just like that, Flagger had her up on the platform with a fist in her hair. He licked her face with his sick slimy tongue and his terrible breath and the only thought Nicole could process was that she didn't want to die like this, not like a piece of meat at the hands of a sicko.

Then she looked into the pit.

It was filled with snakes, hundreds of them.

Flagger must have sensed her horror and decided to amplify it because he suddenly had a rat in his hand, hanging it by the tail. He swung it back and forth in front of Nicole's face and then tossed it into the pit. It hit bottom and immediately jumped as high as it could. Before it came back down fangs had already sunk into the back of its head.

Fallon screamed.

Nicole could see the cage better now. The sides were bars, as was the top. What she didn't know before is that the bottom also consisted of bars. It wasn't a solid surface. When it was lowered into the pit, the snakes could come right in.

Suddenly Flagger pushed her off the platform at the pit.

She grabbed for the side of the cage with all her might.

Her right hand locked onto a bar and held tight while her

body slammed into the bars and jerked to a stop. Her feet were almost within reach of the snakes. Frantic, she got her left hand onto a bar and pulled her weight up.

Suddenly the cage jerked down.

The bottom of it stopped mere inches from the bottom.

Fallon screamed.

Nicole braced for the fangs.

Something brushed against her leg.

Suddenly a gunshot exploded.

It wasn't from Flagger.

It came from off in the shadows.

It was Ash firing.

Then, just like that, Flagger fell towards her. His face was a bloody mess. He grabbed her as he cascaded down and they both fell to the bottom of the pit. She got to her feet, stepped on Flagger's body and jumped up for the side of the cage. Somehow she got a grip, then another, and pulled her body up.

Ash was on the platform now with some kind of controller in his hand.

Suddenly the cage rose eight or ten or twelve feet and swung to the side of the pit.

Nicole's grip came loose and she dropped.

Her head smacked something, hard, and white-hot pain swallowed her brain.

88

Nicole regained focus to the sounds of screaming directly above her. She focused, to see the cage, and realized the screams were coming from Fallon and Danica. Her first thought that there were snakes twisted up in there in the bars with them.

Then she saw what was wrong.

Two men were on the platform, fighting to the death, landing horrible blows to each other.

Flagger must have somehow survived.

He was trying to kill Ash, he was trying to kill Ash for all he was worth.

He was bigger.

He was stronger.

Nicole watched, frozen and horrified, knowing it couldn't go on much longer. Flagger now had Ash on his back with his head hanging over the platform, pounding his face.

Nicole's chest tightened.

She had to do something.

Where was the gun?

She couldn't remember.

Ash had it last. Now it could be anywhere. It could have gotten kicked into the snake pit for all she knew.

She got to her feet.

He head spun and for the first time she realized just how bad her injury was. She fought through it and forced her body towards the fight, step after step after step. Then she was up there with them on the platform. Ash was on his back, face up, being beaten to a bloody pulp. He had no defense left. He couldn't even get a hand up to his face to block the punches.

Nicole looked around for the gun.

It wasn't there.

The only thing up there was the flashlight, lying at the far edge of the platform where it had been dropped or kicked. Nicole got it in her hands, raised it above her head and brought it down with all her might onto the back of Flagger's skull.

Bone shattered.

The flashlight sparked with a terrible violence and went out.

The entire interior of the building immediately fell into total and complete darkness.

DAY SEVEN

September 21
Sunday

89

Nicole woke up Sunday morning to find herself alone in a hospital room with yellow sunshine squirting through a small window. A large bandage was wrapped around her head. Her left leg was also heavily bandaged from her knee down to her ankle. She felt no pain or anxiety and if anything felt good. She suspected she was doped up on painkillers. She looked around for her phone but it wasn't there. Neither were her clothes.

She vividly recalled last night, all the way to the moment when she brought the flashlight down on Flagger's skull. She remembered feeling faint immediately after that and dropping to the platform. She remembered wanting to sleep so, so badly, and closing her eyes.

That was the last thing she recalled.

Whatever happened between then and now, someone would have to explain to her.

She pressed the call button for the nurse. Ten seconds later a young woman walked into the room. She had a nametag, Coco, and also had a smile on her face as if there was nowhere in the world she'd rather be right now than right here.

She said, "How are we?"

"Fine, but I don't honestly don't remember how I got here."

"A man brought you in last night. You had a large gash on

your head and lost a lot of blood. We got you all stitched up but you need to really take it easy. We also gave you Antivenom for the snake bite."

"I was bitten?"

"Yes."

"By a rattlesnake?"

"That's what we believe," she said. "Something venomous, for sure. We caught it in time so you won't have anything to worry about it. You just need to get some rest and let all the good stuff happen."

"The guy who brought me in here—"

"He's outside. He's been waiting all night."

"Can I see him?"

"Possibly. First I need to know if any of your injuries were caused by him."

"No, absolutely not."

"Don't be afraid to say it if that's what happened," the woman said. "If he hit you, you can tell me. You don't have to hide anything."

"He didn't do anything to me. I'm telling the truth."

The woman studied her, looking for lies.

Then she said, "Okay. Let me go get him."

Alone for at least a few seconds, Nicole flashed back to the moment she brought the flashlight down on Flagger's skull last night. She assumed the blow killed him, but maybe not. Either way, as far as she could tell she'd done nothing wrong.

If Flagger died from the flashlight blow, Nicole was justified in doing it. She was protecting Ash, not to mention Fallon and Danica.

She was in the right.

Still, her gut churned.

Whenever there was a homicide, things could go wrong.

People could get blamed.

Words could get twisted.

Intentions could get misconstrued.

Plus, there was still the issue of Pantage. How would Trane react if Nicole made the claim that Pantage was actually half of Hollywood? Would he tell Pantage about the claim and give the man a chance to defend himself? Would Pantage find a way to deflect it as the silliest thing on earth and then silently come after Nicole at some point in the future when it was safe?

Everything was a still a mess.

Ash walked into the room with a swollen purple face, a stitched lip and a left eye that was almost fully closed. He took Nicole in his arms and kissed her as best he could.

"All I remember is hitting Flagger with a flashlight," she said. "Everything else is a blank."

"I know. You passed out right after that."

"So what happened?"

"First off, that wasn't Flagger you hit," Ash said. "It was Pantage."

Nicole's head spun.

"What do you mean? Pantage? What was Pantage doing there?"

"Being half of Hollywood as far as I can figure," Ash said. "He must have come for the party. He and Flagger were meeting there to kill the women together, as far as I can figure. When I shot Flagger and he fell into the pit, he never came back out. I made my way to the platform and swung the cage to the side, to safety. That's when you fell off. Right after that, from out of nowhere, Pantage attacked me."

"That is so strange."

"Yeah, well, strange or not, he would have killed me if it wasn't for you," Ash said.

"So, is he alive, or what?"

"No."

"He's not?"

"No. I don't know if the flashlight killed him or not," Ash said. "All I know is that he collapsed on me and I wiggled out from under him. Then I pushed him into the snake pit. I guess we'd need an autopsy to figure out if he died from the blow or from the snakes. Anyway, at that point, everything was pitch black but I remembered seeing another flashlight up there on the platform, by the control box. I shined it down. Flagger and Pantage were both down there in the snake pit. Snakes were all over them. Neither one of them was moving, not an inch."

"So they're both dead?"

"Yes, no question about it, but nobody knows it yet, including the police. That's the big thing that we need to talk about. After I pushed Pantage into the pit, I got Danica and Fallon out of the cage. They didn't want to call the cops. They didn't want it getting known that Danica was still alive. They wanted to finish the plan just the way it had been started, with Danica getting taken by Hollywood and then never getting heard from again."

Nicole chewed on the idea.

The taste wasn't pleasant.

"I'm not so sure that's a good idea," she said.

"Good or bad, none of us really had any time to think," Ash said. "The car that Flagger came in still had the keys in the ignition. Danica and Fallon got in it and drove off. They told me to never tell anyone what happened."

"What'd you say?"

"I said, okay. Like I said, there was really no time to think about it. My main concern was to get you to a hospital. I carried you to the car and drove straight here. No one knows where we came from."

"So no one knows about any of this?"

"No, not a soul. We all left. No one was planning on calling the cops. As far as I know the place is sitting there exactly as we left it, with the two bodies still in the snake pit. I don't know if what we did was smart or not but we did what we did. You're not part of it though. You need to take whatever action is best for you."

Nicole grunted.

"We're Bonnie and Clyde at this point, Ash. I need to get out of this hospital."

"No, stay here and rest."

She shook her head.

"That's not an option. Trane is going to find out I'm here. I can't afford to get interrogated by him until I know exactly what I'm going to say. We need to figure out exactly what our story's going to be. Is your car down here?"

"Yes."

"Pull around to the front. I'll be out in ten or fifteen minutes."

"You sure?"

"Yes."

He kissed her.

Then he was gone.

Ten minutes later, Nicole slipped out of bed, walked to the door and checked the hall. Her leg hurt more than she realized and her brain was wobbly. To the left, down several rooms, was a nurse station with several people in sight, including Coco. Nicole cinched her gown so that a minimum of her backside would be exposed, then she turned to the right and proceeded calmly down the hall.

90

Back at the loft, alone, Nicole poured a glass of wine and sat down on the couch to weigh her options. The big thing about all this is that Hollywood was dead; both heads of Hollywood, actually. There would be no more murders coming from that direction. That was the good part and it wouldn't change no matter what Nicole did or didn't do from this point on.

There were a lot of loose ends, though.

The big issue was how Pantage died. If he died from the flashlight, Nicole was the one who did it and she was justified. If he died from being pushed into the snake pit, though, then Ash is the one who did it. The big problem with that scenario is that Ash was no longer in danger at that point. He didn't do it to protect himself. He did it because he was pissed, or still hot from the beating, or whatever. Since he was no long in self-defense mode, he no longer had the right to kill Pantage. The DA might well charge him with some degree of murder; possibly no more than involuntary manslaughter due to his agitated mental state, but still, it would be a felony and Ash would lose his license to practice law.

Then there was also the issue of Fallon.

She was guilty of obstruction of justice. If the real story ever came out about how Fallon hired Pantage and set a false manhunt into play, she'd go down hard. She'd end up getting time. So would all the people who cooperated with her, including Ethan Blue. He wouldn't fare well in prison, although he might be able to cut a deal for a halfway house, or even parole. Either way, though, he was a delicate guy and his life would be shattered.

Then there was Danica.

At this point, she was guilty of obstruction of justice in the same way that Fallon was. On top of that, she was at risk of being sucked back into that bank robbery in Atlanta, the one that ended up with a dead police officer, who incidentally was also a mother of two. Before all this, Danica might have been in a position to simply tell the truth and have it believed. Now, though, after all this elaborate scheming, it would doubtful anyone would ever believe her. She looked like someone who was a getaway driver in a failed robbery that ended up with a dead cop. She was so guilty, and she knew it, that she took excessively elaborate schemes to escape, by way of more illegal acts, no less. It was very possible at this point that Danica might spend the rest of her days behind bars.

None of this, of course, was Nicole's problem.

She hadn't directed any of these actions.

She hadn't encouraged them.

She hadn't aided or abetted them.

She didn't even know they were occurring.

All she'd been trying to do was save Danica and not get killed by Hollywood in the process.

Hollywood was dead and the only question left was whether there would be residual damage.

The bottom line was this: if she spoke out, a lot of lives would end up shattered, but she'd probably end up keeping her job. If she didn't speak out, the shattering probably wouldn't occur, but she'd have to quit her job. She wouldn't be able to work with Trane day after day keeping such a big secret from him. It would eventually eat her alive, plus it wouldn't be fair to him. More importantly, though, she wouldn't deserve the job. She'd have to relinquish it for that reason alone.

On top of all that, she'd made a 100% promise to Ethan Blue to never tell anyone what he was going to tell her. The only reason she knew half of what she did was because Ethan Blue told her, based on her promise to him.

She got up out of the couch and hobbled to the windows.

Outside, the sun was bright and the parking lot was full.

Everything was right with the world.

It would be a nice day to go for a drive.

Suddenly a very stray and very scary thought came to her.

It came fast and terrible, like a dark sky full of demon wings.

It made the glass of wine slip out of her fingers and shatter on the floor.

She stepped away from it, called Ash and said, "I want to go back to the scene."

He hesitated and then said, "Why?"

"I want to be absolutely positive they're both dead, and I want to look at Pantage's body," she said. "I want to see if I can figure out if he died from the flashlight or the snakes."

"How will you be able to tell?"

"I don't exactly know yet," she said. "I'm going to do some research this afternoon on postmortem wounds. I'd suspect, though, that if he got bit while he was still alive, there would be swelling because the blood would still be flowing. If there's no swelling, he probably died from the flashlight."

"That might be easier said than done," Ash said. "He was wearing clothes. We might have to pull him out and strip him down."

Nicole pictured it.

Then she said, "Whatever. We'll wait until after dark. Pick me up at eleven."

91

Unbelievably, as nice and sunny as it had been all day, clouds moved in during the evening hours and by eleven a full-blown storm had its fingers solidly around Miami's throat. Nicole didn't like it. She didn't like the lightning. She didn't like the rain. She didn't like the wind. She didn't like any part of it. Every time she'd almost died, it had been on a night like this. That included last night.

The weather could be an omen of some kind.

It might be warning her.

Maybe Pantage would be gone from the pit.

Or maybe he'd be alive and well and sitting in the shadows with a shotgun, waiting.

Ash pulled up exactly at eleven and flashed the headlights. Nicole was already soaked by the time she got down the fire escape and into the passenger seat. It didn't help that she was a lot slower than yesterday on account of the leg.

Ash kissed her and said, "Are you sure you want to do this?"

"Not really."

He smiled.

Then they headed out into the darkness of the world, following the same route as last night. Nicole found herself spitting out words to pass the time, telling Ash all about his potential exposure for a murder charge depending on how

Pantage died, plus all the pros and cons of going to Trane and telling him the whole story.

"I don't want to be a rat," she said, "especially after I made a direct promise to Ethan Blue, but, man, I'm a police officer. I'm supposed to bring the criminals in, not help them get away."

"They're your friends," Ash said. "You're going to be conflicted. You'll figure it out. Whichever way you go, it's fine with me. If it turns out I need to go to jail then I will. I'd rather do that than have you living in guilt or regret or whatever."

"Ash—"

"I'll rebound," he said. "Don't worry about me."

Nicole exhaled and said, "Let's be sure they're both dead, that's the main thing. I got to give you the credit for figuring it out. How in the hell did you find out that Pantage had that cold case involving that girl, what was her name—?"

"—Maddie Fitt—"

"—Right, her. I mean, investigations like that aren't exactly public knowledge."

Ash shrugged.

"I'd like to take credit for that but I can't," he said. "I hired an investigator. He figured it out. Don't ask me how."

"Well, whatever you paid him, he earned it," she said. "What's his name?"

"Scotty Rail."

"Scotty Rail?"

"Yeah, good old Scotty Rail. I've used him for years," Ash said. "A lot of the contracts I get involved in, the studios want people vetted before they hire them, especially the actors. It's not good to find out after the fact that the star of your film may be under investigation for child pornography or whatever. So we vet them as good as we can."

"They don't know it, though."

Ash shook his head.

"Of course not. It has to be done though. Scotty Rail's the best in the business. I have no idea how he works his magic but I do know that his magic does in fact get worked."

"Yeah, well, I hope we have some of his luck tonight."

"We will," Ash said. "I'm sure everything's exactly as we left it. Unless—"

"Unless, what?"

"Well—*this is crazy talk*—unless Danica or Fallon went back for some reason, but I can't think of why they would."

The thought never occurred to Nicole.

"Jeez," she said. "What if they left a cell phone there or something, and didn't remember it until later?"

"Nicole, the storm's winding you up. Calm down."

She felt her hands shaking and grabbed one with the other one.

"You're right," she said. "Keep me in line, all right?"

He smiled.

"I don't have that much energy. Keep yourself in line." He added, "We need to be really careful of the snakes. If we have to pull Pantage out of the pit we need to be damn sure we're not bringing any critters with him, tucked in his clothes or whatnot."

The miles clicked off.

They had another ten minutes to go.

Nicole took the opportunity to pull her phone out and check her emails. She found one from Trane, sent this afternoon. *Pantage has gone AWOL. If he contacts you, please tell him to call me immediately. Thank you.*

As long as she had her phone out, she did a quick Google search for Scotty Rail, curious. No wonder he was good, he had a plain vanilla face no one would ever remember. He didn't have a single remarkable feature that stood out. He was the kind of guy you could watch in a movie all night long and then not recognize the next day if he walked up to you on the street and slapped you in the face with a fish.

She powered off her phone and said, "I've been wondering, when we get there, I'm wondering if I should look around for my gun or not."

"And take it?"

"Possibly."

"Is it registered to you?"

"Yes."

"Then I'd say take it," Ash said. "Now I'm starting to think this trip will actually be worth it."

"I'll still be tied to the scene," she said. "My blood is in the dirt. I probably left prints twenty different places."

"Then maybe we should clean up," Ash said. "It's your decision. Think about it."

"Okay."

"If we're going to do it, though, this would be the time. I don't want to come back for round three."

"Trust me, I hear you."

"You think you want to do it? Clean up?"

She considered it.

"If we do, it's tampering with a crime scene," she said. "There's no going back. We're committed at that point."

"Well, either way. Like I said. It's your decision."

"We'll see if we can figure out how Pantage died. Then we'll decide."

Ten minutes later they pulled into the gravel lane for the junkyard, exactly where they'd been last night. Nicole pulled two flashlights out of her purse and handed one to Ash. She tossed her purse in the back seat, grabbed the door handle and said, "You ready?"

Ash kissed her.

Then he said, "Then let's get this over with. What's wrong?"

"Nothing. I just keep having this strange picture in my mind that Pantage is still alive. If he never moved when he fell into the pit, maybe nothing bit him."

"That's unlikely."

"I know it's unlikely, but it's not necessarily impossible. He might still be there, wounded. We need to be careful."

92

They forced their way through the storm, keeping their flashlights off and using the storage room light as a beacon. They encountered no one and detected nothing in the night that shouldn't be there. The vehicle that Flagger had arrived in last night was gone. By now it was no doubt two hundred miles away, wiped down and abandoned.

They entered the building.

A startled rat scurried behind some kind of metal part on the floor.

They walked through the storage room, then through the office and into the cavern, where they turned their flashlights on for the first time. Everything was exactly as it should be but Nicole couldn't shake the feeling that something was wrong.

"Let's get out of here," she said. "I've changed my mind."

"We're already here. Let's just do it."

They walked towards the pit, one careful step at a time.

Then suddenly something flashed in Nicole's brain, namely an image of the private investigator, Scotty Rail, who she'd pulled up on her cell phone not more than ten minutes ago. She suddenly realized that she'd seen the man before. He was the very same private investigator that she encountered down at the Blue Heron Hotel, the one who was in the room adjacent to the room she and Fallon rented, the guy she thought was

Hollywood and tried to shoot. Now that she thought about it, she saw him two more times too.

What the hell?

He was Ash's go-to guy.

Had he been following Nicole because Ash hired him?

Has Ash been up to something this whole time that he wasn't disclosing?

Ash must have picked up a vibe because he said, "What's wrong?"

Nicole made her voice sound as normal as she could.

"Nothing. This place is just creeping me out."

"Hang in there. It'll be over soon."

They continued walking, getting closer and closer to the pit.

Suddenly another thought flashed in Nicole's brain. Ash's theory was that there were two parts to Hollywood, Flagger and Pantage, who were covering for each other, each doing part of the dirty work while the other was out in the world getting an ironclad alibi. What Nicole suddenly realized is that theory worked equally as well for Ash as it did for Pantage.

Maybe it wasn't Flagger and Pantage who together were Hollywood.

Maybe it was Flagger *and Ash.*

Maybe Ash told Nicole the theory because he actually knew firsthand that there were two parts to Hollywood, because he was one of those two parts.

Days ago, Pantage had made an argument to Nicole that Ash was Hollywood. She'd dismissed it because Ash had an ironclad alibi at the time that one of Hollywood's victims was taken. Ash had been in San Francisco giving a speech at a lawyer's conference. It was actually on YouTube. Pantage commented at the time that the alibi seemed almost too good.

In hindsight, maybe it was too good.

Maybe it was so good because Ash and Flagger made it that

way.

Nicole's heart pounded.

Was Ash Hollywood?

They were at the pit now.

Ash stepped to the edge and pointed his flashlight in. "Bingo," he said.

Nicole looked down.

Both bodies were there, Flagger and Pantage, deader than dead and covered in snakes.

"We need a hook or something to get him out," Ash said. "Let me look around."

"Okay."

Nicole stood at the edge of the pit and waited.

Then she realized something horrible. If Ash was the one who was partnered with Flagger, then Pantage wasn't. Pantage was innocent. So, when Nicole killed him with the flashlight last night, she actually killed an innocent man.

But why would he be there if he was innocent?

At first, the question had no answer.

Then possibilities began to emerge.

Maybe Pantage was closing in on Ash. Maybe he'd figured out that Hollywood had two parts, Flagger and Ash. Maybe he'd put a tracker on Ash's Corvette. Maybe last night he followed Ash to Nicole's loft and then to here. Maybe he'd entered the building to actually save Nicole.

A chill ran up Nicole's spine and straight into her brain.

There was one more question, though.

Ash shot Flagger last light.

If Flagger and Ash were partners in crime, why would Ash kill him?

That answer was easier.

Flagger was on the run. He'd eventually be caught and might implicate Ash to save himself. So Ash silenced him while he had the chance. Ironically, he actually did it while saving Nicole, so the kill was justified. He'd never be charged for it.

Suddenly Ash was at her side with a long metal hook in his hands. He handed Nicole his flashlight and said, "Shine it on his belt. I'll see if I can hook it."

Ash brushed the snakes away with the end of the hook. A lot of them scattered but some of them refused to move. He actually had to lift a few of them up and place them to the side. As soon as some came off others got on.

"I'm not going to be able to get them all off," he said. "Let me see if I can pull the body up a couple of feet and shake them off."

The words sounded like they were coming from the devil.

Ash was Hollywood.

Nicole was sure of it.

She could push him in the pit, right now, so easily. It would hardly take any effort at all. She could get the hell out of there and never come back. If she ever got implicated she could say that Ash lost his balance trying to fish Pantage out. There'd be nothing to contradict that story. Even if someone suspected otherwise, there would be no proof, no evidence. There would be no case. She'd never face charges, so long as she didn't allow herself to get tricked into admitting something.

But what if she was wrong?

What if Ash really wasn't Hollywood?

What if she would be killing an innocent man? What if all her new thoughts were just a crazy trick of the night?

"You're drifting," Ash said. "Keep the light on his belt."

She brought the light back on target.

"Sorry."

Ash managed to fish the hook through Pantage's belt and, with a lot of effort, got him lifted up a couple of feet. Three or four snakes were tangled up in the man's clothes. He shook the body but the stupid things didn't dislodge.

The sight was surreal.

Nicole couldn't help but wonder how she ever got here.

"Find something to scrape them off with," Ash said. "Do it quick, baby. I'm getting seriously tired here."

Nicole set the flashlight down on the edge of the pit, shining it in on the body, then set off with her own flashlight to find a stick or whatnot. In ten steps, she spotted something she recognized.

It was her gun.

It was just lying there on the ground, where Ash must have dropped it after shooting Flagger last night. There should be plenty of bullets in the clip. As far as she could remember, Ash had only fired once.

She picked it up, looked back at Ash, deciding, and then set her flashlight on the ground so as to not give herself away, and ran.

Within seconds she heard shouting from behind her.

"Nicole! Hey, Nicole! Where you going?"

She looked back over her shoulder to see what was going on.

The man was running after her.

He had his flashlight in hand, swinging it wildly.

He was closing the gap.

She'd never make it out of the building.

He'd get to her first.

She jerked to a desperate stop, twisted violently to face him and fired a warning bullet into the ceiling.

The man immediately came to a halt.

He was close, five or six steps away at most.

Nothing happened for a second, and then another, and then another, but then the man brought the light up and shined it into Nicole's eyes.

It was blinding.

She couldn't see Ash's face or body or even the hand

holding the light.

"I know you're Hollywood!" she said. "Don't make me shoot you. I will, make no mistake."

She trained the barrel slightly to the right of the light, to where Ash's body was.

The man said nothing.

Then he slowly started to rotate the light in a circle, keeping the beam fixed in Nicole's eyes.

He said, "Well, this is quite a predicament, isn't it?"

"Just stay back, Ash, I swear!"

"How'd you figure it out, Nicole? You know, that's always been your problem. You're too damn smart for your own good. I was hoping we'd at least get a month or two together. That was going to give me time to plant some souvenirs at Pantage's place, you know, seal the deal and all that good stuff."

The circle of light was getting bigger and seemed like it might be coming closer. What was he trying to do?

Hypnotize her?

Disorient her?

"Ash, stop it!"

The light didn't stop.

Nicole fired another warning shot into the air.

"I mean it Ash! Don't force me!"

The man said, "Nicole, I love you. You know that. You love me too. Let's sit down and talk this through. No more lies. I'm sure we'll be able to figure it out. I love you, baby. Tell me you love me too. Go on, say it. I want to hear the words. You've never said them to me yet. I know they're in there, way down deep in your heart. Now is the time to let them out. Go on, baby, tell me. Tell me you love me. Tell me you love me more than life itself, because that's how much I love you. I have Nicole, from the first time I saw you. Put the gun down, baby. Don't break my heart."

Nicole took a step back.

"Ash, don't!"

Suddenly the light dropped to the ground and Ash charged. Nicole froze.

Then, just as the man's body slammed into hers, she pulled the trigger. Ash made an awful sound as they both fell to the ground. Then Nicole pulled the trigger again and again and again. She could feel the man's blood squirt onto her hands and face and neck.

Air came out of Ash's mouth, so strange sounding.

Then everything got quiet.

She laid there on her back for a long time, not moving, not thinking, just letting the tears silently roll out of her eyes and down her cheeks.

Then she got up and left.

ABOUT THE AUTHOR

Jim Michael Hansen (also writing under the pen name R.J. Jagger) is the author of over 25 hard-edged mystery and suspense thrillers, including the Nick Teffinger thrillers, the Bryson Wilde thrillers, and the Nicole Stone thrillers. In addition to his own books, he also ghostwrites for a well-known, bestselling author. He is a member of the International Thriller Writers and the Mystery Writers of America. His books can be read in any order.

www.ingramcontent.com/pod-product-compliance
Lightning Source LLC
Chambersburg PA
CBHW010535170726
48285CB00008B/2632